# CAPPUCCINO

## A ZION SAWYER COZY MYSTERY

## Volume 1

ML Hamilton

www.authormlhamilton.net

ML Hamilton

# CAPPUCCINO



First print

To my readers, this new series is dedicated to you. I believe I've taken the best of the *Peyton Brooks' Mysteries* and the *Avery Nolan Adventures* to embark on a new cozy mystery series.
As always, thank you for your continued loyalty.
And all my love to my family.

"I like cappuccino, actually. But even a bad cup of coffee is better than no coffee at all."

~ **David Lynch**

# CHAPTER 1

Zion's phone rang on her desk. Staring at her computer screen, she reached up blindly and clicked on the headset, connecting the call, then she said, "Zion Sawyer, *Judicious Insurance*, how can I help you?"

"Ms. Sawyer, I'm David Bennett from the *Bennett, Coleman & Cox Law Firm.*"

Zion stared at the display on the desk phone. She didn't recognize the number. "Excuse me? Who did you say you were?"

"I'm David Bennett. I'm a lawyer in Sequoia, California."

"Sequoia, California?" Zion frowned. She'd never heard of such a place, but then she didn't know a lot of the little tourist towns that dotted the northern part of the state. "Where's that?"

"We're east of Visalia, up in the Sierras."

"I've never heard of it." She smoothed a hand over her straight auburn hair.

"Our population hovers around 15,000 permanent residents, but during summer and ski season, we climb to 20,000 or so."

"Wow." Zion's attention was drawn back to her computer as she reviewed the most current formulary list. "How can I help you, Mr. Bennett?"

"I'm calling on behalf of your mother."

"My mother?"

"Your biological mother."

That got Zion's attention. "I don't mean to be rude, but I'm not interested, Mr. Bennett."

"I understand that, but if you'd just hear me out."

"I'm sorry, Mr. Bennett. That woman gave me up for adoption twenty-six years ago and never had a part in my life.

*My* mother is Gabrielle Sawyer and that's the only mother I've ever known. I appreciate you calling, but I'm not interested in anything to do with that other woman."

"She's dead, Ms. Sawyer."

Zion went still. For some reason, that statement wasn't sinking into her brain. She blinked a few times, then exhaled. "Well, condolences to her family. Thank you for calling, Mr. Bennett, but I'm very busy right now and I need…"

"She named you as her only beneficiary in her will."

That also brought her to a stop. Beneficiary? Why would she do something like that? Zion had never had contact with her, although she knew her parents had kept in touch throughout the years. Zion herself had never felt the need to know anything about her, though.

She shook herself. "Again, I'm not interested." She didn't need anything from a woman who'd tossed her away like unwanted baggage when she was an infant.

"What if I wanted to give you a million dollars?"

"Do you want to give me a million dollars?"

"No," said Bennett in defeat.

Zion thought as much. "Thank you for informing me, Mr. Bennett. I appreciate the call, but I'm very busy."

"Listen, I know this is a bit of a shock."

"Not really."

"Ms. Sawyer, please listen to me. Take down my number and think this over. Then give me a call. Nothing has to be decided today, but I do need you to call me before the week is out."

Zion sighed. Her real mother, Gabrielle, would be annoyed if she didn't show this man the basic courtesy he deserved. She grabbed a pen out of the holder on her desk, dragged her notepad over to herself, and clicked the pen on. "Okay, Mr. Bennett. Give me the number."

He rattled it off. "Please think about this, Ms. Sawyer. You are the beneficiary of your mother's entire estate."

"Estate?" she said skeptically. "Fine. I'll keep it in mind, but I really have to go now. Again, I appreciate the call."

She disconnected the phone and sat staring at the number she'd written on the pad. She wasn't sure how she felt, but she didn't feel grief. How did you feel grief over what you'd never known? She didn't know this woman and her death, while empirically sad, really had no effect on her whatsoever.

Rebekah poked her head around the corner of Zion's cubicle. "Where do you want to go for lunch?"

Zion tore off the paper and pulled open her lower desk drawer, shoving it into her Cartier handbag. "What about *Alta*?"

"Perfect." Rebekah's heavily lashed dark eyes narrowed on Zion. "You look upset. Don't frown. It creates wrinkles."

Zion smoothed her fingers over her brow. She didn't need wrinkles to add to her abundant freckles. Besides, she couldn't lie. She'd always been envious of Rebekah's olive skin and perfect complexion. Her mix of Pakistani and white blood blended to give her straight shining black hair, dark exotic eyes, and creamy naturally tanned skin. She and Zion were nearly the same height at 5'6", neither short nor tall, but Rebekah's curves were in all the right places, while Zion's were…well, bustier. The latest fashions that they both coveted draped over Rebekah's frame, while Zion always looked like she was about to give someone a peep show.

"So, what's wrong?" Rebekah waved a manicured hand.

"That was a lawyer for…" She hesitated. Rebekah knew she was adopted. That hadn't been anything neither Zion's parents nor she hid from anyone, but it wasn't something she discussed regularly either. "…my biological mother. She's dead."

Rebekah gasped and covered her mouth. "Oh, my God, I'm so sorry."

Zion waved her off. “It’s nothing, Becks. I never knew the woman. What’s there to be sorry about?”

Rebekah leaned closer as if she were sharing a secret. “It’s still your mother. If I lost my mother, I’d be devastated.”

Zion raised a brow at that. Rebekah was regularly at war with her mother. Veda wanted her daughter to get married and settle down, but Rebekah was having too much fun in the City by the Bay to do any such thing.

“How are you taking it?”

“I’m fine.”

When Rebekah gave her a skeptical look, Zion held up her own manicured hand. “I’m really fine. Look, Becks, if we want to go to lunch at noon, I’ve got to review these formularies and make sure they’re accurate.”

“Sure. I’ll be just over there if you need me.”

Zion waved goodbye to her and Rebekah reluctantly walked back to her cubicle. Turning to the computer, Zion tried to concentrate on the screen, but her mind kept going back to the conversation with the lawyer. Her mother had made her sole beneficiary of her estate. What the hell did that mean? What estate? What had she left her?

Probably some moldy old clothes and an equally moldy trailer.

She shuddered and drove the thought out of her head. Whatever it was, Zion certainly didn’t need it.

* * *

Zion reached over the counter and snagged a cherry tomato out of the salad, popping it in her mouth before Gabrielle could slap her hand. She crunched it, then lifted her wine glass and took a swig. On Wednesday nights she left San Francisco and drove out to San Bruno where she had dinner at her parents’ house. It was a routine they’d maintained since she returned from college.

She heard the front door open, followed by the scrabble of her parents’ terrier on the wooden floor.

"There's my big boy," came her father's booming voice.

"In the kitchen," called her mother, reaching for the salad tongs.

A moment later, Joseph Sawyer appeared in the kitchen archway, holding a wiggling Rascal in his arms. "Hey, kiddo," he said, moving toward Zion and kissing her on the top of the head.

"Hey, Daddy," she said, taking Rascal from him.

The scruffy brown wiggle worm licked Zion's chin. She settled him on her lap and took another sip of wine as she watched her father circle around the counter to give his wife a kiss. Zion had always envied her parents' marriage. They'd outlasted most of her friends' parents and even a few of her friends. Zion herself hadn't had the best luck in romance. Her latest boyfriend had lasted a full year, longer than the others had, but it had still ended badly. Her parents, however, were still as devoted to each other as they'd been thirty years before.

"How was work?" asked Gabi.

"You know how it is in the salt mines," Joe said, reaching for a cherry tomato himself.

Gabi swatted at him too, but he danced away before she could get him. Not that she tried very hard.

Zion smiled. Joe Sawyer was a hospital administrator. Gabi had been an emergency room nurse until she'd retired last year. Now she'd taken up piano playing, a hobby that caused poor Rascal dismay. Zion had caught the little terrier howling this very night as she arrived at her parents' door, only to hear the discordant tones coming from the living room.

"How did your lesson go today?" asked Joe.

Gabi shrugged. "Roger said I'm improving."

Joe shot a look at his daughter. Zion ducked her head, hiding her smile. Improvement up from abysmal was still in the lower registers of awful. In the last year, Gabi had tried her hand at a number of things. There'd been canning and macramé, and who could forget the disastrous attempts at reupholstering. Her father said many times that he hardly missed his favorite recliner anymore.

Gabi shoved a glass of wine at him. "Try this. Zion brought it."

He took a sip, then smacked his lips. "Very nice bouquet."

Zion rolled her eyes. Her father didn't know a damn thing about bouquet or really anything to do with wine. He was a domestic beer man, always had been.

"I'll be right back," he said and disappeared into the hallway to change out of his business suit.

Zion settled Rascal on the floor, giving his ear a scratch. "Can I help you with anything?"

"Not a thing. We just need the lasagna to finish cooking, then I'll put in the garlic bread." Gabi lifted her wine glass. "So, how was work?"

Zion chewed her inner lip. She wanted to talk to her parents about the strange call she'd received today, but she didn't want to hurt them. Although they'd been open about her adoption and had urged her to talk to them about it, she'd always feared it might hurt them if she seemed too curious about her biological parents.

Gabi set down the wine glass, eying Zion closely from behind her wire-framed glasses. "Zion?"

"I got a strange call today."

"Go on." Then Gabi's face twisted. "Oh, lord, you didn't hear from Lucas, did you?"

Lucas Walters had been Zion's last boyfriend, he who'd lasted that full year.

"No, no." She took another sip of her wine. "God no." The relationship had ended when she caught Lucas stealing from her mother's purse during a weekend visit over the holidays.

Joe came into the room, moving to the refrigerator and pulling it open. He took out a can of beer and popped it open, walking around the counter to take a seat on a barstool next to Zion. "What are we talking about?"

"Zion got a strange phone call today," said Gabi, moving aside the salad bowl and leaning on the counter.

"Oh, from who?"

"Whom," corrected Gabi.

"Whom? Are you sure?"

"Yes, dear, I'm sure."

Zion didn't interrupt them. Maybe if they went off on a tangent, she could avoid telling them about the call, but Gabi had a mother's intuition and she knew something was bothering Zion.

"Back to the call," she prompted.

"It was from a lawyer in Sequoia, California."

Gabi frowned. "Where's Sequoia?"

"I know where it is," said Joe.

"No, you don't," scolded Gabi, "you just think you do."

"You don't know all the places I know."

"Okay, then where is Sequoia?"

"It's in…California," said Joe, taking a swig of beer.

Zion smiled at that. God, she loved both of them so much and didn't want to hurt them.

Gabi shook her head. "I swear," she grumbled, then her attention zeroed in on Zion again. "Go on, dear," she urged.

"Sequoia's east of Visalia," Zion said for her father's benefit.

"Exactly what I thought," he answered.

"Mmmhmmm," said Gabi.

"He said…" Zion's voice faltered and she glanced at the two of them. They'd always been enough for her. She'd never felt the need so many adoptive kids felt to find their biological families, but that didn't mean her parents weren't concerned about it. "He said my biological mother died."

Gabi and Joe went still. Zion felt both of their eyes fixated on her and she wanted to squirm. Then Gabi blindly reached for her wineglass and took a swig.

"I'm so sorry, kiddo," said Joe, draping an arm over her shoulders and pulling her against him. "That must have been a shock."

"How did she die?" asked Gabi.

"I don't know. He didn't say. I mean the lawyer didn't say." Zion leaned into her father and ran a finger over the top of her wine glass. "He said I was her sole beneficiary, but I told him I wasn't interested." She gave her mother a speculative look. "Weren't you in touch with her?"

"We haven't spoken in years. I think the last communication was during your high school graduation. I sent her some graduation pictures."

"Where was she living then?"

Gabi thought for a moment. "I think it was Los Angeles, now that you mention it."

"What do you think it means that I'm her sole beneficiary? What do you think she could have possibly had?"

"Maybe some family jewelry," said Joe.

"She might have squirreled away a little money," offered Gabi.

Zion shrugged, picking up her wine glass again. "It doesn't matter. I don't care what it was. They can give it to charity."

"I don't think it works that way, kiddo," said her father. "I think you'll have to give it away yourself."

"Why?" Zion realized her voice came out sharper than she intended. "She was nothing to me."

"She was your biological mother, Zion," said Gabi in that mother's disapproving tone.

"What does that mean? You're my parents. You're the only parents I've known. She gave me up."

"She gave you to us," said Gabi reasonably. "I have always loved her for the gift she gave us."

"She did what she thought was best for you, kiddo. That was a pretty big sacrifice. She made us a family," said Joe.

Leave it to her parents to get all schmaltzy and emotional. This was the very reason she adored them. They were such nerds. She leaned over and kissed her father's cheek, then covered her mother's hand with her own.

"I love you goofy hippies," she said, laughing.

Gabi smiled in return and Joe hugged her tight. Grasping Zion's hand in both her own, Gabi leaned on the counter. "I think you should call that lawyer back. Do you remember his name?"

"He made me write down his number on a piece of paper at the office."

"Then you call him tomorrow." Gabi squeezed her hand and released her, turning to the stove and grabbing a pot holder. She opened the oven and picked up the garlic bread on its cookie sheet, shoving it on top of the lasagna.

Zion watched her complete these familiar chores, thinking about the lawyer and a mother she'd never met. "What was she like?"

Gabi went still for a moment, then she closed the oven and removed the pot holder, setting it on the counter. Joe's arm slipped off Zion's shoulders and he picked up his beer, swigging it.

Zion glanced between them. "We don't have to talk about this if you don't want to."

Gabi smiled, her eyes crinkling behind her glasses. She was shorter than Zion, about five three and pear shaped, more hips than bust. Her short shag had started to grey, but it was a silvery grey that complemented her dark blue eyes. Her natural hair color had been black, which had always drawn attention when she and Zion went out in public because Zion's own hair trended more toward red/orange unless she added a burgundy wash to it.

"She had the most glorious head of red curls," she said.

"And freckles, so many freckles. They were adorable," added Joe.

Zion scoffed at that. She hated her own freckles and her inclination to burst into flames like a damn vampire if she got the least bit of sun on her.

"She was so young when she had you," said Gabi.

"How young?"

"Seventeen. Her parents weren't supportive at all and the boy…" Gabi stopped. "Uh." She gave a helpless look toward Joe.

"The boy? My father?" Zion prompted.

"Yes, your father, he was just as young. He had a scholarship to play baseball with Florida State, so his parents urged both of them to choose adoption."

"Her name was Vivian, right?" asked Zion.

"Vivian Bradley," said Joe.

"What was his name?"

Gabi sighed. "We never knew. Once they made the decision to adopt, he disappeared from the picture."

Zion did some mental math. "Hm," she said.

"What?" asked Joe.

"She was only 43. Isn't that a little young to die?"

"Very young," said Gabi who'd turned sixty-two in April. "Did the lawyer say what she died from?"

"I didn't give him a chance." Zion frowned. "Maybe I should have listened to him a little more. What if she had a heart attack or some genetic disease?"

"All the more reason to call him tomorrow," said Joe.

Zion nodded, then another thought occurred to her. "Oh, crap."

"What?" said both of her parents together.

"What if she didn't have enough to cover her own burial? What if that's what he wants to ask me to do?"

"I don't think a lawyer would contact you for that, Zion," said Gabi. "She must have had a will. There has to be something she left you."

"You said the adoption was open on her part. How often did you meet with her?"

"We went to the doctor's appointments with her when she was pregnant with you," said Joe.

"And you were there when I was born," prompted Zion.

"We were." Gabi's eyes filled with tears. "It was the best day of our lives, holding you for the first time."

"Did she?"

"Did she what?" asked Joe.

"Did she hold me? Did she ask to see me even?"

Gabi came around the counter and wrapped her arms around Zion, laying her hand against the side of her head and holding her as she had as a little girl. "She did, sweetie. She held you and we all cried. I think it was the hardest thing she ever did, letting you go."

Zion fought her own tears. This was stupid. She'd been so much better off being raised by the Sawyers. "Did my grandparents, her parents, come to the hospital when she went into labor?"

Joe shook his head. "If your mother hadn't been in the delivery room with her, she would have given birth alone."

That made Zion incredibly sad. She'd never spared much thought for the seventeen-year-old girl who gave birth to her, but thinking about having a child without anyone supporting her, that had to be one of the hardest things in the world.

Zion pressed her index fingers over her eyes. "This conversation is getting depressing." She sniffed. "Is the bread burning?"

"Oh, goodness," exclaimed Gabi, throwing her hands in the air. "I plumb forgot about it." And she raced around the counter, grabbing the pot holder as she went.

# CHAPTER 2

"I need some 8d nails for fencing," said Bill Stanley. "Which is better? Stainless steel or aluminum?"

Tate glanced up from the cash register, then moved to the counter and lifted it, stepping through to the other side. "You wanna use screws," he said, motioning Bill toward the bins affixed to one of the rows. "That is if you want it to stay up for any length of time."

Bill studied the overwhelming number of screws of various sizes, materials, and coating. Tate grabbed a box and held it out to the older man. Bill took it, lifting a hand to scratch under his ball cap.

"Don't suppose you'd come out and build it for me?" he said.

Tate chuckled. "That depends. You want it to stay up or not?"

Bill laughed with him and patted his shoulder. "I hear you." He hefted the box. "You retire and suddenly the *Honey Do* list becomes a million miles long."

Tate shrugged, leading Bill toward the register. "I guess I wouldn't know. My wife decided not to wait for me to retire before she found a new honey to do for her."

Bill set the box beside the register as Tate lifted the counter and slipped behind it again. "Young guy like you? Shit, you'll have another wife before you know it. In this town, single men are a hot commodity."

Tate laughed and rang up the sale. As he did so, the buzzer above the door sounded, drawing his attention. Sheriff Wayne Wilson stepped inside, removing his peaked hat and glancing around.

Tate and Bill exchanged a look, then Bill handed him a bank card. Tate kept an eye on the sheriff as he swiped

Bill's card, but Wilson seemed satisfied with wandering around, picking up various items and putting them back.

When Logan appeared from the back, Tate jerked his chin at the sheriff. The teenager lifted the counter and hurried over to him, giving him an anxious smile. "Need some help, Sheriff?" Logan asked.

"Just looking around."

Logan glanced over his shoulder at Tate, then shrugged. Tate offered a nod of acceptance and Logan moved over to an aisle of locks, reaching out to tidy the shelves. Tate passed Bill's card back to him and bagged up the screws.

"I hope you get someone to help you with the fence," he told Bill.

Bill took the bag. "Thanks," he said, pocketing his wallet again. "I'm sure I'll be back before you know it."

Tate gave him a smile and watched him walk toward the door. As he let himself out, Sheriff Wilson turned toward the counter. Logan was now pretending to straighten a row of toilet seats, his eyes glancing up at the Sheriff now and then.

Settling his hat on the counter, Wilson leaned an elbow on it, leveling a look at Tate. "How's business lately?"

Tate shrugged. He wasn't sure where this was going, but he didn't want to show too much interest. Sheriff Wilson was a thin man with a narrow, concave chest, a thin moustache perched on his upper lip. He had watery brown eyes and a severe widow's peak. His hair was a dusty brown, thinning at the top, and he had a hooked nose. He wore his gun belt at his waist and had a tendency to hook his thumbs through it like some 1950's western hero.

In the year and a half Tate had been in Sequoia, this was only the third time he'd talked to Wilson. "How can I help you, Sheriff?" he prompted.

Wilson glanced over at Logan, who was obviously eavesdropping. "I was hoping I could talk to you in private for a moment."

Tate motioned Logan toward the back of the store. The boy hurried, lifting the counter and disappearing through the opening that led to the small storage room. Tate turned back to the Sheriff. "So, what's up?"

"You heard about the accident on Blackrock Road a week ago?"

"Yeah, fatality, right?"

"Right. Vivian Bradley. She owns the *Caffeinator* down the street."

"I've seen the place, but I've never been there. I don't drink those frou frou coffees."

Wilson gave a laugh. "Yeah, me, I can't afford them."

"Well, there's that, but it's a lot of unnecessary fuss."

Wilson played with his hat. "At first, we thought she drove off the road 'cause she was drinking, but…"

Tate straightened, feeling an immediate tightening in his gut. "Look, Sheriff."

"Her tox report came back. Not a drop of booze, no narcotics. She was clean."

Tate fought down the immediate need to ask what else they'd found in the car, what other evidence they'd uncovered.

"When we looked at the car a bit closer, we found dark blue paint on the rear driver's side panel. Bradley's car was a silver Lexus and it was banged all to hell, so we missed the paint on our first pass. She also had some threatening messages on her cell phone."

"She married?" Tate heard himself say without realizing he was going to speak.

"Divorced, 'bout six years ago. Searched her house and found a divorce settlement. Husband's a CFO for a plastic surgery medical office in Los Angeles. They franchised the damn thing. They have about ten satellite surgery centers all over the valley, catering to the beautiful people. She got a lump sum in the settlement, half a mil, and $10,000 a month in alimony. She bought her little cottage outright and owned the building that the *Caffeinator's* in. She was doing pretty good for herself."

"What about here? She involved with anyone here?"

"Not that I can find out. She came out here about five years ago, opened the coffee shop and spent most of her time working it."

"Is the coffee shop still open?"

"Yep. David Bennett, her lawyer, wanted it kept open until her daughter can decide what to do with it. He's the executor. She's got two employees, stoner kid who works the coffee machine, and Dottie Madison, who bakes for her."

"Dottie Madison?"

"Go figure," said Wilson, shaking his head. He rose to his full height. "Here's the deal, Mercer. Something's hinky with this accident, but truth be told, we just don't get a lot of suspicious deaths up here."

Tate looked away.

"I know you left that all behind when you opened this place, but…"

Tate glanced back at him, shaking his head. "I can't, Sheriff. I mean, I'll tell you where I'd start, but I gave that up. I can't get sucked back in."

"I respect that…"

"Then please understand I'm not trying to be rude, but that was a lifetime ago." He tapped his knuckles on the counter. "I just wanna run my store and drink a beer on my deck once in a while."

Wilson nodded, picking up his hat and turning it in his hands. "Got it. So, you said you'd tell me where to start."

"The husband."

They said it together.

"He's got motive and means," finished Tate.

Wilson slapped the hat on his head. "Nice talking to you, Mercer."

"Same, Sheriff."

"If you change your mind, you know where to find me."

Tate gave a lift of his chin, but he didn't respond. No way in hell would he change his mind. He'd left all that two years ago and he sure as shit wasn't getting sucked back in. No way in hell.

* * *

Despite his resolve, Tate found himself standing in front of the *Caffeinator* after he shut the hardware store for the night. He glanced at the hours the store was open, 7:00AM to 6:00PM. Long days this Vivian Bradley woman kept, but then Wilson had said she had two employees.

He knew he should go home. He'd given this up two years ago. He had no business even showing curiosity about it. Still, old habits were hard to break. He'd just go in and see what they offered to drink. He didn't have to do anything else.

He walked to the glass front door and pulled it open. The outside was like the rest of the buildings on Main – shake shingles, A-framed roofs to shed snow, and built in a decade when ornate iron lights and brass door handles were the norm. He turned the burnished old knob and a bell above the door tinkled – a very different sound from his brash buzzer.

The interior was pleasant, if a bit too heavy on the pink. To his left lay a number of Victorian couches with the decorative brass nailheads and the curved wood along the back. They sported rose colored brocade fabric. Flanking them on either side were Victorian armchairs in a striped rose fabric. The fact that he knew they were Victorian style was entirely due to his ex-wife. Cherise had been an interior designer and fabric swatches and paint chips, not to mention catalogues, had littered their house. Beyond the couches were a number of iron bistro sets, offering additional seating in the middle of the room.

A couple sat at one of the bistro sets, staring at each other and ignoring their coffee. They shot him a glance, but then went back to staring, their hands clasped before them. Young lovers. Tate remembered when he and Cherise had been this annoying and for some reason, he missed it.

He looked away and saw another middle aged man sitting on the couches, typing on his laptop, his expression tense. He too glanced up, then went back to staring at the screen, his fingers flying on the keyboard. He wore trendy black framed glasses and a beret, his shirt open at the collar, sporting a gold chain around his neck. In addition to the striped silk shirt, he wore a tuxedo vest and the chain of a pocket watch draped out of his pocket.

Dismissing him, Tate turned toward the glass counter, marking the various baked goods on display. He guessed they were a pared down version of what had been offered earlier in the day, but they still looked delicious.

The swinging door behind the counter opened and a young man stepped out. He had shaggy blond hair, blue eyes, and a ready smile. A five-o'clock shadow darkened his jaw and his sideburns came nearly to his chin.

"Welcome to the *Caffeinator*, dude," he said, stepping up behind the cash register. "What can I do you for?" He gave a dopey laugh.

Tate held out his hand. "I'm Tate. I run the hardware store down the street."

The young man accepted it. "Yeah, dude, I thought I saw you around town." The laugh again. "Man, that's a trip."

Tate gave him a questioning look.

"How come we never met before?" He released Tate's hand. He wore a pink apron over his t-shirt and faded jeans. "Trippy, dude."

"Yeah." Tate wasn't sure what to make of him. "Well, if you ever need any building materials come see me."

"Naw." The young man waved him off. "I don't go in places like that."

"Like what?"

"Hardware stores." He leaned forward and dropped his voice. "Too many hard angles. And nails. Dude, I don't hang with nails."

"Really?" Tate found himself curious, even though this was the strangest conversation he'd had in years. "Why not?"

"Jesus, man. Christ, you know? Oh, man, that was harsh, you know? With the nails and all."

Tate narrowed his eyes, but he didn't respond. He really wasn't sure what the appropriate response might be.

"But you seem like a nice dude. What'd you say your name was?"

"Tate…um…Mercer."

"Tate Mercer, pleased to know you, dude."

"Same here. And you're?"

The young man nodded his head. "Deimos."

"Deimos?"

"One of the two moons of Mars. He was also a Greek god."

"Was he now?"

"Yep, twin brothers with Phoebus, son of Ares and Aphrodite. He represents the pure terror of war." Deimos nodded sagely. "It just felt right, ya know? Of course, the folks didn't really cotton to it, but then they thought Dean suited me, so go figure."

Tate drew a deep breath, filing that little tidbit away. "I honestly didn't know Mars had moons."

"Yeah. Two. Cool, huh?"

"Yeah."

"So, you ordering?"

Tate glanced up at the menu hanging on the wall behind the counter. He'd never bought into the fancy coffee craze and he had no idea what to order. The chalk-drawn list looked more like calligraphy than English to him.

"What do you recommend?"

"Oh, man, I'm really liking the salted caramel Macchiato right now. It's delish."

Tate blew out air. "Okay, hook me up."

Deimos gave his shaggy head a nod and punched some buttons on the cash register. Tate reached for his wallet, rocking on his heels as he waited for the young man to ring up his order. "So, I'm really sorry about your loss."

Deimos' head snapped up and he gave Tate a stricken look. "Dude, thanks. You heard about Viv?"

"Yeah. Terrible accident."

"The worst. I can't believe she lost control of the car like that."

So Wilson hadn't told her employees his suspicions? Hm. He wondered if the sheriff considered someone like Deimos a suspect.

"It must be hard to keep coming to work, not knowing if you'll be paid or not?"

Deimos shrugged, then reached for Tate's bank card. "Viv was so good to Dottie and me. We owe her that. 'Sides, she left the shop to her daughter. Dottie and me decided we wanted to keep things going for when the daughter comes out here."

"You think she will?"

"She's gotta figure out what to do with the store and Viv's house, now don't she?" He handed the card back. "Dude, Viv wanted to be cremated, so they did that, but they haven't released her ashes yet. They're waiting to see if the daughter wants to have a funeral or something. Seriously, dude, I didn't even know Viv had a daughter." He handed Tate a receipt and Tate pocketed it as Deimos moved to the side and started preparing the coffee.

Unable to talk over the sound of the grinder, Tate looked out at the store. The young couple rose and walked out, their arms around each other, but the guy on the couch gave Tate an annoyed glare. Tate turned back to Deimos.

"How's business been?" he asked.

Deimos glanced up as he measured out some milk. "Real good. We get tourists and regulars both. How's the nail business?" He gave a shudder.

"Good." He drummed his fingers on the counter. What the hell was he doing? This wasn't his job anymore. He didn't need to get involved in this. He should just get his coffee and walk away, forget Wilson had ever come to him in the first place. "So, no hassles, no disgruntled customers?"

Deimos pulled a lever and a sharp hissing sound issued from the machine. The hissing stopped and he reached for a dented silver shaker, shaking something onto the top of the coffee. "I mean, you always get some uptight yoyo who thinks you're not moving fast enough, or the coffee's not hot enough, or it's too hot." He reached for a cap and put it on the cup. "That's why I do yoga seven times a week and reiki to channel my chi."

Tate gave a lift of his chin. Cherise would love this guy. She read tarot cards and paid huge sums of money to have her chakras aligned, or some such thing. He'd never been sure what that meant.

"Anyone get…you know, aggressive with…um?"

"Viv? Naw." Deimos reached for a cardboard sleeve and slipped it around the cup. "I don't remember no one."

"What about her ex-husband? You know anything about him?"

Deimos slid Tate's coffee over to him. "Not much. He's in LA."

Tate nodded, curling his fingers around the paper cup.

"I mean, there are the guys from the big box Satan factory."

Tate lowered the cup. He hadn't even had a taste yet. "Wait. What?"

"One of those big box soul-less stores are going in. They want to buy this side of Main Street for it."

"I haven't heard anything about that."

"You're sort of at the end, you know? They want this side – the *Caffeinator*, the *Knitatorium*, the three *B's*, and the double *T's*."

Tate frowned. "Come again?"

"The *Bourbon Brothers' Barbecue* and *Trinkets by Trixie*."

"Got it." Tate lifted his coffee to take a sip, then had another question. "Which big box store?"

Deimos leaned closer and lowered his voice, speaking the dreaded name. Tate couldn't believe the Chamber of Commerce was even thinking of such a store going in here. Sequoia prided itself on keeping its small town feel and a big box store would destroy that.

"They offered Viv beaucoup bucks to sell out, but she wouldn't. Then she and the other business owners agreed to stand together against the Satanic megalith no matter how much they offered them to close down."

"And it worked?"

Deimos shrugged. "Seems to be working, don't it? I mean we're still here."

"Right." Tate lifted the coffee and took a sip. The pleasant combination of salty and sweet struck his taste buds, forcing him to notice it. "Wow, this is good."

Deimos beamed. "Thought you might like it. So how come you never come in here before?"

Tate lowered the coffee cup. "I'm not much on specialty coffee, honestly, but I should have come by and said hi before this. I really am sorry about Vivian." He glanced over at the man sitting on the sofa, but the fella hadn't moved. "Anyone else cause problems for her?"

"Naw. Everyone loved Viv. God, she was great. I miss her so much." Deimos' expression grew grim, then it brightened again. "Can I get you anything else?"

Tate realized he'd probably reached the end of what Deimos knew about Vivian Bradley. He shook his head. "Nope, but thanks for the coffee and the chat. It was nice to meet you, Deimos."

Deimos waved a hand at him. "Call me Dee. Everyone else does. Hope we'll be seeing more of you."

Tate lifted the coffee in a half-salute. "You just might at that," he said, then turned and left the building, hearing the merry tinkling of the bell as he went out the door.

* * *

Tate found himself pinned down behind the car, his hands wrapped around the handle on his gun, his heart hammering in his ear. The crackle of the radio affixed to his shoulder sounded ominous in the darkness.

He reached up to silence it, but he heard the report of the gun and the passenger-side mirror shattered, raining bits of glass down on him. He ducked his head, closing his eyes tight, willing his head to clear of the panic, but the shooting didn't stop. Over and over and over. He heard bullets pinging off the side of the car, slamming through the side windows, puncturing the tire on the driver's side, the whoosh of air loud in the damp night as it deflated.

He knew he had to move or he'd be picked off, so he began to crab walk down the side of the car toward the trunk. Bullets whistled overhead, slamming into the glass around a streetlight and shattering it, pumping into the side of the house. He heard people screaming and the radio kept barking its unintelligible commands.

All training had left him the moment the shooting started. All thoughts of the proper protocols were gone. Everything boiled down to instinct and instinct told him to flee. He halted in the crabwalk, closing his eyes again and trying to regain control. *Count the bullets. Count how many times he fires, then you can judge when he stops to reload.*

But how did you count bullets when they were innumerable? When the gun could fire off twenty or thirty in a matter of seconds?

They were outgunned. No two ways about it. They were outgunned and he didn't hear any backup coming.

He had one chance, one opportunity, and he had to take it.

He continued down the side of the car, feeling with his right hand, his left in a death grip on the gun. The lights had been blown out and it was darker than it had been even a few seconds ago. If he could get around the end of the car, he might get a clear shot. He might be able to neutralize the threat, but he had to get that shot.

He reached the end bumper and sucked in a deep breath, ready to rise over the end of it, firing as he went, but he saw something pooling at the back of the car. Gasoline? Had they hit the fuel tank and spilled its contents?

If they got a shot close to the puddle, a stray spark would send the entire thing up, him included. Shit.

But as he stared at it, he realized it didn't flow like gasoline, evaporating and soaking into the asphalt. It had a viscous quality to it, a way it flowed that could only be one thing.

He realized he was breathing too fast, but he clenched his jaw and braced himself, knowing he had to take a look, knowing he had no other choice.

He gripped the gun with both hands again, easing to the very end of the car, stepping in the fluid, but ignoring it. Then he peered around the end of the bumper.

*Jason's dead eyes stared back at him.*

Tate bolted upright, his heart hammering against his ribs, in his ears, his body covered in a cold sweat. He tunneled his fingers into his hair and braced his elbows on his tented knees. *Just a dream,* he told himself. *Just a dream.*

He waited until his heart rate slowed, then threw back the covers, climbing out of bed. He padded barefoot into the bathroom and turned on the light. His little blue tiled bathroom, desperately in need of a remodel, revealed itself in the soft glow of the light bar over the vanity. He braced his hands on the cracked bowl of the sink and reached for the cold water, then he grabbed a hand towel off the rack affixed to the side of the bowl and dunked it into the water, dragging the cool cloth over his face, behind his neck, and across his bare chest.

He looked at himself in the mirror. His brown hair was mussed, his pupils dilated, the lines of tension stark around his mouth. A day's growth of stubble darkened his jaw. His fingers curled in the towel and he reached to turn off the water, realizing that his hand was trembling.

Leaving the light on, he went back into the bedroom and found his LAPD sweatshirt in the dresser drawer, tugging it on. Now that the panic was abating, he felt chilled. He reached for the matching pair of sweatpants and tugged them over his sleep shorts.

Then he went to the bedroom door and pulled it open, padding his way to the dated kitchen and flipping that light on as well. He grabbed the teakettle off the stove and filled it with water, placing it back on the burner and turning it on. Finally, he grabbed a mug out of a chipped white painted cabinet and reached for the metal canister on the tiled counter, pulling off the top and reaching for a chamomile teabag.

He would have scoffed at men drinking tea just a few years before, but it was the only thing that helped him calm down after one of these nightmares. That and a good book to take his mind off everything.

He tore the bag out of the packet and placed it in the mug, then he left the kitchen and went into the tiny living room, turning on lights as he went. The battered, threadbare recliner sat next to the stone fireplace and he turned on the multipurpose reading lamp/end table he kept there. His book lay on the surface of it with his reading glasses. He reached for the afghan he'd folded over the back of the recliner and swung it around his shoulders, then he heard the kettle whistling, so he went back to the kitchen and prepared his tea.

Finally, he carried the mug to his recliner and sank into the seat. The dream was receding to the back of his mind, but he still couldn't shake the chill that had settled in his bones. He pushed the recliner back and the footrest came out. Bracing his bare feet on the rest, he forced himself to lean back in the chair, breathing in the steam from his tea and deliberately taking slow, deep breaths.

Then he reached for his book. As with many nights since he'd come to Sequoia, he knew he'd spend the rest of this one in this chair, reading until he fell asleep, every light in the house blazing against the darkness.

# CHAPTER 3

Zion sipped at her chai tea and pressed the button on her computer to boot it up. Franklin, her boss, came around the side of her cubicle. His Armani suit and brown leather Ferragamo loafers were impeccable, his frosted blond hair combed back from his strong forehead, his chin clean shaven. He smelled heavenly.

Half the women and a number of the men were in love with him, but whether he trended toward either sex was a mystery. They'd never seen him with anyone and he didn't give any of his secrets away.

"We're getting a lot of complaints about Zavaritram being denied on our formularies. An email went out last night giving you the suggested dialogue you should use when taking a complaint."

Zion clicked on the email icon, watching the program load onto her screen.

"Just wanted to make sure you didn't have questions."

Zion found the email and opened it, scanning the dialogue. It was pretty much the same thing they always said to disgruntled patients. "What's this drug for?"

"Colon cancer."

"And we're denying it because of costs?"

"$11,000 a month." He shook his head in disgust. "These pharmaceutical companies have us by the balls, but they're not gonna call the shots anymore."

"Is the drug effective?"

Franklin's eyes narrowed.

Zion shook her head, holding up a hand. "I know. That's not part of my job description."

He gave her a smile, his teeth dazzling white. She wanted to believe he was straight because she'd love to date such a man, but his sense of style made that seem unlikely.

Still, it would be fun to be seen on the arm of a man like Franklin – she was sure his life was filled with fine dining, first class airline tickets, art shows, and operas – the finest things in life to be had for the right sum.

"You've been doing a good job, Zion. Your days as an administrative assistant aren't going to last long. As soon as we get the go-ahead, I'm looking to expand our field reps. You keep up the good work and you'll rocket to the top of that list."

Zion felt a flutter of excitement. She wanted to be a field rep, taking lunch to the doctor offices, schmoozing them, discussing their products, signing new clients. She'd agreed to the administrative assistant position for this very reason. The opportunities for advancement were endless with *Judicious.*

"Thank you, Franklin, I appreciate it."

He nodded, then walked away.

Zion watched his well tailored backend wander toward his office, then she picked up her tea and took another sip. Honestly, she hated being an administrative assistant. It was simply a glorified secretary's job. She ran errands for the field reps, she answered complaints from clients, and she took messages from the doctors. When she'd been hired, Franklin promised her she'd move up quickly, but his version of quickly was different than hers. She'd been here nearly three years and beyond a promotion to AA II, a promotion without a financial increase, she'd not advanced any further. Rebekah was at least level IV, which gave her an extra hundred a month and a sweeter Roman numeral behind her title.

Forcing the betraying thoughts away, she focused on the email and made sure she knew how to properly respond. At 9:00, Rebekah appeared at the opening of her cubicle, wearing a Vera Wang silk blouse and striped pencil skirt with stiletto heels.

"It's time to set up the coffee for the office meeting," she said.

Zion pushed back her desk chair and rose. "Danishes or muffins this time?"

"Danishes. He wants them heated in the microwave."

Zion followed her friend into the conference room and while Rebekah began arranging the chairs around the huge conference table, Zion pulled the coffee urn out from beneath the counter in the corner, settling it on the granite and plugging it in.

"Did you have dinner with the parents last night?" Rebekah asked.

"Yep, what about you?"

"I went out with Wendel. I think he might ask me to marry him."

Zion glanced over her shoulder at her friend. "Really? Why?"

"He took me to *Saison* in South Beach."

"Wow!"

"Then he asked me to move in with him."

Rebekah and Wendel had been dating off and on for two years now. Zion left the coffee urn and moved toward the table. "What'd you tell him?"

"I'd think about it."

"What's there to think about?"

"He's just a doctor, Zion. I don't know if I can live that lifestyle."

Once being a doctor had been enough for most young women. Zion couldn't help but wonder when it had become undesirable. "What are you talking about? He owns his own condo in the City."

"The hours and the pay." She pointed out the door. "Franklin makes three times what Wendel does."

"Well…"

Rebekah waved Zion off. "Anyway, it doesn't matter. He didn't ask me."

"But he asked you to move in with him."

"I'm not doing that. He's gotta put a ring on it, baby," she said in her best Beyoncé imitation.

Zion smiled, shaking her head. "I gotta get the water." As she started to walk past, Rebekah grabbed her arm, stopping her.

"Hold on. Did you tell the parents about the phone call yesterday?"

"From the lawyer?"

Rebekah gave Zion a *no duh* look.

"We talked about it."

"And what did they say?"

"They think I should call him back."

"Are you going to?"

"I don't know." Zion fussed with the silver chained belt on her skirt. "I don't really want to deal with it right now."

"What if she left you a million dollars?"

"That's what the lawyer said."

"Well?"

"She didn't."

"How do you know?"

"Because I asked him."

"You need to call him back. You need closure."

Zion frowned. "Closure? From what?"

Rebekah put her hands on Zion's shoulders. "Darlin', seriously? You were abandoned as an infant, left to fend for yourself."

Well, not exactly. She'd gone from the hospital to her parents' home, unless you called being showered with love and attention fending for oneself. She sighed, but she didn't pull away. Rebekah's affected behavior was one of the things she actually loved about her.

"Don't you want to know more about your biological mother? Don't you want to get closure for why she abandoned you?"

Zion pulled Rebekah's hands away, cradling them in her own. "No," she said.

"No?"

"No."

"How can it be no?"

"Because I don't care. I had great parents and I don't need closure. Vivian Bradley is no more important to me than any other stranger in the world. I'm sorry she died young, but that has nothing to do with me."

Rebekah frowned.

"Can we just set up for the meeting, Becks?"

"Sure." She gave an airy wave of her hand. "I'll be a reluctant participant to your denial."

Zion laughed and pulled away, walking from the room after the water.

* * *

After a lunch of cottage cheese, a peach, and bottled water, Zion returned to her cubicle and searched her emails, answering the few that needed immediate attention. Then she began typing the report that Franklin had left her.

He kept track of all his contacts, but he wrote his notes in longhand, then gave them to Zion to transcribe. She didn't know why he couldn't keep electronic files for himself, but he refused. He said he thought better with a paper and pen; however, these tasks were the very reason Zion wanted out of the administrative assistant position. Well, that and the money.

Her little studio in the Sunset was barely bigger than a closet. She had room for her bed, a half-assed kitchen, a bathroom where you practically had to straddle the toilet, and no closet. She'd bought an armoire for her clothes, but it took up half the space.

Her phone rang and she automatically pressed the button to connect it on her headset, clicking on the customer call log to open it. "Zion Sawyer, *Judicious Insurance*, how can I help you?"

"I don't know if I got the right place," said the harried male voice on the other end of the line. "You made me push so damn many buttons, I'm not sure where I ended up."

"I'm sorry for the inconvenience, sir. If you tell me what you're calling about, I can direct your call."

He made a grumble of frustration. "Look, I don't want to be transferred to India or any such thing. In fact, I read somewhere that you have to tell me whether you're in Bangalore or Boston."

"Actually, you called the San Francisco branch of *Judicious Insurance*, sir," she said, trying to keep her voice level and engaging.

"Fine." He made another annoyed grumble. "My wife has stage 4 colon cancer."

Zion felt her shoulders grow tight. She'd been dreading this sort of call all day. "How can I help you, sir?" She wanted to tell him she was sorry, but *Judicious* made it very clear that they were supposed to keep the calls professional and never deviate into the personal. Stage 4 colon cancer meant that the customer was using her insurance, costing them money, but it felt heartless not to offer some sort of regret.

"The doctors want to prescribe her Zavaritram, but the pharmacy says that drug isn't part of your coverage."

"That's right, Mr…"

"Harrington."

"Mr. Harrington, Zavaritram is not on our formulary list at this time." Her fingers clicked on the keyboard, logging in the call. "Can I get your wife's member number?" She winced and fought down her own self-loathing at this coldest part of her job.

"What?"

"I need your wife's member number, sir."

He rattled it off and Zion typed it into the contact form. A wheel spun on the program and the woman's name popped up on her screen. Arlene Harrington, age 52, employed by the DMV, member with *Judicious* for the last twenty-two years. She clicked the *add contact* button and Arlene's pertinent information filled the form.

"What are you typing?"

"I'm recording our call, Mr. Harrington."

"What good does that do me?"

Zion's fingers stilled on the keys. She opened her mouth to respond, but realized she didn't know what to say.

"Hello?"

She cleared her throat. "I'm just recording our call, Mr. Harrington."

"I didn't understand what you said. How do I get my wife the Zavaritram she needs? The doctors prescribed it, but your company won't cover it. What do I do?"

Zion briefly closed her eyes. She could hear the desperation in his voice. *Go back to the script. They'd just sent the script this morning. Just follow the script.* "Zavaritram is currently not on *Judicious'* formulary list, but I've taken down your contact information."

"And? And what? What the hell does that matter? Do you know how much this drug costs per month?"

"I am aware of the cost, Mr. Harrington."

"Well?"

Zion swallowed hard. *Just follow the script.* "Unfortunately, Zavaritram is currently not on *Judicious'* formulary list."

"Don't say that again!" His voice rose with frustration and panic. "Are you telling me you people aren't going to pay for her medication? Are you really telling me that?"

"I'm telling you…"

"Don't say it's not on the formulary list again! I need something more. I need answers from you, not some bullshit line you've been told to say!"

Zion flinched. The script said to thank him for calling and disconnect the call. She reached up to do just that, but his voice came back, quieter, more controlled.

"Look, I'm sorry. I don't mean to yell at you. I know you're just doing your job."

"Thank you, Mr. Harrington."

"It's just..." His voice choked off. "I'm desperate. I don't know what else to do. The doctors say this medication has shown promise. It might even give us a few more years. We've been married for twenty-six years. Do you know what a few more years means to me, miss?"

Zion looked out into the office. She could see her fellow workers, each in their own cubicles, typing away or taking calls of their own. She knew if she stood, she'd see the glass walls of Franklin's office, his expensive framed prints of San Francisco, his plush burgundy carpeting, his ebony glazed desk.

"I understand, Mr. Harrington."

"Then help me," he pleaded. "Do something more than tell me this drug isn't on your formulary. *Please*." The please was gut-wrenching.

Zion covered the mouthpiece with her hand and turned back to the computer, lowering her voice. "I took down your complaint, Mr. Harrington. All I can tell you is we've been getting a lot of them lately, which is good. Each complaint logged into the system adds one more consumer demanding we cover the drug."

"But how long will that take? How many complaints do you need to change their minds?"

"I don't know, but if you could get the doctors to call also, that would help. A lot."

Mr. Harrington went quiet, then he sighed. "Thank you for that, miss. I appreciate it."

Zion prayed this wasn't one of the calls *Judicious* was recording. They spot recorded customer service calls and going off script was a quick way to bounce yourself back into training. If you went off script too many times, you'd be filing unemployment.

"I'm really sorry, Mr. Harrington," she blurted out. If they'd recorded this call, she was already in trouble. Might as well make it worth her time. So far, she'd never been caught going off script before.

"Thank you, miss. I appreciate that too." Then he hung up.

Zion typed in the dialogue of his complaint, then saved the log, but the call wouldn't leave her. She looked over her shoulder again, wondering if any of her colleagues felt as horrible as she did at this moment. She hated taking complaints, but usually it was about *Judicious* being slow to pay a claim or mixing something up. Rarely had she had to take a call about them refusing a service to their customers, but that was happening more frequently now. The more the government tried to rein in medical costs, the more the companies fought to get profits anyway they could.

Her eyes chanced on David Bennett's phone number. After talking with her parents last night, she'd made the decision not to call the lawyer about her biological mother's death. And after that last call, she seriously didn't need to hear anything more depressing, but a part of her was curious what Vivian might have left her.

She reached out and ran her fingers over the number, then drew her hand away. Her life was full now. She didn't need anything that woman had left her. What was it her father always said? *No use tickling the tiger with a feather, unless you were itching to lose a hand.*

"Zion!"

She jumped and whirled in her chair. Dear God, they had been listening to her call and they'd already ratted her out to Franklin.

He loomed at the entrance to her cubicle, giving her a speculative look. "Why do you look so scared?"

She placed a hand against her heart. "You startled me."

He brushed that away with a shake of his perfectly coiffed head. "I'm going to meet with a potential client, take him for dinner and drinks at *Quince's*."

Zion glanced at the clock on her computer. It was only two. "So early?"

Franklin rolled his eyes. "Of course not. *Revolver* is having a sale on *Apolis* and I need some new shirts desperately. I can't keep wearing these old rags."

Old rags? Clearly, Franklin had never worn anything remotely resembling a rag in his life, but Zion just gave him a tense smile and nodded. She'd heard about *Revolver*, but she'd never shopped there. One shirt cost over a hundred dollars. She was a long way from being able to afford that and still keep the lights on in her studio.

"See you tomorrow."

He gave a wave over his shoulder, then he was gone.

Zion knew she should go back to typing his reports, but her attention strayed back to the lawyer's number. What did it hurt just to give him a call? Seriously, it might be important. She didn't know what Vivian died from. Maybe it was hereditary and something could be done now to prevent Zion from meeting her demise at 43. In fact, the more she thought of it, the more she realized she owed it to herself to call.

She pulled out her desk drawer and fished in her Cartier handbag for her cell phone. This was her personal call and she didn't want *Judicious* knowing anything about it. Sliding back her desk chair, she rose, deciding to take her afternoon break a few minutes early.

Grabbing the sticky note with the lawyer's number, she walked to the break room. One of the other reps, Steve Pratt, was just walking out with a cup of coffee.

"Hey," he said, giving Zion a jerk of his strong, angular chin.

"Hey, Steve," she said in return. She was pretty sure he didn't know her name. He was one of the few openly straight reps with a wife and two kids. Beyond that, they'd never said an entire sentence to one another in three years.

After he left, Zion had the break room to herself. She took a seat at a table and placed the sticky note in front of her. Then she just stared at it. She didn't know why she was so reluctant to call, but she still felt like she was betraying her parents somehow. However, they'd given their blessing, so what was the problem?

Truthfully, she'd never harbored much interest in Vivian. She knew of her, she knew her name, and she knew Gabi had been in contact with her for years, but beyond that, she didn't give it much thought. Her childhood had been about as idyllic as a childhood could be. She'd never wanted for anything. Her parents had showered her with love and attention. She'd never been bullied in school despite her bright red hair. And the one time she'd left home had been to attend college at UCLA where she earned a bachelor's degree in business. She'd gotten along with her roommate, had a number of handsome college boyfriends, and then returned home to land the job with *Judicious* within a week of graduation. What more did she need or want?

And yet, she thumbed on her phone and dialed David Bennett's number. He picked up on the third ring. "David Bennett," he said in a pleasant, deep baritone. She realized she hadn't really thought about how pleasant his voice was when he called yesterday.

"Mr. Bennett, it's Zion Sawyer. You called me yesterday about my…um…about Vivian Bradley."

"Yes, Ms. Sawyer, I'm so glad you called me back."

"Before we discuss this, Mr. Bennett…"

"Call me David."

Zion frowned. "What?"

"Please, call me David. Mr. Bennett always reminds me of my father. He's sort of the Bennett in *Bennett, Coleman, & Cox*. He just brought me on after I passed the bar."

All righty then. "Okay, um, David, you can call me Zion."

"Nice to meet you, Zion. Again, I'm really glad you called me."

"Sure. Look, David, mostly I'm interested in knowing how she died. I mean, I figured it might be a good idea to know if it was a genetic defect or a heart attack or God forbid, cancer, since knowledge is probably power and…"

"Car accident."

Zion blinked a few times. "I'm sorry, what did you say?"

"She died in a car accident, Zion. I'm so sorry to have to tell you this. She went off the road into a ravine. They believe she died on impact."

"Wow." Zion rubbed at her forehead. Rebekah would scold her that she was going to get wrinkles if she kept frowning. "Um, was she…was she…um…drinking?"

"No, not according to her toxicology reports."

Zion digested that information. She'd never known the woman, but she still hated to think her last moments had been filled with terror.

"Again, I'm sorry, Zion."

"No, it's okay. So…did you call me to make final arrangements or something?"

"Actually, no. Vivian had left clear instructions on what was to happen with her body. As soon as the coroner released it, she was cremated. Her ashes are in my office just awaiting your instructions on what you want me to do with them."

"She didn't buy a niche or whatever they do with…" Zion realized she was sweating. Why was this conversation so difficult? This woman meant nothing to her. "…with remains."

"No, no burial plot, no niche. Beyond cremation, she left everything up to you."

"Okay."

"Do you know what you want me to do about that?"

"No, not right now. No, I—I need to think about it."

"Of course, I understand."

She liked his gentle manner, his way of soothing without being cloying and insincere. Zion drew a deep breath and held it, then she slowly exhaled. "You said she named me as her sole heir."

"She did."

"What does that mean, David?"

"Well, I'd personally like to meet with you to discuss it, give you her will, etcetera. Is there anyway you can come out to Sequoia and meet with me?"

"You can't come here."

"I could, but to be honest, most of what Vivian left you is property. I'd like to show you everything, so that you can make an informed decision on what you want to do with it all."

"Wait. Property? What do you mean property?" It was a house trailer. Shit, she'd known it would be this. A 1970's dark paneled house trailer that would blow over in the first tornado that ripped through Sequoia.

"Your mother had a lovely cottage and a coffee shop on Main Street. There's also about $100,000 in an IRA that belongs to you, but I'd really like to discuss the details in person."

Zion's head couldn't seem to get around what he was saying. "She had a coffee shop?"

"Yes. In fact, she bought the building itself and she paid it off over the last few years. The coffee shop does pretty well for itself. She also bought the cottage with money she got from a divorce settlement."

Zion's fingers tightened on the phone. "She was married."

"Well, divorced, yes."

"Divorced? Did she have other kids?"

"No, she didn't."

"Where's her husband?"

"Los Angeles."

"Is that where she lived?" Her mother had said she thought that's where Vivian was, but she hadn't been sure.

"Yep, she was in Los Angeles for many years, but she's been in Sequoia for the last six, building up the business for herself."

She'd been in Los Angeles. She'd been in the same city as Zion had been in for four years while she went to college. They'd been that close and Zion had never known it.

"Zion, you okay?"

"Yeah," she said, easing her hold on the phone.

"Do you think you can come to Sequoia in the next few days to meet with me?"

Zion didn't know if she wanted to do that. The money was fine. She could use that to maybe get herself a bigger apartment, but what was she going to do with the cottage and the coffee house? She didn't want property in a backwater town like Sequoia.

"What if I want to sell everything?"

"We can talk about that, but I'd like you to see it before we make those arrangements. The cottage in particular is filled with your mother's belongings. I wish you'd go through them before we think about putting it on the market."

Go through her mother's possessions? Dear God, she didn't want to do that, but she guessed there was no one else to do it. She'd make Gabi go with her. Gabi was great in situations that required orchestrating many tasks.

"I need to get a few days off work."

"I'm sure they'll give it to you for bereavement leave.'

Bereavement? What the hell. She wasn't bereaved. She didn't care. And yet, even as she thought this, the image of Vivian dying by herself in a smashed up car intruded in her thoughts. A violent death was bad enough, but to die alone and afraid, that was somehow worse. Zion just couldn't stay detached when she thought of that.

"All right, David, I'll talk to my boss and try to come up the day after tomorrow."

"Excellent. I'm looking forward to meeting you." Then his enthusiasm faded. "I mean, I am sorry for your loss, Zion."

"No worries," she said with a tense laugh. "I'll see you then."

"See you then," he answered and disconnected the call.

Zion sat and stared at her blank phone. She really didn't want to do this, but she didn't have a choice. If there was one thing her parents had taught her, it was not to run away from something unpleasant. Instead, you faced it head on, even if you had to close your eyes to accomplish it.

# CHAPTER 4

Tate entered the *Caffeinator* the next morning just before he was scheduled to open the hardware store. An older woman, nearly as round as she was tall, stood behind the counter, wearing the same pink apron Deimos had been wearing, but she was rolling out dough with a rolling pin. She looked up, blinking at him from behind thick glasses.

Beaded chains affixed to the ears of the glasses kept them in place around her neck. Her purple hair was a loose cloud of curls on her head and her hands were short fingered, covered in flour, the palms broad.

She beamed a smile at him. "Hello, sugar, what can I get for you today?" Her voice was low and melodious, instantly soothing the jangle of nerves inside Tate. He could actually feel his shoulders lower.

He came forward and held out his hand. "I'm Tate Mercer. I own the *Hammer Tyme* down the street."

"*Hammer Tyme*," she laughed, then held up her flour covered hands. "So clever."

He pulled his hand back, feeling silly that he'd offered it when she was obviously working the dough. "Well, I didn't actually name it. The Chamber of Commerce did. It was already the *Hammer Tyme* when I bought it."

She laughed again. "They're all so clever, all the businesses. I love me a good pun."

"I guess," he answered, but he couldn't help smiling. Her smile was infectious.

She picked up a knife and began paring the dough into stripes. "I'm Dottie. Dottie Madison, sugar."

"Nice to meet you, Dottie. What are you making?" he asked, peering over the counter.

"I love to make these cinnamon bread sticks. You dip them in frosting, then take a bite and it's like you've died and gone to heaven. They melt in your mouth."

"Sounds fantastic."

"You come back here in an hour and they'll be hot right out of the oven," she said, glancing up at him with another smile. "I'll save you some."

Tate noticed her eyes were a lavender color as well and blinked in surprise. Was she wearing contact lenses under her glasses?

"So, did you want some coffee too, sugar?"

The happy bell jingled above the door and an older couple entered, immediately bickering about what they wanted to order.

"Good morning," Dottie called. "Be right with you." She left the dough on the counter and walked to the sink, beginning to wash her hands.

Tate glanced at the couple, but they were distracted by the handwritten board, so they didn't bother to acknowledge him.

"I was in here yesterday afternoon and Deimos…"

"Dee, lovely boy, isn't he?" Dottie called over her shoulder. "He's been a rock since poor Viv died. I couldn't run this place without him."

Tate nodded. Here was the opening he'd been looking for, but honestly, he didn't know why he was here. He'd promised himself when he got up this morning he wasn't going to poke around in this case. It was none of his business and it was bringing back the nightmares, yet here he was and he couldn't seem to stop himself from asking questions.

Dottie dried her hands on a hand towel and moved back to the counter. "Can I start a coffee for you, sugar?"

"Um." Tate motioned at the couple. "Go ahead and help them."

"Sounds good." She focused her attention on the couple. "What'll it be, folks?"

They moved to the counter and placed their orders. Tate took the opportunity to wander the store. People were beginning to meander down Main Street, looking at the shops. He didn't have much time, he figured, before Dottie was swamped with customers wanting their first cup of coffee for the day.

The sound of the grinder, the smell of the coffee, the sweet scent of the baked goods, all gave off a calming, serene air and he liked it. He could almost understand why people gravitated to these places. It gave you a bit of relaxation in the midst of your busy day. Even the kitschy decorations in here, the pink furniture, the muzak piped in through the speakers, added to this sense of calm. He could get used to coming here.

Dottie passed out the coffees and took their payment. The couple went on their way as Dottie washed her hands again. Tate wandered back to the counter.

"I'm sorry about Vivian's death," he said, scratching his forehead.

Dottie's smile faded. "She was such a doll. Such a good friend and a fantastic boss."

"Do you know what's going to happen to this place now?"

Dottie shook her head. "She had a daughter. She left everything to her, but she gave the daughter up for adoption when she was an infant. Viv didn't talk about her much, but according to David over at the lawyer shop, the daughter doesn't want anything from her." Dottie gave a sigh. "So, I figure, she'll probably sell the place as soon as she can."

Tate digested that. "You don't think she'd sell to the big box store, do you?"

Dottie shrugged. "Why not? It would be the quickest way to get rid of it."

"Do they bother you much? The conglomerate?"

"Not so much once the stores on this side of the street agreed not to sell, but who knows now that Viv's gone?"

Tate worried that seemed too convenient a reason to get rid of Vivian Bradley. Bump her off, the store goes to a disinterested party, and you have a wedge to drive between the remaining business owners.

"So, what can I get you, sugar?" Dottie asked, her good nature returning.

"I've never tried specialty coffees before yesterday. Dee made me a salted caramel Macchiato yesterday. It was very tasty."

"Dee just loves that drink right now," she said with a laugh. "How about a mint mocha freeze? That's refreshing for starting the day."

"Sounds great. I'll try it."

She set about making the coffee with obvious skill. She was almost as fast with the various machines as Dee had been.

"Shame Vivian didn't have more family. Was she married?" Tate asked conversationally.

Dottie shook her head. "Nope. Divorced. Her ex gave her the money to buy this place and her little house. She loved that little house."

Tate nodded. "You ever meet him?"

"No, he's a big shot plastic surgeon in LA, giving boob jobs to all the little starlets." Moving to the blender, she dumped everything inside and added ice. The whir of the blender stopped all conversation.

Tate rubbed the back of his neck. What the hell was he doing? He'd stopped being a cop two years ago. Why was he getting himself involved in this? It was none of his business. He'd just get his coffee and beat a hasty retreat, and he'd forget Sheriff Wilson had ever come to him for help. This was not his job, this wasn't his case. He needed to move on.

The blender went off and Dottie poured the thick mixture into a clear plastic cup.

"Viv was pretty closed mouth about her private life." She capped the cup and slid it over to him with a straw.

Tate took out his wallet and removed his card, passing it to her.

Dottie smiled at him. "I hope you enjoy that, sugar. I'd love to see you become one of our regulars. You got a nice face, kind and open, but you look like you could use a little happiness in your life."

Tate wasn't sure what to do with that, so he busied himself with removing the wrapper on his straw. "Thanks," he mumbled.

Dottie swiped his card and then printed a receipt. "You come back in an hour and I'll have those cinnamon breadsticks ready for you."

Tate smiled. "I'll send my assistant. I gotta open shop and he doesn't run the cash register yet."

She laughed. "You hired that Logan boy, didn't you?"

"Yep. He's a good kid."

"Yes, he is. Wish he'd go back to school."

"He's sort of going to school. He goes to the charter school over in Visalia. Goes down there twice a week and gets his lessons. He says sitting in desks isn't for him."

"Can he get his high school diploma that way?"

"Apparently, but I feel bad that he's missing out on everything else."

"Yeah, it's a shame, but his mother needs the help."

Tate nodded. Logan's mother had stage four cancer and didn't have much time left. Logan had opted for the charter school, so he could work full time with Tate. Tate understood it, but he hated it.

Dottie patted his hand. "You're a good guy, helping him out like that."

"Wish I could do more," he said, forcing a smile. Then he shifted weight. "Dottie, if anyone from that conglomerate comes around here asking questions or bothering you…"

The bell above the door jangled and a couple of young people stepped inside. Dottie smiled at them. "Be right with you," she said cheerfully, then she focused on Tate again. "Go on, sugar."

"If they bother you or Dee, you tell Sheriff Wilson, okay?"

Dottie frowned at that. "Is something wrong?"

"Just tell Sheriff Wilson if they come around, okay?"

"I will. Is there something you should tell me?"

Tate drew a deep breath, placing his straw in his drink. "I'll tell him to stop by and talk with you, okay?"

"Okay?" Her frown deepened.

Tate didn't feel it was his place to inform her of what Wilson had told him. He lifted the drink and took a sip. The cool, refreshing glide of peppermint bathed his tongue, followed by the slightly bitter bite of the coffee. He shivered in pleasure. "Thank you. This is really nice."

Dottie's smile returned. "I'm so glad. You have a good day, sugar, and send Logan over here for some cinnamon breadsticks, all righty?"

"I will," he answered, waving over his shoulder as he sidestepped the other customers and went to the door, warring with himself over why he couldn't just leave this alone. But he knew, there was something about figuring out puzzles that had him hooked.

* * *

As Tate did inventory, Logan stocked shelves. He watched the boy work. He always looked like a spooked rabbit and if Tate even mentioned he wasn't doing something right, he acted like he might bolt. He didn't share a lot with Tate about his life. Tate had found out about his mother's cancer when Logan applied for the job, and he'd learned about the charter school when Logan had asked for two mornings off a week to head into Visalia, but beyond that, they didn't share much else with each other.

Tate felt a little guilty about that. The boy had worked for him for almost two years now, since he'd come to Sequoia and bought the *Hammer Tyme*, but he didn't even know where he lived or what sort of cancer his mother had.

Hell, beyond the grocery store, Tate hadn't really frequented any of the businesses along Main Street before. Sure, he got take-out from the barbecue brothers once in a while, but the other stores hadn't interested him before.

Since moving to Sequoia, his life had alternated between the store and home, and when he was home, he chose to be alone. It was easier that way. No complications, no one to rely on, and no one who relied on him. He'd thought about getting a dog, but that had seemed like too big a commitment.

Cherise hadn't been wrong when she accused him of cutting himself off from everything but the necessities of life. He'd done it willfully and deliberately. No wonder she'd replaced him the first chance she got. He couldn't really blame her.

"Hey, Logan, you know Dottie Madison at the *Caffeinator*?"

Logan looked up, his brown eyes wide with surprise. "Yep, I know her. Everyone in town knows Dottie."

"She told me to come back and pick up some cinnamon breadsticks. You wanna go get them for me?"

"Really?" The delight on his boyish face was obvious.

"Sure." Tate took out his wallet and held out a twenty.

Logan sidled over to the counter and accepted it. "How many?"

"Get us a dozen. She said there was frosting too. Make sure she includes that, okay?"

"Sure thing. Anything else?"

"Get yourself something to drink on me if you want?"

Logan's gaze dropped as he fingered the bill. "I couldn't do that."

"Nonsense. I told you to. Get whatever you want."

"You want something?"

Tate shook his head. "I've had my one cup of coffee for the day."

The kid ducked his head, then he hurried for the exit, all lanky limbs and loose gait, his jeans hanging off his narrow hips. Tate watched after him, feeling a twinge of guilt. He didn't think the kid had a father figure in his life. He probably could use someone to take some interest in him.

Forcing Logan from his mind, he went back to doing his inventory until the buzzer over the door sounded. Thinking Logan had returned awfully quickly, he looked up. Sheriff Wilson entered, removing his hat as he had the previous day.

Tate set down his pen and closed his log book. "Hey, Sheriff."

"Tate." Wilson settled his hat on the glass front counter. "How are you today?"

"Good, and you?"

Wilson scratched at his thin moustache. "Not bad, not bad. So I got a message you wanted me to talk to Dottie over at the *Caffeinator.*"

"Yeah, I just think they should know what you found out about Viv's death. They still think it was an accident."

"You went over there and talked with her?"

"Well, I actually went there last night, met Deimos. Then I went back this morning."

"And did you find out anything interesting or pertinent?"

Tate blew out air. Here was his opening. He'd tell Wilson what he'd found out, then he'd be done. He could leave the case alone after this. "I found out a big conglomerate wants to buy out the businesses on the same side of the street as the *Caffeinator* to open a big box store."

"You think that's significant?"

Tate shrugged. "Does the ex-husband have an alibi?"

Wilson nodded. "He was home with his latest squeeze. Not rock solid, but right now, it takes him out of the equation."

Tate made an uncomfortable face. "Never liked alibis where the significant other was the cover story."

"I agree, but until I get some evidence, I don't have much else."

"You're right. Personally, I like the big box store angle better anyway."

"Why?"

"With Vivian Bradley out of the way, they might think they have leverage over the remaining businesses."

"Hm, good point." Wilson removed a small notebook from his pocket and flipped it open. "The realtor working this acquisition is Harold Arnold. I think I'll go talk to Mr. Arnold, see if he has an alibi for the night Vivian Bradley died."

Tate nodded. "Good solid start. Did you go through Vivian's phone? Her computer at home? Any threats beyond the text messages you found?"

"We looked through her mail and her computer. We didn't find anything, but that doesn't mean it wasn't there. She could have deleted any emails she got or threw snail mail away."

"Yeah, she could have, but if there was an email trail, you could get a forensic computer technician to look at the hard drive."

Wilson laughed. "You think I have that sort of budget? My forensic computer technician is a college kid named Joel."

Tate laughed with him. "Sorry. Forgot where I was for a moment."

"Yeah," said Wilson, then his smile dried. "So you sure you won't consult with me on this? I sure could use your big city knowledge."

"Naw, I need to stay out of it. I left that behind in L.A."

"Suit yourself, but if you think of anything else, let me know, okay?"

"Sure," said Tate, "I'll let you know."

Wilson picked up his hat again and put it back on his head. "Have a good day now," he said, turning his back on the counter and wandering toward the door.

"You too, Sheriff," Tate called after him.

As he reached the door, Logan yanked it open, almost running into the man. He agilely sidestepped around him, carrying a paper bag that smelled like heaven. "Sorry, Sheriff."

"No problem, kid. Just don't knock me over, you hear? Lord that smells good."

"Yep," said Logan, beaming a smile, "homemade cinnamon breadsticks from Dottie's."

"Well, I may just have to get down there and get some before they're sold out."

Logan breathed in the fragrant steam. "They're still hot too."

Wilson pretended to quicken his pace. "I'm on it," he called over his shoulder and disappeared down the street.

* * *

Business was brisk most of the day and Tate didn't have time to think about Vivian Bradley or her death. Toward late afternoon, he decided it was time to teach Logan how to work the cash register. He had to give the kid credit. He was a quick study and had mastered the credit card machine before they closed the doors for the day.

"Good job," Tate told him.

Logan gave him a rare smile as he untied his apron and hung it on the peg behind the counter. "Thanks, Tate."

Tate wanted to ask the kid about his mother, but he worried that would be too personal. Honestly, he didn't know what was the matter with him lately. He hadn't shown any interest in the people around him before now, but something about Sheriff Wilson asking him for advice had made him rethink his self-imposed isolation.

"So, you have school tomorrow morning, right?"

"Right, but I'll be in by noon, so you can go to lunch," Logan answered, grabbing the broom and starting his nightly chores.

Tate nodded, then began closing out the register, counting the money. "So how long until you graduate?" he asked, conversationally.

Logan gave him a strange look. Tate knew he'd never asked the kid personal stuff before. "Um, a year. I'm a junior."

Junior? Shit, he hadn't considered just how young Logan was. He nodded and went back to counting money. "You thinking of going back to regular school for your senior year?"

Logan shook his head, continuing to sweep. "No, I need to keep working."

He didn't say anymore, but Tate knew it was because of his mother. He started to ask him where his father was, then decided that was too personal. Forcing himself to focus, he finished counting out the cash register, made out the deposit slip for the bank, and locked the necessary change away in the wall safe in the storeroom. By that time, Logan had finished sweeping and had retrieved his skateboard.

"You wanna ride home?" Tate asked him.

"Naw, I'm good," said Logan, stepping out on the sidewalk. He set the skateboard on the ground, then waited for Tate to set the alarm and lock the door. "See you tomorrow."

"See you tomorrow," said Tate and watched him skate off down the street. He sighed, wishing he had some place else to go tonight. He didn't really want to go home.

His gaze followed down Main Street. He could get dinner from the Bourbon Brothers' Barbecue, but he wasn't in the mood for ribs. What he wanted was a drink, to share a beer with someone and watch a football game or something.

Walking down the side of his building, he found his Tacoma waiting for him in the municipal parking lot behind the stores. Climbing behind the wheel, he started the ignition and drove down Main Street toward the opposite end.

The lights were on in the *Caffeinator* and he could see Deimos behind the counter, his shaggy head bopping to music. A few patrons occupied the bistro chairs and the same guy in the vest with the pocket watch sat on the sofa, typing away on his laptop.

Facing forward, Tate turned left and headed toward the freeway and home. About halfway there, as he sat at the light waiting for it to turn green, his attention was snagged by *Corker's Bar & Grill.* A white Cadillac Seville in the parking lot sported an *Arnold Realty* sign on the side panel.

Interesting.

He passed this place everyday on his way into town, but he'd never thought to stop.

On a whim, he flipped a U-turn and pulled into the parking lot, finding a space and putting the Tacoma in gear. Turning off the ignition, he climbed out and walked toward the red painted door and pulled it open.

Country music leached out into the dusk as he stepped inside and he could smell beer and fried foods. To his right was a bar, dimly lit, with a pool table in the center of the room. A few people occupied stools at the long, glossy bar across the back wall and a number of people sat in booths, their drinks in hand, candles in the center of the tables lighting their faces. A single woman sat at a table near the bar, sipping a glass of white wine, but he didn't see anyone who might be Harold Arnold, the realtor. Not that Tate would know what the man looked like.

Even so, he walked up to the bar, taking a seat on a stool, as the pretty bartender smiled, placing a napkin in front of him. "What can I get you?"

"Whatever you have on tap."

"Domestic or foreign?"

"Domestic's fine."

She gave a nod and pulled his beer, setting it on the napkin. He reached for the menu, resting in a metal clip on the edge of the bar, and opened it. Perusing the fare, he lifted his beer and took a sip. *Nothing like a cold beer after a long day,* he thought, pleased he'd decided to stop before going home, even if this Arnold fella wasn't here.

The pretty bartender approached him again. She had light brown hair that she'd pulled up in a clip, dark eyes, and full lips. She wore a white collared shirt and jeans with cowboy boots, silver hoop earrings dangling from her ears.

"Can I get you something to eat?"

"I'll have the bacon cheeseburger and fries," he said, closing the menu.

She nodded and walked away to place his order. He looked around again. A mirror behind the bar let him see the whole room. Glass shelves bisected the mirror, holding bottles of booze, and above the mirror was a massive pair of bull horns.

The booths were made of red leather, the tables highly lacquered. Flashing neon signs advertising various liquors covered three walls. He could see beyond the bar to the podium for the restaurant. A few people had come in and were waiting patiently for a table.

A man appeared in the entrance to the bar, wearing a business suit and carrying a briefcase. He swept the room with his gaze, then zeroed in on the woman sitting at the table behind Tate. The woman was middle aged, about forty something, with platinum blond hair and heavily made up eyes. She wore a silk blouse and a skirt. She'd kicked off her heels as she waited, but the minute the man appeared, she slipped them back on.

Tate watched them in the mirror, curious. He'd bet money this guy in a suit was Arnold. Not many people wore suits in Sequoia.

The man held out his hand when he reached the table and settled the briefcase on the chair to his right. "Mrs. Taylor?" he asked, beaming a too-white smile at her.

She didn't rise, but she accepted his hand with the tips of her fingers. "Mr. Arnold. Please, call me Trixie."

Tate's attention was hooked, but he looked down, taking another sip of his drink.

"Please call me Harold. Thank you for meeting me here," the man said, taking a seat and unbuttoning his suit jacket.

"Well, I wasn't going to meet you in my shop," Trixie said.

"I completely understand. I hope this isn't too far out of the way for you."

She ran a finger along the top of her glass. "I'm not sure this is a good idea."

"Please, don't say that. I think you'll be pleasantly surprised by my client's latest offer."

Trixie shifted uncomfortably. Tate realized he'd never actually seen the proprietress of *Treasures by Trixie*, but he passed her store everyday. "This just seems wrong."

The realtor reached over and touched her hand. "Let me get you another drink. What are you having?"

"Chardonnay."

He rose and approached the bar next to Tate. Tate glanced over at him and gave him a nod. Arnold nodded back. When the bartender approached, he smiled at her.

"I'll have a dry martini and another chardonnay for the lady."

The bartender nodded and started to make the drinks. Tate sipped at his beer, trying to pretend he wasn't interested in this man.

Arnold gripped the edge of the bar with his left hand and Tate marked he had a pinkie ring. He didn't know why, but he always thought of a man with a pinkie ring as smarmy. The bartender passed the drinks to him and he returned to the table.

"So, let me show you the latest offer and we can discuss it," Arnold said, reaching for his briefcase.

Trixie shifted uncomfortably again. "I really don't know. This feels so wrong. We made a pact that we weren't going to sell."

"I know and I understand, but you have to think about what's in your best interest."

Trixie shook her head. "I don't know. Now that Viv's gone, this just seems even more wrong."

Arnold took a folder out of his briefcase and laid it on the table. "We're just talking right now. You're not making any decisions. Just hear me out and then you can think about it."

Trixie chewed on her lower lip. "I guess it doesn't hurt to just look at the offer."

"No, not at all," he said, flashing that smile again. He passed her the papers.

Trixie opened them, then reached for her purse and took out a pair of glasses, placing them over her eyes so she could read the documents. After a few moments, she closed the folder again and lifted her wineglass, taking a sip.

"What do you think?" asked Arnold, giving the folder a nod.

"It doesn't seem that much better than before."

"Well, you have to understand, my clients are buying a number of the businesses on that side of the street, plus the locals are going to protest any sort of big box store going in there, and the Chamber of Commerce is still on the fence. It's gonna take a lot of legal wrangling to get that store on Main in Sequoia."

"I'm just not sure we need it. It's gonna mess everything up on Main." She ran her finger over the top of her glass again. "Besides, I like my store."

Arnold's smile was a little less brilliant. "Is it really making you a profit, Trixie?" He held out his empty hand. "Will you be able to retire in a few years?"

"Retire?" Trixie's back straightened.

*Swing and a miss,* thought Tate, smiling. *Amateur.*

"You think I want to retire in a few years?"

Arnold glanced around the bar, looking for aid, but no one was coming to his rescue.

She shoved the folder back at him. "I need to think about it, talk to my husband."

"Listen…"

"No, you listen. That store was my dream my whole life and I only agreed to meet with you because Joe said I should, that I should know exactly what was being offered, but I made a pact with Viv and the others not to sell."

"Viv's dead," said Arnold.

Tate glanced into the mirror at that. An edge had come into the realtor's voice.

"Her daughter owns the *Caffeinator* now and from what I understand, she doesn't want anything to do with it, so odds are good she's gonna sell." He leaned closer to Trixie. "The best deals go to those who sign up first. I can't guarantee this offer's going to be this good if you wait. Once the rest start to cave, well…my client may not feel the need to be generous."

Trixie stared at him, then she reached for her purse and rose to her feet. "Mr. Arnold, your client may be a big player in the world, but in Sequoia, we take a different view of things. Once they've acquired what they want and you've been paid off, you'll still need the rest of us. Rest assured that I'll let everyone know how you tried to play me."

He sat back, shocked. "What?"

She pointed a finger at him. "I don't like people who think I'm stupid. I know what you're doing and I don't like it."

"Does this mean you're turning down the offer?"

Her gaze strayed to the folder, then her back straightened again. "It means I'm not impressed by their generosity." She hesitated, then her chin lifted. "It also means I'll be telling my fellow business owners what the offer was, so they can be forewarned."

Arnold rose to his feet. "This offer is between us."

Tate zeroed in on the menace in his voice. So did Trixie and she stepped back from the table. Slowly, Tate swiveled in his chair and openly watched the two of them. Arnold shot him a look, then forced a tense smile.

"Please, Trixie, sit back down and let's enjoy our drinks."

She pulled the strap of her purse over her shoulder and shook her head. "We're done here, Mr. Arnold." She put particular emphasis on his name.

"You'll call me after you talk over the offer with your husband, right?" He felt around the pockets of his suit jacket and pulled out a business card. "Let me give you another card."

Trixie accepted it.

"Call me, okay?"

She tucked the card into the top of her purse. "I'll think about it."

"That's all I ask." He held out his hand for her to shake, but she didn't take it, giving him a look of distaste.

"Goodbye, Mr. Arnold," she said and headed for the door.

The bartender settled Tate's burger on the counter behind him, but he didn't turn around, watching Trixie as she walked out of the restaurant. Arnold glanced over at him again and shrugged.

"Women," he said, then lifted his martini and downed the whole amount, throwing himself into his seat. Signaling the pretty bartender, he pointed at his glass. "I'll have another one."

Tate felt his shoulders relax and he swiveled the barstool around to face his meal. Reaching for his burger, he lifted it to his mouth, wondering if he should call Wilson and tell him what he'd heard.

The first bite brought such bliss that he decided it could wait until he'd finished.

"Good?" said the bartender, smiling at him, as she prepared Arnold's second drink.

Tate winked at her in response, his mouth filled with happiness.

# CHAPTER 5

Zion and Gabi arrived at the offices of the *Bennett, Coleman, & Cox Law Firm* around 10:00AM. The firm sat on Black Diamond Road in the middle of other professional buildings – a chiropractor, a dentist, and a divorce attorney. The sign over the door proudly declared Bennett, Coleman, and Cox as probate attorneys. The picture window on the front of the building sported a dapper man in a top hat and a suit, holding a briefcase. A thought bubble rose from his mouth and declared, *Don't let Uncle Sam take what belonged to Gran.*

"Oh, goodness, that's awful," said Gabi.

Zion laughed and reached for the door, pulling it open.

They entered a very masculine reception room with brown leather furniture, a horsehair sofa, and forest green carpeting with black diamonds arranged in geometric patterns. A massive desk occupied the center of the room and a bottle blond with false eyelashes and Zion suspected, other false parts, sat in a brown leather swivel chair, filing her nails. She wore a good deal of blue eyeshadow and glossy red lipstick.

She looked up as Gabi and Zion entered, then gave them a smile. A spot of lipstick marred her front tooth. Gabi made a motion at her own mouth, but Zion caught her hand and pulled it down.

"Good morning," she said, "I'm Zion Sawyer. I have an appointment with Mr. Bennett."

The woman gave a high laugh and laid her nail file on her desk blotter. "Which one? There are two Mr. Bennetts here."

"Right," said Zion. "I'm here to see David Bennett."

"The younger. That's what we call them. Older and younger. Such a kick." The receptionist reached for the desk phone and pressed a button, a task made difficult by her unusually long nails. They were also glossy red with a diamond in the center of each bed. "David, you have a…" She paused and flashed the lipstick stained tooth again. "Sorry, forgot your name already."

"Zion Sawyer."

"Right. Zion Sawyer is here to see you." She listened, nodding her head. "Okey dokey, I'll send her right on back." She rose to her feet, her skirt riding up her thighs. Pulling it down, she gave Gabi and Zion a glimpse of her straining bra. "Come with me. I'll show you to his office."

She opened a door behind her desk and ushered them into a long hallway with photographs of serious men adorning the walls. The geometric carpet continued into the distance as they started walking.

"Do you want a coffee or anything to drink?" she asked as she ambled down the hallway.

"Actually, I'd love some herbal tea," said Gabi. "I'm particularly fond of a breakfast blend if you have it."

The woman stopped and turned on her high heels to face Gabi, her hands waving beside her shoulders. "We have coffee."

Zion pulled Gabi's arm through her own, patting her hand. "Coffee's great."

The receptionist shuffled back around and continued walking, her hips swaying, her hands waving with each step. Zion shot a quelling look at her mother, but Gabi merely shrugged. "I prefer tea," she mumbled.

The receptionist stopped at the last door on the right side of the hallway. A metal name tag affixed to the door read *David Bennett, Esq*. She knocked sharply.

"Come in," came the same pleasant, calm voice Zion had listened to on the phone.

The receptionist turned the knob and pushed the door open, waving Zion and her mother inside. "Your 10:00 o'clock," she said, announcing them.

A tall young man with cultured good looks, straight stylish brown hair, and pleasant brown eyes rose from behind a glass desk and stepped into the room. He held his hand out first to Zion, laying his free one over the top of their clasped ones. His touch was firm and warm.

"Miss Sawyer, so nice to finally meet you in person."

"Zion's fine," she said, smiling at him.

"And this must be your mother?" He reached for Gabi's hand, also clasping it in both of his own.

"Gabrielle Sawyer," she told him, giving him a quick perusal.

Zion knew exactly what she was doing. She was measuring him as a potential son-in-law.

His eyes lifted to the receptionist. "Thank you, Rose."

"I'll just see about that coffee. You want anything, Mr. Bennett."

"No, thank you, Rose." He motioned to two armchairs before his desk. "Won't you both sit? I hope the drive wasn't too long." He guided them forward, then went back to his seat, settling into it.

"It wasn't bad," said Zion, although she'd hated it. She didn't drive much, living in the City, and neither did Gabi. After this trip, she was beginning to wonder if Gabi should drive at all.

Gabi made a snort and looked out the window to her right.

David followed her with his eyes, then focused back on Zion. "I'm glad you could come here in person, Zion. I know it was difficult to get away, but I really think you need to see the property before we decide what to do with it."

"Sure."

"I thought we'd talk about what Vivian left you, then the sheriff should be here and..." He hesitated and shifted uncomfortably.

Zion frowned at the sudden change in his demeanor and Gabi looked over, sensing it as well.

"Then Sheriff Wilson would like a moment to talk to you," he finished.

"Sheriff Wilson?" asked Zion.

"Yes, he agreed to come about 10:30. He's going to meet us here."

"Why?"

"Why?" repeated David.

"Yes, why is the Sheriff coming here?"

"He just wants to talk to you about a few things." He reached for a folder on his desk, opening it, then slid it across to Zion. "Here's the bulk of her assets. She paid for her cremation ahead of time, so that was taken care of. She had $100,000 in a savings account, which was left in your name, her cottage on Conifer Circle, and then the *Caffeinator*."

Zion looked up from the folder. "The *Caffeinator*? Is that the coffee shop?"

"Exactly. She bought the building when she opened the store, so if you decide to sell, it isn't just the business, but the location too."

Zion passed the folder to her mother and Gabi took it, reaching for her purse to put on her glasses. David swiveled his chair around and picked up a brass urn that had been sitting on the credenza behind him. He settled it on the desk blotter.

Zion's eyes zeroed in on it. "Is that…her?"

David gave her a gentle nod. "I'm afraid it is."

"Oh wow!" she breathed.

Gabi reached over and covered Zion's hand with her own. Zion clutched her mother's fingers, staring at the urn, feeling a tumult of emotions, but none of them grief. Well, maybe a little. She'd never known this woman, but thinking of her reduced to something so insignificant felt awful.

"There's never an easy way to do this," said David, giving her a sheepish half-smile. "I'm so sorry."

Zion nodded, but she couldn't take her eyes from the urn. "She didn't say what she wanted done with her ashes?"

"I'm afraid not. She left that to you."

Gabi's fingers tightened on her hand. "We'll figure it out, don't worry?"

Zion nodded again, but she still couldn't look away.

A knock sounded at the door, drawing David's attention. "Yes, come in."

Rose opened the door and brought Gabi and Zion each a mug of coffee. "The sheriff's here early. He wanted to know if he can come in."

"Of course," said David, rising to his feet and retrieving a smaller guest chair, positioning it next to him. "Bring him in."

Zion tore her eyes from her biological mother's urn and looked over her shoulder as a thin man with a concave chest entered the room. He wore a sheriff's uniform, wide-brimmed hat, and motorcycle boots. A thin mustache perched on his upper lip. He took off his hat and held out his hand first to Zion.

"Miss Sawyer," he said.

Zion accepted his hand. "Zion, please."

Then he offered his hand to Gabi next. "I'm Sheriff Wilson," he said, releasing her and moving to the chair David indicated. Zion realized Rose still lingered in the doorway.

"Would you like some coffee?" she asked Sheriff Wilson.

"Naw, another cup and I'll burn a hole in my belly." He rubbed the spot as he took a seat, setting the hat on the desk. He focused on Zion and Gabi. "I appreciate you letting me come in to talk to you."

"Of course."

"So, here's the thing, Miss Sawyer."

"Zion," she reminded him.

"Right, Zion, there's no easy way to say this, so I won't pretend there is." His eyes strayed to Gabi. "We're actually investigating your mother's death as a…well, a homicide."

Zion frowned and glanced at Gabi, then she leaned forward. "Hold on a minute. I thought she died in a car accident."

"So did we, at first, but we uncovered evidence that she might have been pushed off the road."

"Pushed off the road? By another car?"

"It looks that way, yes."

Zion sat back in her chair, shocked. Scratching her forehead, she tried to process what the sheriff was saying. "I'm sorry, but you're saying my biological mother was deliberately forced off the road."

"Yes, that's what I'm saying."

"How do you know this?"

Sheriff Wilson drew a deep breath. "At first we thought she might have been driving while intoxicated."

"But she wasn't?"

"No, ma'am. Not one lick of anything in her blood, so we took a look at the car again."

"And?"

"There was a mark of darker paint on the rear driver's side panel. Definitely didn't come from her silver Lexus."

Zion didn't know what she felt, but gut-punched seemed like a pretty good description. "She was…murdered."

"It's looking that way." He shook his head. "I know this is a shock."

"Do you have any suspects?" asked Gabi.

"Well, we always start with the significant others."

"She was divorced, wasn't she?" asked Zion.

"Yep. Called him on the phone, but he's got an alibi. He was with his lady friend in Los Angeles the night Viv died."

"He told you that?"

"He did and I spoke with her too."

"What does that prove? She's his girlfriend? Why wouldn't she lie for him?"

"I've already thought of that. I haven't crossed him off my list yet, but I'm trying to eliminate suspects here."

"*Is* there someone here?" Zion glanced at David. He met her gaze, chewing on his inner lip, then he looked down.

"Viv and a number of merchants on Main Street, all on her side of the street, have been approached by a big box store to sell. The business owners made a pact that they wouldn't, but with Viv gone, well, it's looking a little suspicious."

Zion rubbed her forehead again. She couldn't believe this was happening. First, she'd been told her biological mother was dead at the age of 43. Now she was being told she was likely murdered.

"I…" She shook her head. "I don't know what to say."

"It's a lot to take in," David said kindly.

Sheriff Wilson nodded. "I wanted you to know, especially if you hear rumors while you're out and about. I didn't think it was appropriate for you to hear about it from anyone but me."

"We appreciate that," said Gabi, shifting in her chair so she could rub Zion's back. "It's just quite a shock."

David pushed his chair back and rose. "Why don't we give you both a few moments to absorb everything?"

The sheriff rose with him, reaching for his hat. He held it in his left hand and placed the right one on Zion's shoulder. "I really am sorry to tell you this."

Zion nodded woodenly, her eyes fixated on Vivian Bradley's urn.

* * *

As they left the room, Gabi pulled out her cell phone and dialed her husband. Joe picked up on the second ring. Zion could hear his cheerful voice through the speaker. She rose to her feet and walked over to the window behind David's desk, staring out at the redwoods towering overhead.

She couldn't deny Sequoia was beautiful. Gabi and Joe had taken her to see the redwoods many times, but she hadn't been since she returned from college and started working at *Judicious*. In fact, she hadn't taken a vacation in three years. Most of her time off was for genuine illnesses. This was the first time she'd taken a personal leave day.

She could hear Gabi telling Joe about Vivian in a hushed voice. Since Zion had woken that morning, she'd felt anxious and she wasn't sure why. Vivian Bradley had been an occasional thought all these years, something considered with curiosity in passing. Something would trigger the memory that she was adopted and she'd spare a brief moment to think about the woman who'd given her up, but for the most part, it wasn't a daily thought on her mind.

Except now she was confronted with the fact that Vivian Bradley had been murdered. Someone had deliberately stolen her life from her. There was no one who would make sure she got justice, no one who would keep after the case until it was solved. There was only Zion.

She knew she didn't have an obligation to pursue this. She wasn't completely sure she wanted anything from Vivian, not her money, not her house, and especially not her business. Scratch that…especially not her urn. What was she supposed to do with her ashes? What would be proper, respectful, and yet not cause Zion undue grief?

Knowing that Vivian had been murdered, though, changed everything. It put a burden on Zion to get to know this woman who'd given her away, to find out about her life, and maybe discover who wanted her dead. It forced Zion to get involved.

Gabi held out the phone to her. "Your father wants to talk to you."

Zion moved away from the window and took the phone. "Hey, Daddy."

"Hey, kiddo, I'm sorry about the news you just got."

"They gave me her urn."

"Oh, wow! Just like that? How'd they do it?"

"Put it on the desk in front of us."

"They did? Just put it on the desk?"

"Yeah."

"Oh wow, that's dark."

"Then the sheriff came in to tell me they suspect murder."

"I know. Your mother told me."

"They think someone forced her off the road."

"I know, kiddo. I'm really sorry. Did they do that forensic stuff? You know? Take DNA samples and look for insects indigenous to the area?"

Zion laughed, but it turned into a sob. The sob surprised both her and her father. Gabi got to her feet and gathered her in her arms.

"I'm sorry, kiddo, I don't mean to be callous," Joe said.

"No." She swiped at her tears, laying her head on Gabi's shoulder. "I don't know why I'm crying."

"Because it's a shock," he said.

"Because she was your mother," offered Gabi.

But neither of those were true. Zion knew why she was crying and it didn't really have anything to do with her at all. She was crying because Vivian Bradley had died alone, afraid and hurt, with no one to mourn her passing. Not even her own daughter.

* * *

After she'd calmed down and Sheriff Wilson had come back into David Bennett's office, promising to contact her if he found out anything more, Zion gave the sheriff her cell phone number and Wilson departed.

David returned, offering her a sympathetic expression, and asked her if there was anything he could do for her. Zion shook her head. He then suggested they go see the *Caffeinator* first. Zion guessed he figured going to Vivian's house with all her personal effects might be harder than seeing the business she'd built herself. She and Gabi agreed.

"I'll drive," said David, going around his desk and opening the top drawer, taking out his car keys.

Zion's eyes landed on Vivian's urn. She didn't know why she was reluctant to handle it. It wasn't that she feared death. Her parents had always told her death was a necessary part of living, it was just so disconcerting to know all that remained of a person, her hopes and dreams and desires could be bottled up in a vessel smaller than a two-liter bottle of soda. Somehow it was too awful.

Always attuned to her daughter's distress, Gabi took the urn in her arms and held it close. David gave them both a kind smile and held the office door open for them. They passed down the hallway silently. Zion liked David's warmth and the fact he didn't seemed to want to pressure her into anything.

He held the door to the lobby open as well and they filed through. Rose occupied her desk chair, filing her nails again. She lifted a hand and waved as they moved toward the outer door.

"Nice to meet you," Rose called after them.

"Nice to meet you," said Gabi, cradling the urn as if it were a child.

"Thank you for the coffee," said Zion.

David led them to his Range Rover and opened the rear passenger door for Gabi, then held the front passenger door for Zion. Gabi climbed in back, settling Vivian's urn on the seat next to her, then she buckled her seatbelt and picked up the urn again, placing it on her lap.

Zion watched her mother in bemusement, then turned to climb inside herself. David shut her mother's door, then touched Zion on the elbow, stopping her.

"This must be hard for you. If you want to take a break at any time, please just say something."

Zion smiled at him. His kindness and his calm resonated with her. "I appreciate that. You've been very patient and kind."

"Well…" He blushed.

Zion couldn't help but be charmed by that. She hadn't met many men in San Francisco who still blushed.

"Are you going back to the City tonight?"

Zion sighed. "We'd sort of planned on it, but it looks like the situation's a bit more complicated than I thought. Still we didn't make any hotel arrangements or pack any clothes."

David gave a sheepish shrug. "Technically, Vivian's house belongs to you." When Zion pulled away, he shrugged again. "I mean, it's there and it's yours."

"I know, I just don't know if I can stay there. I mean, I didn't think I'd be this affected by her death, but it's all kinda hitting me harder than I thought."

He touched her elbow again. "Vivian was a good person, Zion. She was always kind to me whenever I came into the *Caffeinator*. A lot of people are going to miss her and she didn't deserve what happened to her, whether it was an accident or something more." He gave her a wistful smile. "I know you didn't know her, but she was part of who you are and that's gotta be hard to sort out."

"It is. Thank you for helping me do that."

He made an elaborate bow. "At your service, milady."

That brought a giggle out of Zion that she quickly swallowed. She didn't remember the last time a man made her giggle. She climbed into the passenger seat and David shut the door, then he walked around the front of the Range Rover as Zion buckled her seatbelt.

"He's a cute one," said Gabi behind her, "but he's a lawyer."

"Shh," hissed Zion. "He might be able to hear you." She looked over the seat at her mother.

Gabi stroked the smooth surface of the urn. "You might be right. His ears are a little large."

"Mom!"

Gabi gave a little laugh, then reached out and touched Zion's cheek. "I'm sorry you have to deal with this."

Zion curled her fingers around her mother's hand and squeezed, a flush of love spreading through her for this woman.

David climbed inside and started the SUV. "I called ahead and let Dottie know we're coming in. She said Dee would be there too. Dottie and Dee worked for Viv for years. Dottie does the morning shift and Dee does the midday to closing. I think you'll like them."

Zion released her mother and faced forward as David pulled out of the parking lot and onto the street. "Sheriff Wilson mentioned a big box store was trying to buy up the businesses on the *Caffeinator's* side of the street?"

"Right. Harold Arnold of Arnold Realty is representing them."

"Has he asked you about the *Caffeinator*?"

David shot a glance at her, his fingers tightening on the steering wheel. "He showed up the day after Vivian's car was found."

"Is he a suspect?"

"I couldn't tell you. Sheriff Wilson's keeping this one close to his vest, but Arnold and I got into a heated argument over it."

Zion wouldn't mind seeing that. She had a hard time picturing David getting heated over anything, he projected such a calm, easy going air. "So this big box store wants to buy the *Caffeinator* and they already approached you to get me to sell to them?"

"That's the gist of it."

"What did you tell them?"

"I told Arnold to get out of my office. I hadn't even talked to you yet and that was the last thing on my mind at the moment."

"What do the locals feel about this store going in?" asked Gabi.

David glanced in the rearview mirror. "They're very much against it. They don't like it at all. Like Sheriff Wilson said, Viv and the other store owners made a pact not to sell to them."

"What about now?"

David glanced over at her and his expression was grim. "I don't know," he said.

They fell silent as they made the short ride to Main Street. Zion looked out the windows at the old fashioned wooden buildings, the bright awnings, and the wooden boardwalk. Many of the businesses had large plate glass windows with hand painted signs proclaiming their wares. It was charming and brought to mind a simpler time.

David pulled into a small municipal parking lot and turned off the Range Rover. "The *Caffeinator's* just down the street."

Zion unbuckled her seatbelt and started to get out, but Gabi hadn't made a move. "I don't know what to do with Vivian," she said uncomfortably. "Maybe I should wait here."

Zion climbed out and opened her mother's door. "I want you to come too." Forcing down her aversion, she reached for the urn. "We'll strap it into the seat."

Gabi unbuckled her own seatbelt and climbed out, so Zion could buckle Vivian's urn in her place. "Don't worry. We'll figure out what to do with her," Gabi told Zion, rubbing her arm.

Zion wished she wouldn't keep calling the urn *her* and *Vivian*, but she didn't have the heart to say that to her mother. Shutting the car doors, they met David on the wooden boardwalk and he locked the Range Rover with his remote, then they walked down the street to the *Caffeinator.*

"This is so charming," said Gabi, looking around. "I can't imagine anyone wanting to tear it down and put in a big box store."

"That's what the residents say too," said David. He stopped in the middle of the street and reached for the old fashioned glass door knob. Zion liked the gold lettering on the plate glass window proclaiming the establishment as the *Caffeinator.*

As David pushed open the door, muzak bled out into the street, a soft jazz blend of piano and horns, and a tinkle of bells sounded as she crossed the threshold, looking around. Vivian had chosen a Victorian theme with brocade sofas with a nailhead embellishment around the arms and wood along the backs. Striped Victorian arm chairs flanked the sofas and wooden tray tables made up a very pleasant seating area. The rest of the room was filled with ornate wrought iron bistro tables with striped cushions on the seats and glass tabletops. A few patrons sat at the tables, some typing on laptops or just talking quietly, and a middle aged man sat on the sofa, a laptop open on his lap, his booted feet braced on the edge of the tray table. The walls were a soft pink as were all the fabrics and the pleasant smell of cinnamon and coffee filled the air.

A long glass counter took up the back wall, filled with beautiful pastries, and coffee making equipment lined the wall behind the counter. An older, round woman with surprising lavender colored hair rolled out dough on a cutting board, while a young man in a ball cap and pink apron stood behind the cash register.

Zion felt every eye in the room turn to look at her, especially those of the people behind the counter. David gave her a smile and urged her forward. "Zion, this is Dottie Madison and Deimos Hendrix."

Zion held out her hand to Deimos and he took it, giving her a nervous smile. Dottie reached for a dishcloth and wiped the flour from her hands, then took Zion's hand when Deimos released her.

"This is my mother, Gabi," she said and Gabi stepped forward to shake both of their hands.

"Pleasure to meet you," Gabi said.

"Same," said Deimos, dropping his eyes.

"We're very sorry about Vivian, sugar," said Dottie, wiping her hands on her pink apron.

"Yeah, real sorry. Viv was a great lady," added Deimos.

"Thank you." Zion looked around again. "This place is cute."

"Very charming," said Gabi.

David motioned to the end of the counter. "Vivian had an office back here. I thought you might like to take a look at the accounts. I think you'll see the *Caffeinator* does well for itself."

Deimos glanced at Zion again, then looked down, but Dottie folded her hands over her belly, waiting to see what she would do.

Zion didn't know what to do. She wanted to reassure these people that she didn't want to take away their livelihood, but the truth was, she knew nothing about running a business like this. She didn't even brew her own coffee at home, let alone know how to operate the complicated machinery all around them.

"David," she said, holding out a hand to stop him. "Like I said before, this is much more complicated than I thought it was. I need time to sort through everything I've heard today."

"Of course," he said.

She looked back at Deimos and Dottie. "I appreciate what you've done since Vivian's death, how you've kept her business going."

Dottie ducked her head and Deimos scratched his ear.

"I wish I could tell you what I plan to do, but…" She held out her empty hands. Gabi moved to her side and rubbed her back.

"We understand, sugar," said Dottie and Zion felt a little of the tension ease inside of her. "You got a lotta decisions to make in the next few days. We'll keep things running just like we've always done."

"I will make sure you get your regular pay for this," she assured them.

"Thanks, ma'am," said Deimos, shuffling his feet.

Zion laughed, despite herself. "I've never been called ma'am before. Zion's fine."

He met her gaze and offered her the ghost of a smile. "Can I make you something to drink?"

"I'd love a chai tea."

"Me too," said Gabi. "I've wanted tea all day."

"Coming right up," said Deimos and he hurried to prepare their drinks.

Dottie laughed. "Not me. It's coffee or nothing. I drink the stuff all day long."

"My husband's the same way. He'd drink coffee until bed if I let him," offered Gabi, warming to the lavender haired barista.

David came back to Zion's side. "Just tell me what you want to do now," he said in a low voice.

Zion shook her head. She didn't really know, except it was clear this situation wasn't going to be cleared up in one day. "I need to call my employer and get a few more days off. Then I think I'd like to see Vivian's house. You're sure Mom and I can stay there."

"It belongs to you, Zion."

"Okay. Tonight we'll just deal with that and tomorrow, I'll come back here and take a look at the books. Maybe I'll figure out exactly what I want to do by then."

Gabi rubbed her back some more. "We'll call your dad. He'll have some ideas."

Zion nodded, but her attention was drawn to the man who'd been sitting on the couch with his laptop. He'd set the computer on the tray table and approached them. He gave Zion a sheepish look as if he wanted to talk to her. Zion smiled at him.

"I'm Jackson Van Tiernan, miss."

Zion shook his hand. He had to be in his late thirties, early forties, wore thick rimmed black glasses, a suit vest, black jeans, and Doc Marten boots. His button up shirt was crisply white and he had a thin black tie on that he'd pulled open at the throat.

"Nice to meet you, Mr. Van Tiernan."

"Call me Jackson." He released her and gave her a searching look. "I just wanted to tell you how sorry I am for your mother's death. She was always very kind to me."

Zion shifted uneasily. She still had a hard time thinking of Vivian as her mother. "Thank you, Jackson."

He nodded and looked around the store. "Truth is, this is my second home. I come here everyday."

"That's wonderful." Zion didn't know what he wanted her to say. She was so out of her depth here.

"I work for *Cyclone Games*. I'm an RPG developer."

"How exciting!"

"They're located in the Silicon Valley, but I work remotely. The *Caffeinator's* my office, you might say. Vivian always listened to my ideas. You wouldn't have thought it to look at her, but she knew her RPG's."

Zion nodded, feeling uncomfortable with his intensity.

"Are you planning to have a memorial service for her?"

Zion's gaze flickered to David. He picked up on her discomfort and angled between the two of them.

"Zion just got here a few hours ago. She hasn't had time to think about that yet. I'll let you know if she decides anything, Jackson, how about that? Or Dee can?"

"Sure," he said, never taking his eyes from Zion. "That works. No pressure, but I'd like to pay my respects, you know? If you have something, I mean."

"We'll get word to you," said Gabi, putting her arm around Zion's waist.

"You look like her," he said, backing toward his seat.

Zion's smile dried. That was the last thing she wanted to hear. She turned toward Gabi, unable to answer him, and found both Dottie and Deimos glaring at the man. Deimos held out her chai tea, giving her a kind smile.

"Try it. It's my secret blend."

Zion forced a smile and slipped out of her mother's hold, going to the counter and taking the drink. Lifting it to her mouth, she sipped it and was pleasantly surprised. "Thank you, Deimos. This is excellent."

He beamed at her. "Call me Dee," he said and held out a second drink for Gabi.

* * *

After they left the *Caffeinator*, David drove them to Vivian's cottage on Conifer Circle. It was a small steel blue house with white trim and a sloped roof. A porch ran across the front of it and the yard sported an enormous redwood. An old fashioned mailbox was affixed to a post in front of the picket fence and a whitewashed wooden archway led the way up a granite line walkway. To the left ran an asphalt driveway with a covered carport.

Zion's throat felt tight and she gripped the seatbelt, unable to remove it. Here was her biological mother's house with all her worldly possessions. She'd come to this house at the end of the day, tired and seeking refuge, and she'd spent her quiet moments, reading or watching television or sleeping.

Gabi curled her hand around Zion's shoulder. "It's going to be all right."

Zion nodded, never taking her eyes from the cottage. "I just need a moment."

"Sure," said Gabi, leaving her hand in place, but she turned to David. "Do you get much snow here in the winter?"

"Depends. Sometimes we get quite a few feet. Other times, it's just a dusting. Most folk in this neighborhood have Lewis Tilson on standby to plow out their driveways during a snowstorm."

"Do you live in this neighborhood?" Gabi asked.

"I did. My folks live over on Spruce Place. That's where I grew up. I went to college in Reno, got my law degree in Sacramento, then came home. I have an apartment near the office, but I still spend a lot of time over here."

"This is a really cute neighborhood," said Gabi, looking out at the street.

David nodded.

Suddenly Zion reached for the door handle. "Let's get this over with." She pushed the door open and stepped out onto the sidewalk.

Gabi and David hurried to follow her, Gabi grabbing Vivian's urn. Zion waited for David to go up the walk first, then she followed him, trying to pretend like she didn't feel like vomiting. There was no reason this was so hard for her. She didn't know Vivian Bradley, had no connection to her. This woman meant nothing. She was just an abstraction, an idea that had never fully taken form.

David took keys out of his pocket and inserted them in the deadbolt, then pushed the door open and Zion stumbled to a halt, unable to move forward.

Gabi came up beside her. "Are you all right, darlin'?" she asked gently.

Zion shook her head. "No," she breathed out, willing herself to climb the stairs and go inside, willing herself to have the courage to face a life that she'd been denied, willing herself not to feel like an orphan.

Gabi passed David the urn and gathered Zion in her arms. They must have looked ridiculous, the two of them, Zion so much taller than the other woman, her hair a deep auburn to Gabi's black and grey, but it didn't matter. Zion buried her face in Gabi's shoulder and clung to her, and she knew that she wasn't alone. She'd never be alone as long as Gabi and Joe Sawyer were there for her, her real parents.

# CHAPTER 6

Tate opened the *Hammer Tyme* the next morning by himself because Logan had school, so he couldn't get to the *Caffeinator* to try another specialty coffee. He was beginning to look forward to it, which made him realize how easy it was to become hooked on something other than instant or store-bought ground.

Quite a few customers came in, keeping him busy and distracting him from Vivian Bradley's death. In fact, he didn't think of it at all until Logan showed up at noon for his shift. He tied on his apron and settled his backpack under the counter.

"I got things if you wanna grab some lunch."

Usually Tate ate a sandwich or leftovers from the previous night in the storeroom. That way he could work the register if a customer came in, but he was really wanting to give Logan more responsibility, show the young man that he trusted him.

He reached for the ties on his own apron. "You think you can work the card reader and the register if I go out for a bite?"

Logan's eyes glimmered and he nodded quickly. "Sure I can."

"You can get me on cell if you have trouble. I'll just be on Main, but I thought it might be nice to actually get out of here for a bit, get some sun." He shrugged.

"Go. I got this. I promise. I remember everything you showed me yesterday."

Tate nodded and removed his apron, folding it and passing it to Logan behind the counter. Even if the kid screwed something up, Tate wasn't too worried. Business had been good enough today to weather a mistake or two.

"See you in an hour," he called over his shoulder and headed for the door.

"See ya," shouted Logan after him and it was impossible to miss the excitement in his young voice.

Tate paused on the sidewalk outside the *Hammer Tyme* and let the sun wash over him. He couldn't remember the last time he'd just enjoyed the feel of the sun in the last two years. He'd been so preoccupied putting LA behind him, then starting his business that he hadn't considered anything else.

Tucking his hands in his jeans pockets, he wandered toward Main Street. He was thinking of getting lunch at the *Bourbon Brother's Barbecue*, but he came to *Trixie's Trinkets* before he reached the restaurant. Peering in the plate glass windows, he marked the bric-a-brac, the porcelain dolls, the decorated plates, the small wooden redwood trees. He walked to the door and reached for the door handle, an old fashioned glass knob like the one on the *Caffeinator*. A lilting charm sounded as he stepped inside.

The room smelled of potpourri and soap, pleasant if a bit cloying. Trixie had opted for rustic elegance with wooden furnishings, carved hope chests, quilts, and pinecones, interspersed with collectible dolls and hand-sewn stuffed animals. An entire glass shelf sported miniature plates and bells and spoons emblazoned with a redwood tree and the word *Sequoia* in gold leaf across the front of it. On another shelf were Native American dolls in traditional dress, woven bowls in bright colors, and trade blankets in Native American print. Bundles of sage gave off an earthy, wholesome smell, while flute music played in the background.

"Can I help you?" came a female voice and Tate turned to see Trixie emerge from a back room. The doorway was covered in wooden beads that rustled as she passed through.

Tate moved toward her, offering his hand. "I'm Tate Mercer. I own the *Hammer Tyme* down the street."

She accepted his hand, giving him a smile. "Oh, right. I've seen you driving through town. My husband spends half our pay in your store."

"Does he?"

"Joe Taylor. Big guy, going bald on top. Worked for Caltrans for years, but he retired early. Hurt his back."

"Joe, yes." Tate knew who she was talking about. He did spend a lot of money in Tate's store. Tate scrunched up his face as he thought for a moment. "He was building a bear box for your trashcans, right?"

"Right."

"He ever finish it?"

Trixie gave Tate an arch look, then they both laughed. "I'm Trixie by the way. Nice to finally meet you."

"Same here."

"So? The only time I get a man like you in here is when he's buying something for a special lady." She fluffed her short platinum blond hair. "What's the occasion?"

Tate shifted uncomfortably. "I gotta confession, Trixie."

She leaned away from him. "Sounds serious."

"It is, a little." He stuffed his hands in his pockets again. "I was at *Corker's* last night, sitting at the bar when you came in."

Trixie's smile dried.

Tate knew he was about to lose her, so he hurried on. "I heard some of the conversation with Harold Arnold, the part where it got heated."

"That was you? I knew someone was there, but I was so angry I wasn't paying much attention. I'm sorry if I came off rude or aggressive. He just got me so upset."

Tate held out a hand. "No, you did nothing wrong. He was the ass."

Trixie blew out air in a laugh. "He was, wasn't he?"

"Total ass." He shifted weight. "Which is why I wanted to tell you that I support you and the other business owners. In fact, if it comes to a vote with the Chamber of Commerce, I'm completely on your side."

Trixie gave him a warm smile. "I appreciate that, Tate. That means a lot." She glanced around the store. "For years I worked as a receptionist in a dental office. The pay was steady, the work wasn't hard. I raised two kids doing that job, but once they went off to college, I wanted something for myself, you know?"

Tate nodded.

"So, Joe and I opened this store. I mean, I guess if they were offering a king's ransom it'd be different, but it's just not that great of an offer, not great enough to give up your dream."

"I know. Running the *Hammer Tyme's* been good for me. I really needed the store when I came up here. I get what you mean."

She shrugged. "Not that it matters now."

"Why do you say that?"

"Vivian's gone and her daughter just came up from the City. She wants to sell everything and go back home. She's not going to stay here and run the business, she's gonna take the easy way out. I'll bet Harold Arnold's already been in contact with her."

"Has he bothered you since last night?"

"No, I made it pretty clear I wasn't happy with him."

Tate glanced around the store, rubbing the back of his neck. He knew he had to approach the next question carefully. Sound too much like a cop and people shut down. He'd seen it happen a hundred times before.

"Trixie, you know Sheriff Wilson thinks Vivian was forced off the road, right?"

Trixie gasped, covering her mouth with her hand. "No, I didn't know that."

Tate nodded. "Before that happened, she got some threatening text messages on her phone. Have you gotten anything like that?"

Trixie blinked a few times. "No, I haven't." She leaned close, putting her hand on Tate's arm. "Are you saying Sheriff Wilson thinks it was deliberate?"

Tate had always believed forewarned was best. "Yes, he does."

"She was murdered?"

"It looks that way."

Trixie looked away, worrying her bottom lip. "Does he have suspects?"

"He's looking at her ex-husband and, to be honest, the big box people."

Her eyes whipped back to his face. "Do you think I'm in danger since I told Arnold to get lost?"

"I don't, but just to be safe, if you notice anything suspicious, anything that makes you uncomfortable, contact Sheriff Wilson right way."

Trixie reached out and touched his arm again. "That's just horrible about Viv. I can't believe it. She was such a nice lady."

"That's what I hear."

"How scary!"

Tate nodded.

"Thank you for telling me."

"Sure. It was nice to finally meet you."

"It was nice to meet you too, Tate. I hope I'll see you in here again."

He gave the store a final glance. "You never know. I might just suddenly decide I can't live another moment without a bell that says Sequoia on it."

She playfully swatted at him and laughed. "Go on, now. Don't be charming."

Tate tipped an imaginary cap at her and turned to leave, pausing at the door to look back. "Take care of yourself, Trixie. Keep the sheriff's number close at hand."

"I will," she called after him, "and you do the same."

He stepped back out on the sun dappled boardwalk and shut the door behind him. He hated to make Trixie afraid, but being warned was half the battle.

* * *

Deciding barbecue was exactly what he needed today, he walked a few doors down to the *Bourbon Brothers* and pulled open the door. The smell of cooked pork, spicy barbecue, and beer curled around him, urging him inside.

The interior was dark paneled wood with green glass poker table lamps hanging over the booths. Neon signs advertising various beers shone from the walls and the brothers had decorated with Sequoia's requisite number of wooden barrels, leather saddles, and ropes.

At noon, every booth was occupied with tourists or regulars, their laughter and chatter battling for dominance over the jukebox in the corner belting out 70's R&B.

Daryl, the younger brother, manned the cash register and behind him, appearing in the pickup window was Dwayne, the older brother. Bustling about with Dwayne in back was their short order cook, Al Wong, who'd come on shortly after the Ford brothers opened for business.

Out of everyone in Sequoia, Tate knew the Ford brothers best. He frequented the barbecue and they always talked or watched a ball game together. Both Dwayne and Daryl had been firefighters for years, but in a place as forested as Sequoia and during one of the worst droughts in history, being a firefighter meant long hours, backbreaking work, and excellent pay in terms of overtime. It also meant not being with your family and risking your life on a daily basis. It was enough to make a person age ten years in one.

The brothers were big men, over six feet, broad shouldered, muscular, although Dwayne was developing a bit of paunch. Tate suspected it was too much of a good thing, his own cooking. Dwayne had salt and pepper hair shaved close to his head. He also sported a neat salt and pepper beard and moustache with no sideburns. His dark brown skin gleamed now in the heat off the cooktop, a white apron hanging around his neck.

Daryl, the younger brother, was clean shaven, handsome, with darker skin and warm brown eyes with thick lashes. He wore his hair a little longer and liked to shave lines in the back of it that looked like arrows. Tate had to admit he thought it was cool, even though he'd never be able to pull something like that off.

As he got in the line behind a number of other people to place his order, Daryl looked up and gave him a chin jerk in greeting. Tate nodded back, smiling. He watched Dwayne and the much smaller Al dance around in the back, spinning out of each other's way in some elaborate moves as they dished up plates faster than a tornado.

Finally Tate got to the register and Daryl held out his hand, dragging Tate in for a man hug. "What the hell are you doing getting out for lunch?" Daryl said, flashing a row of brilliant white teeth at him.

"I taught Logan to use the card reader and the register."

"And you left him?"

Tate shrugged. "He's got my cell."

"Man, you're a trusting soul. So, you want the regular?"

"Yep."

Daryl typed in his order and then printed out a slip, shoving it on the tin rolling order rack in the pickup window. Dwayne glanced at it, then looked out.

"Heyya, Tate, my man."

"Dwayne," said Tate, holding up a hand, then he passed his card to Daryl.

"Wanna beer too since Logan's runnin' the show?"

"No, better not. Water's good."

Daryl ran his card and gave it back to him, then filled a large glass with ice from the dispenser behind him and poured Tate's water, passing the glass to him. Tate moved to the counter and took the seat closest to the register as Daryl helped a young couple behind him. Once he finished, he came over to Tate and leaned against the counter.

Tate looked out over the restaurant. "Business is good," he said. He wanted to open up the topic of the big box store, but he didn't want to go all cop on his two closest friends here.

Daryl looked out as well. "Yeah, we were thinking of hiring a kid to buss tables and stuff, but…"

Tate ran his fingers over the condensation on the glass. "But?"

Daryl scratched his chin. "Viv's death's making that slimy leech Arnold put pressure on us to sell."

"He's been in here?"

"Yeah, but Dwayne told him he'd stick him on the barbecue spit if he came back."

"He's been after Trixie too."

Daryl straightened. "Yeah?"

Tate told him what he'd heard at *Corker's* the other night.

"She gonna sell?"

Tate shrugged. "Who knows? She said she doesn't want to, but she's afraid that if Vivian's daughter sells, it'll be harder to refuse."

Daryl nodded, then moved back to the register to take another order. When he returned, his expression was troubled. "Damn, Tate, I hate this shit."

"I know."

"It affects you too, man. If they buy up this side of the street and put in that store, why are the tourists gonna come down here? It'll dry up your business, you watch."

Tate shook his head, taking a sip of his water. "I came here to get away from that shit. I don't want a store like that here."

Daryl tapped a tattoo on the counter. "Preach, brother."

Tate glanced up at him. "What'll you do if it happens?"

Daryl shifted weight. "Go back to the fire department, I guess, but I don't wanna do that. And what about Dwayne? He's too damn old."

"Watch your mouth," said Dwayne, pushing open the kitchen door and setting Tate's pulled pork sandwich and coleslaw in front of him. The two men shook hands before Tate dug into his meal. "You talking about that weasel Arnold?"

Tate nodded, his mouth too full to speak.

"He said Arnold's been pressuring Trixie."

"She-et." Dwayne shook his head. "I knew he'd go after her."

Tate grabbed a napkin and wiped barbecue sauce from his chin, chewing. "She's pretty tough," he said, around a mouthful.

"Yeah, but they offer enough money and..."

Tate made a noncommittal shrug. "She says the offer wasn't that good."

"But what about Vivian's daughter?" said Daryl.

"Well, that's the weak link, ain't it?" said Dwayne.

Tate nodded. "She lives in San Francisco. She's not gonna wanna stay here."

Al tapped the silver bell on the pickup window. "Order up!" he shouted.

Daryl went to get the plates to deliver them, but Dwayne stayed where he was. "Sheriff Wilson told me Viv's death wasn't an accident."

"Doesn't look that way."

"He got suspects?"

"A couple, yeah."

"Arnold."

"He'd be top of my list."

Dwayne looked out at the restaurant, considering, while Tate took another bite of his sandwich. After he chewed, he wiped his mouth and drank a sip of water, then leaned back in his chair. "Damn that's good."

Dwayne smiled at him, showing his chipped front tooth. "You know it."

Tate's expression grew serious. "Would you really go back to the fire department, Dwayne?"

"She-et, Tate. You know I don't wanna do that. Would you go back to being a cop if the hardware store goes under?"

Tate hadn't told anyone, not even the Ford brothers, why he'd left the force. He'd just said he couldn't do the job anymore. He looked away, running his tongue over his teeth. "No, I couldn't do that."

"Yeah, well, there I am. Cheryl would leave me if I went back. I can't do that to her, but here's the thing. Tallah's a sophomore. That girl's real smart. Two more years and she's gonna be going to college. I want her to go wherever she wants. I just don't know what to do."

Tate didn't have an answer and it frustrated him. Vivian's death had thrown everything into turmoil. It couldn't be coincidence that she died just when this conglomerate wanted to open shop. Somehow the two things had to be connected, but you had to have evidence to arrest people and Tate didn't want to get that involved. Asking a few questions was one thing, but actually looking over the crime scene, asking to see what Wilson had gathered, that crossed a line Tate wasn't willing to cross.

Yet.

* * *

On a whim, he detoured into the *Caffeinator* after lunch. He was full and didn't really want coffee, but after talking with the Ford brothers, a niggling worry had started in the back of his mind and grew into a full blown fret. Dwayne was right. He could lose the hardware store if that big box store went in. The big box store would carry a lot of the same things he did and they'd be able to undercut him in every way.

Deimos worked the counter, while Dottie manned the espresso machine. Tate glanced around the pleasant room, marking that every table was filled and a group of four young people occupied one of the couches and the two arm chairs. The same guy in the vest with the pocket watch sat on the opposite couch, staring at his laptop, a frown on his face, his feet braced on the coffee table. He glanced up as Tate entered, then went back to looking at his screen.

Tate got in line behind a couple with two pre-teen kids. The kids were begging their parents for treats from the glass display case bursting with pastries and pretty cupcakes with pink icing. Glancing beyond them, Tate realized the door to the back room was open and he could see Harold Arnold sitting in a chair before a desk, talking animatedly to someone Tate couldn't see.

After the family ordered and moved to the side to wait for their drinks, Tate stepped up to the cash register. Deimos' face lit up and he held out his hand.

"Tate, dude, let me guess, salted caramel Macchiato, right?" he shouted over the sound of the milk steamer.

Tate smiled. "Sure."

Deimos rang up his order, then took his card and swiped it. Tate tried to peer beyond him and see what was happening in the office, but it was hard with so much noise and so much activity in the coffee shop.

Deimos handed back Tate's card, then glanced over his shoulder, following Tate's gaze. Leaning closer, he dropped his voice. "Viv's daughter's back there, meeting with that slimy realtor guy."

"I can see that. Why's the office door open? Doesn't she want privacy?"

Deimos shrugged. "I think he makes her nervous. She's by herself right now and asked me to keep the door open. Earlier that lawyer dude, Bennett, was here with her, going over the books, but he left for an appointment. Her mom came in with her yesterday, but she's not here today."

"Can you hear what they're saying?"

"Not really, only snatches. It's pretty busy in here."

Dottie came to the counter. "Hey sugar, you want whipped cream on that Macchiato?"

"No thank you, Dottie."

"How you doing today?"

"Pretty good. You?"

She also glanced at the office. "Not gonna lie. I'm feeling a little down. It's affecting my baking too. The cinnamon rolls aren't as flaky as I usually make them."

Deimos shook his head sadly, staring at a distant place. "I hate looking for work. Dude, I'm bad at interviewing, let me tell you."

Tate didn't know what to say. He had his own worries, but he wanted to offer Deimos and Dottie some comfort.

"Man, I just wish Viv hadn't died like that," said Deimos.

Dottie patted his shoulder, then went back to making coffees.

"I could look at your resume, if you want," offered Tate.

Deimos gave a sad laugh. "What resume? Got my high school diploma, and I roast a bitchin' cup of coffee. That ain't gonna get me a job as a CEO anywhere, now is it?"

Tate laughed, but his attention was snagged by motion in the office.

Deimos turned to look and Dottie went still.

"I said leave, Mr. Arnold!" came a sharp, feminine voice.

Harold Arnold rose to his feet, holding out a hand. "Just a moment, Ms. Sawyer!"

"I've heard enough! I want you to go!"

"Please, just listen to me, you're gonna want to hear the whole offer. I promise you! You wanna play ball with me,

Ms. Sawyer, 'cause I've got your best interest in mind. Now others, not so much. I can promise you that."

"Are you threatening me, Mr. Arnold?"

The coffee shop had gone surprisingly quiet. The customers were all listening and the regular with the laptop had turned around, trying to see what was going on. Dottie gave Deimos a pointed look, but the barista only shifted weight, his expression pained.

Tate found himself moving before he even realized what he intended to do. He went around the counter and stepped between Dottie and Deimos, headed toward the open office door. To his right was a small kitchen, but the left led straight into the office.

"Sit down, Ms. Sawyer, and let me finish!" said Arnold.

"No, we're done, Mr. Arnold, and you need to go!"

"You don't know what you're doing, girl. If you want the best deal, the best price for this place, we don't need to haggle anymore. I told you I'd get it for you."

Tate stepped inside. "She told you to leave. She better not have to say that again."

Arnold glanced over his shoulder at Tate, but Tate ignored him, focusing on Vivian's daughter. She was tall and slender, although curvy in all the right places. She wore a stylish black skirt, a striped long-sleeved silk blouse, and a silver belt. She had long, straight auburn hair and a smattering of freckles across her nose and cheekbones. Her green eyes were heavily rimmed in black lashes with just a subtle hint of eye makeup to accentuate them. She wasn't traditionally pretty, but something about her high cheekbones, broad forehead, and large eyes gave her an undeniable magnetism. Tate found her stunning.

"This doesn't have anything to do with you," said Arnold, dismissing him.

Tate's gaze snapped to the realtor's red face. "When a woman tells you to leave and you don't, it has everything to do with me."

Her green gaze moved back to Arnold and she crossed her arms. "Leave, Mr. Arnold. We're done here."

He sighed, then reached for a folder on her desk and closed it, shoving it into his briefcase. Clicking the briefcase shut, he stepped back between the armchairs and inclined his head. "Fine, but you know where to reach me when you come to a decision."

"I do," she said, tilting up her chin.

"I wouldn't wait too long. If you make a decision this week, I can get the papers drawn up before you go back to the City, but if not, you'll have to come back out here to sign them." Without another word, he turned and pushed past Tate, moving rapidly toward the exit.

Tate stepped into the office doorway to make sure he left, then he looked back at the young woman. For some reason, he felt nervous facing her and he didn't know what to say.

"Thank you," she offered. "I appreciate you coming to my rescue like that. I agreed to meet with him, but I didn't know he'd want me to make a decision just like that."

Tate gave a tense laugh. "He's been pushy like that lately." He took a step forward and held out his hand. "I'm Tate Mercer. I own the hardware store down the block, the *Hammer Tyme*."

She accepted his hand, but she made a face. "That's truly awful – the name."

He nodded. "Not much better than the *Caffeinator*."

"Touché," she said and laughed. He liked her laugh. "I'm Zion Sawyer."

"Zion? That's…um…biblical."

She laughed again. "My parents named me after their honeymoon location."

"Ah," he said, then an awkward silence fell between them and he shifted weight, pointing over his shoulder. "Now that the crisis has been averted, I'll just get my caramel Macchiato and head back to my place."

She smiled at that. "Thank you again, for intervening."

"All in a day's work, ma'am," he said with an affected southern drawl, then he flinched. "Sorry." He rubbed a hand over his forehead.

Her tinkling laughter followed him back into the coffee shop where Dottie presented him with his coffee. He took it, making eye contact with Deimos. Deimos shook his head.

"Dude, that was rough."

Tate nodded. "Tell me about it. You're bad with interviews and I'm bad with..." He glanced over his shoulder, but he could no longer see Zion Sawyer. "...whatever the hell that was."

* * *

Tate and Logan shut down the *Hammer Tyme* around 6:00PM.

"You want a ride home?" Tate asked the boy.

Logan held up his skateboard. "I like to ride when the weather's nice."

"Okay, then. See you tomorrow."

Logan lifted a hand and dropped the board on the ground.

Tate watched him, then reached for his car keys. "Logan," he called.

Logan looked back at him in question.

"You did good today. With the register?"

The boy shrugged, but Tate could see a half-smile on his lips. "It was nothing."

"Yeah, well, I appreciate it."

"See you tomorrow, Tate," said the boy, then he skated off.

Tate walked around the side of the hardware store and found his truck waiting for him. Unlocking it, he climbed inside and started the engine. Pulling out onto Main Street, he eyed the tourist traffic still meandering around, window shopping or deciding on a place to grab dinner.

Was Dwayne right? Did all this go away once a big box store opened? He hated to admit it, but that was probably exactly what would happen. Reaching over, he turned on the radio and let his shoulders relax against the seat cushions.

Driving out of town, he got on the highway for a bit, then took his exit and turned onto his street. He could see his house in the middle of the street, but something was wrong with the front of it. Turning down the radio, he pulled into the driveway and set the brake, flipping off the ignition, then he got out and walked back to the street, staring down at the remains of his mailbox.

Someone had taken a bat to it and knocked it off the post beside his front gate. Placing his hands on his hips, he tried to reason this out. Most likely it was a bored group of teenagers out to do some mischief, but another worrisome thought intruded. He'd been poking into Vivian's death, talking with the other business owners. What if this was a warning of some kind?

He heard a car pull up behind him, but he didn't pay attention to it, until a familiar voice called to him.

"Hey, neighbor."

He turned and found Zion Sawyer leaning out her driver's side window. A dark haired woman sat on the passenger side. He forced a smile and walked over to her, ducking down to see the other woman.

"Hey, is Vivian's house on this street?"

She pointed to the pretty blue cottage at the end where the street curved into a circle. "Just down the way there."

Tate scratched his head. "I've lived here two years and I never even knew that. Wow."

She pointed to the woman next to her. "This is my mother, Gabi Sawyer."

Tate shook hands with the older woman. She didn't look anything like Zion. She was smaller, darker skinned, with salt and pepper hair. "Nice to meet you, I'm Tate Mercer."

"How do you do, Mr. Mercer," she said, releasing him.

Zion frowned at his mailbox. His attention was drawn to the freckles across the bridge of her nose. They were out of keeping with her big city airs – her clothes and fashionable hairstyle – but for some reason, he liked them.

"Someone took a bat to your mailbox?"

Tate looked back at his smashed property. "Yeah, looks that way. Probably teenagers messing around after school."

"That's a pretty nasty prank," she observed.

Tate put his hands on his hips again and nodded. "Yeah, when I first moved here, I thought the old fashioned mailboxes were charming. Now I see their fundamental flaw."

Both Zion and her mother laughed.

"Good thing I sell them in my store."

Zion gave him an understanding smile and he felt his heart trip a little. He hadn't felt like this in a long time. What the hell! He and Cherise had finalized their divorce a year ago, but he hadn't been interested in dating anyone since then.

"Tate rescued me from the realtor," she told her mother.

Gabi leaned forward again. "Thank you for that. What a scumbag! Zion says he got really pushy."

Tate nodded. "He's been doing that a lot lately. There's a big box store just waiting to go in on that side of Main."

"I see," offered Gabi.

Tate shifted, pointing down the road to Vivian's cottage. "Look, if you need anything, just ask, okay?" He wanted to question her about her intentions, but he knew that such questions might feel like pressure, especially seeing as she got rid of Harold Arnold the minute he tightened the screws.

"Thank you, Tate," she said, flashing that smile again. For some people, a smile transformed their faces from pleasant to magnificent. Zion had such a smile.

"Like I said, all in a day's work."

He grimaced when the southern drawl came out again. What the hell! Why did he want to go all southern gentleman on her whenever he saw her?

Gabi and Zion laughed, then Zion pulled away, headed toward Vivian's cottage. She waved out the open window at him and he waved back. Then he walked over to the mailbox and studied it. Should he call Sheriff Wilson or was he making too much out of a random act of vandalism? Finally, he decided he'd mention it the next time he saw the sheriff, but it didn't merit a phone call.

Bending he lifted the twisted bit of metal and started up the driveway for his garbage can, but he paused at the top and looked down the road where Zion and her mother were getting out of their car. Damn it, the first time he'd been interested in a woman in two years and she lived in San Francisco. Just like him to do some fool thing like that.

# CHAPTER 7

Zion curled up in the arm chair next to the brick fireplace, pulling the throw blanket around her legs, then lifted the photo album into her lap and opened the cover. Reaching for her tea, she took a sip as she studied the pictures of Vivian when she was younger.

Zion couldn't deny there was a strong resemblance between them. Vivian's hair was the exact shade of Zion's if Zion didn't have an auburn wash applied to it every six weeks and it naturally fell into ringlets. Zion paid a lot of money to have hers artificially straightened. Their green eyes were the same as were the annoying freckles.

Zion smiled at the picture of Vivian laughing as she and a girlfriend ate ice cream cones at a zoo somewhere. Vivian looked like a happy woman, easy going and quick to smile. Turning the page, she found a picture of her at the beach.

It had been taken in profile and she was looking out at the surf, her long curly hair flowing over her left shoulder, her expression pensive and at peace, relaxed.

Zion's gaze drifted past the photo album to the urn that sat on the coffee table, a wash of sadness swamping her. She'd never known this woman, but sitting here in her house, going through her belongings made her wish she had.

"You okay?" came Gabi's voice in the doorway of the living room.

Zion looked up. Her mother was a shadow in the darkened room, the light from the table lamp not reaching her. "Yeah, couldn't sleep."

Gabi came over to the ottoman in front of Zion's chair and took a seat on it. "Looking at pictures?"

Zion nodded, smoothing her hand over the page. "She seemed like a happy person. In all these pictures, she's with friends, laughing, exploring different places." She flipped a few pages and found one of a handsome man with blond hair and blue eyes, his arm around a smiling Vivian. "This must have been her husband."

Gabi turned the photo album to look at it. "They look happy. I wonder what went wrong."

"I wonder why she didn't have more kids."

Gabi took Zion's hand. "I'm proud of the way you're handling this, honey. I know it's harder than you thought it would be."

Zion looked around the room. Vivian had decorated it much like she had the *Caffeinator* with antique furnishings and Victorian accents. However, here she'd replaced the pink with beige and blue over polished dark hardwood floors and stained glass in the windows.

"I thought I'd just come here, we'd tell David to sell everything, then we'd have been back in San Francisco yesterday."

"I know."

Today Gabi had started cleaning out Vivian's clothes, something Zion just couldn't force herself to do, while she and David had met at the *Caffeinator* to go over the books. "The coffee house is really doing well and this place…" Zion sighed and gave her mother a sad smile. "I really like this house."

Gabi looked around too. "She had an eye for making things cozy, didn't she?"

Zion nodded, then shut the photo album. Her eyes strayed to Vivian's urn again. "What am I going to do with her ashes, Mom?"

Gabi released her hand. "I've been thinking about that and I think you need to have some sort of memorial. She left you quite a bit of money. Use a little of it to buy her a niche at the cemetery and we'll invite people to the *Caffeinator* to celebrate her life. I'm sure Dottie and Deimos would be willing to help us prepare it."

"That's a good idea." She chewed on her inner lip. "What about the coffee house? Should I just sell it to that smarmy Arnold guy?"

Gabi slapped her hands on her thighs. "I want a cup of tea. Come on, let's go make one and we'll hash this out. You know I'm big on pro and con lists. Let's make us one of those too."

Zion smiled as Gabi padded off to the kitchen after her tea. Her parents had always been big on making lists. When Zion tried to figure out what college was best, they'd made a list. When she wanted to buy her first car after graduation, they'd made a list. When she couldn't decide what companies to apply to, they'd made a list.

Throwing back the blanket, she picked up her own tea and followed Gabi into the kitchen. Wood molding curved over every door and window, stained a dark color, matching the doors themselves. The cabinets in the kitchen were mahogany, sturdy and rustic looking, while the stove's old fashioned look didn't mask its upgraded gourmet quality. The refrigerator, although modern on the inside, looked like an icebox from the 1930's. Zion couldn't deny she loved this house and everything about it. Rebekah, her best friend, would say it was kitschy, but Zion didn't see it that way.

She sat down at the plank board kitchen table and settled her tea before her. Gabi put on the teapot and got down one of Vivian's rough clay mugs, taking a tea bag out of a tin canister on the counter that sported vintage ads from the 1920's. Pulling a pad of a paper and a pen out of the small desk in the corner, she laid it on the table next to Zion and took a seat.

"Let's talk about the business first of all," she said.

Zion sipped at her tea. "Okay. Harold Arnold made an offer for it, but since I have no experience with selling something like that, I don't know if it's fair or not."

"Okay. Well, did you show David the offer?"

"No, we're supposed to have dinner tonight and I thought I'd show it to him then."

Gabi paused in the act of writing on her list. "You're having dinner with the cute lawyer with the big ears?"

"It's just dinner, Mom, not a honeymoon."

"I didn't say it was. Besides, I'm not sure you should date a lawyer."

"Well, we can make a list about that later." Then Zion frowned. "Wait. Why don't you like lawyers?"

"Lawyers, politicians, CEO's, businessmen in general – you know – all the power players, they don't make good husbands. You should look for someone who serves the public. Veterinarian, social worker, doctor…"

"…garbage man," quipped Zion, drinking her tea.

Gabi wagged the pen at her. "You could do worse than a man who keeps the world clean, young lady."

"Okay, can we get back to the list? Why are you suddenly so interested in marrying me off?"

"I'm not interested in marrying you off. I think marriage is an archaic institution that's meaningless now."

"Says the woman married for thirty years."

"I'm just saying that a modern woman can do very well for herself without the entanglement of marriage, but if you're going to go down that route, it's best to stack the cards in your favor."

"With a man who serves the public?"

"Now, you've got it." The teakettle began screaming and Gabi set down her pen, going to turn it off and pour her tea. "Okay, so you're going to show the offer to David tonight."

"Right, but it didn't look like that great of an offer. The coffee house actually makes a pretty good profit each month, even with all the overhead and salaries. And Vivian owned the building outright, so there's no mortgage or rent to pay."

"But you don't know anything about running a coffee house?"

"I know."

"And you have a job in the City?"

"Also true."

"So what other choice is there?"

"He wants to buy the building so they can tear the coffee house down and put in a big box store. David told me they've got their eyes on all the businesses on that side of Main Street. When Vivian was alive, the business owners made a pact not to sell. Everyone's afraid it'll ruin the small town feel if Main Street goes the way of the rest of the state, strip malls every block or so."

Gabi curled her hands around her mug. "Wow, I hate the idea of that."

"I know, right?"

"If you sell, the others will be pressured to sell too, won't they?"

"Yep."

"That's a problem."

"Tell me about it." Zion took another sip. "So what do I do?"

"Is there anyone else interested in buying the *Caffeinator*? Anyone local who'll keep it as it is?"

"Arnold said there wasn't, but I didn't get the sense he had the purest of motives." She worried her lip again. "He was so persistent, Mom. If Tate hadn't come in and told him to leave, I don't know what he would have done. I was actually reaching for my phone to call Sheriff Wilson."

Gabi's eyes grew clouded. "You don't think he's desperate enough to kill Vivian, do you?"

"If I had a suspect, he'd be it."

"I don't like you going up against him then, Zion. Maybe you should just sell and be done with it."

"Take the coward's way out, Mom. Is that how you raised me?"

Gabi rolled her eyes. "Nice, throw my own words back in my face. Still, this scares me. If Vivian lost her life because someone wanted that building, I don't want you standing in the way."

Zion rubbed her temples. "God, I don't know what to do. Your list isn't helping. And we haven't even started talking about this place."

Gabi looked around the cottage. "I think this is the least of your worries. The mortgage's paid off, you only have to come up with property tax and insurance, and Vivian left you money for that. You can keep this place until you decide what to do with it. Have it as a retreat."

Zion felt some of the weight lift from her shoulders. "You're right. I don't have to make a decision on this place right now."

"And maybe that's what we do with the coffee shop."

"What do you mean?"

"I mean being a little passive aggressive isn't necessarily a bad thing. Maybe you tell this Arnold guy you're so torn up about Vivian's death, you can't make a decision, we go home, and let it sit."

"What about the *Caffeinator* though? Dottie and Deimos? If I shut it down, what'll they do?"

"Don't shut it down. Let them run it. They've run it since Vivian's death. So maybe we come up here every couple of weekends and check things out, but until this whole deal with the big box store calms down or until Sheriff Wilson finds Vivian's killer, we just don't do anything with the store."

"Procrastinate?"

"Yep."

"I like it."

They sipped at their tea in silence for a few minutes, then Zion frowned. She thought she heard something coming from the back door. Tilting her head, she listened and there it was again, faint, but unmistakable. She heard the crying of a kitten.

Rising to her feet, she went to the back door and parted the white lace curtain to peer out the window, but she couldn't see anything. Gabi swiveled around in her chair to watch her as Zion unlocked the back door and pulled it open.

A tiny black kitten sat on the wooden doorstep, mewing to be let inside. Zion bent and picked it up, cuddling it close to her chest. It was shivering even though the night was mild. Carrying it back in the house, she found Gabi standing before her, reaching out to stroke the tiny animal's ear.

"Poor baby, are there others out there?"

Zion passed the kitten to her mother and went to the desk, rummaging in the drawers until she came up with a flashlight. Clicking it on, she went back to the door and stepped out on the small porch, shining the flashlight over the yard, then she climbed down the stairs and shone the beam over the remaining yard, under the stairs and beneath the picnic table, but she didn't see any other trace of kittens.

Going back in the house, she found Gabi had wrapped the kitten in a dish towel and was feeding it drops of water from a turkey baster. "What are you doing?"

"I think she's dehydrated."

"How do you know it's a she?"

"She looks like a girl."

Zion rolled her eyes and walked over to her mother, touching the kitten's tiny ear. "How old do you think she is?"

"Very young. Probably too young to be away from her mother."

"We'll take her to the shelter tomorrow."

"Okay, sounds good."

"We should probably try to get some sleep."

Gabi nodded. "There's a shoe box top in the living room. Get that and I'll make her up a bed, then you can take her with you."

"I don't want to take her with me. You take her."

"Why?"

"Because…"

"Because you're afraid of a tiny, lost kitten."

"Because I'll wind up keeping her."

Gabi shoved the kitten into Zion's arms and gave her the turkey baster. "See if you can get her to drink this while I make her a bed and a makeshift litter box."

"What are you going to use for litter?"

"Shredded newspaper. I bought a whole bunch today when I thought I was going to box up Vivian's dishes."

Without another word, Gabi was gone, leaving Zion standing in the kitchen with a tiny kitten, who inexplicably started to purr.

* * *

The next morning, Zion found Gabi in the kitchen, trying to coax the kitten to eat something. She looked up and gave Zion a worried look.

"Is everything all right?"

"She won't eat. I think she's too young to leave her mother."

"Probably." Zion went to the coffee pot and poured herself a cup, leaning against the counter and taking a sip.

"I went back into the yard to find her mother, but I didn't see anything."

"Well, the shelter will know what to do."

"I called a vet."

Zion lowered the coffee cup. "Wait. Why? I thought we agreed it's going to the shelter."

"If she's sick, the shelter will just put her down. Let's at least see if she's well." She tried to coax another drop of whatever she had into the kitten's mouth with the turkey baster. "We have an appointment at 8:00, so you better get ready."

Zion glanced at the clock over the desk. It was already 7:15. "Mom, seriously?"

"Hurry up. You'll have to drive, so I can hold her."

Zion knew better than to argue. Carrying her coffee, she walked to the guest room she'd been occupying. No way was she sleeping in Vivian's old room. Her mother had agreed to take that. Grabbing a clean change of clothes they'd bought at the discount retail store last night after the *Caffeinator* closed, Zion took a quick shower. She didn't have time to blow dry her hair, so she pulled it up in a ponytail and slapped on a little makeup. Staring at herself in the mirror, she knew Rebekah would be horrified, especially as she hadn't accessorized with a statement necklace or a scarf.

She found her mother pacing by the front door, the kitten wrapped in a fuzzy blanket. "Let's go."

The sun was shining as they walked out to the car. The street was quiet and the smell of pine permeated everything. Zion could get used to smelling the freshness of the forest everyday. It beat car exhaust and the smell of cigarette smoke.

"I don't know where this place is," she told her mother, looking at the kitten lying limply in her mother's arms. A pang of worry rose inside of her, but she tamped it down. Her life was complicated enough. She didn't need anything else right now.

Gabi had pulled up directions on her phone. The Bluetooth picked it up as she pulled her car onto the street. The vet was in a small Victorian cottage a few streets over from Main. They had to park on the street and walk to it, Gabi jogging ahead in her worry. Zion followed her into the building and found her mother at the counter, talking to a blond woman with no makeup, her hair pulled into a severe bun, wearing pale blue scrubs. Rebekah would throw a coronary if she saw her.

The woman was leaning on the counter, pulling back the blanket so she could see the kitten and the look of genuine concern on her face soothed Gabi. She handed Gabi a clipboard and Gabi passed it to Zion.

"You need to fill it out."

Zion took a seat on the bench in the waiting area and Gabi perched next to her, her leg jogging with anxiety. Zion touched her arm. "Mom, why are you so worked up about this?"

"She's just a baby, Zion. She needs us."

Zion shifted to study her. "Mom, let's be reasonable. We live in San Francisco. It's no place for a cat. Besides, Rascal hates cats. He always chases them."

"I just want to make sure she's okay before we dump her at the shelter."

"We're not dumping her. We're giving her a chance."

Gabi looked away, clearly indicating the conversation was over, so Zion filled out the form. Under *Pet's Name*, she put *Cat*, then worried that might earn her a scolding from Gabi, but the cat didn't have a name and she sure wasn't giving it one.

A few minutes later, they were called back into a room. Zion sat down on the bench provided, sure they were going to have to wait forever, but a few minutes later, a woman wearing glasses, the same blue scrubs as the receptionist, and bright blue hair stepped inside. She had her hair spiked up on her head and a number of earrings lined both ears. Zion had to admit the people here had almost as crazy a fashion sense as the most outrageous cross dresser in the City.

"I'm Dr. Beningfield," she said, going to the sink and washing her hands. "I understand you found a kitten."

"Yes, Doctor, but she doesn't seem to be doing too well. I can't get her to eat anything. I think she's too young."

Dr. Beningfield approached the examination table and held out her hands for the kitten. The poor little thing mewed piteously as the doctor removed the fuzzy blanket and began to prod her. Lifting the skin at the back of the kitten's neck, she watched it slowly fall back into place.

"She's dehydrated." Making sure Gabi had a hold of her, she stepped to the door and called to a technician.

Zion couldn't hear what the doctor said, so she rose and approached the table, reaching out to stroke the tiny cat's spine. The kitten blinked at her with cloudy eyes.

The doctor returned to the table and began to prod it some more.

"How old do you think it is?" Zion found herself asking.

The doctor pried the kitten's mouth open and looked inside. "No more than three weeks at the outside. Too young to be away from her mother."

"We tried to find the mother, but she wasn't anywhere around," said Gabi.

"She's probably been killed, along with the other siblings. Raccoons or coyotes get them, or they get hit by a car."

Zion had an overwhelming urge to scoop the kitten up and cradle it. Thinking of the tiny thing left all alone was horrible.

"Can you tell if it's a boy or girl?" asked Gabi.

The doctor lifted the little thing and turned it over, glancing between its hind legs. "Female," she said.

Gabi nudged Zion with her arm, and Zion nodded at her.

The door opened and the technician handed the doctor a tiny baby bottle with formula in it. The doctor picked up the kitten and held her against her chest, offering her the bottle. It took a few tries, but suddenly the kitten was greedily sucking at the bottle, making tiny growling noises and kneading the doctor's chest with her paws.

Zion found herself smiling.

"Oh, poor darling," said Gabi, tears in her eyes. "She was so hungry."

"A kitten this small will need a bottle every couple of hours. You can begin feeding her watered down wet food in a few days, but she'll still need the supplement for at least two more weeks."

Gabi looked at Zion. Zion knew what was coming next and grimaced.

"Will the shelter be able to take care of her like that?" asked Gabi.

The doctor's face grew grim. "The shelter? You're planning to take her to the shelter?"

"Well, we live in San Francisco and my mother has a dog who doesn't like cats," said Zion as reasonably as she could.

"I'm gonna be honest. It'd be more humane to put her down then."

"Put her down?" said Zion, surprised by how this news upset her. "Why would we do that? She's a kitten. Someone's bound to want her."

"She already has two strikes against her. Number one, she's too young to eat solid food and the shelter's too busy to give her bottles. If they can't find a foster quickly, she'll die. And number two, she's a black cat. People are superstitious and more black cats are put down every year than any other color."

Zion's eyes went to the kitten, fighting so hard to stay alive.

"Like I said, it would be more humane for us to put her down right now."

Gabi made a sound of distress.

Zion closed her eyes. She knew when she'd been had. "No, you can't do that. We'll take her."

"You'll have to bottle feed her every few hours for a few weeks until she can eat solid food."

Rubbing her forehead, Zion nodded. Sure, why the hell not? Who cared that she had a job and a life and other things to do. "I'll have to move in with you and Dad for a few weeks, so you can feed her while I'm at work," she said, looking at her mother.

"Your father will love that."

"And we'll have to keep her away from Rascal."

"She'll have the run of your room during the day."

The doctor smiled. "If you're careful about introducing the two of them, you shouldn't have a problem. Chasing cats in the yard is very different from having the cat be part of your family."

Zion nodded at that, her eyes coming to rest on the tiny body in the doctor's hands. "You're going to have to show us how to do that."

The doctor held the kitten and the bottle out to Zion. "It's just like feeding a baby."

Sure, it was, although Zion had no experience with that either. She cuddled the tiny body against her and offered her the bottle. Lord knew, she didn't need a cat. Her life was too complicated and busy for an animal. In fact, she wasn't even sure she could have a cat in her building.

But staring into the tiny face with the pointed ears and the cloudy eyes, Zion knew she couldn't leave her at the shelter. This baby had survived the death of her whole family. It was something Zion could relate to.

"This is your fault," she told Gabi.

Gabi put her arms around her and squeezed. "God, I hope so," she said.

* * *

Zion dropped Gabi and the kitten back at Vivian's cottage, so the kitten could have a quiet place to rest and Gabi could feed her as often as she needed to be fed. She also promised to continue cleaning out Vivian's clothes.

Kissing her mother on the forehead, she got back in her Optima and pulled up the directions for the funeral home. She made arrangements for Vivian's ashes to be interred in a columbarium just outside of Sequoia, and she paid extra for a plaque with Vivian's name, date of birth, and date of death on it. Then, because that had her feeling restless and depressed, she detoured onto Main Street and found the *Fast & Furriest Pet Supplies* shop on the opposite side of the street from the *Caffeinator*.

She parked in the municipal parking lot and walked to the store. A cat meow alerted the owners to her arrival. As she waited, a tall, angular man and a heavyset woman appeared out of the back. Zion was instantly reminded of Jack Sprat and his wife.

"Good morning," said the man with a smile, adjusting his glasses on his nose.

"Welcome to *Fast & Furriest*," said the woman.

They both had brown hair, cut in identical bobs, wore jeans and sneakers, and had button up shirts with rolled up sleeves. The man's shirt was blue, while the woman's was pink. Over their clothes, they wore an apron with a cartoon dog and cat painted on it and the words *Fast & Furriest* embroidered in red thread.

"I'm Zion Sawyer," she said, holding out her hand. "I'm Vivian Bradley's biological daughter."

Both of their eyes widened and the woman came forward, clasping Zion's hand in both of her own. "I'm so sorry about your mother."

"Thank you."

The man clasped her other hand. "Me too. You must be in shock. Can we get you coffee?"

"Tea?"

"Water?"

Zion shook her head. "No, I'm fine. Actually, I'm here for two reasons. The first is I'm going to have a memorial service for Vivian at the *Caffeinator* tomorrow night." She mentally flinched as she realized she hadn't asked Deimos or Dottie if that was okay or not. "And I'd like to invite you both."

"A memorial service?"

"How lovely."

"Yes, lovely. What time?"

"Can we bring anything?"

Zion gently extricated herself from the pair and tried to sort through the questions. "I thought we'd have it after the coffee shop closes at 6:00PM and you don't have to bring anything. I'll have refreshments and drinks there."

"That's very nice," said the woman.

"Quite a tribute to a lovely woman," said the man.

"Did you know Vivian?"

"Of course we did. We usually stop by the *Caffeinator* every morning for our morning cup of coffee."

"I love the cinnamon twists," said the man.

Zion smiled. "They are good."

"Delicious."

"A real treat."

"I'm sorry, but I didn't catch your names," said Zion.

"Betty."

"And Barney."

"Brown," they said in unison.

"Very nice to meet you," she said, smiling.

"You said you had two things to ask us," questioned Betty.

"She said she had two reasons for coming inside," corrected Barney.

"Right. My mother and I found a tiny kitten. The doctor thinks she might be less than 6 weeks old. We have nothing for her, not even a litter box. Can you help me?"

The Browns looked at one another, then they sprang into motion, piling things on the counter for Zion. For her own part, Zion found herself drawn to the fluffy beds and the scratching posts. She went through the toys, then asked Betty to select a good wet food to start the kitten out on. Together they picked out a tiny collar, bowls, a litter box and liners, and finally litter. Barney got her a second baby bottle and dry formula that she and Gabi could mix on their own.

"You'll need a carrier," said Betty.

"You have to have a carrier. It's always best to have a carrier for each animal in your family."

"Then I just need the one."

"You can go with the cardboard carrier for now," said Betty.

"Then you can upgrade later when she gets bigger."

Zion was drawn to a pretty pink carrier with rhinestones on the top and sides. She picked it up, realizing she was having a good time accessorizing a cat she hadn't been sure she wanted. "I'll get this one."

"Excellent choice," said Barney.

"She'll be able to use that one for her entire life," said Betty and began ringing up Zion's purchases.

After she paid with her credit card, Zion shook her head in bemusement at how much paraphernalia one tiny creature needed. "I hope it all fits in my car."

"I'll help you load it," said Barney, grabbing the scratching post and a few bags.

Zion put the receipt in her wallet and grabbed the others. "It was a pleasure to meet you, Betty," she said, "and I look forward to talking with you more tomorrow night."

"We'll be there," said Betty, waving to her as she went to the door.

Zion deposited everything in the Optima and then thanked Barney, locked the car and detoured toward the *Caffeinator* to hopefully enlist Dottie's and Deimos' help with Vivian's memorial service. She didn't want to think of how much money she was going through. Vivian's estate hadn't been released to her yet, but it didn't matter. Zion found herself wanting to do these things for a woman most people seemed to hold in high regard.

* * *

Deimos waved to her from behind the cash register as she entered the coffee shop. He was tying an apron around his middle and taking the order of two teenage girls. Zion waved back, then saw Jackson Van Tiernan was in his spot on the couch, laptop open on his lap. He held up a hand to her as well.

She smiled and wandered over to the couches. "Good afternoon."

"Good afternoon," he said, but he didn't smile. "How are you?"

"I'm fine. How are you? Getting a lot of work done?"

"That's the plan. I have a deadline in a few weeks. I'm creating the sequel to *B&E-1* and *Cyclone* wants it for rollout around Christmas."

"B&E?"

His expression grew grim and he adjusted his heavy rimmed glasses on his nose. "Breaking and Entering-1. It's a huge RPG."

"I see. And you're working on the sequel?"

"Right. We're hoping it'll be the most highly anticipated game this holiday season."

He sounded like a walking advertisement. Zion forced a smile. She'd never heard of that game, but that meant less than nothing. She wasn't really a gamer. Deciding to change the subject, she glanced around the coffee house, then took a seat on the couch next to him so she wouldn't be overheard.

"So, I'm planning to have a memorial service for Vivian here tomorrow night. Would you like to come?"

He tilted up his head and looked at her through the bottom half of his glasses. "Seriously?"

Zion cocked her head. "I don't understand."

"You're inviting me?" He shifted on the couch, closing the top of his computer. When Zion continued to give him a bewildered look, he nodded. "Sure, that'd be great."

"Okay, good. Tomorrow night, then. At 6:00."

"6:00, sure. I'll probably be here anyway."

"Right." Zion rose. "Well, I'll let you get back to work."

He nodded, his eyes following her as she headed toward the counter. Zion turned her back on him, giving Dottie a bewildered look.

"He's an odd duck," Dottie muttered under her breath. "So, sugar, can I get you something to drink or eat?"

"I would love a cinnamon twist. Barney Brown at *Fast & Furriest* mentioned them and got my stomach growling."

Dottie beamed a happy smile and hurried to get Zion's order.

"Any coffee?" asked Deimos, finishing up his last customer.

"Chai tea, please," she said, and he set about making it.

When Dottie handed her the cinnamon twists and a small cup of icing, she smiled at her and reached for her purse. Dottie waved her off and went back to mixing up something in the blender. Zion waited for the noise to die down, then she accepted the cup from Deimos. Carrying it and the plate of cinnamon twists behind the counter, she moved toward her office.

"Can you both come in here for a moment please?"

She saw them share a look, then Dottie started washing her hands and Deimos straightened his apron. Zion settled her dishes on the desk and took a seat behind it as her two employees entered the office, looks of trepidation and worry on both of their faces. She hated those looks. Since she'd met them, she hadn't seen many other expressions. She wished she could put their minds at ease, but that wouldn't be fair since she still didn't know what she planned to do.

"Please, take a seat."

They both perched on the edge of the armchairs Vivian had arranged before the massive pine desk. Deimos looked over his shoulder into the coffee shop, but once he'd assured himself there wasn't a new customer, he faced Zion again.

"So, I know this is a tense time for both of you and I wish I could tell you I've made a decision about the store, but the truth is, I haven't. What I asked you in here for is I want to have a memorial service for Vivian tomorrow night and I was hoping you'd be able to help me. I want to have it in the *Caffeinator*." When they just continued to stare at her, she quickly added, "You'll be compensated for the extra time, of course."

"That's not necessary," said Dottie. "We loved Vivian. We're happy to help."

"You got it, Boss Lady, anything you want."

Zion released her held breath. "I'm so glad because I wasn't looking forward to pulling it off on my own."

"Don't you worry, sugar. We'll have everything in top shape before your guests get here. Do you know who you're inviting?"

"Just some of the business people on this street. I asked the Browns and Van Tiernan. I thought I'd go to the rest of the businesses today and see if they'd like to join us. Also David Bennett."

"Of course. What about Harold Arnold?" asked Dottie, not disguising the edge in her voice.

"Old Americano," said Deimos bitterly.

Zion blinked at him. "Americano?"

"I remember people based on their most frequent coffee order. The Arnold dude likes Americanos. The Browns are lattes, and you're Chai tea now. Bennett's a doppio with a splash of cream."

Zion laughed. "That's one way to remember people." She turned her attention to Dottie. "No, Harold Arnold's not invited."

Dottie gave her a slow smile and Zion knew she'd pleased the older woman with that response.

# CHAPTER 8

Before he left home, Tate put in a call to Sheriff Wilson, but the sheriff hadn't come into the office yet. He left a brief message and hung up. Walking out to his truck, he wondered if he should have kept the mailbox and maybe Wilson could pull a fingerprint off it, but honestly, he figured the mailbox had been taken out by a baseball bat from a moving car.

He couldn't help but glance toward Vivian Bradley's house, hoping to catch a glimpse of Zion, but the little white Optima was gone. He hadn't been interested in a woman since his divorce. Not that he hadn't seen attractive women, he just hadn't considered going down the rabbit hole again. Maybe the fact that Zion was going back to San Francisco had him intrigued. There was no way for it to be anything more than a casual flirtation.

Climbing into the truck, he dismissed her from his mind. He had other things to think about – his store, Logan, the fact that someone had vandalized his house, although the more he thought about that, the more he figured it had to be teenagers being…well, teenagers. He almost felt silly for calling Wilson.

Driving into town, he parked in his customary spot and walked down to the store. The sun had risen above the tops of the buildings and wispy white clouds floated overhead. Tate could feel the coming heat of the day. It wasn't going to get as hot as it would come July, but it was going to be in the mid-80's at least.

He pulled his keychain out of his pocket and unlocked the door. The fob to his under-counter gun safe slapped against his palm as he fitted the store key into the lock. Stepping inside, he turned on the *open* sign in the window and started turning on all the lights.

After he'd gone through the entire store, set up the cash register, and made sure the bathroom was clean, he used the remaining time to straighten the shelves. He'd lost himself in sorting the screws back into the proper bins when the buzzer over the door sounded.

He glanced over his shoulder, surprised to see Sheriff Wilson step inside, tipping his hat to the back of his head and then tucking his thumbs into his belt. Tate gave him a smile and placed the screws he was holding in a bin, then he walked over and shook the Sheriff's hand.

"You didn't have to come out," he said.

Wilson looked down, studying the toe of his cowboy boot. He tapped a floorboard by the front window. "The sun's bleaching this spot. You should put up some blinds."

Tate looked as well. "Damn, I didn't even notice it. The sun's always above the buildings when I open shop."

"Yeah, it's that early morning sun. It just blasts down on this side of Main."

"You want some coffee? I put a pot on just a bit ago."

"Sure," said Wilson, following Tate toward the counter.

"I'm serious. You didn't have to come out here. I'm actually feeling a little silly for calling you." He motioned Wilson to follow him into the storeroom where he'd set up a dorm fridge, a microwave, and a coffee pot.

"I like to get out of the office, stretch my legs." Wilson rocked on his boot heels as Tate poured two mugs of coffee and handed him one.

"Cream or sugar?"

"Nope. Gave that up after my last physical. Cholesterol's through the roof. Aging is no picnic."

Tate smiled and added a splash of instant creamer to his coffee. He motioned to the card table and two folding chairs arranged before the shelves of merchandise. "Have a seat."

"What if a customer comes in?"

"I'll hear them. The buzzer rings back here too."

Wilson gave a nod and wandered over to the table, sitting across from Tate. "So, someone busted out your mailbox yesterday?"

Tate curled his hands around his mug, shrugging. "Yeah, but now that I'm thinking of it, it was probably some teenagers just joyriding."

Wilson took a sip of his coffee, then removed his hat and set it on the table. "What did you think it might be before you started talking yourself out of it?"

Tate scratched his forearm. He always rolled up his shirt sleeves when he came to work, so the cuffs didn't get grease on them, but whenever he got nervous, he caught himself scratching the panther tattoo on his right inner arm. He'd gotten it when he was a teenager, his own version of rebellion, and many times over the years he'd thought to have it removed, but he hadn't done it yet.

"I don't know, Sheriff. I mean, I've been poking around a bit in this Vivian Bradley case."

Wilson went still. "What do you mean poking around?"

"Nothing big. Just talking to people mostly, hearing what they have to say, but…" He made a face, then lifted his mug for a sip. He actually found himself missing the rich flavor of the coffee at the *Caffeinator*. That was how they hooked you, damn it all.

"But?"

"I had two run-ins with Harold Arnold."

Wilson tilted back his head. "What sort of run-ins?"

"The first one wasn't a big deal. I saw his car at the *Corker* the other night when I was going home, so I went in to grab something to eat. Trixie Taylor was in the bar, meeting Arnold. He got a little aggressive with her, but she shut him down pretty good. Still we made eye contact, Arnold and me, so he knows I was there."

"And the second?"

"Was yesterday in the *Caffeinator*."

"What happened?"

"I went in to get coffee. He was meeting with Zion."

"Zion?"

"Vivian's daughter?"

"Right."

"They were back in her office, but she had the door open. Dee told me she was nervous about meeting with him alone."

Wilson absorbed everything he said, taking another sip of his coffee. "Go on."

"I don't know what happened, but all of a sudden, I could hear Zion shouting, telling him to get out of her store. He started arguing with her, refusing to leave. Before I even realized what I was doing, I went around the counter and stepped into the office, telling him to get lost. He wasn't happy about it."

Wilson sat and listened, nodding.

"I don't know why I got involved, but I did."

"The cop in you came out."

"I guess." Tate shrugged and tapped his fingers on the coffee mug. "Anyway, he left and I didn't think anymore about it, until I got home and my mailbox was smashed."

Wilson glanced away.

"See, it's ridiculous, isn't it?"

"I don't know about that. I think it's a bit too coincidental. You know I told you Vivian had some threatening messages on her cell phone, right?"

"Right."

"What I didn't tell you is some of them were voicemail."

"Voicemail?"

"Yeah, but the voice is unrecognizable. In each one the voice was distorted. Whoever left them used a voice program or something."

"What were they about?"

"Idle threats. Name calling. Really juvenile stuff."

"Like smashing a mail box?"

"Exactly."

Tate scratched the tattoo again. "You don't think Arnold would stoop to stupid intimidation tactics, do you?"

"I think Harold Arnold works for some deep pockets who are used to getting what they want. I think those deep pockets don't like the fact that the other merchants didn't immediately fold when Vivian Bradley died."

"Does that mean he's your top suspect?"

"It means I can't put the ex-husband in Sequoia no matter what I do, so I'm down to one suspect, unless you've uncovered something more."

"Nope." Tate shifted uncomfortably. "You don't have enough to arrest Arnold, Sheriff."

"I know."

"So now what?"

Wilson shrugged. "I get enough."

The buzzer sounded. "Tate?" came Logan's voice from the front of the store.

"Back here," Tate called to him. He focused on Wilson again. "So what next?"

"You need to fill out a formal complaint at the station."

Tate nodded, knowing that was true.

"Then I keep trying to find evidence to connect Arnold to this thing." He gave Tate a wry smile. "Still sure you don't want to come on as a consultant?"

"Nope." Tate laughed. "Getting my mailbox smashed was an effective warning. This morning, I checked to see if I had the fob to my gun safe just to be sure."

Wilson chuckled. "'Tis strange times we're living in. I took this job because I figured I'd never have to investigate a murder. You came out here to get away from the crime back home, and here we are, both of us, sucked in again."

Tate sighed. "Not me, Sheriff. I'm happy to let you have that honor."

"Mmhmm," said Wilson, lifting the mug to his lips.

* * *

Tate pulled a set of mini-blinds out of the storage room for the front window. No use letting the antique wooden floor get more damaged than it already was. He enlisted Logan's help to put up the blinds, showing the teenager how to use the power tools.

Logan might work in a hardware store, but the way the boy handled tools told Tate a lot about his upbringing. Logan never talked about his father. Tate hadn't felt comfortable asking him, so they'd ignored the topic completely, but it was clear male role models were lacking in Logan's life.

Tate's own father was a hard sonuvabitch. An ex-cop who measured male masculinity by the traditional means, Tom Mercer thought every man should be able to do three things: pick up women, hold his liquor, and use power tools. Tate hadn't been very good at the first two, but he'd absorbed everything his old man had to tell him about the latter.

Like with everything Tate taught him, Logan was a quick study and delighted in the whir of the drill. Tate couldn't help but feel a pang of remorse that Logan wasn't in school, that he might give up on getting his education. He was too smart to settle for a life of minimum wage jobs as a retail clerk.

The buzzer sounded and the door opened. Zion Sawyer walked into the store, looking around. Tate handed the drill to Logan and moved toward her, unable to keep the smile from his face. She had her hair pulled up in a ponytail and wore a pair of jeans and a frothy silk top with spaghetti straps. Her freckles stood out in the sunlight streaming through the windows. Looking at her, he realized he was immediately enchanted.

"Zion, hi?"

She lifted her hand and pulled away a pair of sunglasses, glancing over at him. "Tate, good afternoon."

"Good afternoon." He tucked his hands in his pockets, suddenly feeling uncommonly nervous around her. "What brings you to this part of Main?"

"Well, I wanted…" Her green eyes shifted to Logan. "Hi, I'm Zion."

The boy's mouth was agape and he was still holding the drill as Zion moved toward him, holding out her hand.

"That's Logan Baxter, my assistant."

"Hi, Logan."

"Hi, Zion," he said, taking her hand.

Zion glanced over their work. "Putting up blinds, huh?"

Tate shrugged. "Yeah, the sheriff pointed out the floor's getting bleached. It's antique, so I thought we ought to protect it."

"Of course." She moved toward him again, taking a look around. "This place is…uh…"

"It's a hardware store," he offered.

She laughed. "I was going to say tooly, but then I thought that's probably not a word."

He laughed with her. "No, it's probably not, but I'll start using it and maybe we can make it stick." He caught Logan's pained expression from the corner of his eyes and clamped his mouth shut.

Zion smiled at him. "It's a very masculine place, Tate, and if I ever needed a doodad, this is where I'd come."

"We carry doodads, right over there," he said, pointing behind him.

Logan closed his eyes and turned away. Tate looked down. God, he didn't know why he got all tongue tied around this woman.

"So you're out and about bright and early?" he said.

She gave him a bewildered look. "It's almost noon."

"Right, but that's probably early somewhere."

Logan bumped his forehead on the molding around the window a few times.

She laughed. "Sure. Actually I have been out since early this morning. Mom and I found a tiny kitten on the back porch of Vivian's house. We took her to the vet."

"Is she all right?"

"She's too young to eat solid food, so we have to bottle feed her. I thought about taking her to the shelter, since I live in a condo in the City, but the vet said she'd die. Now I have a cat. We always had dogs growing up."

"Well, I don't think they're all that different, are they?"

"Sure they are. You can't walk a cat on a leash to do her business."

"No, that's true."

"And the paraphernalia alone – scratching posts, carriers, food dishes."

"I hadn't thought about that, but you don't have to worry about her biting the mailman."

Zion laughed, but Logan smacked his forehead with the heel of his hand. She reached out and touched his arm, and Tate almost stopped breathing. "Look, I actually came in here to invite you to Vivian's memorial service."

"Really?"

"Yeah, it'll be low-key, just a few of the people who knew her. I'm having it at the *Caffeinator* after it closes tomorrow night. I'll have some food and drinks, but it's nothing big."

"Can I bring anything?"

She looked around the store. "I think we're covered on the doodad end of things."

He laughed. "Well, if you change your mind…"

Her smile turned wistful. "It's not a big deal, I just want to celebrate her memory."

He nodded. "I'll be there."

"Well, I'll let you get back to the power tools and other masculine pursuits." She glanced over at Logan. "Nice to meet you, Logan."

"You too, Zion," he said, holding up the drill in salute.

"See you tomorrow, Tate," she called and then she walked from the store.

Tate watched her until she disappeared around the corner of the building, but he felt Logan's eyes on him. "What?"

"Dude, that was painful to watch."

"Yeah, well, I'm out of practice."

"Practice for what?"

Tate walked back to the window, taking the drill out of Logan's hands. "Everything, apparently," he said.

* * *

The day passed in a blur as customers came in frequently enough to keep him and Logan hopping. After they closed and Logan rolled away on his skateboard, Tate realized he didn't feel like going home to his lonely bachelor pad to heat up a bowl of chili like he'd planned.

Looking down Main, he could see the *Bourbon Brothers* had arranged their outdoor tables on the small wooden patio they had outside their door and they'd turned on the lights Tate had helped them string from the eaves. Candles winked from the tabletops and people's laughter drifted out into the evening.

Tate wandered down the street toward the restaurant, knowing he shouldn't eat the rich barbecue twice in the same week, but also knowing he would get some lively conversation from the brothers. He entered the restaurant, finding it filled with tourists and regulars both. Walking up to the line, he waited while Daryl took orders.

Cheryl, Dwayne's wife, came by, carrying two pitchers of beer and nudged him with her arm. "Heya, handsome, what's up?"

He smiled at her. Cheryl only worked the evening shift when the restaurant got particularly crowded. About fifteen years older than he was, Cheryl Ford had a trim, curvy figure, a dazzling smile, smooth dark skin, and captivating brown eyes. She always wore her hair cropped close to her head, but on her it looked exotic and sexy. He had to admit he envied Dwayne a little. Cheryl didn't take crap from anyone, but she was also sweet and welcoming if you behaved yourself. And she adored her husband.

"Hey, Cheryl, how'd they drag a classy lady like you in here?"

"Aw, aren't you a charmer," she said, winking at him.

*Not where Zion was concerned,* he thought.

"Go sit in your regular spot, honey, and I'll take your order. You don't have to wait in line."

Tate smiled at her and stepped out of line, going to his place at the counter and taking a seat. Daryl gave him a chin nod and continued taking orders. As usual, he could see Dwayne and Al cooking away through the order window, their steps choreographed in perfect sync.

Dwayne's pretty teenage daughter came out of the kitchen, wearing a *Bourbon Brothers* apron, and grabbed a dish towel, wiping down the counter in front of him. "Mr. Mercer, nice to see you," she said.

Tallah Ford wore her hair in braids down to her shoulders, a few strands of pink woven into the mix of black, a pair of dangling earrings and a nose ring, but beyond that small rebellion she was the most centered, focused teenager Tate had ever seen. Tate, himself, didn't know exactly what he wanted and where he intended to go at the age of thirty-three, but Tallah did. She wanted to get into UCLA to study medicine and he didn't doubt she'd succeed. She was a straight A student, took all honors and AP classes, played volleyball, and had no time for the nonsense most fifteen year olds got caught up in.

"Tallah, nice to see you. I just saw your mom. How'd they get both of you working tonight?"

She laughed. "Tour bus just came through from Kings Canyon and Uncle Daryl sent out the all-hands on deck call." She leaned closer to him and dropped her voice. "I hate when he gets all nautical."

Tate laughed with her. "He told me he wanted to fly a jolly roger outside the restaurant."

Tallah rolled her eyes. "Of course he did. So, what can I get you?"

"He'll have his regular," said Daryl, sliding a frosty beer over to Tate. "Won't cha?"

Tate gave Tallah a shrug. "He knows me."

She nodded and smiled, moving off to pick up an order that her father set on the window.

"Order up!" he shouted.

"I hear ya! I hear ya!" Tallah said, gathering the plates and walking off.

When Tate reached for his wallet, Daryl waved him off. "This one's on me. Consider it your frequent flier rewards."

"Thanks," Tate said, putting the wallet away, and picking up the beer. "My first heart attack is also on you."

Daryl waved him off. "Gotta go someway, man."

Tate nodded in agreement and sipped at the cold brew. Turning on his stool, he looked over the restaurant. "This has got to be good for your bottom line."

Daryl leaned on the counter. "Yep, gives us more ammunition to fight the big box guys."

"You'd think…" Tate started to say, then his gaze chanced on the woman with the auburn hair, sitting in a booth on the other side of the restaurant. He recognized the man sitting across from her. David Bennett. Not that Tate had had much occasion to talk with Bennett, but he had paid for an hour consultation with the man after he moved here, trying to protect the *Hammer Tyme* from Cherise. "Shit," he said, curling his fingers around the beer mug.

"What?" asked Daryl, then his eyes tracked to where Tate was looking. "Oh, yeah, that's Vivian's daughter, Zion. Crazy names you white folks call your kids."

Tate gave him a look that said *seriously*. "I know who she is. What's she doing here?"

"Eating dinner." Daryl frowned. "She invited me and Dwayne to her mother's memorial tomorrow night."

"Yeah, I know. She invited me too."

"You going?"

"I was."

"What's that mean?"

Tate shifted back around on his stool. He couldn't deny he felt disappointed. She was leaning on the table, bringing herself closer to Bennett, and the two of them were laughing. It sure didn't look like a business meal.

"Oh," said Daryl, nodding.

"Oh what?"

"You like her."

"What the hell! We're not in grade school."

"Doesn't matter. I get you. She's cute."

She was more than cute to Tate, but he didn't answer, just took another sip of beer. "Whatever."

Daryl leaned on the counter again. "Come on, admit it. You like her."

Tate glared at him. "Obviously she's on a date with Bennett. Besides, she lives in San Francisco."

"You're right," said Daryl, straightening. He moved to the cash register to help a customer. "What'll it be?" Two older women placed their order and Daryl rang them up, then he came back to Tate. "At least you're lookin' again," he said as if there hadn't been an interruption in their conversation.

Tate didn't answer, staring at the beer in his mug.

"You're gonna go to the memorial service still, right?"

"I don't know."

Daryl hit him in the shoulder. "You have to go. It'll be rude if you don't."

"Why are you her fan all of a sudden? If she sells out to Arnold, he's just gonna up the pressure on you and Dwayne."

"She says she hasn't made a decision yet."

"Yeah, well, I bet she does before she leaves here."

"Don't get pissy with me, man."

Tate held up a hand and let it fall. "Sorry. You're right."

"Damn straight I am."

Dwayne dinged the bell on the window and shouted, "Order up."

Walking backward, Daryl grabbed the basket without looking and set it in front of Tate. "Look, man, this is good. It means you're coming out of your coma. Next time you get the hots for a woman, maybe she'll be available."

Tate sighed, feeling foolish that he'd let himself get worked up over something so trivial. "You know, it was fine when I first got here. I mean, I wanted my privacy, but now, it just seems like there's no reason to go home at night. I don't even have a cat."

Daryl frowned. "What?"

Tate waved him off and picked up his sandwich. "Forget it." What the hell was he doing? Getting all touchy feely with Daryl. Shit.

Daryl shook his head and went back to the register to ring up another customer. Tate finished off his meal and drained the rest of his beer, then slipped out of the restaurant without looking over at Zion. He knew it was childish, that he should go over and say hi, but he didn't want to make an awkward situation even worse. Not that it would be awkward for her. For some reason, everything he did around that woman was awkward. It was probably a good thing that she was going home soon, or he'd really make a fool out of himself.

# CHAPTER 9

"I know Rascal doesn't like kittens. She's Zion's kitten. She and Zion will just be staying with us until the kitten can eat solid food." Gabi made a talking motion with her hand and shook her head at Zion.

Zion laughed, glancing down at the tiny ball of black fluff in her arms. The kitten made a strange growling noise as she sucked on her bottle, grasping it with both front paws as if it might escape her. Zion stroked the tiny head between the ears with her thumb and couldn't deny this little bit of nothing was quickly stealing her heart.

"No, you're not allergic to cats. That wasn't the cat. You had a reaction to shellfish," said Gabi, pouring herself another cup of coffee. "Yes, I do know that. I went into the doctor's office with you. No, the Morgans didn't even have a cat. You ate the shrimp. No, it wasn't prawns. It was shrimp. I'm not sure what the difference between a shrimp and a prawn is." She gave Zion a questioning look.

Zion shrugged.

"Yes, I'm sure they were shrimp. No, that wasn't a cat, it was their daughter's beanie. Right." Gabi's voice trailed off as she carried her coffee into the other room. Zion watched her leave, feeling a surge of love for her parents. They had a relationship she couldn't deny she envied.

The kitten finished the bottle and Zion got up, carrying kitten and bottle to the sink and setting the bottle inside, then she held the kitten close as she refilled her coffee mug, stroking her hand along the tiny back until she started to purr. Carrying kitten and coffee to the back door, she opened it and stepped out into Vivian's overgrown backyard.

She should probably hire someone to whip this bit of wilderness into shape, but she didn't know any gardeners here. She could ask David. He seemed to know everyone and everything in this town since he'd grown up here.

Taking a seat in one of the Adirondack chairs Vivian had placed on the edge of the stone patio, she settled the kitten in her lap and continued to pet her. The kitten kneaded Zion's cotton capri pants with her front paws and continued to purr as Zion looked out over the yard.

The focal point was a massive redwood, towering above the little cottage and offering a bit of shade to the rest of the plants. Ferns grew in a raised planter bed along the back wall and closer to the house, Vivian had planted carpet roses. The sun was up, although there was a slight breeze and the temperature was a pleasant 70 degrees already. It was going to be a beautiful day.

Gabi found her a few minutes later, holding the sleeping kitten and sipping her coffee. She took a seat in the Adirondack chair next to Zion and settled her phone on the little side table. "Your father sends his love. I told him we'd be home sometime in the afternoon tomorrow."

Zion couldn't deny she felt a pang of regret. It was peaceful here and she was beginning to enjoy herself, despite the sad occasion.

Gabi reached over and stroked the kitten's back. She made a chirping sound and flexed her paws, but didn't wake. "She needs a name. I was thinking Kate."

Zion gave her mother a bewildered look. "Kate?"

"For Kate Middleton. She may be a princess, but she's also independent and a badass."

"I thought you were all about the proletariat."

"I am, but that kitten was meant to be a princess."

"Well, I was thinking of Cleo, short for Cleopatra. Who's more independent and badass than she is?"

Gabi acquiesced the point. "Good choice. Cleo it is." Gabi tapped her fingers on the arms of the chair and looked out over the yard. "So, how was your date with the lawyer?"

"It was dinner and it wasn't a date."

"It could have been a date. Did you have wine?"

"Well, I did, but he had a beer."

"Then it was a date."

"It was barbecue."

"Still. Do you like him?"

Zion considered that. "I do. He's a nice guy, Mom."

"Well, then…"

"Well, then nothing. I live in San Francisco."

Gabi fell silent. Finally, she shifted in her chair. "Can I venture an observation?"

"Can I stop you?"

"No."

Zion lifted a hand and let it fall.

"You seem reluctant to leave."

Zion laid her head against the chair back. "It's not that. I'm not reluctant to leave. My home's in the City and I love it, but…"

"But?"

Zion rolled her head on the chair and looked at her mother. "Sometimes I feel as if I'm spinning my wheels."

"How so?"

"I've been at my job for three years now, but I'm not getting the promotion I wanted, and…" She bit her bottom lip. "I'm beginning to wonder if I even want it anymore."

"It's hard working for the man."

Zion frowned at her mother. "You know that sounds ridiculous when you say it."

Gabi waved her away. "You're too old to be embarrassed by your mother anymore. You're supposed to think I'm adorable and quaint."

"Like a rusty old antique."

Gabi stuck her tongue out. "Anyway, maybe all of this stuff with Vivian's a wakeup call."

"What do you mean?"

"I mean, maybe you need to evaluate where your life is going and make a change if it isn't going in the direction you want."

Zion considered that. "You're pretty insightful for a rusty old antique."

Gabi swung her legs over to Zion's side of the lounger. "Don't be disrespectful to your..."

"Antique?"

"Elders," Gabi said, then swatted her leg. "Come on. We've got food to order and paper products to go shopping for."

Zion nodded and watched her mother enter the cottage, but she couldn't get her words out of her mind. *Maybe you need to evaluate where your life is going and make a change.* Hm, that was pretty interesting advice.

* * *

While Gabi made calls to order sandwiches and a dessert platter, Zion took the picture of Vivian at the beach and drove into town. She found the *Cut & Print* copy shop and walked inside. An older man with a paunch and thinning salt and pepper hair pushed himself off his stool and came to the counter. He had a full moustache and beard.

"Hi," said Zion, smiling.

"Hi, yourself," said the man.

Placing the photo down on the counter, Zion slid it over to the man. "I was wondering if you could blow this up to an 11x17."

He lifted the picture and studied Vivian's features. "Vivian Bradley?" He gave Zion a closer look. "You must be her daughter."

"She was my biological mother," Zion heard herself say. "I'm Zion."

"Jim Dawson." He laid the picture on the counter again. "Such a nice lady, your mother. When I had my gall bladder surgery, she brought me a plant and visited me in the hospital."

"Did she?"

He nodded, then picked up a pair of glasses from beneath the counter and slipped them over his eyes. "You look a little like her, freckles and all, but your hair's darker and not as curly."

Zion gave him a forced smile. She didn't want to go into her beauty secrets with this man. "I'm having a memorial service for her tonight at the *Caffeinator*. It'll be low-key, but I'd love for you to come."

He studied Zion's face for a moment. "I hear you're planning to sell out to the big money."

Zion shifted uncomfortably. "I haven't decided yet."

"Well, you better give it some thought, missy." He pointed a finger at her. "A lot of people built their dreams on this town for you to swoop in here and just cause a bunch of turmoil."

"I'm not trying to cause turmoil, Mr. Dawson, but I'm not from Sequoia. In fact, I didn't know anything about it until David Bennett contacted me after Vivian's death."

"She was a fine woman, your mother."

"That's what I hear from everyone. I'm not disputing that."

"You better think twice before you destroy everything she built here." The finger was back, jabbing at her. "You better think."

"I am thinking, Mr. Dawson, but I live in San Francisco. What do you want me to do?"

He considered that a moment. "Lot of people pinned their dreams on this town. Shame to just throw that away for some money."

Zion reached for the picture. This wasn't getting her anywhere. "Thanks for your help," she said, drawing it back to her.

"Where you going?"

She gave him a confused look. "I got the impression you'd prefer I leave."

"What gave you that impression, girl?" He grabbed the picture. "11x17 you said."

"Yes, but…" Zion frowned in confusion.

"Is this for her memorial service?"

"Yes, if you have time to do it."

"I told you I had time, didn't I?"

*No, no you didn't,* Zion wanted to say, but she bit her tongue and kept quiet.

He shuffled back to the huge machine in the middle of the room. "Come back at 2:00PM and I'll have it done."

"Thank you, Mr. Dawson," she said, but he waved her off, turning his back on her.

Zion left the print shop, glancing at her cell phone to see the time. She needed to get out to the convenience store and buy the paper products, then she had to see what time Gabi ordered the pickup for the sandwiches and desserts.

As she left the shop, she ran smack into David Bennett. He caught her elbows, giving her a dazzling smile. "Hey, Zion, how are you this morning?"

She slid her phone back into her purse and gave him a smile in return. "I'm good, how are you?"

"Excellent. Just coming to see Jim about some fliers we had printed up."

"Well, I'm afraid I may have put him in a bad mood. He gave me quite a scolding about selling Vivian's coffee shop."

David waved that off. "Don't be silly. Jim Dawson's always in a grumpy mood. He's the original curmudgeon. I can just picture him on his porch in a rocking chair, shouting at the kids to get off his lawn." David waggled a finger at her, making his voice deeper.

Zion laughed. "Well, that's good to know. I hate to be the cause of someone's bad mood."

David gave her an intimate look, leaning closer to her. "That could never happen," he said.

Zion felt a flutter at his look. "Very charming, Mr. Bennett." She touched his arm. "You're going to be at Vivian's memorial tonight, aren't you?"

"I'll be there. In fact, I was wondering if I could pick you and your mom up from Vivian's place."

"Oh, thank you, David, but we have to get there a little early to set things up. Still I appreciate it."

"Any time." He pointed over her shoulder at the print shop door. "Well, I should probably get those fliers."

"Right," she said, feeling a blush steal into her cheeks. "See you tonight."

"See you tonight," he answered, reaching for the doorknob.

Zion moved toward her Optima parked on the street and clicked the button to get inside. Digging her phone out of her purse, she pulled up the directions to the convenience store and settled the phone on its magnetic holder. Then she started the car and pulled out onto the street.

* * *

As she pulled into the parking lot of the convenience store, she couldn't help but wonder why a company wanted to open a big box store here. Sequoia already had this strip mall outside of town with a relatively large supermarket and the convenience/drug store. Would anyone really frequent the other location since it was downtown with limited parking?

As she mused this over, her phone rang. She glanced at the display and saw Rebekah's name flash on the screen. She thumbed it on, lifting it to her ear.

"Hey, Becks, what's up?"

"Zion, thank God. I thought you'd dropped off the world."

"No, I'm sorry I haven't called, but I've been so busy. I adopted a kitten."

"You adopted what? I thought I heard you say kitten."

"You did. She's a tiny little thing. We have to feed her with a bottle. I'll send you some pictures."

"A kitten? Zion, what in the world are you going to do with a kitten? It'll get hair all over your work clothes, and…" Zion could almost see her shudder. "They have fleas."

"Not if you treat them, they don't."

"Well, then have you thought of the litter box."

"I have."

"And?"

"And I've also thought that she's adorable, and fuzzy, and she purrs, and she likes me already."

"Seriously? God, you need another man, not a cat. You know this is a slippery road, right?"

Zion surprised herself by the flash of annoyance she felt. Becks was her dearest friend and she rarely got annoyed at her. Pushing open the car door, she stepped out. "Look, Becks, I'm really glad you called, but I've got a lot to do today. We're having a memorial service for Vivian and I need to pick up paper plates and stuff."

"Wendel didn't ask me to marry him," Rebekah blurted into the phone, then made some strange hitching sound that might have been crying, but Zion wasn't sure. "I really need you here. We need to eat ice-cream and drink Daiquiris and watch chick flicks."

"I'm sorry I'm not there, Becks, but I'm a little confused. He asked you to move in with him, right?"

"And I told him I'd think about it."

"And?"

"And nothing. I told him I wouldn't move in with him unless he put a ring on it, and…"

"And?"

"He didn't." Now she was crying, loud and dramatic.

"Becks, are you at work?"

"Mmhmmm."

"Are you in your cubicle?"

"Are you kidding me?" Her voice sounded a lot less emotional. "You think I want anyone to see me all torn up like this?"

"Well…" Zion dragged the word out. Torn up wasn't the impression her friend was giving over the phone.

"What does that well mean?"

"It means I'm not sure this is a bad thing."

"What?"

Zion started walking toward the store, grabbing a red shopping cart and bracing the phone between her shoulder and ear. "You did say you weren't sure about marrying him."

"When did I say that?"

"The other day. You said you weren't sure you could live the lifestyle of a doctor."

Rebekah blew out air. "I did say that, didn't I?"

"Yep."

"Well, I'm not sure, but I wanted him to at least ask me."

"Why?"

"You should have a minimum of three engagements before you settle on the man you marry."

"Where did you hear that?" Zion turned down the picnic aisle and eyed the paper products. She didn't want anything dismal, but she didn't want it to be too cheery either. She selected a pink paisley plate with matching napkins that reminded her of Vivian's style.

"*Cosmo.*"

"I don't believe that."

"Okay, it was on the internet."

"Well, then it must be true."

Rebekah laughed. "I miss you."

"I miss you too."

"You better get back here soon."

Zion started to tell her they were returning tomorrow.

"Franklin's been on the warpath the last few days, threatening all of us with retraining."

Zion hesitated in putting some plastic forks in the basket. "Wait, why?"

"You haven't been watching the news?"

"No, what have I missed?"

"*Judicious* has been all over it. This Zavaritram denial – people are protesting and calling their representatives. There might be congressional hearings over it, Zion."

*Wow, that was bad,* she thought, but a small part of her felt a little elated. It was time someone stood up to these insurance and pharmaceutical companies. "Did he mention anyone in particular?"

"What do you mean?"

"Did he mention anyone who might have said something to a patient that they shouldn't have?" Her mind immediately went to the Harringtons. She'd told the husband to protest to his doctor about the fact his wife's medication was denied.

"No, no one specific, but he did tell us that we didn't need the negative publicity. They're going over all the tapes to see if anyone violated protocol."

Zion felt the blood drain from her face and she laid her head on her arms, closing her eyes. "What?" she whispered.

"They're reviewing the tapes. They do it all the time. But if anyone violated protocol, they're going back to training for a week."

"Just back to training?"

"Or being fired. What's wrong? Your voice got soft."

"Nothing. Look, I gotta go, Becks, okay? I'll talk to you tomorrow."

"I need you here, Zion. We need a girls' night out."

"Yeah, we'll do that. Okay, bye." She disconnected the call, but she didn't lift her head.

"Are you all right, dear?" came a kind voice.

Zion glanced up to see an older woman standing next to her, wearing a knit sweater and polyester pants with an elastic waist. She wore glasses and her grey hair was a mass of tight curls on the top of her head. She had the most remarkable warm blue eyes Zion had ever seen.

"Are you all right? You're looking pale." She reached into her basket and pulled out a bottle of water from a case, breaking the seal and handing it to Zion. "Drink this."

Zion took the water and sipped at it. It helped ease the ringing in her ears. "Thank you."

The woman's blue eyes took in her cart, then roved over her face. "You're Vivian Bradley's little girl, aren't you?"

Zion smiled, despite her feeling of panic. She hadn't been called a little girl in years. "Yes. Did you know her?"

"I'm Beatrice Sanchez." She patted Zion's hand. "I know the last name doesn't fit, but I married me a beautiful Mexican man. He's been dead these last ten years, but we had us a fine life. Four kids, all went to college."

Zion felt the tension ease. "Really? I'm sorry you lost him."

"So am I." She leaned close. "That man was passionate, let me tell you."

Zion felt her cheeks blush and she laughed. "You don't say."

Beatrice put her hands over her cheeks. "Oh, goodness, I did it again. My kids say I'm always giving too much, how do they say it now, the TMI?"

"Too much information," offered Zion.

"That's it." She shook her head in amusement. "By the way, I own the *Knitatorium* on Main next door to your mama's coffee shop."

"I've seen it." Vivian's coffee shop was on the corner of the street, then the *Knitatorium*, the *Bourbon Brothers' Barbecue,* and *Trinkets by Trixie. Fast & Furriest* was across the street with the *Cut & Print* right next to them. Tate's *Hammer Tyme* occupied the opposite end of the street on the corner, two doors down from *Cut & Print.* The store between them was empty. "Beatrice?"

"Call me Bea."

"Bea, I'm having a memorial for Vivian tonight at the *Caffeinator.* Would you like to come?"

"I'd love it. Is that what you're getting all these supplies for?"

"Yes."

"Can I bring something? I make these delightful peanut butter balls. I'd be happy to whip up a batch."

"That would be wonderful." Something occurred to Zion and she frowned. "Who's manning your store right now?"

"Carmen, Raul's sister. We co-own it."

"Oh, I see. So you can take turns?"

"Yes, it works out perfectly. We also share our house together. It's so much better than being alone."

Zion smiled at that.

"You're looking better, dear."

"I feel better." She held up the water bottle. "Thank you for this. Can I pay you?"

"Nonsense. Well, Carmen and I will see you tonight."

"Great. Thank you again, Bea."

"My pleasure, dear." Then she bustled away, waving over her shoulder.

Zion's thoughts returned to Rebekah's news about *Judicious*, but suddenly it didn't have the impact it had only moments before.

* * *

After the convenience store, Zion went home and gathered Gabi and Cleo, taking them with her to pick up the sandwich platter and the dessert tray from a deli on the edge of Sequoia called *Up to No Gouda.* Sitting in the Optima before the little shop with the red and white striped awning, Gabi laughed.

"So clever," she said to Zion, cradling the kitten on her lap.

"So bad. They're all so bad. Why?"

"Why not? Hurry up. We've still got a lot to do."

Zion hopped out and hurried into the store. The smell of musty cheese and cured meats struck her as she moved to the counter. A young woman with pink hair and tattoos up and down her arms, smiled at her.

"Order for Gabrielle Sawyer?" Zion asked.

"It's ready to go." Then she tilted back her head. "Serge, Sawyer order up!" she yelled.

Zion pulled out her credit card and handed it to the young woman, who rang up the order. A moment later the swinging door opened and a huge man with a crooked nose, thick black hair, and arms as big as tree trunks stepped out. He was well over six feet tall. He carried a covered platter in each hand.

"Here ya go. Platter of sandwiches, variety pack, and a dessert platter." He set them both on the counter and pointed with a blunt finger. "You got your pastramis and your turkeys and your hams and your vegetarians." He rolled his eyes at the last one, then he pointed at the dessert platter. "You got your brownies and your chocolate chip cookies and your petit fours." He said the last with a perfect French accent.

Zion gaped. "I'm stunned. You're a deli and a bakery both?"

He shrugged. "You bake bread, you bake cake. What's the difference?"

*Indeed*, she thought. "Thank you. I appreciate you getting this prepared on such short notice."

"Ain't nothing for Viv. She was good people."

Zion smiled at that. "Please feel free to come by for her memorial tonight."

"We got a thing," he said, "but I tell you what, that Harold Arnold gives you any grief, and you can tell him he'll answer to me."

Zion wasn't sure what to make of that. Her confusion must have shown on her face.

"Sheriff Wilson and me go back a ways. We golf on the weekends."

Zion had a hard time seeing the huge man holding a golf club, but who was she to judge?

"He told me that snake's been putting the pressure on. Yeah, I'll give him some pressure. He might find a meat hatchet in his head, if you know what I mean."

The young woman rolled her eyes. "You're a regular Goodfella, Serge," she said, handing Zion back her card. "Sorry about your old lady."

"Thank you," Zion told her and reached for the sandwich platter.

Serge took it from her and picked up the dessert tray. "I'll walk you to the car." He banged through the swinging door in the counter and nudged open the glass door on the deli, then walked to the car and waited while Zion opened the trunk. He gently settled both platters inside.

"You take care, now," he said and headed back to the deli without looking behind him.

Zion slipped behind the wheel and started the engine.

"You get everything?" Gabi asked.

Zion reached over and stroked Cleo's fur. The kitten blinked up at her with blurry eyes. She still didn't know what color they'd eventually be. "You got your pastramis and your turkeys and your hams," she said, wheeling the car back toward Main.

* * *

Jackson Van Tiernan was in his spot on the couch as Gabi and Zion carried Cleo and her paraphernalia, along with the sandwich platter into the *Caffeinator* around 4:30. Deimos rushed out from behind the counter and asked if he could help. Zion gave him her car keys and told him which vehicle parked in front of the *Knitatorium* was hers, then she went around the counter, leading Gabi into the back rooms.

Dottie followed them, showing Gabi into the office where Cleo would be safely ensconced for the evening. As Gabi prepared the kitten a bottle, Dottie fussed over her.

Zion went back out to the car and found Deimos returning, the dessert platter in one hand and the bags from the convenience store looped over the other.

Zion took the car keys from him and pointed across the street to the *Cut & Print.* "I've got to get Vivian's portrait," she told him.

"Sure thing, boss," said Deimos, heading into the store.

Zion paused and looked back at him. Boss? Did he think she intended to keep the coffee shop indefinitely? She didn't want him to get his hopes up. She had no intention of being his or anyone else's boss. Forcing that thought down, she hurried over to the print shop and waited for Jim Dawson to get her order.

He didn't speak as she thanked him, merely grunted, then went back to his computer. Zion didn't let it bother her, hurrying back to the coffee shop to make the final arrangements. She found Dottie putting out the paper products in the small kitchen and Deimos taking orders. After she helped Dottie set up the rest of the food, she looked out to see a last minute rush on in the coffee shop. Dottie went to help Deimos fill orders, but as Zion knew nothing about making specialty coffees, she retreated to the office with Gabi and went back to reviewing the books.

The first guest arrived at 6:00PM. David Bennett poked his head into the office and Zion felt herself brighten at seeing him. She shut down the computer and waved him into the room.

"I'm glad to see you," she said, coming around the desk.

"So this is the famous kitten," he remarked, but he didn't touch her.

Zion lifted her from Gabi's arms and cuddled her a moment, then settled her in her basket between the armchairs. "Let's go out into the main room."

David and Gabi preceded her from the office and she carefully closed the door, so Cleo wouldn't escape. The number of customers had dwindled and while Dee cleaned the espresso machine, Dottie flipped the sign to closed.

David and Gabi helped Zion move the food out of the kitchen and onto the bistro tables. She'd set Vivian's portrait on the counter, leaning against the wall. Deimos came over and studied it with her.

"She was such an awesome lady," he said wistfully.

Zion touched his arm in comfort. "That's what I hear from everyone."

After that the rest of the guests started to arrive. Beatrice Sanchez and her sister-in-law Carmen came first, and Zion introduced them to her mother. Then to her surprise Jim Dawson stepped through the door, going straight for the sandwiches and helping himself.

Trixie Taylor and her husband, Joe, arrived. Trixie clasped Zion's hands in both her own and told her how sorry she was for Zion's loss. Zion smiled at her, but she sensed Trixie had more on her mind.

Shifting weight, Trixie glanced over her shoulder. "Have you made a decision yet about the shop?" she finally asked.

"Trixie," warned her husband.

"I know. I'm sorry. It's a terrible time to ask this."

"Let me get you something to drink," said David, coming up behind Zion and steering the couple away. Zion gave him a grateful smile.

The identically dressed Betty and Barney Brown from *Fast & Furriest* arrived. They both hugged Zion, then hugged Gabi, and finally decided everyone deserved a hug, so they went around the room. When they got to Jackson Van Tiernan, sitting in his spot on the couch, he held up a hand to stave them off. Neither seemed to know what to do then, so they hugged each other.

The Ford brothers arrived, bringing Tate Mercer with them. He ducked his head at Zion. She held up a hand in greeting, but the Browns had returned and were asking after Cleo. She noticed the Ford brothers and an attractive woman were waiting to talk to her, so she thanked the Browns for coming and moved in her other guests' direction, holding out her hand. Daryl, the younger brother, accepted it and smiled. Then she shook hands with the older brother, Dwayne.

Dwayne placed a hand in the middle of the woman's back. "Zion, this is my wife, Cheryl."

Zion shook hands with her. "Nice to meet you, Cheryl." She was about ten years older than Zion, but something about the kind look in her eyes felt welcoming.

"Nice to meet you, Zion. We're very sorry for your loss."

Gabi approached and Zion introduced her to them. "So, you own the barbecue?" asked Gabi.

"Yes, ma'am," said Daryl.

"And the developer's after your store too, aren't they?"

"Yes, ma'am," Daryl repeated.

Gabi started up a conversation with the three of them, so Zion extricated herself and greeted Tate. "I'm glad you came."

He held up a bouquet of flowers in a vase – lilies and carnations in pink. "Vivian seemed to like pink, so I thought it might be more practical than doodads."

Zion laughed, glancing around the store. "She did like pink." She pointed over her shoulder to Vivian's portrait. "I'll just put them over here."

He followed her as she carried the glass vase to the counter and set it next to Vivian's picture. "That's a really nice photo of her," he said.

"Yeah, I really liked it. I got it blown up at the *Cut & Print*. Jim Dawson might be a man of few words, but he knows his printing."

Tate laughed.

"Tate, dude, let me make you a salted caramel Macchiato," said Deimos, coming over and giving Tate a male handshake/hug.

"No, he wants a mint mocha freeze, doncha, sugar?" said Dottie.

"Um…" Tate gave Zion a panicked look.

"I'll have another cappuccino," came Van Tiernan's voice. He stood behind Tate, waiting for one of the baristas to notice him. He glanced at Zion, then looked down. "I just wanted to say, again, how sorry I am for Vivian's untimely death."

Tate frowned at Van Tiernan's strange words, but he plastered a smile on his face and turned toward him. "I've seen you in here a couple times. I'm Tate Mercer. I own the *Hammer Tyme*."

"With the nails," said Deimos, leaning in.

"Right," said Tate with a laugh. "With the nails."

Van Tiernan didn't look like he knew how to respond. He studied Tate's hand, then rubbed his own hand on his pants, but he didn't shake it. Zion couldn't help but wonder if Van Tiernan had a touch of autism.

"I'm Jackson Van Tiernan," he said. "I work for *Cyclone Games*."

"I've heard of them."

Van Tiernan nodded, warming to his topic. "I designed *B&E 1*."

"*B&E*?" said Tate.

"Breaking and Entering, dude," offered Deimos. "RPG."

"Role playing game," said Van Tiernan.

Zion extricated herself from the men. "Dottie, how about you show me how to make a cappuccino?" she said.

Dottie pulled her arm through her own and led her behind the counter. "Go check on that little ball of fluff, while I make the drinks."

Zion felt a wash of gratitude. She didn't really want to get all befuddled with the espresso machine when there were so many people in the coffee shop. She hurried to the office and checked on Cleo. The kitten was curled in a little ball, fast asleep. She didn't want to wake her, but she couldn't resist touching her ear.

Cleo trilled and stretched her little legs out, the toes spreading, then she curled back into a ball. Zion knew she was finished. This little fur ball had captured her heart.

"Here you are," came David's voice. "I wondered where you got to."

"Just checking Cleo."

"You got a good turnout."

Zion rose to her feet and moved toward him. "All of the business owners came. Vivian was well liked."

"How are you feeling about returning to the City tomorrow?"

"I'm glad. I miss my father and my condo, but I've enjoyed being here. I just wish the circumstances had been better."

"So do I." He moved closer to her, his eyes locked on hers. "I know you have to go, but I'm sort of sorry about it."

She felt a flutter of heat at his words. "Mr. Bennett, are you making a pass at me?"

He blushed and she found it charming. "Did it work?"

She gave him a sultry smile. "Maybe."

Gabi poked her head inside the office. "Is Cleo okay?"

Her appearance shattered the mood and Zion broke eye contact to glance at her mother. "She's fine."

"Whew! Good. I was worried about her." She took in the scene. "Sorry, did I interrupt anything?"

"No," said David, moving back a step. "We were just talking about Zion's next move."

"Oh, I see."

"You'll call me if Sheriff Wilson finds out anything, right?" Zion asked him.

"Of course I will."

She touched his arm. "Thank you for all your help."

"I'll also call you as soon as the rest of the estate clears. You'll have to sign some papers, especially for the money in Vivian's account, but we can do that the next time you come up. I hope to have the title to the house cleared, so we can get that in your name too."

"Just let me know when. Well, I better get out to my guests." She eased past David and her mother, striding back into the store, just in time to see Harold Arnold step over the threshold, carrying a briefcase.

His gaze landed on her and he moved in her direction. Zion's guests parted before him like Moses parting the Red Sea. No one seemed interested in coming into contact with the realtor, watching him warily without making eye contact.

"Ms. Sawyer, I wanted to come to express my condolences and pay my respects to your mother."

"Thank you, Mr. Arnold. I appreciate that."

He gave a nod, then glanced around. The room had fallen ominously quiet. "I was hoping we could talk. I understand you intend to leave tomorrow."

Zion felt David move up behind her. "You want to talk? About what Mr. Arnold? This is Vivian's memorial."

"I understand that." He shot a look at Tate. "But you are leaving tomorrow, right?"

"Yes," she said, a warning edge in her voice.

"I have a counter offer from my clients and…"

"I told you I wasn't selling at this time, Mr. Arnold." She could see how intently the other business owners were listening.

Arnold removed a handkerchief from his suit pocket and wiped it over his wide perspiring forehead. His short-cropped black hair gleamed with sweat. "I understand, but I think you'll be pleasantly surprised by the offer."

Tate started to open his mouth to speak, but he hesitated, watching Zion.

Zion felt her anger rise. "This is a completely inappropriate time, Mr. Arnold."

"Well, to be honest, you haven't left me with any other choice. You won't return my calls and you wouldn't come to my office like I requested."

"I reviewed the last offer with my lawyer," she said, indicating David, "and we determined it wasn't a serious offer."

"It was a very serious offer, Ms. Sawyer. My clients have been both patient and generous. They're taking a risk developing this property, but they've been very clear they're interested in the future of Sequoia."

"Are they? And yet they want to rob the residents of the very things that make this place so unique."

"In what way?"

"This street is a tourist draw, Mr. Arnold. People come here not to shop at a big box store, but to shop at places like *Trinkets by Trixie.* They want something unique like home cooking at the *Bourbon Brothers.* In a world filled with instant coffee and stale burgers in styrofoam boxes, they want something that takes them back to a simpler, more genuine time."

Arnold gave a bitter laugh. "To be honest, Ms. Sawyer, that's all folderol."

"Excuse me?"

"Nonsense. You can't wait to get out of this quaint, little town, can you? You can't wait to get back to San Francisco, so spare me your bleeding heart notions about preserving simplicity. I don't buy it."

Suddenly, she realized she wasn't selling to this man or his clients no matter what the offer might be. "To be honest, Mr. Arnold, we're done. I wouldn't sell to your clients under any circumstances now."

"You tell him, girl," said Cheryl Ford.

A smattering of approval filtered through the room.

"If I sell, it'll be to someone who wants to build a life here in Sequoia, someone who wants to preserve it, not pave it over with strip malls and fast food joints. Vivian Bradley came here to start a new life, to build something that had meaning, and I won't profane her memory by selling out for a quick profit, Mr. Arnold. So, sir, with all due respect, I ask you to leave. This is a gathering of people who cared about Vivian and you are definitely not included."

Spontaneous applause broke out. Harold Arnold glanced around, then gave a nod. "You have my card, Ms. Sawyer. Call me when you get back to the City."

And with that, he left.

# CHAPTER 10

Tate left Vivian Bradley's memorial later than he'd expected. Daryl had shamed him into going, but he'd expected to pop in, say his condolences and get out again. It was pretty clear that Zion had made more than a lawyer/client connection with David Bennett. He'd certainly come to stand behind her when Harold Arnold had made his appearance.

Still, it had been a pleasant event, with the exception of Arnold, and once he'd been sent packing, Zion had managed to put everyone at ease again, laughing and socializing. It was a good send-off for Vivian – upbeat, celebrating her life, rather than focusing on her death. Tate figured all memorials ought to be more like that.

As he climbed behind his Tacoma and drove down Main toward the highway, Tate couldn't deny he was impressed by Zion Sawyer. For all her polish and urban ways, she had a natural grace about her. And the way she'd handled Arnold – he'd applauded louder than anyone when she put the realtor in his place.

Smiling, he pulled onto the highway. This late at night he had the entire four lane roadway almost to himself. A few cars meandered toward Sequoia on the other side of the median, but he couldn't see anyone ahead of him. Worrying about deer, he turned on his high beams and then reached over to switch on the radio.

A country/western station filled the car with twangy notes and steel guitar strings. He left it on, thinking the soulful sound fit his mood pretty well. The moon had risen and he could see it shining through the trees, illuminating the forest. His shoulders relaxed and he realized that for the first time in the last two years, he was happy.

He liked his work. He liked the people around him. He was starting to make real friends. And the nightmares came only occasionally. And although it wasn't going to work out with Zion, he'd discovered that he wasn't dead in that regard either. He could feel something for a woman, enjoy her strength and wit and intelligence. Plus he found her physically fascinating as well. At some point in the future, he might actually think about having another relationship. Boy, that hadn't been a consideration for so long now.

He lost himself in thought so completely that he didn't realize another car had come up behind him, until the shine of their headlights bounced from the rearview mirror, nearly blinding him. He squinted up into the mirror, realizing that they had their high beams on.

He flashed his own high beams to warn them and flipped his mirror up, so the beams weren't blazing directly into his pupils, but the car didn't take notice. In fact, it crept closer to him, easing right up on his bumper until its lights filled his truck with a phosphorescent glow.

He squinted into the rearview mirror, trying to see the model of car or the license plate number, but all he could see was a painful glare. He could feel his heart beginning to beat faster and he reached over, turning off the radio. His cellphone was in his jeans pocket and he couldn't reach it with his seatbelt on.

The car eased even closer until it was riding so tight on his bumper, he didn't know how they weren't touching. Tate deliberately slowed down, taking his foot off the accelerator. The car slowed as well, but didn't back off. Tate pumped the brakes a few times. The car swerved, then came back, pressing up against him.

Tate's fingers curled on the steering wheel as he began talking to himself. "It's a drunk driver. That's all. Just keep driving."

But the car continued to ride him so close he couldn't see anything beyond its blazing headlamps.

Finally, Tate knew he had to do something or they were going to have an accident. He waited until they came to a stretch of highway with a wide shoulder, then he swerved suddenly onto the embankment and brought the Tacoma to a bumping, grinding halt. Pressing down hard on the brakes, he stared in the rearview mirror, watching the car follow him off the highway, skidding on the gravel, then coming to a stop right on his bumper.

Tate realized he was shaking, but slowly, he reached over to the glove compartment and opened it, curling his fingers around the military grade flashlight he kept there. He wished he had one of his guns, but they were both locked away – one inside a safe under the counter at the *Hammer Tyme* and the other in a safe in his bedroom closet. He pulled the flashlight out and reached for his seatbelt, slowly unbuckling it.

The car idled behind him. He couldn't see anyone getting out of it. He tried to see the license plate again, but he realized there wasn't one on the front. The high beams made seeing inside the car impossible.

Suddenly, the car backed up violently, kicking gravel, its wheels spinning, then it swerved around Tate's truck and back onto the highway. Tate looked through his driver's side window, trying to see who drove it or catch the make of the car, but the windows were tinted and it moved too fast for him to get anything more than a brief impression of it. As it sped down the highway, Tate realized it didn't have rear license plates either. What the hell!

Closing his eyes, he lowered the flashlight and let out a whoosh of air. Cold sweat peppered his hairline and dotted his chest. His tattoo itched and he scratched at it, throwing the flashlight onto the passenger side seat. Wiping a hand over his forehead, he cradled his head in his hands and waited for his heart to return to normal.

As soon as he felt calm enough, he pulled back onto the highway and made his way home. Pulling into his driveway, he sat for a moment, staring at his dark house. For some reason he was reluctant to go in. Someone had busted his mailbox and now had followed him from Vivian's memorial. What if they were waiting for him inside?

Finally, he grabbed the flashlight and climbed out of the Tacoma, locking the door, then he crept to the gate and opened it, going around back and climbing the back stairs to his kitchen door. He unlocked it and pushed it open, listening in the darkness for any sounds. When he was sure no one was inside the kitchen, he slipped inside and locked the door behind him, then he eased to the hallway and peered through the archway into the living room. Nothing.

Turning left, he hurried down the hall, holding the flashlight curled in his fist, until he came to his bedroom. Gliding across the dark interior, he tossed the flashlight onto the bed and pulled open the closet door, pressing the key fob for the safe. It popped open and he took out his service revolver.

Once he had it in his hand, he could feel his shoulders relaxing. Carrying the gun, he went through the whole house, turning on lights as he went. He thought about calling Sheriff Wilson, but vowed to himself that he'd stop by the office before he opened the *Hammer Tyme* the next day.

Moving to the window in his living room, he pulled back the curtains. The street was empty. He shifted and looked down to the corner at Vivian Bradley's house. Lights shone from the windows, so he figured everything had to be all right.

Going back to his room, he changed into his sweats, then carried the gun into the kitchen and prepared himself some tea. Finally, he carried the tea to his favorite recliner and sat down, pressing the button to extend the footrest. Reaching for his reading glasses, he set the gun on the end table and picked up his book. No use trying to go to sleep now. His nerves were zinging.

* * *

Tate woke, his neck cramped, his legs aching. He rubbed a hand over his face and blinked, trying to remember why he was asleep in his recliner. Memories coalesced and he groaned, easing forward to snap the footrest of the recliner in place again. Placing his book and his glasses on the table, he stared at his gun and felt foolish, getting so spooked last night, but someone had definitely followed him off the highway and onto the shoulder. He reached for the gun and carried it to his room, locking it back in the safe.

Going into the kitchen, he brewed some coffee and stood, waiting for it, looking out over his small backyard. He should really do something about sprucing the place up, getting a barbecue and some patio furniture. It might be nice to have the Fords over for dinner sometime.

The rich smell of coffee filled the room and he went to the pot, pouring himself a cup. He added a splash of milk from the fridge and carried it out to the living room, opening the front door and stepping onto the porch. He sipped the coffee and grimaced. It tasted nothing like the rich blend served at the *Caffeinator*. Surprising how quickly he was becoming addicted to the stuff.

Thinking of the *Caffeinator* made him think of Zion. He leaned on the porch post and looked down the street toward Vivian's cottage. Gabi appeared, carrying a pink cat carrier and placing it in the Optima, then she climbed into the passenger's seat. Zion appeared a moment later, dressed in a frilly pink and blue top with capris and sneakers. Her auburn hair was pulled up in a long ponytail. She got in the driver's seat and started the engine.

Tate wondered if he should go back inside the house, he didn't want to be caught spying, but it was too late as she backed out of the driveway and turned up the street. When the Optima passed his house, Zion leaned forward and then she and her mother both waved at him. He waved back, smiling. He actually felt a pang of regret that she was leaving.

Once the Optima was out of sight, he turned back into his house and carried the mug to his bedroom. Grabbing a clean set of clothes for the day, he went into the bathroom, shaved and showered, then ran a comb through his hair.

Carrying the mug into the kitchen, he dumped the rest of the coffee and washed the mug, then he checked to make sure everything was locked and went out to the Tacoma, climbing behind the wheel.

He drove into town, arguing with himself along the way. In the light of the day, he wondered if he was making too much out of his encounter the previous night, but he couldn't shake the reality that someone had pulled off the highway onto the shoulder behind him. That wasn't typical behavior.

Had he cut someone off on his way out of town and they were responding by following him down the highway? That seemed a far stretch, but road rage was a real phenomenon. He'd seen it as a cop in LA. Things quickly got out of control when traffic and bad driving combined, but he didn't remember seeing anyone on the road as he left town last night.

Deciding it was too strange an occurrence, especially in light of his mailbox being smashed, he drove to the sheriff's office and pulled into the parking lot. Putting the truck in park, he walked to the glass door and pulled it open. A long counter with a frosted glass barrier covered the back of the room with a single door on the far left. A few metal chairs with cracked vinyl seats were scattered around the waiting room and formica end tables sporting magazines at least five years old lay between them. A dusty silk plant occupied one corner and a water cooler the opposite side.

Tate walked up to the sliding window and pressed the bell embedded in the counter. He could hear it ring behind the glass partition and a moment later a woman with short cropped blue/grey hair pulled it open and squinted at him. She wore a sheriff department uniform exactly like Sheriff Wilson's.

"How can I help you?"

"I'm Tate Mercer," he said, rubbing his hands against his pant leg. "I was wondering if Sheriff Wilson was in yet."

"Hold on," she said and shut the partition again. Tate wandered to the windows and looked out at the street. The sheriff's office was a few streets over from Main in a strip mall that also housed a dry cleaner and a Chinese take-out. An auto parts store occupied the large space at the opposite end.

Behind him, the partition opened and the woman poked her head out. "I'll buzz you in," she said, pointing at the door to her right.

Tate walked over to it and waited until he heard the buzzer, then he pushed open the door. He found himself in an open area with a couple of desks, occupied by sheriff's officers with the front counter to his right.

The woman met him in front of the door. She was tall and angular, wore no makeup, and had a no-nonsense look about her. Tate wouldn't want to tangle with her. She hooked her hands on her gun belt and gave him a cool once over.

"Sheriff says you were a cop."

"Yep," he said, glancing away. He found it hard to meet the penetrating stare of her intense gaze.

She held out a hand. "Nice to meet a fellow man in blue."

Tate accepted her hand and she squeezed it hard. "Thank you."

She released him and put her hand back on her belt. "So, you worked in LA."

"Yeah, I did."

"Bet this seems sort of boring, right?" She tilted her head as if challenging him.

Tate glanced at her and away. "Not lately, no."

She gave a bark of laughter, then shot her hand out, indicating the room. "This way. Can I get you some coffee?"

Tate followed her. "I'll pass, but thank you."

"Good idea. Bet you remember the lead they serve in a precinct."

"Actually, lately I've been spoiled by the coffee at the *Caffeinator*."

"Yep, that'll do her."

She wove through the desks, moving toward the back of the room. A few of the officers glanced up and nodded, then went back to whatever they were doing. Tate counted five officers in all. Not bad for a small community. He figured some were off duty and others were out on calls, but Sheriff Wilson had a fairly good sized force at his command.

Stopping before a white door with a silver placard that read *Sheriff Wayne Wilson*, she knocked once, then turned the handle and poked her head inside. "Got your man here, Sheriff."

"Send him in," came Wilson's voice.

The officer pushed the door open and motioned for Tate to go inside.

"Thank you," he told her.

She nodded, then turned and went back to what she'd been doing. Tate stepped into Wilson's office and held out his hand for the sheriff to shake. Wilson rose from his desk chair and accepted Tate's hand, then motioned to the metal chairs on the other side of his desk. Tate marked that they were the same sort of chairs as in the lobby.

He sank into the one on the left and glanced around. Framed commendations hung from the white walls, along with newspaper clippings showing Sheriff Wilson shaking hands with various politicians and important business owners in the community. A bookcase held legal manuals and a folded American flag in a glass case was mounted above the window. The shades were up on the window, allowing sunlight to fill the space. Besides Wilson's desk, the bookcase, his desk chair, and the two visitors' chairs, there was no other furnishing in the room.

"Nice to see you, Tate. What brings you by?"

Tate shifted in the chair. Once again he was worrying whether he'd made too much of the situation or not. "It's probably nothing."

"Why don't you let me decide?" said Wilson, steepling his hands. His hat lay on the table next to a picture frame of a woman and two children.

Tate shifted again. "You know last night was Vivian Bradley's memorial, right?"

"Right. Ms. Sawyer held it at the *Caffeinator*."

"Right."

"And did something happen?"

Tate considered that. Had anyone told the sheriff about Harold Arnold showing up? "Harold Arnold came and demanded Zion talk with him. She told him to leave. It got pretty heated."

Wilson shook his head. "That man just doesn't take a hint, does he? Did he leave when she asked?"

"He didn't have much choice. There were quite a few of us there."

"I see."

"But it was after the memorial that something strange happened."

"Go on."

"I was driving home and…" Tate scrubbed his hands on his jeans, hesitating.

"Go on, son. I'm listening."

"I'm just not sure it's anything. I mean, last night I was spooked, but today, it doesn't seem like that big of a deal."

"What happened?"

"A car came up behind me, riding right on my bumper, shining their high beams into my truck."

"Did you get a license plate?"

Tate shook his head. "No, that's the strange part. Well, one of the strange parts. It didn't have either a front or rear plate, the windows were tinted, so I couldn't see inside, and I really have no idea what color the body was."

"Hm," said Wilson, frowning.

"It rode my tail for a long way until I finally decided I had to do something. I swerved onto the shoulder and brought the truck to a stop. The car swerved onto the shoulder right behind me."

Wilson dropped his hands and leaned forward. "What did you do then?"

"I reached for the flashlight I keep in the glove box and prepared to get out, but the car suddenly went into reverse and pulled back onto the highway, disappearing."

"What did you do after that?"

"I went home, but it shook me up."

"Yeah, I'll bet. You're sure it didn't have a license plate?"

"I'm sure, Sheriff. I remember looking for one."

"Did you get a sense of the model or make of the car?"

"No, it had no emblems or anything. Like I said, I can't even be sure of the color."

"If you had to guess, what would you think?"

"Black, but that's a pure guess."

"Okay." He reached into his desk drawer and pulled out a pad of paper. "Let's go back to the beginning, all right?"

* * *

Tate worked in the store until Logan came in around noon. They didn't speak much, but Tate let the boy work the register while he ate lunch in the storeroom. Grabbing a notebook, he drew two columns down the page. In the first column, he wrote the things he knew about the Vivian Bradley case. In a second column, he jotted down his mailbox and the car following him the previous night.

Pulling up a map on his phone and slipping on his reading glasses, he tried to pinpoint the location where he'd had his encounter, then he searched for Blackrock Road, where Vivian had been killed. The distance between the two was too close for it to be coincidence, but where he'd been driving on the highway, there weren't any steep embankments like there'd been on Blackrock Road. Beyond shoving him into the embankment and totaling his car, his assailant wouldn't have been able to push him much farther. So what was the motive? To scare him off? But why him? Who knew he was looking into Vivian's death? Not Harold Arnold.

His only encounter with the realtor had been when he asked him to leave Zion's office. That certainly couldn't be grounds for messing with him. Except, his mailbox had been busted that night and then he'd had the car tailing him after Arnold showed up at the memorial. Both events seemed suspicious.

Placing the pen in his mouth, he chewed on the end of it. He didn't want to get involved in this case. He didn't want to be brought on as a consultant, but he was starting to think he needed to see those messages that had been on Vivian's cell phone. What exactly had been the nature of the threat?

Wilson wouldn't tell him, and Tate knew he never would unless he agreed to Wilson's terms.

He slammed the pen down on the table and raked both hands through his hair. He didn't want to get back into this. He'd left this two years ago. He didn't want to awaken the nightmares again, the cold sweats, the hours spent in the dark, shivering, rocking himself in terror. It was starting to get better.

"Tate?"

Tate jumped and looked over. His expression must have been wild because Logan took a step back.

"I'm sorry," he said.

Tate shook his head, scrubbing a hand over his jaw and pulling off the glasses, shoving them in his shirt pocket. "No, I'm sorry. I was just thinking."

"Bill Stanley's here and he was wondering if you could help him with some plumbing stuff."

"Yeah, yeah, I'll be right there." Tate closed the notebook, then carried it to the file cabinet and stuffed it inside behind his invoices. Then he grabbed up his lunch wrappers and threw them in the garbage, walking out to meet the retired Caltrans worker.

"Hey, Bill, what does the wife have you doing now?"

"She wants a new sink in the downstairs bathroom. It's one of them fancy above the counter dealies." Bill scratched at his temple beneath the brim of his ball cap. "I connected everything, but I still got me a leak. You got something to fix that?"

"You know I do." Tate smiled and lifted the counter, stepping out into the store.

After Bill left, they had a steady stream of customers, most of them wanting landscaping tools due to the warmer weather. Tate and Logan rang up orders, helped load cars, and demonstrated how to set up sprinkler systems half a dozen times. Logan was particularly good at talking customers through the process, even drawing diagrams for them.

Tate didn't have any more time to worry the Vivian Bradley case, but as soon as he and Logan closed up for the night, he found himself standing on the sidewalk, looking down the street at the *Caffeinator*.

Pocketing his keys, he headed for the coffee shop. Two construction workers pushed past him as he opened the door, both carrying frozen coffees with whipped cream on top. The only other customer this late in the day was Jackson Van Tiernan, the computer game designer. He glanced up as Tate entered, slowly closing his laptop. He had a faraway look in his eyes. As usual, he wore a vest, a bowtie, and the chain of his pocket watch draped down his side. He had his wing tipped shoes braced on the coffee table.

Tate gave him a nod and Van Tiernan nodded back, leaning forward to pick up his coffee cup and draining the last amount.

"Hey, Tate," said Deimos from behind the register. "Dude, do you mind turning off the *open for business* light?"

Tate flicked the switch and the light flickered off.

"You wanna lock the doors for me and I'll start something for you." He tossed Tate the keys. Tate turned them in the door, then carried them with him to the counter. "What'll it be, bromide?"

Bromide? Tate shook it off and handed the keys back to Deimos. "Would it be too much trouble to make the mint mocha freeze Dottie makes me? I don't really want anything hot."

"Dude, here I thought you were a caramel Macchiato, but you're really a mint mocha freeze." He gave a shrug and laughed. "Whatever floats your boat man! Namaste."

Tate smiled. "So, how's it been today?"

"Busy, man." Deimos filled a blender with ice and began the process of making his drink. "I love it when it's busy. The day just flies by."

"Dottie was in this morning?"

"Yeah, she opens. It's been a little hard. Things get real busy in the morning. Usually Vivian came in, helped with the morning rush, did some paperwork, then went home for a few hours. She'd come back in the afternoon after Dottie left and help me out." He hit the blender, but shouted over it so Tate could hear him. "Now that it's just the two of us, we're getting slammed!"

"Did you talk to Zion about that?" Tate shouted back at him.

"Yeah. She said she'd put an ad in the local paper for part-time help until she decides what to do with this place."

"She didn't tell you…" The blender cut off and Tate stopped shouting. "She didn't tell you what she planned to do?"

"Alls I know is the same as everybody else. She won't sell to that snake Harold Arnold." Deimos poured the blended coffee into a plastic cup.

Tate glanced out at the coffee house. Van Tiernan hadn't turned around, but he was listening, his hands flattened over his laptop.

Deimos slid Tate's drink to him and handed him a straw, then he punched in some numbers on the register. Tate took out his wallet and removed his card, handing it to the younger man. "Dee, do any of the other business owners come in here for coffee?"

"Almost all of them. A couple times a day."

"Has any of the others told you about weird things happening to them?"

"Like what?" Deimos handed back his card and tore off his receipt.

"Like having their houses vandalized, getting prank calls, someone following them in their cars."

Deimos' face clouded over. "No one's said anything. Why? Did they say anything to you?"

Tate shook his head, lifting the straw and tearing off the wrapper. "No, nothing."

"Trixie said someone followed her to her car the other night," said Van Tiernan. He didn't turn around, just spoke to the room in general.

"What night?" Tate shoved the straw into his drink and picked it up, carrying it toward the man on the couch.

Van Tiernan's face scrunched up as he thought. "Musta been three nights ago. She said he followed her all the way to the parking lot. She got her pepper spray out of her purse."

"Did she get a look at him?"

"No." Van Tiernan glanced up at him. "She said it was too dark."

"Did she report it to Sheriff Wilson?"

"I don't think so. Her husband said he'd come down when she closed and walk her to the car from now on, but she said she'd be just fine."

"When did she tell you about this?"

"Last night at the memorial," he said, "after Arnold left."

Tate looked over at Deimos. The barista shrugged.

"Did she remember any distinguishing characteristics about this guy?"

Van Tiernan tilted his head, contemplating. "Not that she mentioned." His eyes widened and he held up a finger. "Except she said he was heavyset and not too tall."

Harold Arnold couldn't be taller than five eight and he had a bit of a paunch. Tate needed to ask Trixie herself about this.

"Thanks, I appreciate it."

Van Tiernan gave a nod, then reached for his laptop case and shoved the computer inside, rising to his feet. "See you tomorrow, Deimos."

"Later, gater," said the barista, moving around the counter. He walked his last two customers to the door and unlocked it, letting them out. Tate stood next to Van Tiernan on the sidewalk as Deimos bid them goodnight and locked the door again.

Van Tiernan walked over to a bicycle locked up in a stand between the *Caffeinator* and the *Knitatorium*, bending over to unlock it. He dangled the chain over the handlebars and climbed onto the seat, slipping the strap to his laptop case overhead.

"Well, thanks for the information," Tate said.

Van Tiernan looked up at him, reaching for a helmet that had been locked onto the handlebars. "Sure."

Tate glanced at the deepening shadows. The days were getting longer, but darkness wasn't far away. "Look, I have a truck. Do you need a ride home?"

"No," said Van Tiernan, putting the helmet over his head. "I like to ride. I ride in the snow even. Cars and trucks are killing the planet."

"Right." Tate forced a smile. "Well, good night."

"Night," said Van Tiernan, pulling away from the curb and dropping into the street.

Taking a sip from his mint mocha freeze, Tate started walking toward the parking lot.

# CHAPTER 11

Zion made it into *Judicious* a few minutes before 8:00AM. She actually found herself hating to leave Cleo. The tiny kitten was quickly stealing her heart, but Gabi assured her she had it covered. Zion didn't doubt that. Even Rascal had been on his best behavior. He'd sniffed the tiny ball of fluff, but he didn't growl or show any inclination toward hurting her. Still, Gabi promised to be vigilant in supervising any interactions between canine and feline.

Zion's father Joe had been relieved to have his women back. Gabi scolded him for half an hour about the takeout cartons she found in the garbage can. Clearly Joe hadn't been cooking for himself or eating from Gabi's carefully prescribed menu she'd tacked to the fridge.

Zion had whispered to him in the living room, while Gabi cleared the refrigerator of all offending foods. "Why didn't you take the cartons to work and throw them away there?"

Joe shook his head in consternation. "You'd think I'd learn by now. Hoisted on my own petard."

"Sure," Zion said, rising and kissing him on the forehead. "I missed you, Daddy."

"I missed you too, kiddo."

"I'll just go see if I can smooth things over with Mom."

"Put in a good word for me too."

Zion gave him a frown, but he nodded at her and shooed her on her way.

The only thing that would settle Gabi was practicing on the piano, forcing Zion to retreat to her girlhood room and sending Rascal into caterwauling. Poor Joe sat in the living room, listening to it, suffering his penance with grace. God, she loved her parents.

Staring at her computer screen now, Zion realized she felt out of sorts this morning. It wasn't staying with her parents. It was coming to work. She pulled up her emails, then gave a groan at the number that filled her in-box. She didn't even know where to begin.

Clicking on the first one, she forced herself to read it and concentrate, but it was hard. She kept thinking about Cleo and the way the kitten made growling noises as she ate, and then her thoughts wandered to David Bennett and his smile. She thought about the way the morning sunlight shown in the back windows of Vivian's house, warming the breakfast nook.

"There you are," came Rebekah's voice.

Zion blinked and looked up, realizing she hadn't even gotten through one email. "Hey, Becks, how are you?"

Rebekah wore a high-waisted A-line skirt in burgundy, a white button down shirt with a high lace neck, and a pair of platform pumps in pale pink. She looked like a million bucks. "The real question is how are you?"

"I'm fine."

"How did it go in Podunk, California?"

Zion felt herself bristle a little at the comment, which surprised her. "It went fine."

"You get everything settled?"

"What do you mean?"

"I mean, did you find a buyer for the business and the house?"

"Well…"

"Well what? What's there to well over? Did you or didn't you?"

"I didn't put either one up for sale."

"Why the hell not?" Rebekah fixed a hand on her hip. "Wasn't that why you went there?"

"At first."

"Well, what are you thinking? You live here, Zion."

"I know that."

Rebekah tilted her head. "And?"

"I like the house. It's paid off. All I have to pay for is insurance and property tax. Vivian left me enough money to pay that for thirty years. I thought I might keep it as a vacation home."

Rebekah's finely drawn eyebrows lowered into a frown. "What about the coffee house?"

"I haven't found the right buyer yet."

"What does that mean?"

Zion leaned back in her chair. "It means I want someone to take it over who'll give it the dedication that Vivian did."

"It's a coffee house. They come, they go." Rebekah waved airily.

Zion glanced away. She was used to Rebekah's lackadaisical attitude, she'd never been anything less. In fact, Zion found it refreshing. So much of college had been filled with people's daily causes, daily battles, daily hills to die upon. She liked Rebekah's screw the world philosophy. Usually. Today, it grated.

"This one's important to me, Becks."

"You can't be serious?"

"I am."

"What are you gonna do? Run it yourself. You don't even drink coffee."

"I know." She held up an empty hand. "I don't know. I mean, no, I'm not going to run it, but I owe the employees something more than selling to the highest bidder."

Rebekah leaned on the partition. "Sell it and move on. With the money from the business and the house, you might have enough for a down payment on a condo."

"A condo? Vivian had a whole house with a yard and a picket fence."

Rebekah reared away. "Who are you?"

Zion gave a weary laugh. "Anyway, I have about a billion emails to get through, so…"

"Yeah, whatever." Rebekah waved her off. "Where do you want to go for lunch?"

Before Zion could answer, her desk phone rang. She pressed the button on her headset to connect the call.

"My office, now!" came Franklin's voice through the line.

Zion felt the blood drain from her face. She swallowed hard. "I'll be…" Her voice broke and she cleared it. "I'll be right there."

He didn't answer, just hung up.

Zion disconnected the call and looked up at Rebekah.

"Franklin?" Rebekah asked, subdued.

Zion nodded. "He sounded furious."

"It's the Zavaritram fiasco. *Judicious* is taking a beating on it."

Zion drew a deep breath and closed her eyes. Then she pushed herself to her feet. "Here goes nothing," she said, straightening her skirt and turning toward Franklin's office.

"It'll be fine. It's not like you have anything to worry about," called Rebekah behind her.

Zion stumbled, but she tilted her chin up and kept walking. Sure, she had nothing to worry about, except one phone call to a desperate husband where she suggested he protest *Judicious'* decision. That couldn't have started this big mess, now could it?

* * *

Zion knocked on Franklin's glass office door. He didn't bother to glance up from his computer, just waved her inside. She turned the handle and walked through. Her heart had started to beat faster and her hands were sweating.

"Sit," he told her, still not looking at her.

She sank into the chair on the other side of his desk and clasped her hands tight. She felt a little sick to her stomach. "Franklin…"

He slammed his laptop closed and gave her a severe glare. Not a hair was out of place on his blond head and his suit was impeccably pressed, a pinstriped Versace in charcoal grey. "Before we get started, I should probably ask you how you're doing after the death of your mother and all."

Zion blinked at him. She didn't know how to answer that dispassionate display of concern. "I'm fine."

"Everything's in order?"

"Well…"

"Good," he said, cutting her off. He clasped his hands on the laptop. "While you've been gone, *Judicious* has had a difficult week."

"Rebekah told me…"

"We've received quite a bit of negative publicity, there've been protests outside our headquarters, and the press has gotten a hold of it. It's been the scandal du jour, to say the least. We've been trashed on social media and our stocks have taken a hit."

"I'm sorry."

"You know why this happened, don't you?"

Zion felt her face heat and she twisted her hands in her lap. "Um…"

"It's that damn Zavaritram drug. Everyone is clamoring for it because of the stupid advertisements without even knowing what they're asking for."

"If it has good results, shouldn't we take a look at it?" Zion heard herself say. "I mean if it's saving lives."

"Do you know what *Judicious* is, Zion?"

"An insurance company?"

"It's a business."

"A business that's supposed to be about saving lives."

He leaned forward, his expression softening. "Yes, of course it is, and our job is to save the greatest number of lives possible. Wouldn't you agree?"

"I would," she said hesitantly.

"Unfortunately, that means we have to make some difficult choices. We have to pick drugs that will benefit the largest number of people. That means we may not be able to offer drugs that benefit a limited number of people because the cost is prohibitive. Do you understand what I'm saying?"

She understood what he was saying, but she also knew he drove a Ferrari and wore designer suits. "Franklin…"

"Our stocks have taken a hit, Zion, our reputation has been stained, so we had to review our employee call log." His expression grew grim. "I think you know what we found."

Zion swallowed hard, her nails digging into her palms.

"You took a call from a man named Harrington. His wife Arlene has colon cancer."

"Which Zavaritram is very effective against," she said, despite her better judgment. She knew she should shut up, but she couldn't. She eased forward in the chair. "He just wanted a few more years with her, Franklin. Is that too much to ask?"

"You had a script you were supposed to follow, but you told him to have his doctor lodge a complaint with us."

"I was trying to give him some hope."

"We're not in the business of hope, Zion. We deal in numbers and that's the only facts you need to know."

Zion looked away. She'd been here for three years, she'd hoped to move up in the company, become a rep, but for what? So she could buy Armani suits and drive a sports car? Was that all that mattered?

"Am I fired?" she asked wearily.

He swiped his tongue across his gleaming white teeth. "No, you're not fired. I defended you. I said you weren't thinking right. I told them you were processing your mother's death."

Zion didn't think that made it any better.

"But you will have to go to retraining."

Retraining or reprogramming?

"The retraining class begins Monday on the fifth floor. You'll spend a week there before you come back down here. Until Monday, you'll type up my contacts, but you won't answer any customer service calls. Then every call you answer will be recorded and evaluated for the next six months. I can tell you that another screw-up, even one, Zion, and you'll be gone. Nothing I say will be able to save you then."

Zion nodded woodenly. The fear had left her in a rush and she felt drained.

"You had such a bright future here, Zion."

Zion's head snapped up and she stared at him.

"I was going to recommend you for a promotion in the next three to six months."

Three to six months? What the hell? She'd been in this position for three years. She deserved a promotion now.

"Clearly, you're going to have to prove your loyalty before either of us can consider that again. It's a shame. This little escapade has set your career back a bit."

The fear she'd felt was suddenly replaced with anger. She'd given them three years of her life. She'd given them her loyalty. Where was their loyalty? Where was their commitment?

* * *

Zion lay on her childhood bed, staring at the poster of a running horse on the ceiling, stroking her hand on Cleo's back. The kitten purred, kneading her stomach with her tiny paws. A knock sounded at the door and Zion glanced over at it.

"Come in."

Gabi poked her head inside. "Is everything okay?"

Zion sat up, bracing her back against her headboard. The twin bed still had her pink pony bedspread, pony-shaped throw pillows, and puffy, quilted headboard. She'd adored horses until she left for college. Well, horses and boys with motorcycles, but she'd never let Gabi know that, saving the boys with motorcycles for occasional, minor bouts of teenage rebellion.

"Everything's fine."

Gabi came into the room and sat down on the edge of the bed as she had when Zion was growing up and had a problem. She reached out and smoothed a strand of hair back from Zion's face. "Did you have a bad day at work?"

Zion considered that. She supposed it was a bad day, but for some reason, the fear she'd felt in Franklin's office hadn't returned. She really wasn't sure what she felt. "I didn't have a good day."

"What happened? Tell me."

Zion looked away. Her dresser was still covered with her awards – honor roll, mock trial, the stock market game. She'd been so proud of those achievements, but what was it all for. She was a glorified secretary and she likely wasn't going to be anything else for the foreseeable future.

"*Judicious* has been in the news lately."

Gabi nodded. "That drug, Zavisomething."

"Zavaritram, right. It's helps fight colon cancer. It's had some good results, but it's expensive and *Judicious* doesn't cover it."

"Okay?" said Gabi. "So?"

"Well, before we left for Sequoia, I got a call from the husband of a woman dying from colon cancer. The doctor wanted to try Zavaritram on her, but I had my instructions to tell him to basically screw off."

Zion went on to tell Gabi the rest of the story, ending with how she'd been called into Franklin's office and told she needed to attend retraining if she wanted to keep her job. She stroked Cleo as she talked and Gabi listened without interruption.

"I was really afraid in Franklin's office, sure he was going to fire me on the spot. Then, when it was over and he told me I had a chance to keep my job…" Zion hesitated.

Gabi tilted her head in question. "What?"

"I felt disappointed."

"What do you mean?"

"I mean if he'd fired me, I'd be afraid. How will I pay the rent? How will I find another job? I mean, I don't really want to eat cat food with Cleo."

Gabi laughed and petted the kitten as well. "You wouldn't eat cat food. You could move back in with us."

"Oh, that's awesome, Mom. I can move back in with my parents at 26."

"It would only be temporary."

Zion looked away. "But I didn't get fired." Her eyes moved back to her awards. "I didn't get fired and I actually felt disappointed that I didn't."

"Why do you think that is?"

"I don't know. I thought this was the work I wanted to do. I mean, I went to college and got a degree in business, but when I was talking with Mr. Harrington – he's the guy whose wife has cancer – I felt angry that I couldn't help him. I kept wondering what's the point of all of this if we don't actually help people."

Gabi nodded and looked down at her hands, studying the lines and spots on the back of them.

"You know what Franklin asked me?"

"What?"

"He asked me what *Judicious* was. He said *Judicious* was a business."

"Well, it technically is."

"A business that makes money off people's health." She shook her head. "No, not even their health, their illness, their desperation, their fear."

"That's true."

"Instead of making this time easier for people, we make it harder. He said we have to deny drugs that only benefit a small number of people, so we can offer drugs that benefit a large number of people. I used to believe that, Mom. I used to believe that was true."

"And now?"

"I see his Armani suits and I know he drives a Ferrari." She shrugged. "I wanted those things too. I'm not going to lie. I saw that and I wanted to be a rep. I wanted to have the perks."

"And then?"

Zion stared down at Cleo. "I don't know. I don't know what happened. Maybe it was talking to Mr. Harrington. Maybe it was Vivian's death. Maybe it was seeing what she built for herself, the simplicity of it. I don't know, but I know that working as a secretary for a company like *Judicious* isn't what I want to do for the rest of my life. And I know I don't want to be rep anymore."

Gabi smiled at her and folded her hand over Zion's. "Then figure out what you want. Figure out what you want to do and do it. You know your father and I support whatever decision you make."

"What if it's something stupid like, I don't know, becoming a bridge artist."

"A bridge artist?"

"Someone who paints pretty pictures on bridges."

"Is that a thing?"

"Why not?"

Gabi laughed. "Then why not. Be the best bridge artist there ever was. We'll be proud to tell our friends what our daughter does for a living."

Zion leaned forward and hugged her mother, careful not to disturb the kitten. "I'm not going to make any rash decisions," she said, "but I appreciate the support."

Gabi smoothed her hair back again. "You always have that, sweetie. You always have that."

# CHAPTER 12

Tate slowed as he drove down Main Street the next morning. A number of people were gathered out in front of the *Knitatorium* and the *Caffeinator.* A sheriff's patrol car was parked across the front of the businesses, blocking his view.

He drove on to the municipal parking lot behind the *Hammer Tyme* and parked his pickup, then he walked down the street to the gathering, spotting the Ford brothers along with the rest of the business owners.

"What's going on?" Tate asked.

Daryl turned and shook his hand. "Someone spray painted the front of the *Caffeinator* and the *Knitatorium.*" He pointed.

Tate rose on tiptoes and looked over the heads of the business owners. *Go home, bitch!* and *Sell out!* was written in black spray paint across the front of both buildings, along with a host of more profane words. Sheriff Wilson and the woman he'd seen in the sheriff's office the day before were taking statements, but no one had seen anything. Bea Sanchez was shaking her head, her arm around her sister-in-law's shoulder. Carmen was crying into a handkerchief and speaking in Spanish.

"This is getting personal," said Daryl. "Someone went through our dumpster."

"How do you know?" asked Tate.

"We found food and paper products thrown all over the alley behind the building," said Dwayne. "I'm worried they were looking for receipts or other pieces of business information."

"We shred all of that," said Daryl.

"Did you report it to Sheriff Wilson?"

"We haven't gotten a chance. He's been trying to get information from Bea and Carmen."

At the moment, Wilson was talking to Dottie, who shook her purple head and tsked.

"Someone should call Zion," Tate said.

Daryl gave him a searching look.

"To tell her the business was vandalized," he added, giving Daryl back the same look.

"Right," said his friend, rocking on his heels.

"Okay, everybody, go back to work. We'll stop in later today to get a statement from each of you."

Tate watched the business owners dispersing. Daryl and Dwayne patted him on the back before they went back to the restaurant. Tate followed Trixie with his gaze. He wanted to ask her about what Van Tiernan had said the previous night, regarding the man who'd followed her to her car, but she was walking with the Browns, deep in conversation, and he didn't know her well enough to interrupt them.

Bea directed Carmen to their shop and opened the door, while Mr. Dawson of the *Cut & Print* pushed past Tate, muttering about outsiders under his breath. Dottie turned and gave Tate a sad look.

"How about a mint mocha freeze, sugar?" she said.

He touched her arm in comfort. "I'd love one. Hey, when Logan gets in, I'll send him down with some paint to cover up this mess."

She smiled at him. "I'd appreciate it. I hate to bother Zion with this. You think you can match the paint on the outside?"

"I think we can get pretty close."

"Bea and Carmen would appreciate it if he could take care of their mess too."

"I'll have him get right on it."

Dottie squeezed Tate's hand. "Your drink today is on me then," she said and headed toward the *Caffeinator.*

Wilson tilted his hat to the back of his head. "So, still want to stay out of this?"

Tate scratched at his temple. It was getting harder and harder to remain neutral. "You think Harold Arnold would result to such petty pranks, Sheriff?"

Wilson folded his notebook and tucked it in his pocket. The deputy with him started snapping pictures of the graffiti. "Who knows? These businesses should have security cameras outside of them. It would make my life a whole lot easier."

Tate glanced up at the eaves. "I guess they've never needed them before."

"Yeah, well, now they do."

Tate tucked his hands in his jeans pockets. "One of the *Caffeinator's* regulars told me that Trixie mentioned someone followed her to her car the other night. She got so nervous, she pulled her pepper spray out of her purse."

Wilson frowned. "She didn't tell me that."

"Well, I don't know her that well, so I was wondering if you could talk to her."

"Sure. I'll head over there after we finish up with this." He pointed over his shoulder at the graffiti. "I wonder why she didn't mention it."

"Maybe she didn't think it was anything to worry about once it was over, but it seems important to me. The Fords also think someone went through their garbage. They found stuff thrown all over the alley."

"Damn, they didn't say anything either. You sure you won't consult on this? People seem to confide in you."

Tate sighed. "I'm not going to lie. I'm kinda curious about the threatening messages Vivian received. I was wondering if you'd clear me to look at them."

"I'd be happy to."

"I still have some contacts in the LAPD. Maybe I could see if they can trace back a phone number. You'll need a warrant though."

"I can get that, no problem, and I'll get you the messages, but my computer forensics guy…"

"The college kid?"

"Hey, Joel's the best. Anyway, he thought they came from a burner cell."

"Yeah, but if we have the number, sometimes we can trace it back to the store that sold the cell. If we knew it came from LA, then it might lead to Vivian's husband. If it came from around here, well…"

"We start putting some pressure on Harold Arnold."

"Exactly."

"I'll get you that information today."

"Great. You gonna talk to Arnold?"

"I don't have anything on him yet. No one saw who did this." He pointed at the graffiti. "You didn't get a license plate on the car. We can't match the paint on Vivian's car. And we got no evidence from your busted mailbox. It's all pretty sketchy."

"Maybe Trixie can identify her stalker?"

"I'll talk with her, but if she thought it was Arnold, I can't believe she wouldn't have reported it. Anyway, I'll go talk to her."

"I promised Dottie I'd send Logan over to repaint the stores."

"Just let us get the rest of our pictures, then go for it." He patted Tate's shoulder. "Glad to have you on-board. I'm not liking where this case seems to be headed. I'm worried someone else is going to get hurt before we get a break."

"Well, to be honest, that's why I'm breaking my cardinal rule and offering you my help, but this is a one-time deal, Sheriff. We're on the same page, right?"

"She-et, man, this is the most exciting case I've had in my entire thirty-year career. You think stuff like this happens in Sequoia. Not even a chance. This will definitely be the only time I need help like this."

Tate gave him a nod, then headed toward the coffee shop after his mint mocha freeze.

* * *

The buzzer sounded on the front door and Tate stepped out of the storage room. Logan hadn't returned yet from repainting the storefronts, so he was all alone. He smiled as he saw the deputy from yesterday step into his shop. She carried a file under her arm and moved toward his counter.

"Deputy? Nice to see you again," he said. "I realize I didn't get your name yesterday."

"Murphy. Sam Murphy, short for Samantha, but I shoot people who call me that."

"Got it."

She laid the folder on the counter. "Sheriff just got the warrant to search the records on the burner cell. He said to bring the information over to you."

"Thanks. I'll get right on it." She passed him the folder and he opened it, flipping through the pages. "This is the transcripts of her text messages."

"And audio messages too. She had a couple of them. Sheriff wants me to send you the actual audio files so you can hear them. I'll need your email address though."

Tate took a business card out of the holder on the counter and wrote his email on the back. "Wilson said the voice was distorted."

"Yeah, like he was speaking through an echo chamber or something. I'll send the files over to you as soon as I get back to the station."

"Okay. I'll let you know if I figure anything out."

"Great." She tapped the counter with her knuckles. "You know where to call?"

"Yep."

With a salute, she walked to the door and pulled it open, striding out. Tate reached for the stool he kept behind the counter and pulled it over, taking a seat. He looked through the list of phone calls from Vivian's cell phone. Wilson and his staff had identified most of them. A few to her ex-husband, some from the ex-husband to her, and a number to her lawyer. Wilson had identified Harold Arnold's number as well. The realtor had called Vivian at least ten times about three weeks before her death, then suddenly the calls stopped. Either she was blocking him or she'd told him not to call her anymore, or more alarming, he'd decided to switch to a burner cell.

Flipping to the text messages, Tate read through them. They were all similar to the things spray painted on the front of the *Caffeinator. Bitch, you're a sell out. Why don't you go back home? You don't belong here. Take your whorish ways back to where you came from. Outsider.* For the most part, they were juvenile and insulting, but there didn't seem to be an actual threat in any of them.

Reaching for his cellphone, he pulled up his contacts and pressed his thumb to the icon he wanted. The phone rang a number of times, then a cheerful voice came on the line.

"If it isn't the prodigal son. What the hell's happening, Tate?" said Darcy.

Tate smiled. He'd left so many people that he truly cared about in LA and Darcy Reyes was one of them. "Hey, how are you?"

"I'm peachy keen. You?"

"Doing good."

"Running an auto parts store?"

"No, it's a hardware store." He glanced around the *Hammer Tyme.*

"Same difference. What's it called again? Something cutesy."

"*Hammer Tyme.*"

"God, that's awful."

Tate laughed, realizing he missed her. They'd always had an easy camaraderie about them. "How's Mikey?" Darcy's five-year-old son was too smart for his own good, already able to figure out passwords and access things he shouldn't be able to access for his age.

"He's good. He misses his Uncle Tate. When you coming home again?"

"Not for a while."

"I saw Cherise at the grocery store."

"Yeah." Tate felt his smile fade. "I'll bet that was uncomfortable."

"We talked a little. She was with Johnny GQ."

"Yeah." He didn't want to talk about his ex-wife or her new boyfriend. Rubbing a hand across his forehead, he briefly closed his eyes. "How's Rachel? You seen her?"

Darcy fell silent.

Tate opened his eyes and stared at the file before him. Rachel had been his partner's wife. Jason and Rachel were one of those couples who just seemed made for each other, as if they hadn't been whole until they met.

"She's okay, Tate," said Darcy. "We go for a glass of wine once in a while. She's talking about moving back to Nevada where her folks are."

Tate nodded, pressing his tongue against his molars. He realized his palms were sweating, so he rubbed his hand against his jeans. "Hey, Darcy, I need to call in a favor."

"Ask and ye shall receive," she said and he felt the tension ease immediately.

"The local sheriff has a suspicious death out here."

"Huh. They still off people in the boonies?"

"Pretty much a local pastime everywhere, I think."

"So what do you need my genus for?"

"The woman who was killed, Vivian Bradley, had some threatening text messages on her phone. The tech guy here, a college kid named Joel, traced it back to a burner cell, but that's as far as he can go. I was wondering if you could trace it to the store that sold it and maybe we'll get lucky and the idiot would have bought it with a credit card."

"You know I need a warrant for that, bucko."

"I'll send it to you."

"And I'll have to do this on my lunch hour."

"I owe you a lunch."

"How'd you get sucked into this? I thought you were retired, happy selling carburetors and shit."

"It's a hardware store, not auto parts."

"Same difference."

"Not even a little. So, you gonna help me or not?"

She laughed. "You know I'll say yes. Send me the info and I'll get on it as soon as I can."

"Thanks, Darcy. I owe you one."

"You owe me many, buddy, but I'm not keeping track."

"Sure you're not."

"Well, not in writing at any rate. Okay, I gotta get back to work, but send the stuff over and I'll get on it."

"Thanks, Darcy."

"Anytime." Then she disconnected the call.

* * *

Tate left the hardware store and got in his pickup to go home right at 6:00PM. He wouldn't admit it to anyone, but being in on the inner workings of the case had him a little fired up. He pulled into the driveway of his house and set the truck in park, then he gathered the file Sam Murphy had brought him. He hoped she'd sent the audio messages to his email like she'd promised she would.

He opened the front door and walked to the kitchen, setting the file on his table, then he retrieved the laptop from his bedroom and set it next to the folder, pressing the button to boot it up. While he waited for it to load, he grabbed a beer out of the refrigerator and popped it open, taking a swig.

He searched for something to eat and came up with a frozen dinner, tearing back the top and shoving it into the microwave. He hated frozen dinners, but he didn't have time to get any more elaborate tonight.

Finally, he took a seat at the table, settling his beer next to the laptop, and pulled up his email. Sure enough, the first email was from the Sequoia Sheriff's Department, sent by Deputy Murphy. He clicked on it and read the one sentence message.

*Contact us if anything triggers with you.*

Woman of few words, Murphy. Not that Tate was complaining. He'd just as soon keep it business like and professional. He tapped the mouse on the first of two audio files, then he leaned forward, tilting his head as he listened.

The voice had an unmistakable mechanical quality, but more than that it had been altered to sound much lower than normal.

*Bitch, don't mess with me. You know what I want and I always get what I want. People don't deny me. Tell me where it is and no one gets hurt.*

The voice sounded vaguely familiar, so Tate played it again.

"I always get what I want. Tell me where it is." Tate played it a third time.

His dinner dinged in the microwave and he got up, pulling it out. He dug a fork from the silverware drawer and took a seat again, pulling back the cover completely. Taking a bite, he reached for the mouse and keyed up the second message.

*Don't be a hero. Just hand it over. No one needs to get hurt.*

Setting the dinner on the table, he went into his bedroom and grabbed his headphones, then he played each of the messages another time, listening without the distraction of any other noises. He definitely recognized the voice, but it wasn't anyone he could place. Actually, now that he thought about it, he wondered if he hadn't heard this voice in a movie or on television.

Still, he couldn't remember where he'd heard it. It was definitely familiar, but he just couldn't place it in context. If it was on television or a movie, he might never remember it.

Scratching the back of his head, he gave a frustrated groan and reached for his beer. Damn it all, he had nothing to give Sheriff Wilson in the morning and yet, he wanted to be able to offer him something. Anything. Shit.

* * *

Tate found himself crouched on the side of the patrol car, one hand on the vehicle, the other wrapped around his gun. He needed to get around the back of the car so he could get off a clear shot. It was their only chance.

He drew a deep breath, said a silent prayer, and inched forward, trying to count the shots, trying to count the bullets. The frantic chatter over the radio distracted him, kept him from getting an accurate count, but he had to take the shot. He had to neutralize the threat.

Reaching the back bumper, he stared down at the liquid pooling beneath the car. Something in his mind shut off, unable to process what he was seeing, what was before him. He closed his eyes and told himself to remember his training. Remember what he'd been taught.

Forcing himself to keep moving, he slid around the back of the car, listening to the ping of the bullets off the side panel, trying to keep his head below the line of the trunk. Jason lay on his back, blood pooling under his head, a single bullet hole in the center of his forehead.

He saw the bullet hole, he knew what it meant, and yet he reached out and pressed his fingers under Jason's jaw, searching for a pulse.

"Don't do this to me, man," he heard himself say. "Please don't do this to me. Talk to me, man."

A bullet slammed into the asphalt near Jason's outstretched foot and Tate cringed against the back of the car, his fingers still searching for a pulse.

"Please, Jason, don't do this to me," he whispered. "Jason!"

Tate gasped, coming awake. His heart was pounding, but he lay still, staring at the ceiling, trying to remember where he was. Sequoia. He was in Sequoia. He rubbed a hand over his face and then laid it in the middle of his chest where his heart hammered like a drum. Damn it. *Damn it all.* Rolling to his side, he looked at the clock on his nightstand. The green neon letters said 2:30AM.

He couldn't hear anything in the rest of the house, just his own ragged breathing. He was drenched in sweat, a bead trailing down the side of his face. Throwing back the covers, he got up and went to the bathroom, turning on the shower.

As his heart returned to normal, the sweat dried, chilling him. He stripped off his boxers and t-shirt, stepping under the hot spray and scrubbing his hands across his face. Bracing his hands on the shower wall, he let the water beat on his shoulders, easing the tension, his eyes closed.

Scrubbing all over twice, he switched off the water and grabbed the towel hanging from the door. He dried himself, then draped the damp towel over the shower door and padded into his bedroom, pulling out a clean pair of boxers and a t-shirt, slipping them on.

Walking out to the kitchen, he filled the teakettle with water and set it on the stove, then sat down at the kitchen table and powered up his laptop again. He located the audio files and played each one over a few times.

He still couldn't place where he'd heard the voice, but this time he concentrated on the words. They were generic. Nothing about them suggested the messages had been expressly meant for Vivian. No mention of her name, no mention of the coffee house, nothing personal. In fact, they sounded like a canned message, like something you'd hear in…a movie. He was back to that again. But what movie?

He racked his brains for any movie that had cheesy gangster dialogue, but nothing came to mind. It was probably from one of the million police procedurals that littered prime time, but he didn't watch television, so he'd never be able to recognize it.

He jumped when the kettle whistled and rose to pour himself a cup of tea, selecting his favorite chamomile from the tin canister. His hand faltered as he started to lower the bag into the hot water in the mug.

God, Jason would give him such a bad time for drinking chamomile. Jason had been a man's man, six foot two, 250 lbs of muscle, all badass cop with an attitude, who went soft if their call involved a child or an animal. There wasn't a dog or cat on their regular beat that Jason hadn't known and he had a stash of teddy bears in the patrol car's trunk for any scared child.

Tate shook off the memory and dropped the tea bag into the hot water, carrying the mug back to the kitchen table. He put the headphones on again and played the messages, then grabbed a pad of paper and wrote the words down, pulling up Google to search for them.

Frustration rose inside of him as he tried various incarnations of the message without getting a hit. When he finally gave up, he realized it was going on 4:00AM. He had to open the store by 10:00.

Damn. This is why he hadn't wanted to get sucked into this case. He never knew when to leave it alone. He always brought it home with him. Cherise hadn't been entirely wrong. He hadn't been the best husband when he was on the force. Jason had always been able to let it go. Jason had never taken it home with him.

He slammed the laptop lid down and rose, carrying the mug to the sink.

He was going to finish what he'd started for Sheriff Wilson, then he was getting out. He was going to have to make that clear. He wasn't consulting for Sequoia after this case. He was a business owner and that was it. He wasn't a cop and he'd never be again.

# CHAPTER 13

Zion took her seat at the small table in the conference room on the fifth floor. A few people occupied some of the other tables, but no one made eye contact, focusing on their cell phones. She could hear the click click of their nails on the screens.

Settling her purse in her lap, she took out her own cell phone and turned it to vibrate, then she replaced it in her purse and set the purse beneath her chair. Clasping her hands before her, she looked around again.

A table had been set up on the side of the room with a coffee urn and paper cups. She pushed her chair back and got up, walking over to it. She searched for tea, but there wasn't any, so she settled for coffee. Pouring a bit of creamer into her cup, she picked up a wooden stir and placed it inside, then she carried it back to her spot at the table.

No one acknowledged her as she sat again. Glancing up at the clock in the front of the room, she sighed. This was going to be one of the longest weeks of her life.

She let her thoughts wander to Cleo. The kitten had gone exploring this morning while Zion got ready for work and had wound up in the garbage can, unable to get herself out again. Zion had rescued her after she heard her frantic meows over her hairdryer, cradling her close and kissing her fuzzy head. Just thinking about her now made Zion smile.

A woman in a stylish navy suit entered the room. She wore a pair of pale blue pumps that Zion would give her entire paycheck to own. In her arms she carried a number of binders, which she began distributing to the people. Most of the participants barely looked up from their phones.

When she handed one to Zion, Zion smiled at her, setting the lukewarm coffee aside. "Thank you," she said.

The woman gave her a frown, then forced a smile in return. "You're welcome."

When she was done passing out the binders, she moved to the front of the room and clapped her hands once. "My name's Suzanne Livingston and I'm a training and development manager for *Judicious.* Before we get started, let me tell you a little about myself and set the norms for our time together."

Zion tried to look interested. The guy in front of her slumped in his seat. He wore a white shirt and tie, his jacket slung over the back of his chair. He placed his phone face down on his binder and clasped his hands over his belly.

"I've been with *Judicious* for four years now. Before that, I worked for a rival insurance company that shall not be named." She laughed at her own joke and Zion's smile grew brittle. No one else laughed. "Let me tell you, I am very grateful everyday to know that I am now with this company."

Zion looked at her binder, tracing a finger over the *Judicious* logo on the front cover.

"I have a B.A. in Business Administration slash Human Resources from a very well respected university and I am proud to say I have a total of seven years working in Human Resources in one capacity or another."

Her eyes roved around the room, then she straightened her suit jacket. "Now, let's go around and state your name, your position, and how long you've been with *Judicious.*"

Zion glanced up as the woman on the far left began. She barely heard their names, not because she didn't care, but because, honestly, when would she ever see these people again after this week? They were all here because they'd gotten into trouble and this was their penance. Well, she'd do her time, try to have a positive attitude, but she wasn't looking for a new best friend.

When it came to her, she pasted a bright smile on her face. "I'm Zion Sawyer. I'm an administrative assistant slash customer service rep and I've been here three years."

"Very good. Now, let's set some norms," said Suzanne, pressing a button on the podium behind her. A slide show opened up on the screen and she picked up a remote, clicking on it. "We're all here for the same reason." She gave them a smile. "We need a little refresher course on doing our jobs properly."

When a few of the participants grumbled at that, she held up a hand. "Now, don't be offended. Everyone needs reminders once in a while, and at *Judicious*, we're happy to provide it."

"When the military does it, it's called brainwashing," grumbled the guy in front of Zion.

Suzanne ignored him. "Now, before we begin, I just want to set some ground rules for our sessions. Number one, no cell phones. If you'd please turn off your cell phones now, I'd appreciate it."

She waited while everyone complied. Giving Zion a pointed look, she tapped her right foot. Zion held up her empty hands, earning herself an approving nod.

"Rule number two, keep bathroom trips to designated breaks only. Of course, if there is an emergency, you may leave. I wouldn't want any puddles." She laughed, the sound a lonely echo in the silent room.

Zion bit her inner lip. Oh lord, this was going to be torture.

* * *

"So, how did your training session go?" asked Rebekah, spearing a lettuce leaf.

Zion had met her friend in the small sandwich shop on the first floor of the building because she only had half an hour before she had to be back.

She pushed a tomato around with her fork. "That was the longest morning of my life. We went over all of the protocols for answering phones, then reviewed *Judicious'* formularies, and watched a video on proper customer service protocol."

"What's left for the afternoon?" laughed Rebekah.

"I have no idea. What concerns me more is the remainder of the week."

"Well, it's your own fault for going rogue." Rebekah placed the lettuce in her mouth and munched on it.

Zion picked up the tomato and placed it in her own mouth, trying not to feel disheartened.

"So, you didn't tell me much about your trip to the outback."

Zion gave Rebekah a wry smile. "You know it isn't that far away, right? And it really isn't as outback as you think it is."

"Is there a single building over three stories tall?"

"No."

"I rest my case." She dropped her fork into her salad bowl and pushed the remainder away. "I just can't do commercial lettuce. Seriously, how hard is it to buy organic?"

Zion set her own fork beside her plate. Did she sound like Rebekah? Did she complain about first world problems to the same degree? God, she hoped not, but she suspected she might.

"So, what was the coffee house like?"

"It was cute."

Rebekah reared back. "Cute. In what way? Oh God, don't tell me your mother had those kitten plates up on the walls. I can't even."

Zion laughed. "No kitten plates, just real kittens."

Rebekah waved that off. "What about cute guys? All cowboys right? Cowboy hats, leather pants."

"I don't think leather pants are a thing anymore."

"Sure they are."

"Only if you're an 80's rock star."

"Tell me about the guys," said Rebekah, bracing her chin on her hand.

"Vivian's lawyer, David Bennett, is kinda cute. We went on a sorta date."

"What's a sorta date?"

"He took me to dinner, but it was actually to discuss an offer on the coffee shop."

"Did you take the offer?"

"I already told you I didn't."

Rebekah gave her a bewildered look. "Yes, but I didn't understand your reason for that."

Zion shrugged. "I don't really have one, except I don't want to rush into anything."

Rebekah studied her a moment, then she leaned closer. "Was it weird?"

"Was what weird?"

"Being in your biological mother's world."

Zion considered that. "Yeah, it was." She looked out the window at the bustling San Francisco street. "I've never given her much thought, but there in her house and the coffee shop, she was a real person. Everyone I met told me how generous and kind she was."

"So how did that make you feel?"

"At first it was irritating, then…"

"Then?"

"I don't know. I guess I wanted to know her. I wish I could have known her. I mean, not as my mother or anything. That's Gabi. But just as a person, you know? As another soul on this planet."

"Very Zen of you," said Rebekah, grabbing a kidney bean from her salad and popping it in her mouth. "You got all deep on this trip. What happened to you?"

Zion shrugged. "I hate to think I was shallow before."

"No, not shallow, just not…I don't know… concerned with adult crap."

Zion laughed. "You do know that you have to grow up at some point, right?"

Rebekah looked away. "I'll worry about that after I land my first husband."

"Your first husband?"

"Sure."

"How many are you planning?"

Rebekah held up her empty hands. "Who knows. You know what we need?"

"Nope."

"Macaroons. Today feels like a macaroon day." And she bounded to her feet, going to the checkout counter to buy some.

* * *

Zion returned to the training session feeling like she was going to detention. She didn't have much experience with detention, truth be told, but she had gone once in high school, when she'd been talking to a cute boy with a tattoo and a motorcycle during class.

She would have been humiliated, but motorcycle boys with tattoos were sort of a weakness back then. Now it was men in Armani suits, or it had been. She wasn't so sure if that was still her thing or not.

She forced herself to stop daydreaming when Suzanne actually took roll. There were only ten of them in the room. Zion figured a quick head count should be adequate, but Suzanne felt the need to call their names and force them to say *here*.

"Okay, I hope you had a wonderful lunch and feel rejuvenated," she said, clapping her hands again. "Especially since we're getting to the really difficult part of this training."

The guy in front of Zion slipped lower in his seat.

"Before you can get back on the phones, we have to be sure you can handle the most difficult of all situations, a disgruntled customer." Suzanne gave them all a sympathetic look. "I know that's been a problem for you before, but don't worry. When we're done here, you'll feel much more confident."

Zion felt certain that wasn't going to solve their problems, but here she was just the same.

"Please open your binders to the section called *Scenarios*."

Zion flipped her binder open to the requested section.

"In a moment, I'm going to partner you up with another rep and the two of you will act out the scenarios. You all have different situations and you'll see they're very difficult, but if you follow the *Judicious* script on the first page of your scenarios, you'll do fine."

Suzanne went around pairing people up. Of course, she put Zion with the bored guy in front of her. He swiveled around and held out his hand. He had curly brown hair, a boyish face, and a large gold wedding ring on his left hand. His sleepy brown eyes told Zion he'd rather be anywhere else.

"Doug Evans," he said, offering her his hand.

Zion shook it. "Zion Sawyer."

"Zion, huh? Parents pretty religious?"

"Nope. Hippies. They named me after their honeymoon destination."

"Huh," he said with a laugh. "If my wife and I did that, our kids would be Vegas and the Venetian."

Zion laughed with him. Maybe this wasn't going to be as bad as she thought.

"Okay, now that you've met each other, eyes on me," said Suzanne with another clap.

Doug swiveled around and Zion looked up.

"Take turns and read the first scenario in your binder. If you are the customer, try to be as persistent as you can. You want to make the rep slip up. If you're the rep, make sure they don't get you to deviate from your script. Now, go."

Doug swiveled back around and gave her an apologetic look. "You wanna be the rep or the customer first?"

"I'll be the customer. I didn't do so hot on the rep end of this, obviously. Otherwise I wouldn't be here."

"Preach on, sister," said Doug, giving her a wink.

Zion turned the page and glanced over the scenario. "Okay, here goes. So, I guess I'm calling you."

"*Judicious Insurance*, Doug Evans speaking. How may I help you?"

"My name is Margie Allen, Mr. Evans, and I've been a *Judicious* customer for the last five years."

"Excellent. We are delighted to have long term subscribers, Ms. Allen."

"Well, you see, Doug, I have Hepatitis C and I've heard there's a new drug that can actually cure my disease..."

Zion went on to plead her case to Doug, but he stuck to the *Judicious* script, informing her that the drug is in trial stages at the moment and *Judicious* has not authorized it to be a regular drug on their formularies. He never deviated no matter how hard Zion pleaded her case, even when she pretended to get angry.

This last part wasn't much of a stretch for her. The more she argued with Doug, and the more he stuck to his script, the angrier she got. God, it was so frustrating to be rebuffed at every step by someone who was obviously quoting boilerplate.

Suzanne moved around the room, giving pointers to the partners. Zion didn't want her to see how worked up she was becoming, so she pretended to hang up and end her call. Collecting herself, she forced a smile for Doug.

"You did great."

"I feel like an ass," he said, wiping a bead of sweat off his upper lip. "God, that was miserable."

Zion rubbed her hands on her skirt and nodded. "I know, but you stuck to the script. Good for you."

Doug glanced over his shoulder to see where Suzanne was. "I guess we should do you now."

"I guess." Zion felt a flutter of anxiety in her belly. If Doug got as heated with her as she'd gotten with him, would she cave? She didn't want to do this stupid training anymore, but she had no choice.

Unfortunately, a betraying little voice in her head said she did have a choice. She tamped down on it and flipped to the *Judicious* script as Doug turned to his scenario.

"Okay, I'm calling you now," said Doug.

"Good afternoon, *Judicious Insurance*, Zion Sawyer speaking. How may I help you?"

"Ms. Sawyer, my son has chronic lymphocytic leukemia and my wife heard of a treatment where doctors give an immunotherapy drug that helps the immune system attack the cancer cells. Our doctor is recommending it. It's sort of our son's last hope. I can't remember the name of the drug, but I was hoping you could help me find out how to get this treatment covered."

Zion stared at Doug, not answering. He sounded so much like Mr. Harrington when he'd called about his wife that she couldn't think straight. Doug glanced over his shoulder to see where Suzanne was, then he tapped the paper in front of Zion.

"Sorry," Zion said, trying to gather her thoughts. She looked down at the script and tried to read it, but the words seemed to blur. "Um, I, um…"

"Do you want some water or something?"

"No, I'm okay." She looked up and took a deep breath. "I'm sorry, can you tell me your name and the name of your son? I'll also need your medical record number, so I can log in the call."

Doug rattled off the information she requested. "Ms. Sawyer, the doctors say this may be my son's last chance. If we don't get this drug, they don't give him a year. He's sixteen, Ms. Sawyer. He used to play basketball. We thought he might get a scholarship to college, then he got sick."

Zion stared at him. The emotion in his voice could only come from a father, a man who knew what it was like to be so vulnerable, so afraid. Suzanne moved up behind him.

"Please, Ms. Sawyer, we need your help. I've been a *Judicious* customer for seven years now. We haven't used the insurance for anything but physicals. We need your help."

"Stick to the script," said Suzanne, pointing at it. "I know this is hard, but this is why we practice these things. Just compartmentalize it and trust your training."

Zion looked down at the script again. "Um, Mr. Evans, I understand where you're coming from and I'm going to make a note in your chart…"

"What's a note going to do? My son's dying, Ms. Sawyer. We need this drug. My God, this is his last hope. Tell me what I have to do. Tell me how I can get this drug for my son."

"Uh." Zion braced her forehead with her hand. "You see, Mr. Evans, this drug is in trial stages at this time and we're awaiting final approval."

"He doesn't have time to wait for final approval," prodded Doug.

Zion shot him a panicked look.

"Stick to the script," said Suzanne. "Just stick to the script."

"Um, I understand your frustration, Mr. Evans…"

"Frustration! My son is dying, Ms. Sawyer. You have to do something."

"The script, Zion," said Suzanne.

"This drug is in trial stages at this time and we're awaiting final approval."

"We don't have time for that!" said Doug, slamming his hand down on the table.

Zion jumped, her eyes flashing to his face.

"Good, Doug, you're doing a great job. Now, Zion, how do you respond? Remember, stick to the…"

"No."

Suzanne tilted her head in surprise and Doug sat back.

Zion stared at the script and everything came into focus. She didn't want this anymore. If she were honest with herself, this had never been what she wanted in the first place, she just hadn't known what else to do. Both of her parents were in medicine. She'd gotten a business degree. It only seemed sensible to combine the two, but this wasn't her passion. This wasn't what she wanted to dedicate her life to doing.

"Zion," said Suzanne, holding out a hand. "Read the script. It'll be okay. Just read the script."

Zion glanced around the room and realized everyone was looking at her. "He's right."

"I'm sorry."

She pointed at Doug. "He's completely right. What does it matter if something's been approved or not? If someone is dying, you try anything. You do anything you can to save them."

"*Judicious* is a business, Zion. We can only help so many people. We have to put our resources where we can do the most good."

Zion closed her binder and reached for her purse. "I'm glad you said that, Suzanne, because that makes everything easier."

"I don't understand."

Zion looked down at Doug. "You have a family, kids you have to support. I get that. I get why you're here, but I don't have that yet. I wish you the best, Doug. You seem like a nice guy." She glanced up at Suzanne. "For me, well, I have a bit more latitude. I have time to figure out what my passion is and I can tell you, it isn't this." She slung her purse strap over her shoulder and pushed the binder toward Suzanne. "*Judicious* may be a business, but it's a business built on saving lives and it seems to me that one life or a thousand, well, that's a pretty important job and it ought to be done with more consideration than words written on a script. When you're dealing with living people, you ought to be able to give them something…anything…the least of which, Suzanne, is hope."

She smiled at Suzanne and inclined her head to the rest of the room. "I wish you all the best, but for me, I think I'm going to learn how to make a cappuccino."

* * *

Zion walked up to Franklin's glass office door. He was sitting at his desk, talking on his phone, pretending he couldn't see her. She tapped on the door, but he still didn't acknowledge her, swiveling his chair around so his back was presented to her.

Zion didn't know how she'd ever found him attractive. What had she been thinking? It was the suit, the hair, the confidence, but looking at him now, she realized the suit had more to do with the designer, the hair he owed to a talented stylist, and the confidence – well, that was really arrogance.

Reaching for the handle, she twisted it and went in. He swiveled around and gave her a startled look.

"Gotta go. I'll call you back," he said into the phone, then he set it back in its cradle and gave her a tense smile. "Zion, I'm surprised to see you."

She looked over her shoulder at the glass door. "But you just saw me…" She waved it off and stared down at him. "Was that Suzanne on the phone?"

He gave her a curious look, but she didn't buy it for a moment. "Suzanne?"

"Suzanne Livingston. The trainer."

"Oh." He stared at the phone for a moment. "That? That was…"

"Suzanne."

He leaned back in his leather chair and his shoulders dropped. "What's going on with you, Zion? I thought you were on track for big things."

"I've been a secretary for three years, Franklin, how much bigger could it get?"

"Administrative Assistant slash Customer Service rep."

"You do know it's annoying when you say the slash, right?"

He blinked in confusion. "What?"

"Look, Franklin, I appreciate the opportunity to work here at *Judicious*. I really do, but I just don't think this job is for me."

"Just because we made you go to retraining?"

Zion shook her head and realized that that hadn't been it at all. The retraining was simply the event to clarify all the others. "No, this has been coming for a long time." She touched the center of her chest. "I have a degree, but I'm answering phones and typing up your notes. You can type up your own notes, Franklin. That's what people do nowadays."

His mouth opened but nothing came out.

"I thought I'd be a rep by now."

"That's what this is about?"

"Actually, it's not. I thought I wanted to be a rep. I wanted the clothes and the car and the…" She sighed. "The stuff. That's all it is. Stuff. I'll bet you don't even enjoy driving your car because you're so worried someone might smash into it."

"What are you talking about?"

"And did you eat lunch today?"

"Lunch?"

"Probably not because then you wouldn't fit into your $1,000 suits."

"Zion…"

She held up a hand. "I'm not blaming you."

"Blaming me for what?"

"I take responsibility for my own life, but this isn't what I want. I die inside a little every time I take a call and tell a scared or grieving person I can't help them."

"That's a bit dramatic."

"In your world, it probably is, and I really hope you never find yourself on the opposite end of one of those calls, Franklin, I really do."

He flinched.

"But I can't do this anymore. I can't pretend that this is at all what I want."

"Is this about your mother's death?"

Zion considered that. "Maybe. Maybe her death woke me up. Anyway, thank you for your guidance and everything else, but I'm going to leave now."

"You're going to leave?"

"As in quit." She started to turn, then shifted back around. "And since you brought it up, my mother did just die, so I think I'll take the rest of the vacation I have to process her death and we'll call that my two weeks' notice. Do you agree?"

He stared at her, his mouth hanging open. "You're quitting? Just like that?"

"Yes." She folded her hands before her.

He rose to his feet. "You're quitting because we asked you to do your job? Answer phones? Tell people our policies?"

"No, I'm quitting because I'm morally opposed to your policies and my sense of worth is more than this paycheck."

"I'm not sure I can give you a good reference, Zion."

"Well, that's something you'll have to struggle with on your own. About the two weeks notice?"

He thought for a moment. "Look, I know your mother just died, so I'm going to cut you some slack. Take your two weeks off and then come back."

"I'm not coming back, Franklin. I quit."

She knew he thought she was unhinged by her mother's death and therefore, he was a little worried about threatening to not give her a referral to a new job if she asked for one. She should let him down easy, but she wasn't going to. She'd given him three years of her life. This was the least he could do for her.

"Fine. I accept your resignation. We'll use your vacation as your two weeks notice."

"Thank you." She inclined her head and turned back to the door.

"Zion."

She stopped and glanced over at him.

"If this great moral victory becomes hollow, I can't take you back. I hope you know this."

"I know it, Franklin, and I understand."

"I'm serious."

She turned around and faced him, realizing a weight had lifted from her shoulders. "So am I. I've never been more serious. Have a good rest of your day."

And she left his office, letting the door slide quietly back into place on its whisper hinges. Well, that last part wasn't as satisfying as it might have been if she could have slammed it.

* * *

Zion drove to her parents' home and could hear her mother playing the piano from the driveway. To be fair, it sounded a lot more like banging on the instrument rather than playing it, but it was still daylight outside, so the neighbors could just adjust.

She grabbed the champagne bottle off the seat and threw open the Optima's door, stepping out. Walking to the front door, she could hear Rascal howling. Now, maybe that was pushing the bounds of neighborly decency.

She used her keys and let herself into the house. Gabi waved at her over her shoulder, then went back to playing. Rascal stood beneath the piano bench, his head tilted back, his little mouth in a perfect o. Zion shut the door and crossed the living room, headed for the kitchen. She set the champagne on the counter and turned into the hall for her own room.

Cleo had made a nest for herself in the middle of Zion's bed. She stroked the kitten and got a lazy trill for her effort. The kitten's belly was distended, so Zion knew she'd just been fed a short while ago. Sitting down next to her, she touched a tiny ear and smiled.

She kept expecting to feel a wash of panic over quitting her job, but she didn't. She was strangely calm. Rebekah had done the panicking for her, calling after she left *Judicious*, begging her to come to her senses and plead with Franklin for her job back, but she had no intention of doing that. She hadn't realized what a weight *Judicious* had been on her and now that it was gone, the entire world seemed to open up.

The phone rang again. Zion looked at it and saw it was Rebekah once more. She let it go to voicemail and changed out of her work clothes into sweats and a t-shirt. She'd call her back later. Right now, she wanted to tell her parents her decision.

The piano grew quiet and Zion could hear her father's booming voice greeting first his dog, then his wife. Gabi never seemed to mind that Rascal came first. Zion smiled at that, gave Cleo a final stroke, and hurried out of the room.

Her father and mother were just moving into the kitchen where they would both have a cocktail before dinner. They looked up as she entered, Gabi pointing at the champagne bottle. "Where'd this come from?"

"The store," she said. She couldn't help teasing her mother a little as she kissed her father on the cheek to welcome him home.

"I know it came from the store, but did you buy it?"

"I think it's a safe assumption that she bought it, Gabi, since neither of us did."

"You can't deduce that," scolded Gabi, moving toward the refrigerator and pulling out a block of cheese and placing it on the cutting board. "She might have been given it as a gift."

"If it was a gift, it would likely be in a gift bag of some sort," said Joe.

"Not if it was given by the company. Maybe she won a contest or something." She reached for a knife and began cutting slices of cheese.

"What sort of contest would she have won at work, Gabi? You were a nurse for twenty-five years. Did you ever have a contest at work?"

"I'm certain we did."

"And what would that look like? A reduction in the number of people sent to the morgue?"

"You don't know everything. *Judicious* might have been rewarding their workers for signing up a certain number of new clients or for answering calls in a timely fashion or for getting high ratings by the doctors in the practice…"

"I quit."

Silence fell.

Zion watched Joe and Gabi swivel to face her.

"You what now, dear?" asked Gabi, lowering the knife.

"I thought you said you quit," said Joe.

Zion nodded. "I did."

"You quit your job?"

"The job you had?"

"What other job would I quit?" Zion asked.

"Why?" asked Joe, but Gabi slapped him in the chest with the back of her hand. "Ouch," he complained and rubbed it. "Why are you hitting me?"

"Because our job is to be supportive. If Zion says she quit, then we have to accept that she knows best."

"And we can't ask why?"

"No, we can't ask why."

"Why?"

She slapped him again. "Because that doesn't seem supportive, now does it?"

"I guess not." He gave Zion a bewildered look. "Do you feel unsupported?"

Zion burst into laughter. "Not for a moment. And you can ask why?"

"Why?" said Joe and sidestepped before Gabi could hit him again.

"I just couldn't do it anymore. I couldn't take the calls from people asking for medications we don't cover because they're too expensive. I couldn't hear the desperation in their voice and do nothing to help them. I couldn't watch everyone walking around in designer suits, driving sports cars, while we were letting people die."

"What are you going to do instead?" asked Gabi, a worried look on her face.

"And that's supportive?" asked Joe.

She glared at him, then focused on Zion again. "I mean, you'll find something else." She forced a bright tone into her voice. "Do you have any ideas?"

"No, none."

Gabi and Joe exchanged a look.

"And that's okay," said Joe. "We support that decision. Right?" He looked to Gabi for assurance.

"Right," she said.

Zion laughed again, moving forward to hug both of them. "I love you crazy hippies," she said. "Please don't worry about me. I know what I'm doing. I'm going to move to Sequoia for a while and work the coffee shop. Then when I figure out what I'd like to do, I'll sell the store and go back to school for my graduate degree."

Gabi and Joe didn't respond for a moment, then they both let out relieved laughs.

"Well, that's all right then," said Joe.

"Wow, but we'll really miss you when you're so far away. I guess we'll have to come visit you, a lot."

"Right. We'll come up on the weekends."

"I know you will," said Zion, "and I know I'm going to miss everything here, but I think it'll be good for me to get away for a little while. I mean, I've been kinda spinning my wheels here. This is a chance to really do some soul searching."

"Find yourself."

"Figure out who you are."

Zion smiled. God, she was going to miss them. "Right. So what do you say? Wanna have some of that mysterious champagne?"

"Pop that sucker open," said Joe.

"I'll get the glasses," said Gabi and Zion knew everything was going to be okay.

# CHAPTER 14

Tate walked into the sheriff's department the next day, carrying his laptop. He pressed the bell in the counter and waited. A moment later, the frosted window slid open and Sam Murphy looked out at him.

"Hold on, I'll buzz you through."

Tate walked over to the door and waited until he heard the familiar buzz, then he pushed the door open. Sam met him on the other side.

"You listen to those messages?"

"I did, but I was hoping maybe you or Sheriff Wilson could listen to them with me. I feel like I've heard this dialogue before."

"Dialogue?"

"Yeah, I think it's dialogue from something. I don't think it was specifically aimed at Vivian Bradley. I think it's a recording from something."

Sam motioned across the sea of partitions and desks. Tate followed her to a small break room with formica counter tops, yellowed tables, and hard curved plastic chairs. A sink, a microwave, and a dorm refrigerator made up the rest of the space.

She motioned to the table and Tate walked over, settling the laptop on it and taking a seat.

"You want some coffee?" She moved toward the stained pot, sitting on an electric burner.

Tate considered that. He knew police coffee and he wasn't sure his stomach could handle it anymore. "Better not," he said, opening the laptop.

"Good decision." But she poured herself a mug, carrying it to the table. She set it across from Tate. "I'll go see if the sheriff's got a moment." And she disappeared out the door.

Tate pulled up the audio files and leaned back in the chair, looking around the room. Every squad room felt the same – worn-down break room, stale coffee, a few donuts sitting on the counter. He could hear the murmur of voices in the main room, the crackle of the police radio, and the hum of the air conditioner.

A moment later Sam appeared with Sheriff Wilson in tow. Wilson patted Tate's shoulder. "Can I get you anything?"

Tate shook his head.

Pouring himself a mug, Wilson carried it back to Tate's table. Murphy had taken her seat again. "Sam said you thought you might have got something off the messages."

Tate gave a short nod. "I can't place it, but I've heard those words before in that same way."

"What do you mean?"

"I mean they're from a TV show or a movie. It's cheesy gangster dialogue or something. I'm pretty sure this wasn't meant specifically for Vivian Bradley."

Wilson sipped at his coffee, then jerked his chin at Tate. "Play it."

Tate played the message. *Bitch, you're a sell out. Why don't you go back home? You don't belong here. Take your whorish ways back to where you came from. Outsider. Bitch, don't mess with me. You know what I want and I always get what I want. People don't deny me. Tell me where it is and no one gets hurt. Don't be a hero. Just hand it over. No one needs to get hurt.*

Wilson scrubbed a hand over his chin, lowering his coffee mug.

Murphy tilted her head, listening. "Play it again."

Tate clicked on the audio file again. Murphy leaned closer to the laptop, her face scrunched up in concentration.

"I don't know. That first part seems pretty specific to Bradley," said Wilson. "You're a sell out. You don't belong here. Take your whorish ways."

"But that's the thing. It isn't specific. So the sell out applies. It could apply to many different people in many different situations. You don't belong here? Anytime someone moves to a new city that line could be used. And whorish ways? First of all, that's so damn cheesy, but besides that, you said Vivian wasn't seeing anyone here. She hadn't been seeing anyone since her divorce."

"That we know of," said Wilson.

"So what whorish ways?"

"You got a point."

"Then the rest of it. You know what I want? What did he want? What could Vivian have had? The coffee shop?"

"No, that doesn't sound like he's talking about a piece of property," said Murphy.

"Exactly." Tate held out a hand to Murphy. "Besides…" He scrubbed his hand over the back of his neck. "I can't shake that I've heard those words before."

"You mean the voice? Well, it's a mechanical voice, so that might be it," said Wilson.

"But it's not mechanical. It's been altered, but I'd bet money it had a human origin. Besides, I don't mean the voice. I recognize the words. I've heard that dialogue before."

"Like a script?" said Wilson.

"Exactly."

"Maybe you just heard a script that sounded familiar."

"No," said Murphy, shaking her head. "I think he's right. I think I've heard those words before too."

"So, what does that tell us? How does that relate to the case and Vivian Bradley?"

Tate shook his head. "I don't know. I'm sorry. I guess I'm not much help."

"Did you try googling it?" asked Murphy.

"I did. I googled every sentence, and then I googled cheesy gangster movies and studied a whole list of those, but nothing triggered anything. I keep thinking it's a TV show. Does that trigger anything with you?"

Murphy shook her head.

"What about your contact in LA?" asked Wilson. "Were you able to get any information on the phone?"

"Darcy said she'd get back to me as soon as she has anything. She said it might take a few days. She can only work on it during her lunch hour. What about Trixie? Did you talk to her about the guy who followed her to her car?"

"I haven't gotten a chance to do that yet." He looked over at Murphy. "Head out to her shop and see if she'll tell you anything about it."

"On it, Captain," said Murphy, rising to her feet. "I'll keep trying to remember where I heard that dialogue before," she told Tate.

"Thanks." He reached over and closed the laptop, then stood also. "I need to open the hardware store."

"You talk to any of your fellow business owners about putting up security cameras?"

"Not yet, but maybe I'll go to the Chamber meeting and mention it. You might drop by too. It might sound better coming from you."

"Send me a text and let me know when it is. I'll pop in for a few minutes."

Tate picked up the laptop and thought about leaving, but something was nagging at him. "Is Harold Arnold your prime suspect?"

"Right now he is."

"Have you thought about doing a search of his house? Looking for the blue car that struck Vivian?"

Wilson groaned as he rose. "I need more than circumstantial evidence, but it's worth giving it a gander. I'll see if I can get a warrant today." He held out his hand and shook Tate's. "It's nice having a big city cop working with me."

Tate accepted the hand, but he didn't necessarily agree.

* * *

The day was slow at the hardware store. Logan and Tate had time to finish the inventory and repair a shelf that was beginning to wobble. Tate had to admit Logan was a quick study. The kid picked up everything he taught him the first time. As they worked, Tate wanted to ask him about his mother, but he didn't want to step on toes.

When they locked up for the night, Logan pulled the blinds down on the window to protect the floor from the early morning sunlight. Tate took the opportunity to ask him how school was going.

"It's whatever," said Logan, releasing the pulls.

Tate picked up the bank deposit envelope, tapping it on the counter. "You know, if you wanna go back to school for your senior year, we could work something out. I mean, about your job."

Logan's shoulders stiffened and he kept his back to Tate. "Naw. I'm good."

Tate blew out air. Damn he was so bad at this stuff. "Your mom doing okay?"

Logan turned and gave him a stare that said he'd really stepped over a boundary. "Look, Tate, you don't gotta do this, you know?"

"What?" Tate was bewildered.

"Pretend like you care. I work for you, that's all."

"But I do care."

Logan studied him, then held up a hand. "Forget it. I shouldn't 'a said anything." He started to go to the storeroom after his skateboard.

Tate looked out over the store, feeling like an idiot. He'd screwed that up. He tapped the bank deposit again.

When Logan appeared, Tate held out a hand to stop him. "Listen, Logan, I'm not trying to pry."

The kid wouldn't meet his eyes, just held the skateboard against his chest.

"I just think you're a sharp kid and I hate to see you give up your high school career. You might be able to get a scholarship to college."

Logan shot a sideways look at him. "It's too late for that."

"It's never too late. There's junior college and…"

Logan whipped around on him. "You're a cool guy, Tate. I like working for you, but that's all. I just work for you."

"But I thought maybe…" He shrugged. "You might need someone to talk to."

"I don't, okay? I'm good."

"Everyone needs someone…"

"No, they don't. We all have our shit, and we learn how to deal with it. That's all." He looked away, his profile rife with teenage angst. "I gotta go. Later."

"Later," said Tate, watching him hurry from the store. Well, he'd sure bungled that one. What the hell!

Grabbing the bank deposit, he made a final check of the store, making sure the cash register, the wall safe, and his gun were all safely locked away, then he let himself out. Climbing into the truck, he pulled onto Main and headed out of town toward the bank and the evening drop off. He glanced into the windows of the *Caffeinator* as he went, seeing Deimos behind the counter, a few customers sitting at the bistro tables, and Van Tiernan perched as always on the couch.

He drove to the bank on the edge of town, climbed out of the pickup, and slid the bank deposit into the overnight slot, then he headed home. The days were getting longer, so he still had enough light to notice the small moving van parked in front of Vivian Bradley's home.

He pulled into his driveway and parked the truck, then got out and stared down the street. Had Zion decided to sell after all? Was she having Vivian's furniture removed?

Sliding his hands in his pockets, he started wandering toward the house, marking Zion's Optima and another late model BMW in the driveway. He glanced in the back of the moving van and saw a mirror and a few chairs, nothing more.

Walking up to the open front door, he knocked. "Anyone home?"

Zion appeared out of the back, her auburn hair pulled into a ponytail, her face scrubbed clean, her freckles dancing on her nose. "Tate? How are you?"

"Fine. You sell Vivian's house?"

"No," she said with a laugh, coming forward and taking his elbow. "Come in. We just ordered some pizza. Are you hungry?"

He was, and the appeal of another TV dinner vanished with the sight of her smile. "Sure. I've got some beer at home."

"We've got that too," she said, motioning him to follow her.

She led him to the kitchen where her mother Gabi, a middle aged man, and an attractive young woman with long, straight black hair, a perfect olive complexion, and designer skinny jeans, were unpacking boxes.

"Mom, you remember Tate?"

Gabi looked up and gave him a smile. "How are you, Tate?"

"Good and you?"

"Doing well." The microwave dinged and she went to it, removing a tiny bottle. "Cleo needs her milk," she said, and eased past him into the hallway, disappearing from sight.

Zion tugged on his elbow, drawing him towards the man. "Dad, this is Tate. He's one of my neighbors and he owns the hardware store in town."

"Tate, nice to meet you," said the man, holding out his hand and giving Tate a firm handshake. "I'm Joe Sawyer."

He couldn't have been any taller than Zion at about 5'6" with a bit of a paunch and silver grey hair. He wore black framed glasses and his skin tone was a lot darker than his daughter's pale complexion, but the laugh lines around his eyes and mouth spoke to an even temperament.

"And this is my friend, Rebekah Miles."

The lovely young woman wandered over, her eyes roving him up and down. She tilted her head and eyed the tattoo he tried to hide on his forearm. "I have a tattoo," she purred. "You'll never guess where."

"Becks," said Zion, swatting at her.

She smiled at Zion and eyed Tate again. "And I just got my tongue pierced." She stuck her tongue out, showing him.

Tate didn't know how to respond.

"Becks!" cried Zion.

Rebekah laughed. "I'm just teasing." She ran her hands under her hair and arched her back. "I'm bored, Zion. What's there to do in this town?"

Zion gave him an apologetic smile. "You wanna beer?" she said, motioning to the fridge.

Tate followed her over and leaned against the counter as she retrieved a cold bottle and handed it to him. "What's going on? At first I thought you'd sold Vivian's house and were cleaning it out, but it looks like you're unpacking."

Gabi came back into the kitchen, carrying the tiny black kitten. Tate could swear Cleo had grown since he'd seen her last. "She's moving in, Tate. She thinks she can make it all the way out here without her family." She handed Zion the kitten and Zion pressed a kiss to her tiny nose, then settled her against her shoulder. The kitten started to purr.

"I quit my job," said Zion, glancing up at him.

He'd lifted the beer to take a sip, but he lowered it again. "You what?"

"She quit her job. She's our very own Norma Rae," said Joe.

"Norma Rae?" Tate mouthed to Zion.

She shrugged "I just couldn't do it anymore. I've been there three years and I haven't gotten anything out of it, except an ulcer."

"And an apartment in the city," moaned Rebekah. "Do you even have running water out here?"

Zion reached over and turned on the faucet. Water gushed out. Rebekah turned away and Tate tried to hide his smile behind his beer.

"Can I help?" he asked, glancing around at the boxes.

"We're almost done," said Gabi, climbing a step ladder to place glasses in a cabinet. "You've worked all day. Relax."

"Mom, you're gonna fall," said Zion, passing him the kitten and moving toward her mother.

Tate juggled the wriggling little body and settled his beer on the counter.

"Gabi, if you fall, how will you be able to play piano?" asked Joe.

"I'm not gonna fall. You'd think I was ninety years old the way you both act."

The doorbell rang. "Pizza!" called a male voice from the front door.

"Dad, get her down," said Zion, grabbing up some money lying on the table. "I'll pay for dinner." And she disappeared into the hall.

Rebekah sidled up to Tate, who was trying to make the kitten comfortable again. "So, you grew up here?" she said, leaning against the sink beside him.

"Uh, no," he said. "I'm originally from LA."

"LA? Why would you ever move here?"

"Well…"

"LA. We've been to LA many times. Zion went to school down there," said Joe, steadying his wife with a hand on her rear end. "We love LA."

"We hate LA," said Gabi, looking over at him. "You're lucky you got out."

"LA is so much better than this," said Rebekah, her breath fanning against his face.

"We don't hate LA. We don't like Las Vegas," said Joe.

"We don't like LA either. You always get lost there."

"I don't get lost. I just try to be strategic, find the quickest route."

"You get lost," said Gabi, backing down the step ladder.

"Name one time when I got lost."

"Zion's graduation."

"Do you miss the nightclubs in LA? There must be some really cool nightclubs. Not like here," said Rebekah.

"Well…"

Zion appeared with the pizza, setting it on the counter. She tugged Rebekah away from him and pushed her toward the pantry. "See if Vivian has any paper plates in there."

Rebekah gave her a pouty look, but she did as she asked.

"I'm starved," said Joe, hurrying over and lifting the lid on the box.

Rebekah came back with the plates and handed Joe one. He piled four pieces of pizza on the plate, but Gabi removed one, then he went to the fridge and pulled out a beer.

"Come on, Tate. Grab something to eat and let's go chat on the front porch. It's nice and cool now," he said, looking over his shoulder.

Zion took the kitten from him and Rebekah handed him a plate.

"You want me to serve you?" she purred, winking.

Tate didn't know how to answer, but Zion pulled Rebekah away again, so he could grab a slice.

"What's the matter with you?" Zion scolded.

"What? I'm just being a good hostess."

"In a strip club."

Tate got his pizza and picked up his beer, hurrying into the other room, then out onto the porch where Joe was sitting in an Adirondack chair on the deck. Tate left the other chair alone and took a seat on the stairs, bracing his back against the rail. He figured he probably should go home, but he was actually having a good time.

Joe leaned forward, dropping his voice. "We love LA. We went down there every other month to visit Zion when she was in college. We always had a good time."

Tate nodded and lifted a piece of pizza, taking a bite. Gabi appeared a moment later with her own plate and sat in the other Adirondack chair, grabbing Joe's beer and drinking from it.

"So, Tate, how's the business going?" she asked.

"Good. Um, today was slow, but that happens sometimes. Let's us do inventory and repair things."

"You got people working for you?" asked Joe.

"Just one. A high school kid named Logan." Tate glanced up as Zion and Rebekah came out of the house, each carrying their own plates. Rebekah eyed the stairs, then put her hand on her hip. "Where am I supposed to sit?"

Zion handed her her beer. "I'll get you a chair," and she disappeared inside the house.

"Or I could sit on Tate's lap," Rebekah said and giggled.

Gabi swatted at her this time.

Zion set a kitchen chair on the patio and took back her beer. Rebekah didn't take a seat.

"I don't have anything to drink."

"I told you to get a beer," said Zion, sinking onto the stairs across from Tate.

Tate smiled at her.

"I can't drink beer. Dear God, doesn't Vivian have any wine?"

"I thought I saw some boxes in the back of the pantry," said Gabi, her mouth partially full. "Look in those."

Rebekah flounced back into the house.

"What part of LA?" asked Joe

"Reseda," said Tate.

"Reseda?" repeated Joe.

He and Gabi leaned close to each other and started singing, "It's a long day, living in Reseda, there's a freeway runnin' through the yard, I'm a bad boy cause I don't even miss her, I'm a bad boy for breakin' her heart."

Tate and Zion laughed.

"Crazy hippies," Zion muttered under her breath.

Gabi pushed her with the toe of her tennis shoe.

"Did you have a hardware store in Reseda?" asked Joe.

Tate shook his head, lifting his beer to drink. This was getting into an area he didn't want to discuss right now. "It's too hard to own a private shop there."

"Yeah, same in the bay area."

Tate nodded, chewing his pizza.

"So, what did you do down there?" pressed Joe.

Tate met Zion's gaze, then shifted on the stairs.

Zion's smile dried and she turned to her father. "Why the third degree?" she teased.

"Just making conversation."

Gabi had stopped eating and Tate felt her studying him.

"I was a cop," said Tate, staring at the last slice on his plate. "But…I…um…"

Zion laid a hand on his forearm and he looked up at her. The warmth of her touch speared through him. "It's okay. You don't have to talk about it."

He nodded and blindly reached for the beer again. Damn this was bad. He couldn't deny he was attracted to her, but it was easier when he thought she was going back to San Francisco. Now that she was staying here, how was he going to keep up the pretense of being her friend?

"Dee and Dottie will be glad you're staying. They've been saying they need more help."

"I know. They asked me to put in for a part-time person to float between their hours. I might still hire someone. I won't be much help until I learn how to make all those fancy coffees."

Rebekah appeared in the doorway, carrying a glass of wine. "Eureka. I don't know if it's any good, but at least it once saw a grape." She held up the bottle. "How about it, hardware man, you wanna glass?"

Tate politely declined.

They finished eating, talking about what else they needed to move and any other changes Zion wanted to make to the house. Rebekah remarked more than once that she thought Zion was making a terrible mistake.

After the meal was over, Tate offered to move the rest of the stuff in from the truck. He and Joe took care of it, then Zion walked him down to the street. He tucked his hands in his pockets, trying to not notice the way the moonlight caressed her freckles or made her green eyes look darker.

"So, I thought I'd give you my number in case you need anything," he offered. "Move a bookcase or hang something. You know, those manly chores?"

She laughed. "Right." She took her phone out of her back pocket and swiped her finger over the display, then she pulled up her contacts. "I'm ready."

He rattled off his number and she entered it, then she motioned to him.

"Let me give you mine in case you need someone to move a bookcase or something."

He smiled and pulled his phone out. When he was ready, she gave him her number and he entered it. After he was done, he slipped the phone back in his pocket and rocked on his heels, not sure what to do now.

"Welcome to Sequoia," he said, and then flinched. What a cheesy thing to say.

She laughed. "Thank you. I keep waiting for the panic to set in. You know, the oh my God, what have I done."

"But it hasn't?"

She shook her head. "No, this feels right. I mean, I might feel that panic in a few weeks, but for right now, this feels right. I'm looking forward to the change."

He nodded. "Sometimes change is good."

She gave him a warm smile. "Sometimes it is. Goodnight, Tate."

"Goodnight," he answered and watched her turn and hurry back up the walkway into her house.

# CHAPTER 15

Zion got up the next morning at 6:00, gave Cleo her bottle, and started the coffee. Before it had brewed a full pot, she poured herself a mug and carried it and the kitten to the patio in back, walking down the stairs and taking a seat at the picnic table. She set Cleo on the table top and watched her explore, making sure she didn't fall off the edge.

Gabi appeared a short while later, carrying her own mug and taking a seat across from her. "Penny for your thoughts," she asked, redirecting the kitten when she came too close to the edge.

"Wondering if I should go talk to Sheriff Wilson about Vivian's case."

"I wish you wouldn't. He'll come talk to you if he has anything."

Zion considered that. "I kinda thought that Harold Arnold would be calling me before now, bugging me to sell the business, but I haven't heard from him."

"Did he have your number?"

"No, but he knew David represented me. He could have asked David to call. I haven't heard from him either."

"Well, I'm just as glad. That Arnold fella worries me a little. I'm still not sure he's not involved in Vivian's death."

"If he was, why hasn't Sheriff Wilson arrested him?"

"Because he needs evidence."

"I guess."

Gabi eased the kitten back to the middle of the table and Cleo protested with an annoyed meow. "You know, I could stay for a few days and make sure you're settled."

"What about Rascal?"

"Dad can get him out of stir." *Stir* being a fancy dog kennel where he would have his own room with a television.

"And your piano lessons?"

"Well, I have missed a few and I do have that recital next month."

"Then you need all those lessons and more."

Gabi glared at her.

"Just saying," laughed Zion. She reached over and covered her mother's hands with her own. "I'm fine, Mom. I'm actually excited about this. Please don't worry."

Cleo had made it to the edge of the table and was trying to decide if she could make the jump to the seat. Gabi watched her, then reached over and pulled her back, cuddling her against her chest. "It's hard to let your baby go. I'll worry about you."

"And you didn't when I was in the City?"

"No, I worried then too." She wagged a finger in front of Zion's face. "You just be careful, you hear me? And watch out for those men."

"What men?" asked Zion, frowning.

"Those lawyers and ex-cops. I wish you'd stay away from all those types of men."

"Right. You want me to find a good garbage man."

"Dear God," said Rebekah, coming down the stairs into the yard, wearing pink, frothy baby-doll pajamas. "A garbage man? Do you want to give me a heart attack?"

Zion and Gabi laughed.

* * *

Zion saw her parents and Rebekah off, then took a shower, fed Cleo again, and called to make an appointment with the vet. She figured Cleo had gotten big enough now that she might be able to start on regular kitten food in addition to her bottles.

Gabi had hugged her a million times and told her how to take care of Cleo at least a trillion. Zion couldn't deny that she felt a little worried once the moving truck and Rebekah's BMW disappeared down the street. She and Cleo were now alone and beginning their grand adventure.

Deciding she needed to check in at the *Caffeinator*, she packed Cleo into her carrier, made up another couple of bottles, grabbed a plastic bag of kitty litter and a makeshift litter box, then loaded everything into the Optima and drove into Sequoia.

The sun was out, the day was warm, and white fluffy clouds floated overhead. She rolled down the window and breathed in the pine scent, feeling her shoulders relax. She couldn't remember the last time she'd dressed in jeans and a t-shirt during the week. And she hadn't bothered to unpack her heels yet. She wore a pair of Converse with pink sparkle shoelaces, her hair in a ponytail, and only a bit of mascara on her eyes. She felt happy.

Driving down Main, she marked the happy bunting hanging from the businesses, the community flower pots draped over the decorative lighting, and the old western store facades. This was her new home and she intended to enjoy it.

Pulling in front of the *Caffeinator*, she got out and removed Cleo and as much of the kitten's paraphernalia as she could in one trip. A middle-aged man held the door open for her as she entered and she thanked him, then looked up.

"Zion!" shouted Deimos, hurrying around the counter. He threw his arms around her and hugged her fiercely. "Dude, it's so good to see you."

She laughed, unable to extricate herself with her hands full. "How are you, Dee?"

"Great."

He finally released her and bent down, peering into the carrier. "Little dude, how are you?" He waggled his fingers in the cage and Cleo pounced on them.

While he played with the kitten, Zion took a look around. Jackson Van Tiernan sat in his usual spot on the couch and the rest of the bistro chairs were occupied by customers, chatting or typing away on electronic devices. Dottie held up a flour-covered hand.

"Hey, sugar, what brings you by?" Although she sounded cheerful, Zion could hear the edge in her voice.

She smiled at Deimos, then moved around him, carrying the kitten and her stuff toward the counter. She gave Van Tiernan a nod. He nodded back, then focused on his computer once more. "Let me put Cleo in the office and move the car to the municipal lot, then I'll tell you."

"I can move the car. I was just about to take my break," said Deimos, pushing open the counter so she could pass through.

Zion deposited the kitten in the office, then turned and handed Deimos her keys. "I'd appreciate that, but before you go, I want to talk to you and Dottie."

Dottie stepped into the office doorway, wiping her hands on her pink apron. "What's up?"

Zion clasped her hands before her. "I quit my job in San Francisco."

Dottie tilted her head, her lavender curls sliding to the side. "You did what now?"

"I quit. I just couldn't do it anymore. All I did all day was deny people medication they really needed and it was killing me. So I thought, maybe I could use my business degree and learn how to run a coffee house. That is until I figure out what I want to do with my life."

Dottie and Deimos exchanged pleased looks, then Deimos hurried forward and captured her in a bear hug again, swinging her around. "Dude, that is a huge weight off my shoulders."

Zion laughed, hugging him in return. "I'm glad, but you're going to have to show me how to make all those fancy coffees."

"Easy peasy, pumpkin squeezy," said Deimos, releasing her. He shook the keys. "I'll just go move your car before it gets a ticket." Then he raced out of the office, stopping only long enough to plant a kiss on Dottie's cheek. "I told you our girl, Zion, would come through for us."

Dottie watched him disappear, a fond smile on her lips, then she faced Zion again. "You sure about this, sugar? You're giving up a lot."

"Actually, I'm not giving up as much as you think. I just couldn't do it anymore, Dottie, and I realized I had a way out. So many people don't. I'm lucky that way."

Dottie came forward and put her hands on Zion's shoulders. "We're glad you're back. We really need the help."

"I don't know how much help I'll be, but I'm willing to work hard."

"I know. That'll be enough." She glanced over her shoulder. "Well, I better get back to my baking or you're gonna be out of half your inventory before the afternoon rush."

When Deimos returned from his break, Zion had him begin the task of teaching her how to make the various coffees people ordered. There were so many different varieties, and so many ways people complicated it, that she felt a headache hammering in her temples long before Dottie announced she was leaving for the day.

Dottie pulled her aside, removing her apron and folding it. "We could really use some help in the afternoons still. Once I leave, Deimos gets slammed."

"I know. I'm thinking of putting out an advertisement for part-time help. Maybe a high school kid."

"That'd be great." Dottie squeezed her arm. "It's sure good to have you on-board."

Zion smiled, feeling happy she'd decided to keep the coffee shop. After Dottie left, she found it was more efficient for her to work the register and clean the tables, leaving Deimos to make the coffee. They fell into an easy rhythm and the hours flew past. Zion didn't even realize it was nearly 4:00PM until the door opened and David Bennett stepped inside.

His polished shoes, pressed suit, and brilliant smile made Zion feel disheveled, but she pasted a smile on her face and found she was actually glad to see him. He made a little flutter of pleasure blossom in her belly.

"What can I get for you, sir?"

"A nonfat latte, no whip," he said, leaning his tall frame on the counter. "A little bird told me you were back in town."

"Who would that be?" she said, giving him a coy smile as she rang him up.

"Rose came in for coffee a little while ago."

Rose, his secretary. Zion had hardly recognized her, they were so busy at the time.

"Right. I'm sorry. We've been slammed since I got here."

He looked around. The crowd had thinned and only one couple occupied a bistro seat apart from Van Tiernan. "Can you take a break and have coffee with me? I'm buying."

"Sure."

"If I remember, you're a tea drinker, right?"

"Right." She looked over at Deimos. "Do you mind if I take a break?"

"Nope. What do you want?"

"Chai tea," she said and moved around the counter, untying her apron. She stuffed it under the counter, then eased through the swinging door and motioned to a bistro table nearest the couch.

David held out her chair for her. "So, how come you're back?"

"I decided being a barista was a lot less taxing on my soul."

He laughed and sat down across from her. "What does that mean?"

"I quit. I'm gonna try running the coffee shop and see where that takes me." She shrugged. "Maybe I'll go back to grad school, but for right now, I just want to live on my own."

He gave her a smile. "And leave the City? I didn't think people did that. I'd give just about anything to go there and here you want to leave."

"I love San Francisco, but I want to try this for a while."

"Well, I'm not gonna lie. I'm glad you're back."

Deimos brought the two drinks over and settled them on the table, then he went back behind the counter, but Zion knew he was listening to their conversation. Glancing over at Van Tiernan, she marked he was also listening, although he had the decency to pretend he was studying what was on his computer screen.

"Did you come in to talk about Vivian's estate or anything?" Zion asked, lifting her drink for a sip.

"Nope. This is a purely personal call. I wanted to see if you'd go out to dinner with me tomorrow night. I thought we could go to *Corkers*. It's actually got reviews on Yelp."

"Oh, well then it must be good."

He laughed.

"I'd love to go. What time?"

"This place closes at 6:30, right?"

"Right."

"Is 7:30 too early?"

"Nope. That gives me time to get Cleo home and change."

"Cleo?"

"My kitten. I found her on Vivian's back porch." She made a sound of amusement. "My back porch. Boy, that sounds weird."

"Good weird or bad weird?" asked David.

"Good weird."

He picked up his latte and saluted her. "Well, I better get back to the office. I'll see you tomorrow night at 7:30."

"Great," she said, and watched him walk out of the building. Gabi might not think she should date a lawyer, but Zion wasn't going to lie, there was something about a man in a suit that got to a twenty-six-year-old Zion the way a boy in a leather jacket had gotten to a sixteen-year-old Zion.

She felt Van Tiernan's eyes on her and met them. He immediately looked away.

"Are you still working on the sequel to that game?"

He nodded, not making eye contact. "I need to have the rough to the production team in two weeks."

"It's a lot of work, huh?"

"Yeah, I mean I'm responsible for the story, the characters, the whole thing. I've even got to give them ideas for the voice talent."

"Wow, I didn't know that much went into it. What's it called again?"

"*B&E-2.*"

"Is it about breaking and entering?"

He pushed his glasses up on his nose. "Yeah. So you're Griffin Davis and you're a small time thug."

"Okay."

"You work for the Ginger Boys."

"The Ginger Boys?"

"It's a gang. You know, drugs, racketeering, prostitutes."

"Okay." Zion tried to keep the judgment out of her voice.

"They send you on jobs, so you gotta get in and get the stuff for them. The more B&E's you do, the better your skills get – you know, stealth, pickpocketing, lock picking – that sort of thing. With the money you earn, you get to buy upgrades, better gear, better clothes, better weapons."

"I see. And you created this game?"

"Yeah, I'm one of their top designers."

"And you don't have to go into the office?"

His expression clouded over and he looked away. "Most of this stuff's done on the computer, so if I make my deadlines, they don't care where I do it."

"I'll bet it's a popular game," she said, trying to smooth over whatever insult she'd inadvertently given him. "Seems like it takes a long time to create it."

"It does. I pour my soul into it. It's like a vampire, sucking my blood."

Zion glanced up at Deimos. He was frowning. "I'm sure it's a competitive field."

"You have no idea. There's always someone younger, someone with more tech skills, someone who discovers some new way to do something. If you don't stay cutting edge, well..."

Zion could feel his frustration. "It was that way at my job too," she said. "The competition got exhausting."

"Exactly." He shifted and met her gaze. "It's exhausting."

Zion picked up her tea and smiled at him. "Can I get you another coffee?"

"Sure."

"What'll you have?"

"Cappuccino," he said and turned back to the screen.

Zion walked to the counter and eased behind it, touching Deimos on the shoulder. "Make this one on me," she said, feeling for the game designer.

"Coming right up, boss," said Deimos and started working the press.

* * *

Zion bolted out of sleep, her heart hammering. She couldn't remember where she was for a moment, then she recognized the exposed beams in the ceiling and the pine knots in the wood. Vivian's house. Vivian's bedroom, in fact.

She blew out air and closed her eyes, trying to calm the panic. She thought over the sound that had brought her awake and her eyes flashed open again. Pushing back the covers, she climbed out of bed and crept over to Cleo's box.

The kitten stood on her hind legs, giving Zion a meow. Zion picked her up, holding her close, and tiptoed out into the hallway. She could see bright light coming from the living room and frowned. Wishing she'd thought to bring a baseball bat or a golf club, she eased to the wooden archway and peered around into the living room.

The headlights of a car blazed into the front windows of the cottage and glittered against a ragged hole in the glass where something had been thrown. Zion felt her heart kick against her ribs. The lights of the car were so bright, she couldn't see the car itself or make out the license plate.

Trying to remember where her cell phone was, she hurried back down the hallway to her room and snatched it off the nightstand where she'd been charging it. For some reason, she pulled up Tate's number and pressed the call button.

A few moments later, she heard his voice. "Hello? Zion?" The strain in it was unmistakable.

"Tate, someone broke out my front window. Now the guy's sitting out there in his car, shining the headlights into the cottage."

"I'll be right there," she heard him say. "Call the cops, Zion. As soon as I hang up, call the cops." Then he was gone.

She dialed 911 as she crept back toward the living room. Cleo struggled to get out of her arms, but Zion wouldn't let her go. She listened to the ringing and peered around the archway, trying to see if she could make out a license plate, but it was too hard in the glare of the headlights.

"911, what's your emergency?" came a woman's voice on the line.

"Someone threw something through my window. He's just sitting out there, shining the headlights into my living room. I can't see him or the make of the car."

"You said someone threw something through your window, ma'am?"

"Yes."

"Are you hurt?"

"No, but he's just sitting out there. Or maybe he's not. I don't know if he's still in the car."

"Tell me your name and address."

Zion started to tell her, but suddenly the car revved its engine and spun its tires, squealing away. She watched it disappear from sight, moving cautiously into the living room.

She saw a lump on the carpet before the window and eased over to it, staring down.

A large rock lay on the flooring.

"Ma'am, do you hear me? I need your name and address."

Zion gave her the information she requested, then she said, "He just drove off, he just sped away. I don't know where he went."

"An officer is on his way right now, ma'am. I'll stay on the line with you until he gets there."

Zion saw Tate run across the street and she felt a wash of relief spill over her. "It's okay. My neighbor's here now. He'll stay with me until the cops arrive."

"Are you sure? I don't mind holding on the line."

"No, I'm sure. Thank you."

"The officer should be there any moment."

"Thank you," said Zion, disconnecting the call. She set the phone on the coffee table and settled Cleo on the couch, then she hurried for the front door and tugged it open just as Tate bounded up the outside stairs.

She threw herself in his arms and he wrapped one arm around her back, the other held at his side. "I couldn't get a license plate," she said into his neck.

"I couldn't get one either. There wasn't a plate on the back."

She eased away from him, realizing she wore only a tank top and sleep shorts. He wore sweatpants and a t-shirt, his feet bare. In his right hand, he held a gun.

"You have a gun?" Zion said, surprised her voice came out so high. "I mean, of course, you have a gun."

"Ex-cop," he said sheepishly. "I have a permit."

"Of course you have a permit." She pushed back her hair and gave a hysterical laugh. "I don't know why I'm talking like I swallowed helium."

He gave her a sympathetic smile. "Did you call the cops?"

"Yeah, they're on their way."

He looked down. "Maybe you want to grab a bathrobe then."

She wrapped her arms around her chest and felt a blush paint her cheeks. "You won't leave, will you?"

"No, I'll stay until they get here."

She pulled him into the house and locked the door, then she hurried to the master bedroom after her robe. When she came back, he'd set the gun on the end table and held Cleo cradled against his chest as he inspected the window. When she came over to him, he held out his free hand. "Be careful, there's glass all over here."

"Oh, I'll get the broom."

He caught her elbow. "Not before the police have a chance to look at it."

"Right." She reached for the kitten. "I'll just put her in bed."

He handed her over and Zion hurried back to her room, placing the kitten in the box and shutting the door behind her. She went back into the living room and found Tate had taken a seat on the couch, the gun resting on the coffee table before him. She studied the gun and realized she'd never seen one up close before.

"What is it?" she asked.

"A Glock 19. That's my service pistol."

She sank onto the opposite end of the couch, pulling the bathrobe around her. "I've never seen a real gun before."

"I'm sorry. I didn't know what might be happening and with everything…"

"No, it's okay. I was pretty scared." She glanced over at the broken window. The upper part was original stained glass. She wondered if they could save it when they repaired the clear part.

"Zion." He shifted on the couch and gave her a serious look. Her eyes traveled over the panther tattoo on his forearm. She wanted to ask him about it, but she wasn't sure he would welcome such a personal question. He seemed like he wanted to hide some things. "There's something I haven't told you," he said.

Zion's eyes snapped to his face. "Okay."

"I'm sort of consulting on your mother's murder investigation."

Zion frowned. "What does that mean? Consulting?"

"I'm helping Sheriff Wilson. I listened to the messages on her phone, read her text messages, and I looked through Wilson's file on the case."

"Do you have any suspects?"

He blinked at her as if he were surprised she wasn't upset. "Wilson thinks Harold Arnold is a suspect. He was going to get a warrant for his house, see if he could find the car that caused Vivian's accident."

"I see. Well, I'm glad someone's looking into it."

"That's not the main point."

Zion waited for him to speak.

"After Vivian's memorial, someone tried to run me off the road. When I pulled over, they pulled right behind me and shined their high beams into my car. I thought I was going to have to fight my way out of it, but suddenly they pulled away. I didn't get a license plate number or a make of the vehicle that time either, but I think it was the same car – black sedan, no plates."

Zion nodded. "God, I'm so sorry that happened to you."

He shrugged it off. "The businesses around the *Caffeinator* were vandalized a few days later, black spray paint. And Van Tiernan told me someone followed Trixie to her car."

Zion shivered, despite herself.

"I know you want to start over here, but maybe it isn't a good idea right now. Maybe you should go home. At least until Wilson catches Vivian's murderer."

Zion thought about that for a moment. "What's he doing to catch this guy?"

"He brought me onto the case and I contacted someone in the LAPD to see if she can trace the phone that sent the messages to Vivian. Honestly, Wilson's doing the best he can with the resources he has, but I don't like what's happening. Now, you've become a target too."

Zion chewed her inner lip. She heard a car pull into the driveway and looked out the broken front window.

"It's the cops," said Tate, rising to his feet.

Zion's gaze dropped to the gun and she clenched her jaw. "I'm not running away. Vivian deserves justice and I'm going to make sure she gets it."

Tate regarded her without speaking, then he went to the door and opened it, allowing a woman into the house. The woman walked over to Zion and held out her hand, squeezing with force. "Deputy Sam Murphy," she said, releasing Zion, then she reached for a notebook in her front pocket and pulled it out. "Do you mind if I take notes while we talk?"

"Not at all."

"So someone threw something through your window?" she asked.

Zion's eyes rose to Tate pleading for him to take over. He smiled and motioned for Deputy Murphy to follow him.

"A rock. We didn't touch or move anything until you got here."

Murphy studied the rock, then pressed the button on her radio attached to her shoulder. "How far out are you?"

"'bout ten minutes," came a male voice.

"Good." She glanced over at Zion. "We have one crime scene investigator. He's on his way over."

Zion nodded, clasping her hands between her knees.

"So someone launch the rock through your window, then shined his headlights into the room? Is that right?"

"Yeah. I called Tate and he came over. I think he scared the guy away."

Murphy looked over at Tate, then eyed the gun. "Your service revolver?"

"Yeah, I have a permit if you want to see it."

"I can look it up in the database. What did you see?"

Tate shifted weight, his eyes sliding past Zion. "It looked like the same car that harassed me after Vivian's memorial service."

"You sure?"

Tate shrugged. "Pretty sure. Black sedan. Tinted windows. No plates."

Murphy scratched her upper lip. "The car that forced Vivian off the road had blue paint."

"I know."

"Anything else?" she said, looking over at Zion. "Any threatening messages? Any strange phone calls?"

"No, nothing."

"Did you talk to Trixie about the guy who followed her to her car?" asked Tate.

"I didn't get over to her shop," said Murphy. "We got a multi-car accident right as I was heading out, and by the time I got that all squared away, she'd closed up for the night."

"What about the warrant to search Harold Arnold's place?"

"Sheriff's working on it. We just don't have enough hard evidence against him. It's not illegal to be an annoying ass."

Zion stared at her hands, feeling frustrated and a little afraid. She'd almost convinced herself the attack that took Vivian's life was a horrible accident, that someone had forced her off the road without realizing what they'd done, but after hearing about Tate's experience, the vandalism on the businesses, and now her own involvement, it was getting harder to pretend something wasn't going on.

"What's this all about?" she asked.

"If we knew that," said Murphy with a sigh, "solving crimes would be a cakewalk, now wouldn't it?"

# CHAPTER 16

Tate waited until Logan showed up for work, then he filled the cash register with money and made sure everything was okay before he told the teenager he was going to the *Caffeinator*.

Logan rolled his eyes, but didn't argue.

Tate started to explain that it wasn't to flirt with Zion, but then he figured he'd have to tell Logan what happened the previous night and he just wasn't ready to do that yet. He paused on his way out the door and realized he wanted Logan to open up with him about his life, but he wasn't doing the same. He scratched at his tattoo and turned back around.

"It's not for the reason you think," he said.

Logan looked up from sweeping behind the counter. "What?"

"The reason I'm going to the *Caffeinator*."

"What's the reason I think?"

Tate bit his inner lip. "To see Zion."

"Right. Seriously, I wasn't thinking that. I figured you wanted one of those froufrou coffees you're so crazy about lately, but dude, whatever. You're legal."

Tate frowned. "I'm legal?"

"Over 18."

"Oh, right." He laughed and looked away. Damn, they had it right in the 60's. Never trust anyone over 30. When had he stopped speaking teenager? "It's just, someone threw a rock at her house last night, broke out the front window, and then shined his headlights into the living room."

Logan's face grew grim. "No shit?"

"No shit."

"Why'd they wanna do that?"

"Why'd they wanna take out my mailbox or run me off the road?"

"Someone ran you off the road?"

Right. Tate hadn't told him about that. "Yeah, after Vivian's memorial. Look, I'm telling you this because I want you to keep an eye out, okay? Watch yourself. I don't think anyone is gonna mess with the *Hammer Tyme*, but…"

"They be crazy. Straight up."

Tate digested that. "Yeah, they be crazy."

"I gotcha. I'll keep my eyes open and my ears too."

"Thanks." Tate gave him a smile and Logan gave a hesitant one in return. "See you in a bit." He started to turn around, then paused. "How about some of Dottie's cinnamon breadsticks?"

"Do you even have to ask?"

"Guess not." Tate lifted a hand in farewell, then went to the door.

He jogged down the street to the *Caffeinator*. The plants the Chamber had hung along Main Street were starting to bloom and added some much needed color and charm to the weathered buildings. He breathed in the fragrant scent and thought, as he had many time before this, that it would be a shame to replace the small businesses with a big box store. There were so few places like Sequoia left in the world.

He pushed open the *Caffeinator's* door, listening for the tinkle of the bell. The interior was crowded with people getting their coffee, talking on telephones, or typing on laptops. He was surprised to see Jackson Van Tiernan in his spot on the couch. He usually didn't come in until after the morning rush, although this was a little late for a morning rush.

Van Tiernan lifted his eyes and studied Tate behind his black-rimmed spectacles, not showing the least bit of recognition. Tate approached him, seeing that Zion was trying her hardest to help Dottie with the customers.

A wisp of auburn hair had escaped her ponytail and trailed down her cheek, her freckles stark against her pale skin, dark circles under her eyes. He knew she probably hadn't gotten any sleep last night, but here she was, trying to learn how to make complicated coffees for people needing speed and caffeine in that order.

"Hey, you're here early," he said to Van Tiernan, glancing at him, then watching Zion again.

"Yeah, deadlines, you know?"

Tate focused on him. "I thought you had to have the game finished by Christmas."

"No," said Van Tiernan levelly. "*Cyclone* wants to market it for Christmas – the must have game on everyone's list."

"So, how close are you to being finished?"

"The main programming's done. They're just putting the finishing touches on it, but I'm trying to add a bit to the story itself."

"Story? Isn't it all shoot 'em up and car crashes?"

Van Tiernan's expression shuttered. "It's so much more than that. If you want to be the top selling game, you've got to give people an experience. They have to feel like they're there. Like they're the ones committing the B&E. They have to care about the characters, they have to live it. It has to be a completely immersive experience."

Tate felt chastised. He'd never considered it that way before. "That's a tall order. You've got some sophisticated players, don't you?"

Van Tiernan looked out the front windows of the coffee house. "That's the problem with technology. The more it comes to look like reality, the more real people want it to be." He blinked and looked at Tate again. "They want the Star Trek holodeck experience. They want to forget their boring, mundane lives and become the hero they always envisioned themselves to be." He looked back at the laptop. "Problem is there are no more heroes."

Tate blew out air. "I didn't mean to take it lightly."

Van Tiernan glanced up at him and shrugged.

Tate forced a smile and moved toward the counter. Van Tiernan was a bit intense for him. Besides, the customers had begun to thin and now only half the tables were occupied and the line had been served. Dottie was just putting the finishing touches on some drinks, but she looked over her shoulder and smiled at Tate.

"How are you, sugar?" she called.

"Alive and kicking," said Tate, then he leaned on the counter.

Zion smiled at him, pushing back the escaped strands of hair. "I haven't worked this hard in my entire life."

"But she's a quick study. She's got latte and espresso and cappuccinos down pat," said Dottie with pride.

Zion laughed. "As long as people aren't picky which of the three they get."

Tate laughed with her. "Well, that's better than me. If I owned this place, it'd be instant."

Dottie gasped in outrage and a woman waiting for her drink gave him an arch look. Tate shrugged, focusing on Zion once more.

"How are you this morning? You look like you didn't get much sleep last night."

She pushed her hair again. "That bad, huh?"

Tate motioned to his own eyes. "Dark circles."

"The curse of Irish blood or whatever Vivian was." She leaned on the counter next to him. "I'm okay. Still a little shaken up. I have someone coming to the house today to give me an estimate on the window. I want them to try to save the upper part."

"The stained glass part?"

"Right. Thank you for boarding it up for me last night and for waiting with me until the police finished their work."

"No problem."

Dottie handed the two customers their drinks and wiped her hands on her apron. "I'm not a nosy person, mind you, but what happened last night and why were police involved?"

Tate smiled at her comment. Not nosey, huh? "Someone threw a rock through Zion's window."

"What? Who?"

"We didn't see. He also flashed his high beams into her living room. The car I saw had no plates," said Tate.

Dottie pulled Zion into her arms. "You should have called me. You must have been terrified."

"I was a little afraid." She hugged Dottie in return. "But everything was all right as soon as Tate came over."

Tate looked away. He caught Van Tiernan watching over his shoulder, listening to Zion's story.

"Maybe you better start over at the beginning. Why was Tate there?" asked Dottie, leaning a hip against the counter.

Zion told the entire story from the moment she was startled awake until the CSI guy showed up, collecting evidence. Tate couldn't remember his name right now. Dottie listened, covering her mouth at appropriate intervals, gasping when required, then dragging Zion into another hug. When Zion was finished, Dottie clapped her hands.

"What is this world coming to?" she remarked.

Zion shrugged.

"I'm buying your drink today, sugar," she told Tate, hurrying to the machine.

"That's not necessary," said Zion. "It's on me."

He smiled at her, but sobered when her eyes slid past him into the room. He turned around to see where she was looking, but except for Van Tiernan and a couple at a bistro table, the *Caffeinator* had emptied.

He shifted back to face her. "You okay?"

She blinked. "Yeah, fine. How's the hardware store?"

"Good." He dragged the word out. He felt that was a strange question to ask. "So, I thought I'd go by Sheriff..."

"Do you want whipped cream on your coffee?" she interrupted him.

Tate straightened away from the counter. She was acting oddly, making it clear she didn't want to talk about Vivian's case. "No, no whip," he said.

She nodded, then reached for the ties on her apron. "Well, I have to get Cleo to the vet for a checkup and her first shots. Dottie, you can hold down the fort while I'm gone?"

"Sure thing, sugar. I got this."

"I'll stop by the paper and put in a want ad for help while I'm out."

"Good idea," said Dottie, continuing her preparation of Tate's drink.

"I'll talk to you later," Zion said, looking him directly in the eye. "Okay?"

"Sure." He was a little bewildered by how quickly she'd turned things around.

She stuffed the apron under the counter and waved at him as she hurried to the office for her purse and, he suspected, Cleo's carrier. Dottie turned to the counter as she hurried away.

"One mint mocha freeze," she said, settling it before him. "This has become your signature drink now." Then she winked at him.

* * *

Rather than head back to the *Hammer Tyme*, Tate detoured into *Trinkets by Trixie.* The platinum haired woman with the heavy eye makeup and the ridiculously long nails looked up from her spot behind the register. She was reading a fashion magazine and smiled at him.

"Tate, right?" she called.

"Right," he answered. He glanced at the displays, but headed in her direction. It always made him nervous coming in here with the bric-a-brac sitting precariously on the glass shelves just waiting for him to knock it off. "How are you?"

"I'm doing well." She closed the magazine and gave him a smile. "How are you?"

"Fine. So no more Harold Arnold?"

Trixie rolled her eyes. "That man…he never gives up. If he doesn't come in here everyday, he calls on the phone. I finally told him I was blocking his calls."

Tate nodded. "He's persistent, all right."

"Did you come to get your girlfriend a gift?"

Tate laughed. "No girlfriend and no gift, I'm sorry. Look, Trixie, I'm going to be honest with you. I agreed to consult with Sheriff Wilson on Vivian Bradley's murder."

She looked down her nose at him. "Why you?"

"I used to be a cop in L.A."

Trixie nodded. "I remember something about that now." Then her eyes lit with a shrewd light. "The sheriff doesn't suspect Harold Arnold, does he?"

Tate shrugged. "I can't divulge any information on the case." He shifted weight and stepped closer to the counter. "I wanted to ask you about the situation the other night."

Trixie frowned. "What situation?"

"The one where a man followed you to the municipal parking lot."

"What man followed me?"

Tate shook his head. "Wait. What do you mean?"

"What do *you* mean?" She rose to her feet. "Who followed me to the parking lot? Do you have it on surveillance tape or something?"

"No. Wait. Are you saying you weren't followed to the parking lot?"

"If I was, I didn't know about it."

"But you had to take out your pepper spray."

"I had to do what? What are you talking about? I don't own pepper spray."

"But Van Tiernan said…"

"He said what?"

Tate went back over the conversation he'd had with Van Tiernan. "Jackson Van Tiernan, the guy who designs computer games in the *Caffeinator*…"

"Right."

"He said you mentioned that someone had followed you to your car and that you pulled your pepper spray out of your purse, prepared to use it, but the guy walked away."

"Tate," said Trixie, giving him a serious look, "that wasn't me. Maybe he mixed me up for someone else, but I've never said more than three words to that man."

Tate filed that away. "Yeah," he said to placate Trixie. "He must have mixed you up with someone else." But he didn't think so.

"Look, I'm sorry."

"No, don't be. I'm glad it didn't happen." He gave Trixie a wry smile. "I'm actually very glad it didn't happen." He looked around the store, but he didn't really see anything, his mind was whirling. "I'll let you get back to work. I probably should see how things are in my own business."

"I wish I could help you with the case."

"No worries. We'll figure it out," he said, backing away from the counter. "See you later." He turned and hurried to the door, yanking it open, then he hesitated on the street, staring three doors down at the *Caffeinator*.

He distinctly remembered the conversation with Van Tiernan. Why would the man tell such a lie, and such an easy lie to prove was a lie?

Tate sighed and turned toward the hardware store. Because Van Tiernan wanted to fit in, that's why. Same reason people did anything. They wanted to be accepted, even if it meant telling a bald faced lie. He wasn't much better himself. He was working a case, when he'd swore he'd never do anything in law enforcement again, just so he could feel useful and involved.

Pathetic.

* * *

Tate's cell phone rang. He'd laid it on the counter while he helped Bill Stanley find oil for his chainsaw. Logan picked it up and brought it to him.

"Excuse me, Bill," Tate said, taking the phone and heading toward the storeroom when he saw who came up on the display. He thumbed it on and pressed it to his ear. "Hey, Darcy, how's smoggy SoCal?"

"Smoggy. How's the boondocks?"

"Boonie."

"I don't think that's a word."

"You're probably right." He sat down at the table and opened the notebook to the place where he'd written his notes. Pulling out his reading glasses, he slipped them on. "You got anything for me?"

"Not a lot. The phone was bought in Visalia, one of them big box stores. Guess you don't get many of those out where you is?"

"You'd be surprised," said Tate with a sigh. "Visalia, huh?"

"Yeah, I guess that's the biggest town near you?"

"Pretty much. Tell me we got a credit card number."

"Nope. Paid in cash."

"Shit."

"I got the store name. Maybe your sheriff can get a warrant to pull the video footage. Here's the date the phone was purchased and the store number." She rattled off the date and number. Tate wrote them in his notebook. "Sorry I couldn't be of more help."

"No, you did great. I owe you a bottle of wine."

"Make sure it's white. Red gives me a hangover."

"White it is."

"You coming down here any time soon?"

Tate felt his stomach clench and he gripped the pen hard. "No, Darcy, I'm not planning to go down there. Sorry."

"Suit yourself, but a lot of people would be happy to see you."

Tate doubted that. When he'd decided to quit, many of his fellow officers thought he was betraying the brotherhood, betraying Jason's memory. He scrubbed a hand across his face. "Hey, if you ever get up this way, you got a place to stay, you know?"

"I might take you up on that if I get a wild hair to go huntin' or somethin'."

"It's not a requirement, Darcy."

"Really? They don't make you gut a deer at least once a year to prove you belong."

"Well, I did forget about the deer gutting ordnance, but it's the bear wrestling that's a real bitch."

Darcy laughed. "I miss you, Tater Tot," she said.

He swallowed hard. He hadn't heard that nickname in years. Jason had always called him that, slapping him on the back. God, he hated it.

Bowing his head, he took off his glasses and pressed his fingers against his eyes, unable to answer her.

"Tate," came Logan's voice in the doorway.

Tate looked up. "Yeah?"

"Daryl's here and he says he needs one of them snaky doodads for drains?"

Tate sighed. "I'm coming," he said. "Hey, Darce, gotta go."

"Sure thing. Go find your snaky doodad. I'll talk to you soon."

"Hey, thanks again," he said, ending the call, then he pushed himself to his feet and walked out into the store. "You want a snaky doodad, really?" he scolded Daryl.

"Hey, man, don't bust my chops. Dwayne's got his panties in a bunch because the toilet in the bathroom's backed up. He says the plunger ain't working."

"It's because you serve all that heavy red meat and shit," said Tate, moving into the plumbing aisle.

"You ain't got no problem eating our red meat and shit on a regular basis, man."

Tate laughed. "Be careful. I just might go vegetarian on you, then what'll you do?"

"Make a damn profit," said Daryl, pushing him in the shoulder. "All the free meals you charm out of Cheryl, she-et!"

* * *

Tate and Logan were closing shop when his cell phone rang again. He laid the cash back in the register and picked it up, surprised to see Sheriff Wilson's name on his display. He thumbed it on and took a seat on the stool behind the counter.

"Sheriff Wilson? I was going to call you in a bit."

"Well, I just wanted to tell you we're bringing Harold Arnold in for questioning."

Tate frowned. "Wait, why?"

"We got a search warrant to search his house and we found black spray paint canisters in his garage."

"Black spray paint? You arrested him for having black spray paint?"

"No, we haven't arrested him yet. We're just bringing him in for questioning."

"So you think he did the vandalism on Main Street?"

"It's looking that way."

Tate scratched his tattoo. "Did he admit to it?"

"He hasn't admitted to nothing yet. Murphy just went to collect him." Wilson cleared his throat. "God, I hope this is it. I'm getting sick of this case."

Tate wasn't sure. This was pretty slim evidence, if you asked him. He had spray paint in various colors in his own garage.

"So you said you were going to call me?" asked Wilson.

"Right. I got a call back from my contact in LA. Darcy traced the phone to a store in Visalia. Unfortunately, whoever bought it paid in cash, so we can't trace it any farther. However, she suggested you get a warrant for the store's video surveillance."

"Not a bad idea," said Wilson.

"I have the name, number, and date the phone was purchased."

"Text it to me."

"Got it."

"I'll let you know if we get anything solid out of Arnold."

"Thanks."

Without saying goodbye, Wilson hung up. Tate settled the phone on the counter and thought about Harold Arnold. The fact he had black spray paint in his garage wasn't good, but it didn't exactly scream guilty. And it certainly didn't say he'd murdered anyone.

"Everything okay?" asked Logan.

"Yeah, just this Vivian Bradley case."

"You're helping Sheriff Wilson with it?"

"I thought I was, but I'm not so sure."

Tate couldn't deny he could get to a logical place where someone like Arnold would think murdering Vivian Bradley wasn't a bad idea if he wanted to break the pact between the business owners. Or maybe he hadn't even wanted to kill her. Maybe he thought by scaring her off the road, she'd sell and get out of Sequoia. Add the text messages, maybe the entire thing was geared to scare her into putting the business up for sale. Maybe her death had been a terrible accident. He figured Harold Arnold was greedy enough to make an unfortunate miscalculation, which resulted in someone's death, but was he capable of outright murder?

"So, I think I'll head out," said Logan, pointing over his shoulder toward the front door.

Tate nodded absently and picked up his cell phone, shoving it in his pocket. He tugged the keys out of his other pocket and followed Logan to the door. When he got to the pickup, he decided to detour toward the sheriff's office.

Something bothered him about this entire case. Wilson had said he hadn't charged Arnold yet, but to bring him in for questioning on something as flimsy as black spray paint seemed premature. Of course, admittedly Sequoia didn't get many murders, so maybe it made sense to act quickly. Wilson didn't have the luxury a large precinct with a lot of manpower, nor did he have the resources. People wanted answers and they wanted them now.

Tate parked in front of the station and climbed out. Inside the reception area, he pressed the button. Murphy pulled open the window as she always did. Didn't they have anyone else to do that, Tate wondered.

"Hey," he said, smiling.

"Hey. This is becoming a habit."

"I wonder if I can talk to the Sheriff."

"He's questioning Arnold."

"Did Arnold ask for a lawyer?"

"Yep. Andrew Cox of Bennett, Coleman and Cox."

"I thought they handled probate."

"Cox has a criminal law background and he's a lot closer than the guy in Visalia Arnold first called."

Visalia, again. "Is anyone listening in on the investigation?"

"Vasquez. He's senior officer here."

Tate nodded. "Look, can you tell me what all was found in Arnold's garage?"

"Black spray paint. Damn near a case of the stuff."

"Did he say what he had it for?"

"He said he was painting some patio furniture, but we looked. The furniture's redwood, not painted."

"What about a car?"

"Cadillac Seville with an Arnold Realty sign on the side."

"Yeah, I've seen that car. It's white."

"Yep."

"Could he have another car registered to him?"

Murphy considered that. "You mean one he's hiding somewhere else?"

"Yeah."

She pressed the button and buzzed him in. "We can run it through the DMV database."

Tate figured that probably should have been done the moment Arnold became a suspect, but then again, Sequoia didn't get a lot of murders and he was supposed to be consulting. He probably should have suggested it long before now.

Murphy led him to her desk. A picture of her with a huge man with a grey beard that came nearly to his belt buckle took up one corner. They were standing under some redwood trees and both wore flannel, checked shirts. They looked like lumberjacks.

Hiding his smile, Tate nodded at it. "Your husband?"

Murphy glanced at the picture. "Naw, he's my boyfriend. We been together fifteen years."

"Never married, huh?"

"Don't see the point. Duke always says it'd just end in divorce."

Tate laughed at that. "Yeah, tell me about it."

Murphy glanced over at him as she began typing on her computer. "How long were you married?"

"Six years."

"No way. You don't look old enough. You get married in high school?"

Tate laughed. "Nope. I was 27."

She considered that for a moment. "Sorry it didn't work out."

He shrugged.

She spent the next few minutes typing on the computer. Tate looked around, taking in the feeling of the precinct. The sheriff's office was about a fourth the size of his old department, but many of the elements were the same – a stale smell of burnt coffee, metal furniture, computers that had seen better days, and a couple of moveable white boards. On one he saw a picture of Vivian Bradley with her name under it, followed by some scribbles he figured were notes on her case. A few deputies moved about the room, talking on phones, or filing stuff in metal cabinets along the walls.

"You want coffee or something?" Murphy asked.

Tate shook his head. "Naw, I'm good." He shifted around. A hallway led directly behind him, disappearing around a corner. "What's back there?"

"The john. You gotta go?"

"Just the john?"

"You're not sitting in on the interrogation, Mercer, so leave it, will ya?"

Tate slumped in the chair.

"It gets under your skin, doesn't it?"

"What?" he asked.

"Not being in the loop anymore."

Tate waved that off. "I don't miss it, if that's what you mean."

"Really?"

"No." He looked away, afraid she could see more than he wanted her to see.

She continued typing away. "Why'd you leave it?"

His eyes whipped back to her face. "What?"

"Why'd you leave the force?"

He rubbed the tattoo on his arm. "My partner died. Seemed like a warning, you know?"

Murphy met his gaze. He tried to maintain eye contact, but he couldn't. He looked away again, swallowing hard. She went back to typing. "That's a bitch," she muttered.

Tate nodded. Yep, it was a bitch.

"Huh," she said, letting her hands relax on the keyboard.

"What?" He reached for his reading glasses in his shirt pocket and put them on, then he leaned forward to see the screen.

"Arnold just has the one car registered to him – the Seville."

"Any traffic violations?"

"Nothing."

"No speeding tickets, DUI's?"

"Nada."

"Parking tickets?"

"The guy's squeaky clean. Registration up to date, everything."

Tate braced his chin on his fist. "Then what car was it that pushed Vivian into the ravine?"

Murphy shook her head, biting her bottom lip.

"What car forced me to the side of the road?"

She shook her head again.

"And what car was idling outside of Zion's house last night?"

She leaned back in her chair. "Well, it wasn't a Cadillac Seville, I can tell you that."

"So that begs two questions."

"Go on."

"If he's your man, where'd he get the other car or actually, two cars, 'cause I'm sure the one I saw both times was black?"

"And your other question?"

"If he's not your man, who the hell is?"

Murphy touched her nose with her finger. "Bingo."

# CHAPTER 17

Zion just couldn't get the different coffees in her head. And then people wanted to alter the basic recipe with changes of their own. It frustrated her and confused her and made her very slow, which frustrated them. She could handle the monetary part of running her own business. She could handle the customer part if she wasn't making coffee. And she could handle the frenetic energy of it – she was high energy herself – but she couldn't handle the damn machine.

It spit at her or sputtered or made such horrible grinding noises, she was sure she'd done it permanent damage. Deimos had told her yesterday he'd never heard it make such a noise before. Awesome. Just fantastic. She wasn't even a week into her new life and already she felt like a failure, and yet she was loving it.

The day sped past and she enjoyed working with Dottie and Deimos. Dottie took everything with a calm, easy-going stride, while Deimos was fun. He made jokes or sang silly songs or did ridiculous impressions that had her laughing so hard her mascara ran.

Today, Dottie suggested they switch roles and she'd operate the blasted machine, while Zion kneaded the dough for the sweets Dottie made every day. Zion actually found she enjoyed the baking and had an affinity for it. She'd never known that before.

Gabi had tried to teach her to bake, but like most things Gabi did, she did with great enthusiasm and little talent. After burning batches of cookies, nearly giving them salmonella from undercooked piecrust, or creating cakes that fell like a petulant soufflé, Gabi declared baking a bust and never endeavored to teach Zion again.

Today the morning rush passed quickly. Zion pulled out the first few batches of baked goods and refilled their display cases, then looked around for the next chore, but Dottie put a chai tea in her hand.

"We're good. The morning rush is over. You deserve a break, sugar."

Zion smiled and sipped her tea. "Today went better, don't you think?"

"I think it went splendid. It also gave me a much needed break." She held up a hand. "I think I've got a little arthritis in my hands, so you taking over some of the baking might be good for me. And you're a natural at it. Tomorrow I'll show you how to make my famous cinnamon sticks."

Zion flushed with pride at the compliment. It felt so good to be appreciated for what she did, and even better, to be making money at it. "Is this pretty typical of how busy things are all the time?"

"It gets worse in the summer when the tourists arrive and if we get a heavy snow, Lord have mercy. Then it's the skiers." Dottie laughed. "Yeah, it's pretty busy most of the time."

Zion laughed with her, then sipped her tea. "I put in the ad for part-time help."

"That's good. We can use it."

"Will you help me interview the candidates? I don't really know what I'm looking for."

Dottie touched her arm. "I'd be happy to help, sugar. You got it."

Zion looked out over the nearly empty shop and blew out air. It felt good to see a tangible accomplishment for a change. "Do you mind if I run down to the *Hammer Tyme* to see Tate?" She wanted to talk to him about Vivian's murder, but for some reason, she didn't feel comfortable talking about it in the coffee house. She just wasn't sure who she should trust.

Dottie gave her a speculative look. "The *Hammer Tyme*, huh?"

"I just want to thank him for what he did the other night and get his suggestions on some things I want to do with the cottage."

"Right," she said and winked. "Go on and take your time."

Zion set her tea down, untied her apron and put it under the counter, grabbing her purse. "I won't be long. I have to get back and feed Cleo."

"I'll feed her. I get a kick out of it. She's growling now when she drinks from her bottle."

"I know. She's a fierce little tiger." Zion started for the door. "Don't worry about it though. If it gets busy, Cleo's big enough to wait. She has a few kibbles in there to tide her over. I'll be on cell if you need me."

"Don't fret, sugar, and get going."

She enjoyed the walk down to the *Hammer Tyme.* Carmen was out in front of the *Knitatorium*, sweeping the walk. She waved at Zion. "Buenos días, chica," she said.

"Buenos días," Zion called back. "How are you this morning?"

"Bueno, very good, yes."

*The Bourbon Brothers* weren't open yet, but the spicy sweet scent of barbecue wafted out of their shop. It made Zion's stomach growl and she realized she hadn't had breakfast in all of the rush. She was going to have to make time for that if she was going to be working this hard.

Glancing in the windows of *Trinkets by Trixie*, she saw some new blown glass hummingbirds hanging from fishing line in the window. As they caught the light, they glowed iridescently. She thought Gabi might like one. She'd have to pick one up before she went home tonight.

The hanging pots bursting with colorful flowers created a festive atmosphere on Main and she was glad she hadn't taken the easy way out and sold to the first bidder, which would have been Harold Arnold and his conglomerate clients. That would have been a mistake.

Her cell phone rang and she fished it out of the pocket on her purse, thumbing it on without looking at the display. She figured it was probably her mother. Gabi had called her twice a day since she went back to San Bruno. If she'd known about the broken window, she would have packed her up and taken her home post haste.

"No, I didn't leave the stove on and the water isn't running in the bathtub," she said.

"Well, that's a relief," came a male voice.

Zion puzzled for a moment, then recognition dawned and she felt her cheeks heat with pleasure. "David, how are you? I'm sorry. I thought it was my mother. She calls constantly to make sure I'm still alive."

"You are, aren't you?"

"Close as I can tell," she said and giggled. Giggled? Her? Goodness. "What's up?"

"Well, I was just confirming our dinner for tonight. Remember, I thought I'd take you to our fanciest restaurant here in town."

"You mean the *Bourbon Brothers* isn't the fanciest?"

"God no. *Corkers Bar and Grill* is. You gotta wear pants for that place."

"I don't know if I have anything that formal."

He laughed. "So what do you say? Still up for me picking you up at 7:00?"

"I say yes. See you at 7:00."

"Bye, Zion," he said, caressing her name.

She felt another flush and smiled. "Bye, David."

Replacing her phone, she hurried across the street and pulled open Tate's door, wincing when the buzzer sounded. He looked up from behind the counter, his face lighting when he saw her. She glanced around the store, marking that it was darker than usual.

"Is a light out?"

"What?" he asked. He'd been scribbling on a notepad, but he shut it and took off his glasses, laying them on the cover.

"It's dark in here."

"Oh." He hurried out from behind the counter. "I forgot to put up the blinds. We're trying to save the antique floor." He stepped beyond her and lifted the blinds on the window by the door, letting the light in.

Zion surveyed the sun-damaged floor. "Antique, huh?"

"Well, you know, that's what you call anything old if you don't want to say it's just…old."

She smiled at him. "Where's Logan?"

"School. He goes twice a week in the mornings."

She nodded. It didn't seem right that he wasn't in school full time.

"So, what brings you by? Did you need a doodad or something?" he asked.

"No, I think I've got all the doodads I need, but I might need a whatchamacallit."

"Well," he said, shaking his head. "Those are hard to find." He led the way back to the counter. "I'd offer you some coffee, but mine tastes like road tar."

"You have a lot of experience drinking road tar?"

"I was a cop, remember."

Perfect opening, she thought. "Speaking of that."

He paused in going around the counter and his expression grew wary. She figured he wasn't much older than she was, but there was something ancient and tired in his eyes. Immediately he started scratching at his tattoo.

"Speaking of what?"

She placed her purse on the counter. "I want to help you with Vivian's case."

"You want to…"

"Help you with Vivian's case."

"Zion…"

"Hear me out. I may not have known her, Tate, but she was my mother."

"Which is why you shouldn't be involved."

"But I am involved."

"How do you figure?"

"Someone threw a rock through my window last night."

"Which should scare you enough to keep you far away from this."

"Well, you don't know me very well."

His brow arched.

"I don't scare easily."

He sank down on his stool and sighed. "You should. This is a murder investigation, Zion. Someone wanted Vivian dead, and someone's trying to terrorize you."

"Harold Arnold."

"I'm not sure it's him."

"Why not?"

"It's just so obvious."

"Sometimes obvious is…"

"Is?"

"Well, obvious. You said it yourself, this wasn't done by a professional."

"I don't remember saying that."

"You said the attacks are juvenile."

"I don't remember saying that either."

"That's because I just did."

He tilted his head in question.

"See, I can help you. I can give you an outside perspective."

"Zion."

"Tate, I'm not asking to carry a gun. I'm not asking to go interrogate some perps."

"You need to never say that again," he answered, narrowing his eyes.

"I'm just asking to go over paperwork with you. I have a business degree. If there's anything I know, it's paperwork. I won't get in the way. I won't be in any danger. And I won't cause any trouble, but right now, you and Sheriff Wilson could use another set of eyes on this."

"Sheriff Wilson will never agree to this."

"Which is why he doesn't need to know. You said you were brought on to consult. Well, let me consult with you."

He considered for a moment. "I'll tell you what. We'll start small. I'll play the tapes for you and you can listen to them, see if they seem familiar to you in any way. Then I'll think about the rest of it."

"Can we hear the tapes now?"

"Now?"

"Yes, now. Vivian's case isn't solved, is it?"

"Zion," he groaned.

"Please, Tate. Let me hear the tapes. I know I'll figure something out."

Tate shook his head wryly, but he led her back into the storeroom and played the tapes for her. He played them a few times over and she listened with her nose scrunched up in concentration. Clicking the mouse to stop them, he gave her a wry smile.

"Did you figure something out?"

She scrubbed a hand across her nose. "Not yet. But I will."

"Mmmhmm," he said.

The voice wasn't familiar. In fact, she wasn't sure it was a human voice. And the words weren't really directed at Vivian. They were sort of generic as far as threats went. Something else bothered her about the messages, but she couldn't put her finger on it.

The buzzer over the door rang. Tate rose and she followed him back into the hardware store, but it was only Logan coming in for work.

"Heya, Zion," said the teenager, holding up a hand.

"Heya, Logan. How are you?"

"Fine. What're you doing here?"

"I'm helping with the investigation."

"No, you're not," said Tate.

She glared at him, then beamed a smile at Logan and grabbed her purse off the counter, moving toward the door.

"I am. He just doesn't want to admit it yet." She patted Logan on the shoulder. "Talk to you soon, partner," she called back to Tate.

"You're not my partner."

"Sure thing, buddy," she said and pulled open the door.

"We're not buddies either."

"Soon," she said and winked at him, enjoying his look of frustration. "Very soon," she said and walked away down the street.

* * *

When Zion got back to the *Caffeinator*, Deimos had arrived. He and Dottie were dancing around to some 70's funk and having a good time, making macaroons. A few customers occupied the tables, their head bopping to the music, and Van Tiernan sat in his place on the couch, his laptop balanced against his thighs. He looked up and just stared at her as she stepped into the store.

"Howdy ho, boss lady," called Deimos, raising a flour-covered hand.

"Howdy ho, Dee," she called back, then smiled at Van Tiernan. "Is all this funk disrupting your concentration?" she asked him.

He didn't bother to look around. "I tune it out."

"So I heard you tell Tate you were working on the story for your game? Don't they have to have that first before they can do the CGI or whatever it is?"

"I'm working on some backstory, giving the main character some history, some motivation for what he does. How does a good kid go dark? What pushes him to step outside the law?"

"You mean the B&E."

"Right."

"Can you show me?" She took a seat on the edge of the coffee table before him.

"Hold on," he said, clicking away at the keyboard, then he turned the laptop and showed her a city street with houses on both sides. A boy walked up to the front of the closest house and studied it, then he looked away. Some words appeared on the screen. "Those will be voiced over soon."

She nodded.

The boy turned and started running toward the side of the house, disappearing down a dark, narrow alley.

"He's going in through an open window on the second floor. The player has to figure out how to get up there."

"I see. Clever."

The screen went blank. Van Tiernan turned the laptop, so he could click some more. The scene showed the same street. Suddenly the boy came racing out of the alley and into the street, running fast. A black sedan pulled up next to him and the door opened.

Zion narrowed her eyes on it. Black sedan? Well, it was pretty cliché for gangster movies and such.

"Who's that?" she asked Van Tiernan, pointing at the car.

"His posse." When she gave him a skeptical look, he shrugged. "His gang."

"Oh, I see. Well, it looks like the story's coming together."

Van Tiernan frowned. "Why wouldn't it be?"

"No, I mean, it looks good."

He stared at her unblinking, then went back to the laptop. Zion sighed. So much for making new friends. Pushing herself to her feet, she wandered over to the counter and stashed her purse under it, then she pulled out her apron, tying it around her.

"I need to feed Cleo."

"Already done," said Dottie, removing her own apron. "Now that you're back, if you don't mind, I'm gonna head out. I have a doctor's appointment today."

"Oh, I hope everything's all right."

Dottie gave her a disarming smile. "When you're a woman of a certain age, doctors like to see you a lot. I think they're trying to get as much insurance money out of you before it's too late."

"Oh, Dottie," said Zion, laughing and touching her arm.

"I'll see you in the morning, sugar," she told Zion, then she slapped Deimos in the rump. "I'll see you in the afternoon."

Deimos rubbed the spot with the back of his hand. "That's sexual harassment and I'm pressing charges, dude."

"No, you're not," said Dottie.

"You're right," he said, "I'm not."

Zion smiled at their exchange, feeling a flush of happiness. Going to the sink, she washed her hands. "So what can I do?"

"Dust those wedding cookies with powdered sugar," he said, pointing at the small white cookies on a baking sheet.

Zion picked up the powdered sugar dispenser as Dottie moved out of the back, waving as she headed for the door. "Toodles," she called.

"Toodles," called Zion in return.

"Later gator," said Deimos as Dottie disappeared from sight.

Zion and Deimos worked silently together for a while. A few people came and a few people left. Zion let Deimos work the espresso machine while she took money and fetched stuff from the kitchen. During a lull, Van Tiernan got up from the couch and went to the bathroom.

Zion watched him go, then she edged closer to Deimos. "You ever play his B&E game?"

Deimos glanced over at the hall, then rocked on his heels. "Once or twice. It didn't have good ratings."

"*B&E-1*? It didn't have good ratings?"

"Naw, you can look them up yourself. People said it was stiff, didn't have heart. Just a bunch of car chases and shooting, but not a lot of story. People who play RPG's want a story too."

Zion nodded, considering that. Van Tiernan appeared from the back and Deimos made a locking motion with his fingers at his lips to keep her from saying anything more, but he'd just piqued her curiosity.

* * *

When the afternoon rush was over, Zion excused herself and went into her office. She fed Cleo a bottle and then sank down at her desk, turning on her computer. The black sedan in Van Tiernan's game bothered her a little, but she was sure he was just using a gangster trope for effect.

She searched for *B&E-1*, locating it in an online gaming store. Pulling it up, she read the reviews as she stroked Cleo's black fur. The kitten settled on her lap, purring and kneading Zion's jeans with her claws.

The reviews of the game were brutal. *No heart. No soul. Mindless gunfights and car chases.* Another read, *Did Cyclone employ a robot to make this game? Seriously, no emotion whatsoever and the dialogue is the worst cheese.* The lowest rating made Zion wince. *B&E-1 just proves that old axiom about a monkey typing on a typewriter eventually producing the next great American novel. The same idea holds true that a million Cyclone game designers typing on a computer will eventually produce a decent* RPG *game. This is not that game.* Ouch, she thought.

Zion searched for *Cyclone Games.* A newspaper article appeared on the search engine. She clicked on it. *Cyclone Games* had gone through a restructuring period about a year ago due to poor sales. The article talked about their stocks dropping in value and the CEO being asked to resign.

She chewed on her inner lip. Interesting. That meant there was more pressure than ever for Jackson Van Tiernan to make *B&E-2* the best game it could be. His career could literally be riding on this.

She picked up Cleo and planted a kiss on her head before depositing her back in her bed.

"Hey, boss lady," said Deimos, poking his head inside. "The gambling grannies have just pulled in and we're swamped."

"The what?"

"The gambling grannies? You know those busses that take old folks to South Shore to play a little blackjack and slots."

"Oh, right. A tourist bus just pulled in."

"Isn't that what I said?" asked Deimos, tilting his head at her.

She laughed. "'Fraid not, but I got your back, Jack."

He laughed at that and they both went back to work.

* * *

Zion dressed in a black sheath dress and red pumps for her dinner with David. She pulled her hair into a French twist and put on a little more makeup. In the middle of primping, Rebekah called, so she pulled her up on video chat and had her critique her outfit.

Rebekah suggested a red scarf to match the red shoes. "So you're not going to dinner with the ex-cop?"

"Tate? No, we're just friends."

"What does this Bennett guy do again?"

"Lawyer."

"Oh, that's so much better. Yeah, go for that one. A cop turned hardware store owner is just asking for you to be a housewife in slippers."

"Why slippers?"

"Don't all housewives wear slippers?" she asked.

"Wow, you have so many stereotypes, it's amazing they let you stay in San Francisco," she scolded Rebekah.

"Pshaw," said Rebekah. "Someone needs to say it like it is."

A knock at the door distracted Zion. "He's here. I gotta run."

"Put on a little perfume. It doesn't hurt to smell nice either. Remember, we like lawyers – they're better than doctors."

Zion waved her off and disconnected the call, then she hurried into the living room and opened the door. David stood on the porch, inspecting the plywood Tate had nailed over the hole in her window.

"What happened?"

She shrugged. "Just some punk kids, I'm sure. It'll be fixed by the end of the week."

He shifted his focus to her. "You look very nice. Are you ready to go?"

"Yeah, just let me get my handbag and check Cleo one last time."

"Cleo?"

"Cleopatra, the kitten I found."

"Right."

"Come in," she said and hurried back to her room to check on the kitten. She was sleeping in her box, her little belly full of formula and cat food. Zion stroked her ears and she trilled in her sleep, flexing her paws. Grabbing the red handbag off the bed, Zion shoved her phone inside. Realizing that it might get cold later, she went to the closet and pulled out a pashmina in red and orange, slipping it around her shoulders.

She found David inspecting the hole from the inside of the living room. He turned at her approach. He wore a suit, but it was a bit less formal, the lapels wider, the tie a paisley blue and tan. She couldn't deny he was handsome.

"Are you sure this was done by kids?" he asked.

She took his arm, directing him to the door. For some reason, she didn't want to talk about it tonight. "Sure. Who else would it be?"

He stepped onto the porch and she followed him, locking the door behind her. He led her down to the large

Range Rover parked in her driveway, a hand in the small of her back, and opened the door for her, shifting the hand to her elbow to help her climb inside. She smiled at him as he shut the door for her and hurried around to the driver's side.

"I hope you're hungry," he said.

"Definitely," she answered and turned to face him. As they drove down the street, she glanced at Tate's house. His lights were on, but his curtains were closed. She wasn't sure if he was home or not.

"So, let me preface this by saying I'm really glad you moved to Sequoia, but it must be hard to leave everything behind like you did."

"I miss my family and friends, but I definitely don't miss the job."

"Really? But it had to be so much more satisfying than this one."

"You'd think, right? But it was mostly telling desperate people they couldn't have medications they needed and I hated it."

"But San Francisco? God, I'd give anything to work in the City."

"I do miss that. San Francisco's so vibrant, so alive, but right now, this feels right. I actually enjoy smelling the forest rather than car exhaust in the mornings."

"If I could, I'd move to San Francisco in a heartbeat."

"I think you said you went to college in Reno?"

"Undergrad. Got my law degree in Sacramento."

"Did you like Reno?"

"I guess. I don't know. Something about it always felt temporary to me."

"And Sacramento?"

"I thought of maybe going into politics for a while, but Dad had a heart attack, so I came home to help him run the practice. I honestly didn't think I'd still be here after three years."

"I know the feeling. I was at my job for three years too."

He pulled into a parking lot filled with cars. A neon sign proclaimed the place as *Corkers*. Dusk was just beginning to fall as they got out of the Range Rover and moved toward the restaurant. David had called ahead and reserved a table for them.

The hostess quickly settled them in their spot and gave them menus. Zion looked around at the pleasant atmosphere – the wood paneling, the subtle western accents like a wagon wheel, a barrel, and rope-edging on the partitions between the booths.

"So, they're famous for their fried chicken and cornbread."

Zion gave a lift of her brows and opened her menu. She didn't remember the last time she'd eaten fried chicken. It was probably at her grandmother's house before she died. Joe Sawyer's mother had been a regular southern bell, who liked most things deep-fried.

A middle-aged waitress came over wearing a black apron that read Corkers across the front in white cursive. "Can I get you something to drink?" She smiled at David. "Good evening, Mr. Bennett."

"Good evening, Rose."

"How's your daddy?" she asked.

"Doing well. Thank you for asking." He motioned to Zion. "This is Zion Sawyer. She inherited the *Caffeinator* in town."

Rose's dark eyes shifted to her. "Oh, you're Viv's daughter. She was a wonderful lady."

"Thank you," said Zion, feeling a pang as she always did when people mentioned Vivian. They always said nice things about her, but Zion had no frame of reference and it made her increasingly sad.

"So, how about a bottle of wine? We have a few more bottles of that Cab you liked so much, Mr. Bennett."

"Red okay?" asked David.

"Sure."

Rose nodded and hurried away.

"Mr. Bennett, huh?"

He shrugged. "It goes with the territory. At least she didn't call me esquire."

Zion laughed and looked at her menu.

"So, what looks good?" asked David.

"I think I might have the salmon."

"Good choice. It's usually fresh and the chef cooks it in wine and capers. I've never had it that way before."

Zion smiled at him and felt herself relax as Rose returned and poured their wine. They placed their orders, then spent their time talking about their families. Zion talked a lot about Gabi and Joe, how hard it had been to be so far away from them in Los Angeles while she was at school.

David listened attentively, his hands curled around his wine glass, the candle in the middle of the table highlighting the breadth of his cheekbones. He told her about his father's heart attack, how his mother had no idea about the state of the family's finances, and how he'd had to step in and review everything, despite his father's protest. As an only child, he felt it was his responsibility to keep the family together during such a difficult time.

"But he's much better now, right?" Zion asked.

"Like a cantankerous old bear. He's dropped weight and exercises regularly, and we try to keep him away from the *Bourbon Brothers Barbecue*, but that's almost impossible."

Their dinners arrived and they began to eat. Zion was surprised to realize how hungry she was. The salmon flaked apart and melted in her mouth, leaving behind a subtle taste of wine. Just as they were finishing up, a figure loomed beside their table, startling both of them.

Zion placed her hand against her throat, feeling her heart pounding.

Harold Arnold glared down at her. "You did this to me!" he said, and his breath reeked of alcohol. "Why? What did I ever do to you?"

"I don't know what you're talking about," she said, looking around in embarrassment. "I didn't do anything to you."

"You got me arrested!" he said loudly.

"Okay, I think that's enough," said David, tossing his napkin onto his plate. "You're causing a scene, Harold."

"Outsiders shouldn't be allowed to come in and disrupt everything. You could have just sold the business and gone home."

"That was my decision and I had a right to make it," said Zion.

"I gave you a reasonable offer. How hard was it? But you had me arrested instead."

"I'm not discussing this with you, Mr. Arnold. You're obviously drunk." Zion could see other patrons shifting around to watch the exchange.

"It was so easy. Just accept the offer and get out, go home. That's all you had to do and the other business owners would have caved. That's all you had to do."

David rose to his feet. "I said that's enough, Harold. Let me escort you to your…"

Arnold shook him off. "Get off me, traitor. How can you work for this woman?"

David reached for his cell phone. "I'm gonna call Sheriff Wilson, Harold."

For the first time, Arnold's face drained of color and he held up his hands. "Okay, don't do that. Just don't do that. I'll leave. I'll go." He shot a final look at Zion. "You should have just taken the offer," he said and turned, walking unsteadily away.

Zion stared at the table for a moment, her heart pounding. "Maybe you should call the sheriff just to keep him from driving under the influence."

"You're right. Give me a minute, okay?"

She nodded and watched him walk after Arnold, his phone to his ear. She felt humiliated and a little scared. Should she have taken the offer? How desperate was he to please his deep pocket clients? What would he do to get his way? And now he blamed her for Sheriff Wilson arresting him? But that didn't seem right. No one had told her he'd been arrested. Just that he'd been questioned about the spray paint.

David returned a few minutes later. "One of the busboys was leaving and offered to drive him home. He finally agreed." He touched her shoulder. "You okay?"

"Yeah, I'm fine, but would you mind taking me home?" She just wanted to be in the safety of her own cottage with her kitten, not that she'd felt that safe just a few hours before when someone had thrown a rock through her window.

"I don't mind taking you home. I'm sorry about that."

"So am I, but it's not your fault. I had a nice time until the end."

David took her hand, squeezing lightly. "I had a good time too, Zion. Maybe you'll agree to do it again? But next time, we'll go out of town a bit further."

She forced a laugh and gathered her things. "I'm really sorry, David."

He placed a hand in the small of her back, directing her toward the door. "Stop saying that. You have nothing to be sorry about. Harold was just drunk. He didn't mean what he said."

Zion considered that. She wasn't sure she believed the same thing. There was definitely something strange about the man – that was obvious.

# CHAPTER 18

Zion came through the door of the *Hammer Tyme* about noon. Logan waved to her. "Hey, Zion," he called.

"Hey, Logan."

Tate looked up from his laptop where he was checking the electronic inventory against what he'd physically counted himself. She looked more rested today, her auburn hair back in a ponytail, her green eyes sparkling. She wore a light pink pair of capris and a floral sleeveless collared shirt. A pair of white lace tennis shoes completed the ensemble. Tate knew he shouldn't be noticing what she wore, but it was hard when she smelled like springtime and sunlight.

"Hey," she said, placing her hands on the glass counter. "Can I talk to you?"

"Sure," he said, pointing to the storeroom. "You wanna step into my office."

She looked around the store. A couple of customers meandered, searching for things in the aisles. "Is this a bad time?"

"Nope. Logan can hold down the fort. Right, Logan?"

"Right." He gave Tate a speculative look, but Tate ignored it, lifting the counter so Zion could walk through.

The scent of her peppermint shampoo tickled his nose as she passed close to him. "Bring your laptop," she said, stepping through the archway into the storeroom. He caught up the laptop and followed her, setting it on the table.

She looked around. "I gotta say, this is more industrial, than private eye. The atmosphere, I mean," she proclaimed.

"Well, what did you want? Film Noir?"

"You mean like with a big oak desk, dark mood lighting, cigarette smoke curling around the fixtures, and you in a Fedora with suspenders." She eyed him as she took a seat at the table, pulling the laptop towards her. "I could see you in a Fedora."

"Then you'd have to be in a red dress with a hat, sporting a black lace veil and white gloves," he said, taking a seat across from her.

She studied him a moment without speaking and he felt his cheeks redden. He hadn't meant to be flirty with her, but there it was. "I see." She braced her chin on her hand. "So, I had an altercation with Harold Arnold last night at *Corkers*."

"Wait." He sat up straight. "What?"

"I was at dinner with David Bennett."

Tate felt his stomach roil at that.

"And he came to our table, telling me I got him arrested."

"Did you contact Sheriff Wilson?"

She waved it off. "He was drunk. David got him a ride home with a busboy."

"Zion, he's a suspect in your mother's murder."

"But you don't think he did it."

"I didn't say that. I said I didn't think you could prove his guilt because he had some spray paint in his garage, but this is different. You've got to tell Sheriff Wilson about this."

"Okay, I will after we're done, but I wanted to show you something."

Tate blew out air in frustration as she began typing on his laptop. Finally, she turned it around to face him. "Look at this."

He squinted at the game. He'd left his reading glasses on the counter in the shop. "What is it? A video game?"

"Not a video game. *B&E-1*."

Tate shook his head in bewilderment.

"Jackson Van Tiernan's game, the one he designed."

"Oh, yeah, so?"

"Look at the reviews."

"Let me get my glasses."

"Forget it. I'll summarize. It didn't get good reviews, and look at this." She pointed to another screen where a newspaper article appeared. "His company, *Cyclone Games*, is struggling. They let their CEO go and are downsizing."

"Why?"

"Their games aren't selling well."

"What does that have to do with anything?"

She turned the laptop and clicked some more, then she spun it around to face him again. "Look at that. It's a black sedan. The main character goes into a black sedan and speeds away from the crime scene."

Tate sat forward, staring at the sedan. "What are you saying?"

"I'm not saying anything, but don't you think it's interesting?"

He really wasn't sure what she meant, but he decided he might run the rest of the evidence by her again since she was here. He took the computer and pulled up the audio files Sam Murphy had given him. "Listen to this again and tell me if you recognize it now." He played the recording for her.

She always scrunched up her face as she listened and he found, even that, endearing. Man, he was hopeless. She was obviously interested in David Bennett. She'd gone to dinner with him at least twice that he knew of, possibly more.

"I still don't recognize it."

He sighed. He'd hoped she'd pick up something. "It doesn't sound familiar to you at all?"

"No, I'm sorry. In fact, it doesn't sound natural at all."

"You mean you think the voice is altered?"

"Maybe," she said, shrugging. "But the words themselves are…"

"Are?"

"Kinda ridiculous."

"I know. I keep thinking it's a gangster movie or television show, but I can't place it."

She braced her chin on her fist. "There's something…"

"What?"

"I just thought it'd be personal. Not so generic."

"Yeah, that's what I thought too."

"Well, I'll keep thinking about it, but what do you think about Van Tiernan's game?"

"It was a black sedan in a game about committing crimes. It doesn't exactly scream motive, does it?"

Zion's shoulders slumped. "No, but we've got no leads and I'm getting frustrated."

"That's police work, Sawyer. It's mostly boredom and spinning your wheels."

"Well, I don't like it."

"Sorry."

She leaned back in her chair. "Now what?"

"Now nothing. Van Tiernan told me he only rides a bicycle. He doesn't even drive a car."

"And because he told you he rides a bicycle, you took that to mean he's never driven a car in his life."

Tate considered that. "Point taken."

"I mean I don't own a horse, but I've ridden one."

"Okay, I got it."

She laughed.

He couldn't help but smile at the sound. "I'll call my friend in the LAPD and see if she can run Van Tiernan's driver's license. It's worth a look."

"Thank you," she said, pushing herself to her feet. "Well, I've got job interviews to conduct, so I better get back."

"You're hiring?"

"Just part-time. Someone to help cover the shift between Dottie and Deimos. I'm just not very good with the machine and it gets so busy in there."

Tate nodded. "Well, good luck."

"Thanks," she said, turning her back on him. "See you soon."

"See you," he said, watching her stroll out of the storage room. Then he pulled the laptop around and clicked back to the reviews of the game, squinting at the screen. Damn if it wasn't a black sedan just like the one that had forced him off the road.

* * *

Tate waited until late afternoon before he called Darcy. He played around on the laptop a little, trying to find out more about Van Tiernan's game, but there wasn't much. As far as he could see, the game was only available in used copies through online gaming stores that specialized in "vintage" fare.

He pulled up Darcy's number and called her. She picked up at the last minute, just before he was sure it would go to voice mail. "This is getting to be a habit, Tater Tot," she said.

"Can you tap into the DMV records and see if a man named Jackson Van Tiernan has a car, any car registered to him?"

"Hold on." He could hear her shuffling papers. "Give me the name again."

"Jackson Van Tiernan."

"I thought you were giving up all this crime fighter stuff, Tate. Why are you getting sucked back in?"

"I'm just trying to help solve a murder for a friend."

"Is the friend female?"

"What?"

"You heard me. Is the friend female?"

"What if she is?"

"Mmhmm."

"It's not like that. We're just friends. In fact, she's seeing a lawyer."

"Oh, we hate lawyers," said Darcy, clicking away at her keyboard. "All cops hate lawyers."

"So, will you look up this Van Tiernan guy?"

"Sure, but it'll have to wait until I'm off duty."

"Gotcha. Just let me know whenever you can."

"I will. So this is a lunch and two bottles of wine now and I want a Napa label, not something you picked up at the bargain bin."

"Fine. Two bottles and a lunch. You're the best, Darce."

"I've heard that one before. Later, Tater Tot."

"Later," he said and disconnected the call.

* * *

After he closed the hardware store, Tate didn't want to go home. Knowing that Zion was only a few doors down from his house made him want to go over, order a pizza, hang out and talk, but knowing he might see David Bennett's Range Rover in her driveway made him feel annoyed. He hated the thought of her seeing the lawyer, not that he had anything in particular against David Bennett. He'd met him a few times and he seemed a decent enough guy; he just hated the thought of Zion with anyone.

He wasn't sure why he found her so attractive. She was pretty, but she wasn't the most beautiful woman he'd seen. She seemed smart, but she wasn't the most intelligent woman he'd met. She made him laugh and that was pretty much it. He hadn't had much to laugh at in a few years and he enjoyed her easygoing personality. She didn't seem to take herself too seriously, certainly not as seriously as Cherise had, and she seemed to enjoy life, even when it sent her some bumps.

Since he didn't want to go home, he went to his standby for the last two years – he went to see the Ford brothers. Stepping into the barbecue, he breathed deeply of the spicy aroma. As always it was choked with tourists and regulars, nearly every seat taken.

Daryl saw him and waved him to his spot at the bar, shaking his head to indicate he didn't want him to wait in line.

As he sank onto the stool, Cheryl came over and placed a glass of water in front of him and wiped off the spot with a dishrag.

"Hey, baby, how are you today?"

"Good, Cheryl. How are you? Busy, I see."

"Yeah, seems like the summer season starts a little earlier each year. Can I get you a beer?"

"I'd love one."

"And the usual?"

"You know it."

She smiled and moved behind Daryl to pull the beer as he waited on people in the line. He jerked his chin at Tate, flashing him a smile from white teeth. Through the window into the kitchen, Tate could see Dwayne and Al moving around, Al humming something under his breath.

Cheryl placed the beer in front of him and wrote out his order on a pad, slapping it on the order wheel. "The Tate Special," she called to Dwayne.

Dwayne looked out the window and held up his spatula in greeting. "Coming right up," he bellowed.

Cheryl moved back and leaned on the counter as Tate sipped his beer. "Dwayne said you were consulting on the Vivian Bradley murder?"

Tate set the beer down. "Yeah, Sheriff Wilson wanted some new eyes on it."

She gave him a speculative look. "Are you sure that's a good idea?"

He looked down into the beer mug. "What do you mean?"

"I mean are you sure that's healthy for you?"

He glanced at her and shrugged. "Had a few nightmares, but that happens no matter what."

"Are they worse?"

"Maybe, but…" He leaned closer to her and dropped his voice. "I don't know, Cheryl. It's kinda good too, you know, getting back into it, looking at evidence. I can't explain it."

"Facing your demons?"

Tate considered that. "Yeah, maybe." He sighed. "I always like the puzzle of a case, figuring it out. I just didn't like the guns, the shooting, the violence."

She covered his hand with her own. "Just make sure you know what you're doing, okay?"

He nodded.

The kitchen door opened and Dwayne stepped out, carrying his order. He set it down in front of Tate and shook his head. "I got a bone to pick with you."

Tate sat up straighter. "What'd I do?"

"Not you, your girlfriend."

"What girlfriend?"

"Daryl says you're sweet on the *Caffeinator* chick."

Tate glared at Daryl, but Daryl just laughed and shrugged.

Cheryl swatted her husband with her towel. "Don't go bending his ear about Tallah."

"You know what your girl did?"

"She's not my girl," protested Tate.

"She stole my daughter."

Tate frowned. "She what?"

"She put up an ad for part-time help. Tallah went for an interview today and she offered the job to her."

"Wait. So Tallah's gonna work for Zion?"

Dwayne nodded, looking menacing in his stained apron with a ham-sized fist on the counter. "She doesn't want to work here anymore. She's going to be a vegetarian and she can't keep slinging barbecue pork." He said the last in a mockery of Tallah's voice. "Can you believe that?"

Tate laughed.

"Do you see me laughing?"

"I'm sorry, but that's awesome."

"How do you figure?"

Tate took another sip of his beer. "Tallah's growing up."

Dwayne glared at him, but Cheryl said, "Mmhmmm," in agreement. "I think it's good she has something to put on her college applications besides working in her daddy's store," she added.

Tate held out a hand.

"It's a family business. Slinging barbecue pork is gonna pay for her college," protested Dwayne.

Tate gave his friend a sympathetic look. "If this is the only thing you've got to worry about, you ain't got no problems."

"What do you mean?"

"I mean Tallah's the most together teenager I've ever met. She's a straight A student, she holds down a part-time job, and she's respectful. You're one lucky guy, Dwayne, and you know it, so let her go work for Zion. It's what…two doors away, but it's good experience."

Dwayne pushed the pulled-pork sandwich at Tate. "Eat your pig."

"You could use some vegetables yourself," said Cheryl, studying his fare.

"I got coleslaw," said Tate, lifting the sandwich and taking a big bite.

Cheryl glared at him, then glared at her husband.

"He's got coleslaw," said Dwayne, then he retreated back into the kitchen.

* * *

The night was cool, but the stars were out as Tate walked down the sidewalk to the municipal parking lot and pressed the button to open the door of his pickup. His phone rang as he slid behind the wheel and he dug it out.

Darcy's name flashed on the display.

"Hôla, chica," he said.

"You been drinking?" she asked.

"Just a beer with dinner. You got anything for me?"

"So this Jackson Van Tiernan?"

"Yeah?"

"You know his car is registered in San Jose. Are you sure it's the same dude?"

"Wait? He has a car?"

"Yeah, but the car is registered in San Jose, not Podunk, Johnny-Get-Your-Gun Ville."

"Johnny-Get-Your-Gun Ville's in the next county."

She laughed.

"You looked up Van Tiernan?" Tate spelled out the name, fitting the key in the ignition.

"Yes, I double checked it too. It's not like it's a common name, Tate. It's not Bud Smith or nothin'," she said in a country accent.

"Man, you city slickers is all the same," he drawled back at her. "Just moufy, is what you is?"

She laughed again.

"So, can you text me the address registered to Van Tiernan in San Jose?"

"Tate, this is crossing some lines here. I could get in trouble."

"It's public record."

"Not entirely."

"Okay, can you tell me what sort of car it is?"

"Nissan Sentra."

"Sedan," he said, starting the engine.

"Yep. Four door too."

"What year?"

"Tate…"

"Please. There's another bottle of wine in it."

"You're gonna turn me into a wino."

"Naw, wine is culture. You can't get addicted to it."

"Right. The car's a 2010."

Tate felt his heart begin to speed up and he curled his fingers around the steering wheel, pressing the phone between his shoulder and cheek. "Color?"

Darcy sighed. "If I lose my job, you're paying me child support," she said.

"Please, Darcy, tell me the color."

"Graphite blue."

Tate slapped a hand on the steering wheel. "You're the best, Darce. You know that."

"Right. What makes you think this is the same guy, Tate? Jackson Van Tiernan with the graphite blue Sentra lives in S-a-n J-o-s-e!" she said, enunciating each syllable.

"I'll get back to you on that." Tate put the truck in reverse and pulled out of the municipal parking lot. "Be on the look out for your case of Two Buck Chuck."

"Hey, that wasn't the agreement…"

"Bye, Darcy."

"Bye, Tater Tot."

Tate mulled over the case as he drove out of town. If Van Tiernan was the owner of a blue sedan, he might have been responsible for Vivian's accident, but what was the motive? Harold Arnold had a motive, but he didn't have the vehicle. Van Tiernan hung out in the *Caffeinator* everyday and he was definitely strange, but that didn't make him a killer. Arnold had cans of black spray paint in his garage. That might make him a vandal, but it didn't make him a murderer. Van Tiernan had a black sedan in his B&E game, but that was a game and even Tate wasn't sure the car that had forced him off the road was black. Still, he knew it wasn't graphite blue. Where was the graphite blue car? Still, Van Tiernan didn't live in San Jose. He lived here, in Sequoia.

Tate pulled into his driveway and got out, walking to the street and peering toward Zion's house. He wanted to tell her what he'd found out, but the Range Rover in the driveway stopped him. David Bennett was there and there was no way Tate was going to intrude on whatever they were doing.

A wash of disappointment went through him, but he tamped it down and turned for his door, trying to banish the wave of loneliness that swept over him.

# CHAPTER 19

Zion washed up the few dishes she had left over from the previous night. David had called and told her he had some papers for her to sign and wanted to know if he could bring dinner. She'd agreed and he picked up sandwiches at *Up to No Gouda.*

The visit had been pleasant. She signed the papers, they ate, then they talked about their college days. At the end of the night, she thought he might kiss her, but he pulled back at the last moment and told her he wanted to get her mother's business all finished before they became more than client and lawyer. She agreed, but she was a little disappointed. She liked David and enjoyed spending time with him, but she also admired his ethics. A lawyer with ethics. Her mother would be surprised.

Her phone rang as she put Cleo in her carrier, loaded up her bottles and the wet cat food, and grabbed her keys. She pushed the phone on and braced it on her shoulder as she grabbed her purse.

"Hey, Mom, just heading to work."

"It's not even 7:30AM."

"Yeah, but the *Caffeinator* opens at 7:00AM. I try to get there to help Dottie before the morning rush." She stepped outside the house and set Cleo's carrier down as she locked the door, then picked it up again and carried it to the car.

"She doesn't need you at 7:00?"

"She likes to have an hour or so to make her dough before I come in. By the way, I'm learning how to bake and you'd be surprised at how good I am."

Zion could hear the amusement in Gabi's voice. "You sound happy?"

"I am. This is so much better than what I was doing before." She unlocked the Optima and settled Cleo in the backseat, strapping the carrier in with the seatbelt. Cleo mewed in protest.

"How's my grandbaby?" asked Gabi, hearing her through the phone.

Zion shut the door and got behind the steering wheel, starting the car. "She's getting so big, Mom." She put the phone on speaker and backed out of the driveway. "The vet thinks she can go to just cat food in a week."

"That's fantastic."

"How's Daddy?"

"He's doing great." She paused. "I miss you. I miss our Wednesday night dinners."

"I know. I miss you too."

"But you're not coming home."

"Not right now. I'm happy."

"That's all that matters. Well, I have a piano lesson later, so I need to practice. Talk to you soon."

"Bye, Mom." She disconnected the call and concentrated on driving into town. An Arnold Realty sign distracted her on a small Victorian house just on the edge of Main and she wondered if Sheriff Wilson had made any more progress on her mother's case. Just as she thought to call him, her phone rang again. She pressed the button on her steering wheel to connect the call. "Hey, Becks, this is early for you."

"Wendel asked me to marry him."

Zion gasped, pulling onto Main. "He did? When?"

"Last night. He made us a romantic dinner in his condo and he put the ring on my plate. It's a Tiffany's princess cut platinum gold…oh, I'll send you a picture of it."

Of course Rebekah would know exactly what kind of ring he bought. "Becks, forget the ring. What did you say?"

"What?"

"What did you tell him? Are you going to marry him?"

"Oh, I don't know."

"What do you mean you don't know? You've dated this man for two years. You told me not that long ago that you thought he was going to ask you. You must have thought this through, right?"

"Not really. I mean I knew he was going to ask eventually, especially after I refused to move in with him, but I haven't really thought much about my answer. He's a doctor, Zion, a doctor."

Zion pulled into the municipal lot and grabbed the phone out of the stand, pressing it to her ear. "You make it sound like he's unemployed. Do you love him?"

"Love him?"

"Yes, Becks, do you love Wendel?"

She was silent, which was something significant for Rebekah. Zion gathered her things out of the car and picked up Cleo's carrier. Finally Rebekah sighed. "I don't know," she said.

Zion hesitated. "Then that's a problem." She shut the car door with her hip and pressed the button to lock it, then she started down the street. "If you don't love him, you need to tell him no."

"But that's so hard. The ring is beautiful."

"Becks!"

"I know. I know. I've got to think about it."

"What would you feel if he weren't in your life? Would you be sad?"

"I'd be sad, sure."

"Devastated?"

No answer.

"You need to figure it out." A thought occurred to Zion. "Hold on. Did you take the ring?"

"He gave it to me."

"But you didn't give him an answer?"

"I said I'd think about it."

"And you took the ring?"

"That's part of thinking about it."

Zion laughed, pausing outside of the *Caffeinator*. She pushed the door open with her shoulder and saw Dottie behind the counter kneading dough. A few people were sipping coffee at the bistro tables. The smells, the sights, the soft piano music filled Zion and she drew it in, realizing she felt happy.

"I gotta go. I just got to work."

"You mean you got to the coffee house. That's not work, Zion."

No, it wasn't. Not really. She enjoyed it too much. "You're right. Hey, call me tonight, okay?"

"Okay."

"And Becks?"

"What?"

"Whatever you decide, I'm behind you."

"You'll be beside me as my maid of honor, but we can talk about that later."

"Okay, love ya."

"Love ya. Go make some coffee."

Zion hung up and hurried through the swinging counter. "Just let me settle Cleo and I'll be back out to help you."

"Take your time, sugar. Nothing's on fire out here."

Zion smiled at her and carried Cleo to the office, realizing that Dottie was right. Lord, she was beginning to like this freedom.

* * *

"And if you hold the spoon just so, you can make a little heart on top," said Deimos, showing Tallah how to create a design on the cappuccino.

Tallah was a beautiful girl, cocoa colored skin, big dark eyes, black braids with just a hint of fluorescent pink woven into the strands. She had a nose ring, but her clothes were properly conservative for work, black t-shirt with a rose decal in the center, jeans and sneakers. She didn't balk at wearing the pink apron that said *Caffeinator* on it. Zion wondered if she should think about getting some t-shirts with the shop's name on them too.

"Ugh. It looks like a blob," Tallah complained and then laughed with Deimos. "Maybe I can give it eyes."

"Practice, practice and more practice." He expertly drew a flower on the next coffee and held out his hands in triumph, then he passed it to the waiting woman, earning a bright smile. "Dude, you gotta just keep practicing and you'll get it." He nudged her with his shoulder and she laughed again, her attention focused on creating her next work of art.

"Look, I put a tail on this blob," she said, looking up at him with sparkling eyes.

Zion felt sure Tallah was going to fit in and Dottie was happy to get off a little earlier than usual. She mentioned she'd like to start coming in at 6:30 to get the baking started, then take off at 1:30. Zion didn't mind.

Picking up the bucket for dirty dishes, she carried it beyond the counter and began bussing the tables. She smiled at a couple of college aged girls who were focused on their laptops, then moved to the couches and reached for Jackson Van Tiernan's cup.

"Thanks," he muttered without looking up.

"No problem. Can I get you anything else?"

"Nope," he said, focusing on his screen.

Zion hitched the bucket up on her hip and moved around him toward the counter. Suddenly she heard a low voice coming from Van Tiernan's computer. "You know what I want and I always get what I want. People don't deny me. Tell me where it is and no one gets hurt. Don't be a hero. Just hand it over."

Zion stumbled to a halt and whipped her eyes over her shoulder. Van Tiernan had his game open on the screen, and a huge bald man with bulging muscles had a young kid pressed against a brick wall.

"Don't be a hero. Just hand it over," the hulking brute said again.

Van Tiernan clicked the mouse and the game went silent. He looked up at Zion. "Something wrong?"

Zion's gaze snapped from the game to Van Tiernan's face, but she couldn't find her voice. Her heart was pounding. "What?"

"Is something wrong?"

"What is that?"

"It's *B&E-1*. I was just playing it again to get some ideas for the next game." He shifted on the couch. "What's wrong?"

Zion shook her head, hurrying to the counter and setting the bucket on it, then she went through the swinging gate and pulled off her apron, shoving it under the counter. "I have to run an errand," she told Deimos.

Deimos and Tallah gave her strange looks. "Okay?" said Deimos.

"Watch Cleo for me. I'll be back to shut up, okay?"

"Okay. Everything all right?"

"Yeah, I just remembered something…um, an appointment I have." She hesitated, glancing over at Van Tiernan. He was still watching her, his eyes narrowed. "You're okay here, right?"

"Of course. You sure everything's all right."

"Fine. I'll have my cell if you need anything." She grabbed her purse from under the counter, then without hesitating, she hurried for the door and threw it open, turning down the street.

She almost ran to the *Hammer Tyme*, pulling open the door and hurrying inside. Tate wasn't behind the counter, but Logan waved to her. "Hey, Zion."

"Hey, Logan, where's Tate?" A few customers wandered up and down the aisle, but glanced up when she arrived.

"Getting some turpentine out of the storeroom."

Zion hurried toward the storeroom, lifting the counter and ducking under it.

"Is everything all right?" Logan asked, shifting toward her.

She almost ran into Tate in the entrance to the storeroom. He was carrying the tin of turpentine. "I need to talk to you." She pushed him in the chest and he took a step back, holding out the turpentine to Logan.

"Can you take care of that?" he asked the boy.

Logan gave them a bewildered look. "Sure," he said, accepting it.

Zion shoved past Tate and went to the laptop on the table, setting her purse beside it. "Play those audio messages for me again," she demanded.

Tate followed her, giving her a bewildered look. "What's going on?"

"Just play those messages, please."

Tate bent over the laptop and began clicking. He pulled up the messages and the two of them listened as they played. When it got to the part Zion wanted, she motioned for him to stop the tape. "Right there. Listen to that."

*You know what I want and I always get what I want. People don't deny me. Tell me where it is and no one gets hurt. Don't be a hero. Just hand it over.*

Tate listened, then shook his head. "I've heard it a million times, but I don't know where it comes from, Zion."

"I do. *B&E-1*."

"What?"

"Van Tiernan just played that same dialogue in my shop. I heard it. Every word."

"Are you sure?"

"Of course I'm sure. Download the game."

"You can only get it from used game stores."

"I heard it, Tate." She paced away from the table and back again. She knew it was the same dialogue. "You said it yourself. The messages seemed too cheesy to be real. That's because it wasn't. It was written by Van Tiernan for that awful game of his."

Tate sighed. "We need to talk to Sheriff Wilson."

"No, it isn't enough. We need more evidence."

Tate stared at the laptop. "Look, I called my friend in LA and asked her to see if Van Tiernan owned a car."

"And?" Zion moved in front of him, her eyes widening.

"Someone named Jackson Van Tiernan has a car registered to him – a Nissan Sentra, graphite blue."

"Get out!" she said, clapping her hands.

"Hold on. He's registered in San Jose."

Zion pointed at Tate. "*Cyclone Games* is headquartered in San Jose."

"Are you sure?"

"Completely."

"But the car registered to him is graphite blue. The car that forced me off the road and that was in front of your house had to be black, Zion."

"But the car that forced Vivian off the road was blue."

"I know."

"Maybe he had it painted to cover the damage."

Tate considered that. "But how can we prove it?"

Zion went to the computer and pulled up a search engine, punching in words. Tate took a seat across from her. Glancing up, she gave him a serious look. "When did you find out about the car?"

"Last night."

"Why didn't you come by and tell me?"

He looked down at the table. "David Bennett's Range Rover was in your driveway."

Zion studied him a moment curiously. So? That didn't mean he couldn't come over. Unless he thought something was going on between her and David. Did he care if she was seeing the lawyer?

"What are you looking up?" he said, jerking his chin toward the laptop.

Zion blinked and went back to her search. "Body shops."

"I'll bet they're all down in Visalia."

Zion chewed on her lower lip as she searched, then she pointed at the screen. "Nope. One here in Sequoia on Canyon Ravine Road. *Perfect Ten Auto Body Repair. We're the plastic surgeons of auto repair.*"

Tate frowned. "Wow."

Zion grabbed her purse. "Come on. We're going out there."

"What? Why?"

"To get evidence. If we can get them to tell us Van Tiernan got his car repaired there, we have evidence to present to Sheriff Wilson."

"They're not going to tell us anything, Zion."

She headed for the door. "You coming or not?"

"Zion." He hurried to follow her. "They're not going to tell us that."

"You don't know how persuasive I can be," she shot over her shoulder and headed for the outer door as well.

* * *

They rode in Zion's Optima. She pulled up a block away from the autobody shop and they sat, staring at the small building with the kelly green sign hanging from the facade. A garage stood to the left of it and they could see mechanics moving around, working on the cars.

Zion started to open the door.

He caught her arm. "You can't just go in there and demand to know if Van Tiernan had his car repaired. They'll never give you that information."

"Of course they won't." She climbed out, snatching her phone off the holder, and popped the trunk. Then she began rummaging through it, looking for something. She found a scarf and placed it over her hair, tying it beneath her chin.

He frowned at her. "What's that for?"

"People remember red hair, so I'm gonna hide it."

"And you're gonna tell them you arrived here from the 1950's, wanting information on auto repair."

"No, silly. We're going to pretend you have a convertible and I was protecting my hair from the wind."

Tate gave her a skeptical look. "And you think they won't remember you if you cover your hair?"

She put a pair of large sunglasses over her eyes. "What do men notice about women?" His eyes tracked involuntarily down to her chest. She shoved him. "Besides that."

"Hair?" he questioned skeptically.

"And eyes."

"What about my disguise?"

"They won't be looking at you."

He nodded in agreement at that.

She threw her purse over her shoulder, hooked her arm through his, and led him toward the autobody repair shop. The interior was a small one room waiting area that smelled of grease and gasoline. A man with oil stained hands and an oil stained shirt stood behind the counter. Except for a few chairs with cracked red cushions and an end table, there was no other furniture in the room.

"Hello," she said brightly.

As she expected, the man stood up, smoothing a hand over his protruding belly and snaking another hand through his thinning hair. His eyes tracked over her, ignoring Tate.

"Hey," he said and smiled, showing smoke stained teeth. "How can I help you?"

She fussed with the scarf. "We just rode over in my husband's convertible. Darling little car, but it's hell on my hair."

"No doubt," he said, smiling again. Zion read the patch over his left breast. *Darren.*

"Since he has such a cute little sporty thing," she said, turning to Tate and slapping him in the chest lightly. "I thought it might be fun to spruce up my car."

"Sounds good." He nodded, sparing a glance at Tate. "Darren, right?"

"Right."

She leaned forward. "It's my birthday next week and he does like to spoil me. Don't you, darling."

"Anything for the little woman," Tate said, gritting his teeth. He snaked an arm around her waist and gave her a warning squeeze.

She pushed away from him and approached the counter. "I'm just not sure what's possible or what I want. Can you answer some questions for me, Darren?"

"Sure."

"Do you have testimonials or reviews or anything that I can take a look at? I mean, I'm just not sure what can be done."

"No problem." He reached behind him and pulled out a photo album. "We do before and after pics, so customers can see what we can do and the results we get. Are you looking to change the color?"

"Yes, but it's a tricky one. The car's red and I want to go black."

Tate made a coughing sound.

"Can you do that? Can you completely change the color?"

"Is the pope Catholic?" said Darren, smiling again.

Zion giggled and accepted the album, leafing through it. The before and after pictures of cars in an accident were impressive. "Wow, you can make a car look like new, can't you?"

"Yes, ma'am, so changing the color's no problem."

She put her hand on her throat, studying the pictures. "I don't know. This car's my baby. I mean I'd really like to change it, but I'd hate to mess it up. It's such a pretty color of red right now." She turned toward Tate. "Your friend changed his car, didn't he? Jackson?"

Tate's face lost color. "I'm not sure," he said, clearing his throat.

"You remember, dear." She smiled at Darren. "He forgets things." She beamed at Tate. "He came here, didn't he? He said this was the best autobody shop in town."

"The only autobody shop in town," said Darren.

"That's right. I'm sure he had the work done here. He had a little body damage from an accident and then he wanted the color changed."

Darren shrugged. "We got lots of colors." He picked up a placard and held it out to her with swatches of color on it.

"These are lovely, but I'd really love to see the befores and afters of someone I know."

Darren leafed through the album. "Maybe it's in here."

"This was just a few weeks ago. He has a blue Sentra and he went to black. It had some damage to one of the front wheel wells. Right, darling?" She turned back to Tate.

"Yeah, um…" He scratched at his tattoo. "Right front, right behind the fender."

Darren moved over to his computer. "What was his name again?"

"Jackson Van Tiernan," Zion said.

Darren typed on the computer. "I can't give you any personal information."

"Of course not," said Zion. "Do you think you have pictures of the work though?"

"Yeah, for insurance. We take before and afters, upload them into the computer to send to the insurance companies. Then we print out the good ones for our book. I'll see if I got any pictures I can show you. I shouldn't be doing this, but if he recommended us."

"He did. He said you were the most professional autobody shop he'd ever worked with."

Darren glanced at her, his eyes traveling over her again, then he screwed his mouth to the side in concentration. Zion could hear Tate swallow hard behind her. He was rocking on his heels, scratching the tattoo furiously.

She reached over and took his hand, pulling him up beside her so he would stop.

She jumped when the printer suddenly started up. Darren gave her a speculative look, so she laughed. "It's so quiet in here." She leaned on the counter. "Did you find anything?"

"Yeah, right front wheel well damage, just like you said. He also wanted to take the car darker, tint the windows." He looked at the monitor. "Damn, we did a nice job." He reached down and pulled out the printer paper. "Sorry it's just black and white, but you can see how much darker it is now. And you can see where the damage was. Just like new."

Zion's hand shook as she reached for it. "This is amazing."

Tate tugged her back from the counter. "Thanks. We'll be in touch."

"You want me to write up an estimate for the work?"

Zion's eyes whipped up to his face and she stared at him from behind her sunglasses. Did they want him to work up an estimate?

"Not yet. We just wanted to get some information," said Tate, taking a step back.

"What?" Darren straightened.

"Yeah, you know, now that I think of it, I might want a diamond ring instead, darling," she told Tate, turning toward him.

"What's going on?" asked Darren.

Tate pulled open the door and ushered her outside. "The lady gets what the lady wants," he said and then hurried out after her. Letting the door close behind them, they ran to the car.

Zion was laughing as they dropped into the seats and she started the engine. Looking up, she could see Darren standing on the sidewalk outside his building, staring after them.

She reached up to remove the scarf, but Tate stopped her. "Don't. Not until we're away from here."

"He's probably taking down my license plate number anyway."

"Probably. Guess you won't be having any work done on your car here in Sequoia, now will you?"

"Guess not," she said, pulling away from the curb and speeding back toward town. "Oh well." She held up the paper. "We got what we wanted anyway."

"Damn near gave me a heart attack in the process," Tate grumbled, then they both pealed off into laughter.

# CHAPTER 20

Zion drove directly to Sheriff Wilson's office and parked. Tate waited for her to come around the car, her eyes shining with excitement.

"Do you think we solved it?"

"Solved it?"

"The case."

"You mean Vivian's murder?"

Her face fell as the realization of what they were talking about sank in. "Oh, God, he's sitting in the *Caffeinator* right now." She gripped Tate's arm. "Tallah and Deimos are there. Maybe we should go there first and make sure they're okay."

Tate caught her and stopped her from heading back to the car. "The best thing we can do is get Sheriff Wilson to bring him in for questioning. Provided we have enough. It's pretty slim evidence, to be honest with you, Zion."

"No smoking gun," she said, then reached for her purse. "I need to warn Dee though."

"Warn him what? You tell him to watch Van Tiernan and he gets spooked. Let's talk to Sheriff Wilson. It's still early. The *Caffeinator's* probably filled with customers. I'm sure the sheriff will send someone by just to keep an eye on things."

"Okay." She tried to tamp down on her anxiety. "I just can't believe it's him, Tate. Do you really think Van Tiernan did this?"

"I don't know. I think it's more likely things got out of control and he didn't mean to hurt anyone."

"So you think it was an accident?"

"I do."

"Then why the phone messages and following you and throwing a rock through my window?"

"He got scared and wanted to cast blame elsewhere."

"The messages to Vivian happened before she died."

"I don't know, Zion. Let's go talk to the sheriff."

She nodded wringing the handle on her purse. Tate pulled open the door and ushered her in, then he pressed the buzzer. A tall, lean Hispanic man opened the window and narrowed his eyes on Tate.

"Can I help you?" he asked.

"We need to see Sheriff Wilson right away. It's important."

"Can I tell him who's asking for him?"

"Tate Mercer and Zion Sawyer. It's about the Vivian Bradley case."

"You're consulting with him on it?" said the man.

"Yeah."

The deputy held out his hand. "Emilio Vasquez."

"You were with the sheriff when he interrogated Harold Arnold the other day."

"Yep." He pressed the buzzer. "Come through."

Tate directed Zion to the door. Emilio led them through the precinct to the long hallway off on the left side. He came to the sheriff's office and knocked on the door.

"Enter," came Wilson's voice on the other side.

Vasquez opened the door and motioned them inside. Wilson rose to his feet when he saw them. "Ms. Sawyer, what a pleasant surprise," he said, directing her to a chair before his desk. "Tate."

"Sheriff Wilson."

Zion sank into the chair, clasping the printer paper in one hand. She settled her purse on her lap and moved to the edge of the chair. He knew she was about to launch into her story without waiting to be directed. He couldn't really blame her. It made him edgy thinking of Van Tiernan sitting in the *Caffeinator* all these days, and especially now that Tallah was working there.

"We're pretty sure this is the car that forced Tate off the road and was parked in front of my house the other night.

We're also pretty sure it's the same car that caused Vivian's accident." She set the paper on the desk before Wilson.

Vasquez had been leaving, but he stopped and turned back around. Wilson looked from Tate to Vasquez. "Come again. Who does the car belong to and how did you find it?"

Zion shared a glance with Tate, then she straightened. "It belongs to Jackson Van Tiernan and I'd really appreciate it if you'd send someone to my shop to bring him in for questioning. I don't like him being there with my employees."

Wilson held up a hand. "Hold on a minute. Jackson Van Tiernan? The gaming guy?"

"Yes. That's his car."

"How do you know?" He turned his focus on Tate.

Tate shifted uncomfortably in his chair. "She's right, Sheriff. We'll tell you, but could you send someone to the store? I know you can't arrest him right now, but it's really important that we keep an eye on him."

Wilson frowned. "Does someone want to explain to me what the hell is going on?"

Zion leaned forward. "It all started when I saw *B&E-2*."

"B&E?" asked Wilson.

"Two," supplied Zion. "There was a black sedan on the screen, just like the one that had been in front of my house the other night."

"Hold on. The sedan was in the video game?"

"Yes."

Wilson rubbed at his forehead. "This otta be good," he told Vasquez. Vasquez nodded and shut the door, moving around the desk to his side.

"I asked Deimos what he thought of *B&E-1* and he said…"

Tate leaned back in his chair and let her talk. Sheriff Wilson and Vasquez humored her, until she got to the part where she'd heard the dialogue that matched Vivian's phone messages. Now she had them.

He had to admit, the more he heard her talk, the more smitten he became. She really was something special, he thought and braced his chin on his hand, letting her paint her pictures.

* * *

After they finished outlining their investigation, Vasquez did his own DMV search and found Van Tiernan's car for himself. Wilson went to work on getting a warrant to search Van Tiernan's home, telling Zion and Tate to go back to their businesses and basically dismissing them from the case. Zion fumed at her dismissal, but Tate felt relieved. Catching the perp was up to Wilson now and he was finished with it. He could go back to his non-crime fighting life and relax again.

Zion drove them back to Main. He walked her down to the *Caffeinator*, where they were both surprised to learn Van Tiernan had left shortly after Zion had gone to Tate's store.

Tate warned her not to walk to her car alone and Deimos promised to escort her to the parking lot when they closed shop, then Tate went back to the *Hammer Tyme*, searching the side streets for Van Tiernan's bicycle. He saw nothing.

Logan had a lot of questions when he got back. Tate deflected most of them.

"Anything exciting happen here while I was gone?"

Logan shook his head. "Been kinda dead. Guy bought a tape measure, another some clippers, but other than that it's been slow."

Tate shrugged. Some days were just like that. He headed for the register, planning to count out the day's receipts. Maybe if he closed a little early, he could get back down to the *Caffeinator* to walk Zion to her car himself. Wilson had promised to call as soon as they figured anything out, but he was still nervous.

He punched the key on the cash register and the door popped open. He reached for the money just as Logan moved to the other side of the counter.

"Oh yeah, something weird did happen."

Tate stopped counting and glanced up at him. "What?"

"That gamer dude?"

"Yeah, Van Tiernan?"

"I guess. Anyway, he came in here about two hours ago."

Tate felt the color drain from his face. "What do you mean he came in here?"

"He walked through the door," said Logan, speaking slowly as if he were an imbecile.

"What'd he want?"

"He wanted to talk to you, but I told him you were out, so he left."

Tate released the breath he'd been holding. Okay, that was all. Nothing to get worried about. Even so, he reached over and touched the under-the-counter safe that held his gun.

"Oh, and he asked to use the bathroom." Logan shrugged. "I hope that's okay."

Tate's fingers stilled over the money in the cash register, then he closed the drawer and hurried into the storeroom. What the hell had Van Tiernan been looking for? His laptop? But it sat on the table where he'd left it that morning. He went over and touched the mouse pad, bringing up the log-in screen. It asked for his password. He typed it in and it went to the start screen. So no one had tried to get into his computer while he was gone. He looked around at the shelves, but he couldn't imagine there was anything there that would attract Van Tiernan's attention. He couldn't see anything at any rate.

Logan came to the doorway. "Is something wrong, Tate?"

"You said he wanted to use the bathroom. Did you notice if he did anything else back here?"

"Nope. Except I was with a customer at the time. Still, he wasn't back there long. He came in, asked for you, then asked to use the toilet. He was back a moment later and left."

"He didn't buy anything?"

"Nope, nothing. Did I do something wrong?"

Tate felt his stomach roil, thinking of Logan here all by himself, working alone. He had to be better than that. He couldn't keep leaving a kid to run his business. "No, you did nothing wrong." He moved toward Logan, placing a hand on his shoulder. "If you see Van Tiernan again, just avoid him, all right?"

Logan frowned. "Why?"

He didn't know what to tell the boy. He wanted to warn him, but Van Tiernan was only a suspect at this point. They really had no solid evidence that he did anything wrong. "Sheriff Wilson's taking a look at him. Just avoid him for now. How about I give you a ride home tonight?"

For the first time, Logan didn't argue. "Okay."

"Just let me cash out and we'll lock up. How about you sweep and close the blinds, while I clear out the cash register?"

"Sure." Logan went to do what he asked.

Tate took another look around, then for good measure, checked the wall safe to make sure it wasn't tampered with before he went back to the cash register.

* * *

Tate sat in front of Logan's house, watching the kid skateboard down to the door, hop off, kick the skateboard up into his hand, and bound up the cement steps. He turned at the top and waved to Tate. Tate waved back and watched him pull open the screen, unlocking the front door.

The entire house gave off an air of neglect. Weeds choked the small front yard, the trees were overgrown, and a rusted bicycle lay propped against the porch railing. A few slats in the railing had been broken out and the paint was peeling. One gutter hung off the front of the house, rusted through, and the screen door shut crookedly. Tate made a plan to come back and fix some things for Logan as soon as this mess with Vivian Bradley was solved.

He put the truck in gear and pulled away from the curb, thinking about the boy forced to grow up too quickly. No father, his mother sick with cancer, unable to attend school because he had to work. It was more than most kids dealt with and it made him feel all the more guilty for leaving him for so long today. The thought of Van Tiernan coming into his store sent a chill up his spine.

He jumped when the cell phone rang. He pushed the button on his steering wheel and connected it. Sheriff Wilson's gravelly voice came through the truck's speakers.

"Where are you?"

"Dropping Logan off. What'd you find out?"

"A lot. While we were waiting on the search warrant, Murphy and I decided to drive out to Van Tiernan's rental house."

"Okay?"

"He had a house in San Jose, but it was foreclosed on two years ago. Bank's been forwarding all his stuff here since then."

"Hm."

"But he's not living here either, Mercer."

"What do you mean?" Tate stopped at a traffic light, looking at the phone.

"He was evicted a month ago, moved all his stuff out. The owner agreed to let us in the place without a warrant. Nothing's here. No furniture, no clothes, no car."

"Shit." Tate swore and pulled off to the side of the road, running a hand through his hair. "Does the owner know where he went?"

"No idea. No forwarding address. Mail's piling up, but this guy's got nowhere to send it."

"Why'd he evict him?"

"Behind in his rent. Hasn't paid for two months."

Tate rubbed his temples. He was getting a headache. "Where's he been staying for a month and where did he stash the car after he got it repaired? I've only seen him on a bike."

"Well, you can figure he spends most of his days at the coffee shop."

"But his clothes are always clean and he's showered."

"Laundromats? We got truck stops a little ways out of town that have showers in them. You pay a few bucks and you can clean up."

"That's a start. Maybe someone would recognize him at one of those."

"I'll send Vasquez out with Van Tiernan's driver's license photo."

Tate realized he wished he could go. Shit, he was getting dragged back into this mess. "If you can locate where he gets cleaned up, you might be able to figure out where he spends the night."

"Yep."

"Sheriff?"

"What?"

"He came by the *Hammer Tyme* today."

"He what?"

"Yeah, when Logan was there. He asked to talk to me, but Logan told him I was out, so he asked to use the bathroom."

"The bathroom?"

"Yeah, it's through the storeroom. I checked everything and nothing's missing. My laptop was sitting on the table back there and I thought he might have tried to get into it, but it's password protected and that wasn't tampered with. The wall safe's also fine."

"So why'd he want back there?"

"No idea."

Wilson made a grumbling noise. "This guy wasn't even on my radar until today, Mercer."

"I know."

"Do you really think a stupid car in a game is going to unravel everything?"

"Stranger things have happened."

"I seriously don't like him coming by the *Hammer Tyme*. That means he knows you're involved somehow."

"I'm more worried for Zion. He threw a rock through her window. Why's he targeting her?"

"No freakin' idea. Warn her to watch out, okay?"

"I will."

"I'll call you as soon as I get anything."

"Thanks, Sheriff."

"Yep." Then he was gone. Tate replaced the phone in its holder, clicked on his turn signal, and pulled back onto the road. Part of him wanted to go to the truck stops and check them out, but the other part wanted to make sure Zion was all right.

In the end, Zion won out.

* * *

Tate knocked on Zion's door, grateful there was no silver Range Rover in her driveway. She opened on the second knock, holding Cleo in her hand. She wore a pair of capri sweats and a tanktop, her auburn hair pulled up in a messy ponytail. He noticed it was starting to show waves near her hairline.

"Tate, is everything all right?" She stepped back to let him in.

"I just wanted to make sure you were okay. I won't stay. Sheriff Wilson called with news about Van Tiernan."

"Come in."

He stepped over the threshold and she pointed at the couch. He walked to it and took a seat. She perched on the opposite end as they'd done the night he came over when her window had been broken out. She settled Cleo on her lap, stroking the kitten's back. Cleo began kneading Zion's sweats with her tiny claws and purring. Tate smiled at the animal.

"What did the sheriff say about Van Tiernan?"

"They found the house Van Tiernan's renting here in Sequoia and went out there. The house is empty. The landlord let them search it without a warrant. He evicted Van Tiernan for not paying rent. He had a house in San Jose, but that was foreclosed on."

"Wow, he's really having financial difficulties."

"Seems that way."

"It must be because the game company, *Cyclone*, isn't doing well."

Tate nodded. "That could be."

She thought for a moment. "But where is he now?"

"That's the problem, Zion. Sheriff Wilson doesn't know."

"I wonder if he's living out of the car."

"I'm not sure, but I remarked that Van Tiernan always has clean clothes. He's clean himself."

"That's true. In fact, he's always dressed like he's going to the office." She leaned forward. "He buys cappuccinos every day, Tate. How can he have money trouble?"

Tate smiled at that. "He probably sold off everything in the house, except his clothes. He might have had some savings put away. Not enough to keep a house running, but enough to tide him over until the *B&E* game comes out at Christmas."

"So he must have been pretty desperate. He spent most of his days in the coffee shop, but where does he go at night? How does he keep so clean?"

"Sheriff Wilson said there are a few truck stops, gas stations, around here that have shower facilities for truckers. A couple dollars and you can get clean."

"Should we go check them out?"

Tate felt alarm skitter through him. "No, we're done. It's up to the Sheriff's department now."

She gave him a coy look, chewing on her inner lip. Cleo had fallen asleep. "You gotta admit it was fun today in the autoshop."

"Zion," he warned.

"Just admit it. It was fun to go undercover."

He laughed. "That wasn't going undercover, but yeah, it was fun."

Her eyes sparkled and he realized he'd probably like doing anything with her. He liked spending time with her no matter what it was.

"But you've got to realize Van Tiernan's dangerous. We don't know what happened with Vivian, but if he caused her death…"

"I know." Her mischievous attitude shifted and she rubbed the back of her neck. "You're right." She looked toward the front window where the new glass glimmered in the last rays of sunlight. "You want some coffee, something to eat. Are you hungry?"

He realized that she probably didn't want to be left alone, not until they heard about Van Tiernan from the sheriff. "Sure, what do you have in mind? Pizza?"

"No, I made lasagna the other night. I can heat us both up a slice in the microwave."

"Lasagna? You cook?"

"Yeah, you don't?"

"I eat barbecued pork sandwiches a lot."

She laughed and settled the kitten on the cushion between them, jumping to her feet. "At the *Bourbon Brothers*, you mean?"

"You found out my dirty secret," he said, rising and following her into the pleasant kitchen. He took a seat at the kitchen table while she washed her hands and prepared their meal. "Can I help you?"

"Nope. Just gonna heat it up and it'll be ready. So, I'm really excited that Tallah's working with us."

"Dwayne wasn't happy about it."

She paused and gave him a worried look. "Oh, should I not have hired her?"

"Don't be silly. Tallah needs to get some independence. She's the best kid I've ever met. Straight-A student, plays sports, takes the hardest classes, but Dwayne watches her like a hawk."

"Sort of the opposite of Logan," she said, dishing up slices of lasagna onto two plates and putting them into the microwave side by side.

Tate sighed and fussed with the lace tablecloth. "It's not Logan's fault. His mother's really sick and his father's MIA."

She pulled a salad out of the fridge and tossed it with some salad dressing, then left it on the counter. "That's a lot for a kid to deal with at his age."

"Yeah, it is."

She took a bottle of wine from the fridge as well. "How about a glass with dinner?"

He smiled at that. "Sure."

She grabbed two wine glasses on her way to the table and poured for both of them. "White okay?"

"Sure."

The microwave dinged. She retrieved the plates and set them down, then grabbed silverware and the salad, handing the latter to him. "Dig in."

He dished up the salad and picked up his fork, taking a bite of the lasagna. The melted cheese, the spices, and the sauce filled his mouth with pleasure. He made an approving noise and reached for the wine, chewing and swallowing. "Wow, that's excellent."

She smiled at him and he was transfixed by how pretty she was. "So tell me all about Tate Mercer," she said, digging into her own food.

He'd just taken a bite of the salad and it lodged in his throat. He coughed a little and forced it down. "That's not a topic I like to discuss," he answered.

She looked up at him and he sensed the mood immediately shift. He almost knew it would happen. This was what always happened when people tried to get close to him. And he didn't blame them. It was human nature to share lives, swap stories, tell about war wounds, but he wasn't ready to go there. Not yet. Maybe never.

He looked down at the food, not sure how to smooth things over.

She started eating again. "The vet says I can stop feeding Cleo a bottle. She's already gained a half pound. Of course, she wasn't even quite a pound when we found her, but that's pretty amazing progress, don't you think?"

"I do," he answered, reaching for his wine, grateful for the change in subject, but he knew the spell had been broken. Any hope he had of making headway with her was gone and they were back to small talk. Score one for David Bennett, he thought, gulping his wine.

* * *

Tate didn't stay much past dinner. He kept hoping Sheriff Wilson would call and tell him they'd found Van Tiernan, but that call never came, so after helping Zion wash dishes, checking the locks on all the doors and windows, and admonishing her to call him if anything strange happened, he went home.

He tossed and turned in his bed, unable to get her out of his mind. He was attracted to her, he didn't like her seeing David Bennett, but he wasn't ready to open himself up to her yet. The memory of Cherise walking away when it got too hard still haunted him. Not that his marriage had been whole before Jason died. It had already started to disintegrate.

Finally, he threw the covers off and climbed out of bed, going to the living room and sitting in his favorite rocker. He picked up his reading glasses and put them on, then lifted the book and tried to concentrate, but he couldn't.

He found himself listening for cars going down his street, worried about where Van Tiernan might be hiding.

He fell asleep in the chair and woke with a start, his body drenched in sweat, hearing his own voice calling Jason's name. He sat up and stared around, confused by where he was. His glasses had fallen onto his chest and tumbled to the floor. His book lay there already.

He sat forward, bracing his arms on his thighs and snaking his hands through his hair. Morning light filtered through the front windows. He drew a deep breath to still the pounding of his heart and rose to his feet, picking up the glasses and book and laying them on the side table. Then he walked to the window and looked out.

The street was quiet and the sun was already shining. It was going to be another beautiful late spring day. Wandering into the kitchen, he started the coffee brewing. He knew he could go to the *Caffeinator* for his mint mocha chip freeze, but he felt a little embarrassed to see Zion. While the coffee brewed, he climbed into the shower, washing away the cold sweat of his dream.

Sleepy, but refreshed, he poured the coffee into a travel mug, grabbed his wallet, phone, and keys, shoved his glasses into his shirt pocket and walked to the door. He looked down toward Zion's house, but the Optima was no longer in the driveway.

Taking a sip of the hot coffee, he climbed behind the wheel of the pickup and started her, driving into town. He wondered if he should detour by the sheriff's office, but he'd been spending a lot of time on the Vivian Bradley case and not much time on his store. Sheriff Wilson would call him if he got anything.

Pulling into the municipal lot, he put the truck in park, set the brake, and sat watching Zion's car and sipping his coffee. Something made him want to go to the coffee shop and smooth things over with her, but he knew that seemed desperate.

Shoving open the pickup's door, he locked the vehicle and carried the coffee to the shop, unlocking the door. The interior of the shop was dark, but he knew each row and aisle like the back of his hand. He navigated over to the counter and set the coffee and his keys on it, then he backtracked to the door, reaching for the pull on the blinds.

The blinds did help protect the floor, but he hated the darkened interior, especially today. It was gloomy and he already felt tired and dissatisfied with his situation. Tugging on the pull, he watched the sunlight begin to seep into the room, flowing across the floor, rising as he drew the shade upward.

If he hadn't been so focused on the sunlight, he might not have noticed the shadow appear behind him, blocking the light. He caught motion in the corner of his eye and threw himself to the side. A hammer slammed down, striking a chunk out of the molding on the door, as Tate stumbled away.

Van Tiernan whipped around, holding the hammer before him. "I don't want to do this," he said, shaking his head. Tate had a moment to realize he wore his usual vest, bowtie, and collared shirt, freshly pressed, before Van Tiernan lunged at him, swinging the hammer.

Tate threw himself backward, feeling the hammer swipe past his face. He landed on his backside and scrambled toward the counter as Van Tiernan followed him, raising the hammer again. Tate's hand curled around a standing display of gloves and kneepads for gardening just as Van Tiernan lunged at him once more. Yanking it toward himself, the display crashed into Van Tiernan, taking him down as Tate rolled to his knees, scrambling to regain his feet.

He could hear Van Tiernan cursing as he tried to untangle himself from the display and Tate knew he had only a moment to get out of this before he was bludgeoned to death. He slid on the floor, rounding the counter and threw up the section that lifted, then he dove behind the counter, slamming his hand on the case that held his gun.

Keys! He needed his keys and the fob that unlocked the case.

Van Tiernan threw the display off and grabbed the hammer. Tate thought to reason with him, but his cop instincts told him this had gone too far. He lunged for the keys as Van Tiernan advanced on him, fumbling to pull the fob into his hand.

The lock on the case clicked and the case popped open. Tate's hand scrambled to grab the gun and he lifted it, pointing it in Van Tiernan's face just as the other raised the hammer for the final blow.

Bracing the gun with both hands, Tate stared into Van Tiernan's eyes. "Please don't make me do this, Jackson," he said. "Please!"

Van Tiernan let out a sound that was almost a sob, then his shoulders relaxed and a moment later…

…he lowered the hammer.

# CHAPTER 21

Zion hurried behind Sam Murphy as she led her down the long hallway to the observation room. Tate looked over at her as she stepped inside. He was standing before a two-way mirror, watching what was happening in the room on the other side of the wall. She wanted to hug him, make sure he was all right, but she wasn't sure he'd welcome that display of affection.

"Are you all right?" she asked, surprised her voice cracked.

"Yeah, I'm fine." He motioned to the window. "Sheriff Wilson's just getting started."

Zion moved to his side and peered through the window at Van Tiernan. He wore his usual attire, but a cut on his scalp bled and he pressed a napkin to it. Wilson sat on the other side of a stainless steel table while Deputy Vasquez leaned against the windowsill behind him. A bottle of water sat on the table before Van Tiernan with an old fashioned recording device. Sam Murphy stepped up on Zion's other side, her eyes fixed on the three men in the room.

Tate reached over to a speaker on the wall and turned a knob.

"…to an attorney. If you can't afford an attorney, one will be provided to you. Do you understand your rights?" said Sheriff Wilson.

"Yeah," mumbled Van Tiernan, removing the napkin and looking at the blood.

"Do you want a doctor?"

"No."

"What about a lawyer?"

"No, I can't pay for one and a public defender isn't going to do shit for me."

"Just so we're clear. We're not denying you the right to talk to an attorney," pressed Wilson.

"Yeah, I get that."

"So, you wanna tell us what happened."

Van Tiernan looked up. His eyes behind his heavy rimmed glasses were bleak as if there was nothing left for him. "What do you want to know?"

"Did you kill Vivian Bradley?"

He nodded.

Sheriff Wilson shifted in his chair. "I'm gonna need you to say it out loud."

"Yeah, I killed her."

Zion heard herself make a sound of distress. Tate glanced over at her, then to her surprise, he took her hand, linking their fingers together.

"I didn't mean it."

"How so?"

"I just wanted to scare her. I just tapped her with the bumper and she freaked, drove off the road."

Zion closed her eyes, trying to control herself. She felt like Van Tiernan had sucker punched her, his voice was so dispassionate.

"Why did you want to scare her?"

He drew a deep breath and exhaled, removing the napkin from his head. "That's complicated."

"I got all day," said Wilson.

Zion opened her eyes and stared at the man who'd killed her biological mother. His voice was level, unmoved, lifeless. She realized she'd never heard it any different. He stared at Wilson, then he stared up at the two-way glass, finally he laid his hands flat on the table and stared at the back of them.

"People want reality. They want to feel emotion – excitement, dread, fear."

"I don't understand," said Wilson.

"You mean in your games?" asked Vasquez.

Van Tiernan nodded, then pointed behind his shoulder at him. "Yeah, that's it. In the games. They want it to be like real life, like the Star Trek holodeck."

"What does this have to do with Vivian Bradley? With your attack in the *Hammer Tyme*?" asked Wilson.

"I could do the coding. I could design the gaming system. I could even write the action, but I couldn't get to that other…that feeling."

Tate swallowed hard and Zion moved closer to him, covering his hand with her free one.

Van Tiernan rubbed a hand over his chin. "At first it didn't matter. People were so awed by the graphics, by the reality of the games, they didn't care, but they got more sophisticated. They wanted to feel things."

"Go on," said Wilson, adjusting the recorder.

Van Tiernan studied it. "There's so much money in that industry. We were raking it in. I had a house and the latest model car…clothes." He ran his hands down his vest. "It was really good."

"But?"

"But things started coming apart. Then I got the idea for *B&E-1*. Breaking and Entering. It was top of the line, the Cadillac of gaming systems. No one was doing things the way we did them. We poured everything we had into it. The graphics were like real life. When you got shot, you could see the blood splatter."

Zion took an involuntary step back. He was so intense. Tate glanced over at her and squeezed her hand.

"And?"

Van Tiernan shook his head, his eyes going distant again. "It wasn't enough. The reviews were horrible. They said the game had no heart, no emotion. That players just felt like we were going through the motions. Things changed. It wasn't enough to have the best graphics. They wanted a story. They wanted to feel things. They wanted to connect with the character."

"But you weren't connecting with them?" said Vasquez.

Van Tiernan half-turned toward him. "No. It was a bust. The company floundered. A lot of people got let go."

"Including you?"

He nodded, bracing his head on his hand. "I lost the house, the car."

"Why'd you come out here?"

"My grandparents had a place out here when I was growing up. I hated it then. It was so quiet, but I thought maybe if I got to a quiet place, it would come to me. I could make the game they wanted."

"So you started *B&E-2*?" asked Vasquez.

"Yeah, but this time I was going to do it right. I was going to have the story first. I was going to make the characters come alive."

"But it didn't work?"

Van Tiernan studied Wilson for a moment without speaking, then he shook his head. "It didn't work. I just couldn't get that feeling, no matter what I did. I didn't feel the fear or the excitement. I just felt numb and desperate, but people don't want desperate."

"How does this lead to Vivian Bradley's death?"

Van Tiernan nodded. "I got to thinking there was something wrong with me. You know, maybe I'm autistic or something. I just didn't feel like other people. I went out, but I didn't really have friends. I've never had a relationship that lasted more than a few weeks, you know? With a woman?"

Wilson nodded.

"I've always been a loner."

"So, you…" prompted Wilson.

"So I thought maybe I could see it in other people. Maybe if I could duplicate what they said they felt, I could get what people wanted."

"Is that why you sent Vivian the threatening messages?"

He nodded, chewing on his lower lip. "That's the start. She gave me her phone number one time to send her an article I found on the best coffee. You know, how to roast it and all."

"Okay."

"I didn't want her to know it was me, so I bought a burner phone."

"In Visalia?"

"Right."

"Why did you text her dialogue from the game?"

"I didn't know what to say to her. I'd never done anything like that."

"But that wasn't enough?"

"It was a start. She'd come into the coffee shop and tell Dottie about it. I could hear the concern in her voice, but it wasn't enough. She wasn't scared enough. In fact, she got annoyed."

"So you decided to follow her?"

"Yeah." He gave a strange little laugh. "I followed her so many times, but half the time, she didn't know I was there. She just didn't seem to care."

"Did that make you angry?"

Van Tiernan considered that. "No, nothing made me angry. It made me desperate. I needed to get the game done. It's got to go out by Christmas or we're finished."

"Who's we?"

"*Cyclone* and I."

"But you don't work for them anymore."

"But if I could get the game up and running, if I could show them…"

"They'd hire you back," said Vasquez.

"Exactly."

"So you upped the pressure on Vivian?"

"Yeah."

"Why her?"

"I saw her everyday. I heard her talking everyday."

"Did you have feelings for her? Did she reject you?" asked Wilson forcefully.

Van Tiernan gave him a bewildered look. "Haven't you been listening? I don't feel things that way."

Wilson made a sound of annoyance. Tate shifted weight.

"So you upped the pressure," prompted Vasquez. "You followed her up the highway and you tapped her car with your bumper?"

"I just wanted to scare her, but she was going the wrong way, right along the edge of the ravine. She panicked and overcorrected and went off the edge."

"Did you stop to see if she was all right?"

Van Tiernan didn't answer, just blinked at Wilson.

"Mr. Van Tiernan, did you think to check and see if she was all right? Did you think to call for help?"

"No."

That and nothing more. Zion felt tears burn in her eyes for a woman she'd never known. How terrified she must have been. How alone. No one to help her and all for what? For nothing.

"Did you spray paint the businesses?"

He nodded.

"Why?"

"Once you zeroed in on Harold Arnold, I thought it was a good way to keep suspicion off me. I don't like him anyway."

"Did you smash Tate Mercer's mailbox?"

"Yeah, he had no business poking his nose in this. Why'd you bring him in?"

"He's an ex-cop."

"So. You shouldn't have brought him in." Van Tiernan leaned back in his chair and stretched out his legs. He almost seemed bored. "You could have gotten him killed."

"And Zion?"

"She's a good kid. Coming in here and taking over her mother's shop. Keeping the coffee house open."

"Did you break out her window?"

"Yeah."

"Why?"

"I was still trying to get that feeling, that terror. She's younger than Viv was, so I was hoping she'd be more vocal about it, but she wasn't. She just shut it down."

"Did you deliberately play the audio for her? Did you know she'd recognize the dialogue from the game?"

"I had to know. I suspected she knew something about it. She freaked out when she saw the black sedan in the game. I had my car painted to match it after Viv died."

"Why did you attack Tate Mercer in his shop today?"

Van Tiernan drew a deep breath and released it. "You really shouldn't have brought him in. He could have been killed."

Wilson slammed his hand down on the table, losing his patience. "Because you attacked him."

"You left me with no choice."

"How do you figure?"

"You brought him onto the case to solve it. Let's be honest, Sheriff. You weren't even looking at me. You were focused on Arnold."

"That's true," Wilson agreed. "So how did you get into the *Hammer Tyme*?"

"I'm the author of a game called *B&E.* Really? I've thought up so many ways to get into places, it's amazing."

"How did you get in there?"

"I went by yesterday, asked to use the bathroom, then I opened the window in the bathroom and left. It was still open when I went back early this morning. It was a tight fit, but I got inside, then I waited. I was really worried the kid might get there first. I didn't want to kill him, but I figured it was one of his late days. You know, when he goes to school."

"You didn't want to kill the kid?"

"No, he didn't do anything."

"Neither did Mercer. *We* were coming after you. He was off the case."

"But I couldn't go after you, now could I."

"Why not?"

"You have guns."

"So why go after anyone? You must have known Mercer's an ex-cop. You must have known he'd fight you."

Van Tiernan's eyes widened and glittered with some undefined emotion. "Yeah, I did, but it didn't matter. Not after I was there. Not after I took the first swing." He leaned forward, spearing Wilson with his gaze. "For the first time, Sheriff, for the first time in my life, I felt it."

"You felt it?" Wilson leaned away from him.

Van Tiernan nodded. "I felt it."

"What? What did you feel?"

"What it means to be alive."

Tate looked down. Zion tightened her hold on his hand.

"He's insane," she whispered.

Tate nodded, then he glanced over at Murphy. "He needs a lawyer, Sam."

Sam Murphy nodded as well, her eyes never leaving Van Tiernan's face. "I'll call Andrew Cox," she said and left the room.

* * *

Zion sat on the floor in the living room, watching Cleo romp around, pouncing on the little fuzzy mice she had bought her from *Fast & Furriest.* After a moment, Zion reached for the photo album in the bookshelf, opening it on her lap. She'd found this one the first day she and Gabi had entered the house, but she'd shut it again and hadn't looked at it since.

She opened it now. Inside were pictures of Zion from the time she was a baby until her high school graduation. Pictures at Christmas, Easter, birthdays, special events at school – every milestone Gabi had marked in the daughter's life the two women shared.

And there were letters, folded in the pages, letters from Gabi to Vivian, telling her of Zion's accomplishments. Zion opened one, smiling as she saw Gabi's blocky script.

Dearest Vivian,

I wanted to write and tell you our girl just got her acceptance letter to UCLA. She'll be a Bruin in the fall. We are so proud of her. She has graduated with honors from high school and she plans to major in business.

Can you believe it? I remember the precious baby you laid in my arms eighteen years ago, so fragile, so small, the greatest gift you could have given me and this fall, I'll be taking her to college, leaving her to explore a whole world without us to guide her.

Nothing will ever repay you for the gift you've given us, Vivian, but I want to tell you in the purest words a mother can say to another – thank you! Thank you for letting me know what it's like to be a mother. I will owe you for the rest of my days for this gift of all gifts.

Yours,

Gabi

Zion folded the letter and pressed it to her heart, letting the tears fall, and as she sat there in the middle of Vivian's living room, the sunlight streaming through the stained glass windows, she sobbed for everything that might have been.

Until Cleo pounced into her lap, carrying a mouse in her mouth.

Then Zion laughed through the tears and grabbed the kitten, cuddling her close.

# EPILOGUE

Tate accepted the cold draft beer Daryl poured him and took a sip, wiping away a mustache of foam. Coming around the counter, Daryl patted him on the back and directed him over to the private party in the booth across the room.

The Ford brothers had closed up early tonight, agreeing to host a celebration dinner for the business owners on Main. They'd provided the barbecue and coleslaw, while Dottie and Zion had baked a couple of cakes. Even Jim Dawson from the *Cut & Print* had agreed to come, grumbling that he couldn't get his car out of the parking lot with so many people staying late.

Zion sat in the booth next to David Bennett, but she smiled up at him. He lifted his beer in salute to her. Tonight she had her auburn hair loose around her shoulders. She wore a sundress in a floral pattern, her shoulders bare and showing a dusting of freckles. He thought she looked beautiful and he felt a stab of jealousy toward the lawyer; however, the laughter in the restaurant was infectious and he decided not to get upset about the proprietary arm David had thrown across the back of the booth behind her.

Deimos came over and draped an arm across Tate's shoulders. "I think we need a toast," he said, slurring his words. "To my man Tate, the dude who escaped a crazed killer."

"Hear! Hear!" shouted the crowd.

Tate shook his head, looking down, but Dwayne took the middle of the floor, holding up his own mug. "I wanna make a toast too."

Everyone listened.

"To the businesses on Main who stood up to a massive conglomerate and said, hell no, not in my backyard."

"Hear! Hear!" shouted everyone again.

Cheryl slipped under her husband's arm. "Well, I'd like to make a toast to eating. I'm starved."

Everyone laughed and began moving toward the tables set up across the room, groaning under the weight of so much food. Tate started to move with them, but the outer door opened and Sheriff Wilson stepped through.

Tate slipped away from Deimos and approached him, still holding his beer. "Sheriff?"

"Mercer."

"You wanna beer?"

"No, I'm still on duty."

Tate nodded.

"Just wanted to come by and tell you Van Tiernan's in a hospital in Visalia."

"Really?"

"Yeah, he tried to kill himself in his cell."

"How?"

"Tried to hang himself with his jumpsuit. My men just turned their backs for a few minutes."

"Is he going to make it?"

Wilson shrugged. "If he does, he'll be severely brain damaged."

Tate blew out air. "I'm actually sorry to hear that."

"Yeah, I know. Anyway, I wanted you to know, so you can stop looking over your shoulder."

"Thanks."

Wilson lightly punched him on the arm. "You ever want a job as a consultant, I'll make some room for you in my budget."

Tate laughed. "No thank you. I'm gonna go back to pushing tools and doodads."

Wilson laughed with him. "Just watch out for those hammers, okay?"

Tate lifted his beer in salute. "Touché," he said and watched Wilson leave the restaurant, waving over his shoulder.

As he turned to go back to the party, he came up short.

Zion had moved up behind him.

"What did Sheriff Wilson have to say?"

"He just wanted me to know that Van Tiernan won't be hurting anyone else, ever again."

"Why?"

"He tried to commit suicide and almost succeeded. He's brain damaged."

She frowned at that. "I actually feel sorry for him."

"Yeah, well, that's because you're a good person."

She smiled at him, then her look grew sultry. "Why, thank you, Mr. Mercer, but you don't really know me half at all."

He smiled with her. "Since we're neighbors, don't you think we should do something about that?"

She turned her back on him, her auburn hair sliding over her shoulder and down her back. "I don't know. I'm not really into the strong, silent type." She gave him a wink. "But then again…" With that, she sashayed away.

Tate felt a rush of heat as he watched her and he had a feeling Zion Sawyer was going to make his life very interesting after all.

**The End**

**Now that you've finished, visit ML Hamilton at her website: authormlhamilton.net and sign up for her newsletter. Receive free offers and discounts once you sign up!**

**The Complete *Peyton Brooks' Mysteries* Collection:**

*Murder on Potrero Hill Volume 1*
*Murder in the Tenderloin Volume 2*
*Murder on Russian Hill Volume 3*
*Murder on Alcatraz Volume 4*
*Murder in Chinatown Volume 5*
*Murder in the Presidio Volume 6*
*Murder on Treasure Island Volume 7*

**Peyton Brooks FBI Collection:**

*Zombies in the Delta Volume 1*
*Mermaids in the Pacific Volume 2*
*Werewolves in London Volume 3*
*Vampires in Hollywood Volume 4*
*Mayan Gods in the Yucatan Volume 5*

***Zion Sawyer* Cozy Mystery Collection:**

*Cappuccino Volume 1*

**The Avery Nolan Adventure Collection:**

*Swift as a Shadow Volume 1*
*Short as Any Dream Volume 2*
*Brief as Lightning Volume 3*
*Momentary as a Sound Volume 4*

**The Complete *World of Samar* Collection:**

*The Talisman of Eldon Emerald Volume 1*
*The Heirs of Eldon Volume 2*
*The Star of Eldon Volume 3*
*The Spirit of Eldon Volume 4*
*The Sanctuary of Eldon Volume 5*
*The Scions of Eldon Volume 6*
*The Watchers of Eldon Volume 7*
*The Followers of Eldon Volume 8*
*The Apostles of Eldon Volume 9*

**Stand Alone Novels:**

*Ravensong*
*Serenity*

Made in the USA
Monee, IL
12 July 2020